A Dublin Anthology

A DUBLIN ANTHOLOGY

Douglas Bennett

GILL & MACMILLAN

Published in Ireland by

Gill & Macmillan Ltd

Goldenbridge

Dublin 8

with associated companies throughout the world

© Introduction and selection Douglas Bennett 1994

0 7171 2122 4

Index compiled by Helen Litton

Print origination and design by Identikit Design Consultants, Dublin

Printed by ColourBooks Ltd, Dublin

1   3   5   4   2

CONTENTS

SOCIAL AND CULTURAL CONDITIONS

BIOGRAPHY

HISTORY

ACKNOWLEDGMENTS

For permission to reproduce copyright material, grateful acknowledgement is made to the following:

The Samuel Beckett Estate and The Calder Educational Trust, London, for the extract from *More Pricks than Kicks* by Samuel Beckett, Calder Publications Ltd, London. Copyright (c) Samuel Beckett 1934, 1966, 1967, 1970, 1973 and copyright (c) The Samuel Beckett Estate 1993;

Raven Arts Press, Dublin, for the Michael O'Loughlin poem from *Invisible Dubliners*;

The O'Brien Press, Dublin, for extracts from *Gur Cakes and Coal Blocks*, *The Last of Mrs Murphy* and *Your Dinner's Poured Out*;

The Mercier Press, Cork, for the extract from *Malachi Horan Remembers Dublin* by Dr George A. Little;

Hutchinson Publishers, London, and Brian Behan for the extract from *Mother of All the Behans* (Arena Books);

The Society of Authors for the extract from *John Bull's Other Island* by George Bernard Shaw;

Mary Daly and Cork University Press for the extract from *Dublin: The Deposed Capital*;

The Estate of the late John D. Sheridan for the extract from *Paradise Alley*;

Mr Brian Cleeve for the extract from *Cry of Morning*;

Mr Tony Farmar for the extract from *The Lofty Clattery Café: Bewley's of Dublin*;

Peters Fraser & Dunlop Group Ltd for the extract from *The Life of Reilly* by Anthony Cronin;

Curtis Brown Ltd, London, on behalf of the Estate of Sir Winston S. Churchill for the extract from *My Early Life* by Winston Churchill, copyright the Estate of Sir Winston S. Churchill;

Benedict Kiely for the extract from *Three Poets on Dublin*;

Ms Maeve Binchy and her agent, Ms Christine Green, for the extract from *Maeve Binchy's Dublin*;

Curtis Brown Ltd, London, on behalf of the Estate of Terence de Vere White for the extract from *The March Hare* by Terence de Vere White, copyright the Estate of Terence de Vere White;

Constable Publishers for the extract from *Foreign Affairs* by Sean O'Faolain.

The Publishers have used their best efforts to trace all copyright holders. They will, however, make the usual and appropriate arrangements with any who may have inadvertently been overlooked and who contact them.

The Gilbert Library is the natural repository of books and documents any researcher on Dublin must consult. My special thanks are due to its librarian Máire Kennedy and her senior library assistant Thecla Carlton for steering me through all aspects of the collection. There is a feeling of discipline and reverence on entering Marsh's Library and a state of tranquillity prevails among the treasures of this extensive collection due directly to the Keeper Muriel McCarthy. Aideen Ireland, archivist, National Archives has for many years supplied extracts and dainty morsels that have contributed significantly to areas of investigation. That great institution Dublin Corporation has archivist Mary Clark to protect its historical records. She regularly supplied extracts from antiquated papers. An expression of gratitude is proffered to Fergal Tobin and the marvellous staff of Gill & Macmillan Ltd for producing this collection, also to my friend and publicity officer Eveleen Coyle who made sure that I was neither ignored nor forgotten. Many thanks to them all and finally to my wife and companion Sandra: only a kindred spirit could or would put up with such anomalous behaviour.

INTRODUCTION

I began commuting to school in Dublin at the age of twelve when my exiguous pocket money did not permit indulgence in large capital outlays. So many items were as much beyond my dreams as beyond my cash, but fortunately it was possible for a few pence to purchase books of Dublin interest and I learned at an early age to admire the Dubliners' genius for the spoken and written word. Willingly I developed a ravenous hunger for information contained within tattered journals and faded dust jackets and my frozen literary mind blossomed under the happy stimulus of searching through second-hand book stalls along the Liffey and probing the contents of Joe Clarke's barrow on O'Connell Bridge. This absorbed me in a way that the classroom had never done and when Joe's tired body—eventually deprived of the power of action—surrendered its spirit back to its creator, an era for me came to a close in the city. Having developed a fascination for authors who could construct such flowing, glowing sentences I threw myself into reading with almost barbaric zest. The school reports of the time reflect this in the marks for literature, composition and poetry much of which was pillaged and paraphrased shamelessly. Alas, the same documents do not reflect similar results for geometry, algebra and mathematics. Again, during a torpid year passed in a tuberculosis sanatorium, reading was like a draught of some generous wine, rich and full of flavour that helped me to forget the conditions in that institution. With the restriction of activities, to be able to perceive and understand the meaning of the printed word helped to preserve my sanity.

There is a limit to life but no limit to knowledge and when Fergal Tobin of Gill & Macmillan asked me to put *A Dublin Anthology* together I realised that it would be a labour of love after my own heart, and very soon the book became an indulgent companion. This city becomes a world when one gets to know and love its inhabitants, real or imaginary. Within these covers is a cry across the centuries. As Richard Kain expressed it, 'From the time of Barrington to that of Brendan Behan, Dublin has cherished personality. The city is small enough for individuals to be known as individuals. People are news and the only thing worse than being talked about is not being talked about.' This is the way to a happy life. May you the reader find happiness delving into this little volume finding some new and unfamiliar authors. My hope is also to send you back to the originals to rediscover well-known writers that you once loved and lost awhile.

The anthology is divided into five sections: fiction, social and cultural conditions, biography, history, then finally travel.

Choosing the fiction seemed a pleasant enough challenge until I realised the astronomic amount that would have to be laid aside and many of the omissions are due to the limitations of space. From this great bulk of material I selected books that gave me the most gratification and that appeared to be more pertinent and representative of the intelligent, skilful, entirely enjoyable novels that were written over two centuries. Much condensed literary work is encapsulated in this section. It includes authors of exalted reputation—Joyce, Beckett, Stephens, Behan—together with some pieces produced merely for money. Sharing with these are authors not generally known, in company with some new writers that have as yet not made the grade but were chosen because their use of language is unpretentious, imaginative and precise.

The term biography is somewhat ambitious as it is usually intended to cover the whole extent of the person's life. What I have included here are stories told by many gifted men and women who have contributed something to the history of this city. Winston Churchill recalls three years of childhood spent at his home in the Phoenix Park and remembers the unveiling of the Lord Gough statue in 1878. Brian Behan tells us that the Granny always said that when she died she wanted 'fine fat-arsed black horses to take her to the cemetery, not skinny old knackers'. John Mitchel recalls his life in a Dublin prison as a convicted 'felon'. As in other parts of this book a cross-section of views from all segments of the community is included. For those interested in Joyce, Louis Hyman supplies another dimension to some aspects of the Jewish background of *Ulysses*. Yeats, the mystic bard, Nobel prize winner and senator who devised his own epitaph also contributes.

Dublin is a city of violent contrasts: the inequalities of wealth and the social and sanitary conditions of the poor quarters of the city bear no resemblance to the red brick squares of the eighteenth century where socialites dined, gossiped, drank their claret and dipped into their morning papers. Miss Herbert, writing in 1782, concurs: 'Nothing can be so gay as Dublin is—the Castle twice a week, the opera twice a week, with plays, assemblies and suppers to fill up the time'. An opposite comparison made by Hawkins in his *Medical Statistics* states that 'Dublin appears to have suffered more continually from epidemic fever than any other great city in Europe. The causes of this calamitous state are attributed by the resident physicians to want of employment, poverty, and sometimes famine amongst the lower classes'. There is plenty of material here for urgent consideration and I have included contributors with very varying offerings on social and cultural conditions.

Ireland has always been a source of great anxiety to England and the records of bitter, bloody destructive wars and rebellions I have kept to a minimum. Perhaps this part should be named 'A Historic Guide to Dublin' as it is popular history at its most compelling, covering as it does literary giants in the manner of Shaw and Barrington. Dubliners have always had a fondness for and a devotion to blowing up statues representing notable public persons whether standing, seated or equestrian mounted. It therefore seemed appropriate to include the demolition of Nelson and his column while another form of destruction is recorded by Mary Byrne, who remembers the bombing of the North Strand by a German aircraft in May 1941. Happier events are also recorded including the *Evening Mail's* reporting of the 1932 Eucharistic Congress and the opening of St Stephen's Green as a public park in 1880.

Dublin is a momentous place for the compulsive day tripper and traveller; once visited the experience is not forgotten. I am of the opinion that it is obligatory on my part to close the anthology with an intellectual or mental survey from those who have come to see the city together with those who live and journey around its streets and suburbs. Chiang Yee, a native of China, tells of a visit to the bird market. James Collins, author of a purely factual work, inspects Croppies Acre and gives its exact location. Oliver St John Gogarty, that eloquent and challenging surgeon, states that Dublin has one advantage: it is easy to get out of. The attentive capacity of the reader will be held by Douglas Goldring's tautology of the delightful aspects of the frugality and lack of ostentation in the city. Another truly relevant element is echoed by Eric Whelpton who observes that you cannot spend ten minutes in Dublin without being struck with the unforgettable beauty of the women.

Dubliners thrive on words and for a city of its size there is an enormous outpouring in terms of literature from the impressions left by sensuous experience to divagations into cultural expressiveness. There is a great and exciting complexity of speech in the anthology. The writer of Ecclesiastes says 'of making many books there is no end'. Try not to be irritated or disappointed therefore if your familiar or favourite author is omitted. Distinguished writers have been neglected and I hope that this will not be a source of controversy. Rather, I trust that the work will be of interest to the common reader and that it will encourage further exploration into this vast, huge and boundless subject.

Throughout this anthology, I have changed as little as possible in the way of spellings or style from the originals which are excerpted here. Archaic spellings and stylistic usages have their own charm and authenticity. In the minority of cases where I have detected obvious errors, I have corrected them silently.

Douglas Bennett
Dublin 1994

JANE BARLOW

A Creel of Irish Stories

LONDON ❧ METHUEN ❧ 1897

The little stream which flows southward through Ballyhoy must be one of the smallest contributions accepted anywhere by the sea, so insignificant in quantity is the water trickling over the smoothed stone step under the low arch on the shore. Yet the course of its channel can be traced, when the tide is out, in gleaming sky-coloured loops far across the mud-flats. As a rule the tide there *is* out: some of the neighbours indeed, have a theory, no doubt scientifically untenable, that it comes in only about once a week. For this narrow creek, cut off from the Bay by the great grassy sandbank of the North Bull, is steadily silting up, so that its soundings grow shallower every year, and rarer the occasions when we see a plain of sapphire or mother-o'pearl, threaded with paths of silver rippling, spread all the way between us and the cliffs at purple Howth. It looks as if the Bull would ultimately join the mainland without intermission. Even now, at low water, the passage to and fro can be effected fairly dry-shod by well-chosen routes. These are known to the cattle who graze on the salt herbage among the bent-grown sandhills; and at the fitting time and place, a procession red and white and black may be watched making its way thence in single file towards the strip of common-like pasture beside the sea-road. But the transit, if under-taken by the unwary or ignorant, is beset with serious peril, owing to sundry treacherous mud-holes, which lurk around. Their smothering toils have in time past engulfed much vainly floundering prey, both man and beast, and at the present day several of them are called by the names of their respective victims—Byrne's Hole, Clancy's Hole—obscurely commemorating tragedies not less piteous perhaps than those of the Kelpie's Flow and the Sands of Dee.

I have never heard of any such disaster befalling a class of people who might be supposed peculiarly liable to it, since so much of their time is spent on the dangerous ground. All the shore from Ballyhoy to Portbrendan is haunted by cockle-pickers, who come out from Dublin,

1

where they lodge among the Liberties or other purlieus, climbing down into subterranean cellars, or perhaps mounting wide oaken stairs to spacious upper chambers with the carven panels and mantelpieces and ceilings of the past commenting ironically on the inartistic rags and squalor and famine of today. They time their arrival to correspond with low water, so that when you meet a batch of them jogging along the road, you can infer the state of the tide from the contents of the baskets they shoulder, according as these include a heap of grey-fluted shells and a trail of brown seaweed, or nothing except a dull tin measure and a grimy little pipe. Nobody ever sees a cockle-picker apart from his or her basket, yet one of them would be recognised without it, so constant is the type in the species. All are neither young nor old, all are wind and weather beaten, all are short of stature, any original excess in height being compensated for by a more pronounced stoop, and the garments of all reproduce the tints of blackish mud and greenish slime as accurately as if the wearers were animals whose existence depended upon the power of going invisible. This is not the case, however. Unaggressive and inoffensive in their habits, the cockle-pickers have no especial enemies save the seasons' difference, and the dwellers by the shore regard their proceedings with hardly more suspicion than those of the white seagull flocks which sprinkle the neighbouring dark fields, when the lea is broken up and disturbed grubs abound. A favourite fishery is the strand along by the Black Banks, a little to the eastward of the Ballyhoy river; and on most days of the year sombre figures are to be seen there, paddling and poking, barefooted, in the mud, even when the pools have ice at the rim, and the green weed is stiff instead of slimy.

SAMUEL BECKETT

More Pricks Than Kicks

LONDON ❧ CHATTO & WINDUS ❧ 1934
ALSO CALDER & BOYARS LTD ❧ 1970

Emerging, on the particular evening in question, from the underground convenience in the maw of College Street, with a vague impression that he had come from following the sunset up the Liffey till all the colour had been harried from the sky, all the tulips and aerugo expunged, he squatted, not that he had too much drink taken but simply that for the moment there were no grounds for his favouring one direction rather than another, against Tommy Moore's plinth. Yet he durst not dally. Was it not from brooding shill I, shall I, dilly, dally, that he had come out? Now the summons to move on was a subpoena. Yet he found he could not, any more than Buridan's ass, move to right or left, backward or forward. Why this was he could not make out at all. Nor was it the moment for self-examination. He had experienced little or no trouble coming back from the Park Gate along the north quay, he had taken the Bridge and Westmoreland Street in his stride, and now he suddenly found himself good for nothing but to loll against the plinth of this bull-necked bard, and wait for a sign.

There were signs on all hands. There was the big Bovril sign to begin with, flaring beyond the Green. But it was useless. Faith, Hope and—what was it?—Love, Eden missed, every ebb derided, all the tides ebbing from the shingle of Ego Maximus, little me. Itself it went nowhere, only round and round, like the spheres, but mutely. It could not dislodge him now, it could only put ideas into his head. Was it not from sitting still among his ideas, other people's ideas, that he had come away? What would he not give now to get on the move again! Away from ideas!

Turning aside from this and other no less futile emblems, his attention was arrested by a wheel-chair being pushed rapidly under the arcade of the Bank, in the direction of Dame Street. It moved in and out of sight behind the bars of the columns. This was the blind paralytic who sat all day near to the corner of Fleet Street, and in bad weather under the shelter of the arcade, the same being wheeled home to his home in the Coombe. It was past his time and there was a bitter look on his face. He would give his chairman a piece of his mind when he got him to himself. This chairman, hireling or poor relation, came every evening a little before dark, unfastened from the beggar's neck and breast the placard announcing his distress, tucked him up snugly in his coverings and wheeled him home to his supper. He was well advised to be assiduous, for this beggar was a power in the Coombe. In the morning it was his duty to shave his man and wheel him, according to the weather, to one or other of his pitches. So it went, day after day.

This was a star the horizon adorning if you like, and Belacqua made off at all speed in the opposite direction. Down Pearse Street, that is to say, long straight Pearse Street, its vast Barrack of Glencullen granite, its home of tragedy restored and enlarged, its coal merchants and Florentine Fire Brigade Station, its two Cervi saloons, ice-cream and fried fish, its dairies, garages and monumental sculptors, and implicit behind the whole length of its southern frontage the College. Perpetuis futuris temporibus duraturum. It was to be hoped so, indeed.

It was a most pleasant street, despite its name, to be abroad in, full as it always was with shabby substance and honest-to-God coming and going. All day the roadway was a tumult of buses, red and blue and silver. By one of these a little girl was run down, just as Belacqua drew near to the railway viaduct. She had been to the Hibernian Dairies for milk and bread and then she had plunged out into the roadway, she was in such a childish fever to get back in record time with her treasure to the tenement in Mark Street where she lived. The good milk was all over the road and the loaf, which had sustained no injury, was sitting up against the kerb, for all the world as though a pair of hands had taken it up and set it down there. The queue standing for the Palace Cinema was torn between conflicting desires: to keep their places and to see the excitement. They craned their necks and called out to know the worst, but they stood firm. Only one girl, debauched in appearance and swathed in a black blanket fell out near the sting of the queue and secured the loaf. With the loaf under her blanket she sidled unchallenged down Mark Street and turned into Mark Lane. When she got back to the queue her place had been taken of course. But her sally had not cost her more than a couple of yards.

Belacqua turned left into Lombard Street, the street of the sanitary engineers, and entered a public-house. Here he was known, in the sense

4

that his grotesque exterior had long ceased to alienate the curates and make them giggle, and to the extent that he was served with his drink without having to call for it. This did not always seem a privilege. He was tolerated, what was more, and let alone by the rough but kindly habitués of the house, recruited for the most part from among dockers, railwaymen and vague joxers on the dole. Here also art and love, scrabbling in dispute or staggering home, were barred, or, perhaps better, unknown. The aesthetes and the impotent were far away.

These circumstances combined to make of this place a very grateful refuge for Belacqua, who never omitted, when he found himself in its neighbourhood with the price of a drink about him, to pay it a visit.

When I enquired how he squared such visits with his anxiety to keep on the move and his distress at finding himself brought to a standstill, as when he had come out of the underground in the mouth of College Street, he replied that he did not. 'Surely' he said 'my resolution has the right to break down.' I supposed so indeed. 'Or' he said 'if you prefer, I make the raid in two hops instead of non-stop. From what' he cried 'does that disqualify me, I should very much like to know.' I hastened to assure him that he had a perfect right to suit himself in what, after all, was a manoeuvre of his own contriving, and that the raid, to adopt his own term, lost nothing by being made in easy stages. 'Easy!' he exclaimed, 'how easy?'

But notice the double response, like two holes to a burrow.

Sitting in this crapulent den, drinking his drink, he gradually ceased to see its furnishings with pleasure, the bottles, representing centuries of loving research, the stools, the counter, the powerful screws, the shining phalanx of the pulls of the beer-engines, all cunningly devised and elaborated to further the relations between purveyor and consumer in this domain. The bottles drawn and emptied in a twinkling, the casks responding to the slightest pressure on their joysticks, the weary proletarians at rest on arse and elbow, the cash register that never complains, the graceful curates flying from customer to customer, all this made up a spectacle in which Belacqua was used to take delight and chose to see a pleasant instance of machinery decently subservient to appetite. A great major symphony of supply and demand, effect and cause, fulcrate on the middle C of the counter and waxing, as it proceeded, in the charming harmonies of blasphemy and broken glass and all the aliquots of fatigue and ebriety. So that he would say that the only place where he could come to anchor and be happy was a low public-house and that all the wearisome tactics of gress and dud Beethoven would be done away with if only he could spend his life in such a place. But as they closed at ten, and as residence and good faith were viewed as incompatible, and as in any case he had not the means to consecrate his life to stasis, even in the meanest bar, he supposed he must be content to indulge this whim from time to time, and return thanks for such sporadic mercy.

All this and much more he laboured to make clear. He seemed to derive considerable satisfaction from his failure to do so.

But on this particular occasion the cat failed to jump, with the result that he became as despondent as though he were sitting at home in his own great armchair, as anxious to get on the move and quite as hard put to it to do so. Why this was he could not make out. Whether the trituration of the child in Pearse Street had upset him without his knowing it, or whether (and he put forward this alternative with a truly insufferable complacency) he had come to some parting of the ways, he did not know at all. All he could say was that the objects in which he was used to find such recreation and repose lost gradually their hold upon him, he became insensible to them little by little, the old itch and algos crept back into his mind. He had come briskly all the way from Tommy Moore, and now he suddenly found himself sitting paralysed and grieving in a pub of all places, good for nothing but to stare at his spoiling porter and wait for a sign.

To this day he does not know what caused him to look up, but look up he did. Feeling the impulse to do this strong upon him, he forced his eyes away from the glass of dying porter and was rewarded by seeing a hatless woman advancing slowly towards him up the body of the bar. No sooner had she come in than he must have become aware of her. That was surely very curious in the first instance. She seemed to be hawking some ware or other, but what it was he could not see, except that it was not studs or laces or matches or lavender or any of the usual articles. Not that it was unusual to find a woman in that public-house, for they came and went freely, slaking their thirst and beguiling their sorrows with no less freedom than their menfolk. Indeed it was always a pleasure to see them, their advances were always most friendly and honourable, Belacqua had many a delightful recollection of their commerce.

Hence there was no earthly reason why he should see in the advancing figure of this mysterious pedlar anything untoward, or in the nature of the sign in default of which he was clamped to his stool till closing-time. Yet the impulse to do so was so strong that he yielded to it, and as she drew nearer, having met with more rebuffs than pence in her endeavours to dispose of her wares, whatever they were it became clear to him that his instinct had not played him false, in so far at least as she was a woman of very remarkable presence indeed.

Her speech was that of a woman of the people, but of a gentlewoman of the people. Her gown had served its time, but yet contrived to be respectable. He noticed with a pang that she sported about her neck the insidious little mock fur so prevalent in tony slumland. The one deplorable feature of her get up, as apprehended by Belacqua in his hasty survey, was the footwear—the cruel strait outsizes of the suffragette or welfare worker. But he did not doubt for a moment that they had been a gift, or picked up in the pop for a song. She was of more than average height and well in flesh. She might be past middle-age. But her face, ah her face, was what Belacqua had rather refer to as her countenance, it was so full of light. This she lifted up upon him and no error. Brimful of light and serene, serenissime, it bore no trace of suffering, and in this alone it might be said to be a notable face. Yet like tormented faces that he had seen, like the face in the National Gallery in Merrion Square by the Master of Tired Eyes, it seemed to have come a long way and subtend an infinitely narrow angle of affliction, as eyes focus a star. The features were null, only luminous, impassive and secure, petrified in radiance, or words to that effect, for the reader is requested to take notice that this sweet style is Belacqua's. An act of expression, he said, a wreathing or wrinkling, could only have had the effect of a dimmer on a headlight. The implications of this triumphant figure, the just and the unjust, etc., are better forgone.

At long last she addressed herself to Belacqua.

'Seats in heaven' she said in a white voice 'tuppence apiece, four fer a tanner.'

'No' said Belacqua. It was the first syllable to come to his lips. It had not been his intention to deny her.

'The best of seats' she said 'again I'm sold out. Tuppence apiece the best of seats, four fer a tanner.'

This was unforeseen with a vengeance, if not exactly vaudeville. Belacqua was embarrassed in the last degree, but transported also. He felt the sweat coming in the small of his back, above his Montrouge belt.

'Have you got them on you?' he mumbled.

'Heaven goes round' she said, whirling her arm, 'and round and round and round and round.'

'Yes' said Belacqua 'round and round.'

'Rowan' she said, dropping the d's and getting more of a spin into the slogan, 'rowan an' rowan an' rowan'.

Belacqua scarcely knew where to look. Unable to blush he came out in this beastly sweat. Nothing of the kind had ever happened to him before. He was altogether disarmed, unsaddled and miserable. The eyes of them all, the dockers, the railwaymen and, most terrible of all, the joxers, were upon him. His tail drooped. This female dog of a pixy with her tiresome Ptolemy, he was at her mercy.

'No' he said 'no thank you, no not this evening thank you.'

'Again I'm sold out' she said 'an' buked out, four fer a tanner.'

'On whose authority ...' began Belacqua, like a Scholar.

'For yer frien'' she said 'yer da, yer ma an' yer motte, four fer a tanner.' The voice ceased, but the face did not abate.

'How do I know' piped Belacqua 'you're not sellin' me a pup?'

'Heaven goes rowan an' rowan ...'

'Rot you' said Belacqua 'I'll take two. How much is that?'

'Four dee' she said.

Belacqua gave her a sixpence.

'Gobbless yer honour' she said, in the same white voice from which she had not departed. She made to go.

'Here' cried Belacqua 'you owe me twopence.' He had not even the good grace to say tuppence.

'Arragowan' she said 'make it four cantcher, yer frien', yer da, yer ma an' yer motte.'

Belacqua could not bicker. He had not the strength of mind for that. He turned away.

'Jesus' she said distinctly 'and his sweet mother preserve yer honour.'

'Amen' said Belacqua, into his dead porter.

Now the woman went away and her countenance lighted her to her room in Townsend Street.

But Belacqua tarried a little to listen to the music. Then he also departed, but for Railway Street, beyond the river.

BRENDAN BEHAN

After the Wake

DUBLIN ❧ O'BRIEN PRESS ❧ 1981

THE LAST OF MRS MURPHY

Over Mrs Murphy's bed hung a picture of a person wearing a red jacket and a white head. When I was small I thought it was a picture of herself, but she laughed one day and said no, that it was Pope Leo. Whether this was a man or a woman I was not sure, for his red cloak was like Mrs Murphy's and so was his white head.

The day I was five, Mrs Murphy said we must go over to Jimmy the Sports for a quick one, the day that was in it.

'While I'm putting on me clothes, you can be giving the cat her bit of burgoo.'

I got up the saucerful of porridge and put the milk on it, and called under the bed, 'Minnie Murphy, come out from that old shoe box at once, and eat your breakfast'.

'Before *he* eats it,' muttered Mrs Murphy to herself putting a skirt on over her head.

I was caught once, sitting the far side of a plateful of lights with the cat, but that was a long time ago, when I was only three: we eating, share and share alike.

We got out of the parlour all right, and into the hall. Someone had left a pram in it and Mrs Murphy gave it a blessing when she nearly fell over it. She supported herself going round it, and opened the hall door. Going down the steps into the street, she rested her hand on my head. I didn't mind for she was very light, and it was easy for her to reach me, though I was not that tall, for she was bent nearly double since the winter.

Half-way up the street, she sat on the steps of 16 and said I was to run on up to the corner for a quarter ounce of white snuff.

I had to wait my turn in the shop. There were women in front of me.

'I says to myself when I seen her,' says one woman, 'the dead arose and appeared to many.'

'It's all very fine and large,' says the other old one, 'but I've had her in the Society since before the war. If she dropped dead this minute, God between her and all harm, I'd still be losing money. When she got over the Spanish 'flu, and was missed be the Tans on Bloody Sunday, I said it was only throwing good money after bad, and I'd cut me losses and let the policy lapse, for nothing less than an Act of God or a hand grenade could make a dent in her.'

'Ah sure, what nicer am I? And we're not the only ones. There's more money invested in old Murphy nor the GSR.'

The shopman looked over the counter at me,

'Well, me little man?'

'A quarter ounce of white snuff.'

The women nudged each other, 'And how's poor Mrs Murphy today, *a mhic*?'

'She's powerful.'

'God bless her and spare the poor old creature.'

'Barring the humane-killer,' muttered the other old one, and they went out.

In the pub she sat in the corner and ordered a bottle of stout for herself and a dandy glass of porter for me.

'An orange or something would be better for the child,' said Jimmy the Sports.

'The drop of gargle will do him good,' said Mrs Murphy, 'it's only a little birthday celebration.'

'You must be the hundred,' said Jimmy the Sports.

'I'm not,' said old Murphy, 'nor nothing like it. I was born in the year eighteen hundred and thirty-seven.'

'You'd remember the famine then,' said Jimmy the Sports.

'We were respectable people round this street and didn't go in for famines. All shut hall-doors that time. Down in Monto they had the famine. They didn't do a stroke of work for months only unloading the stuff off of the boats. The people that brought it over didn't mind. It was for the hungry Irish, and it saved them the trouble of going any further with it. They had the life of Riley down on the quay, while it lasted.'

Jimmy the Sports ground his teeth and looked as if he might cry. 'God forgive you, and you an old woman. My poor mother fell from her own dead mother's arms outside Loughrea workhouse.'

Mrs Murphy took a pinch of snuff. 'Well, we all have our troubles. If it's not an ear, it's an elbow. What about the gargle?'

Jimmy the Sports put them up and she paid him. 'Sorrow sign of famine on you anyway, Jimmy. The land for the people,' she muttered to herself, 'will you ever forget that?'

We spent a bit of time in Jimmy the Sports and then went back down the street. I walked in front for her to lean on my head, slow and in time with her. The pram was still in the hall, and she muttered a few curses getting round it, but the baby from the back drawing room was in it this time, and she leant a minute on the side looking in at him.

'What's this the name of that crowd that owns this child is?'

'It's Rochfords' baby,' said I. 'Out of upstairs. He's only new out of the Roto this week.'

'How do you know he's out of the Roto?'

'I heard my mother and them saying it. That's where all babies are from. They have pictures there too.'

She waved her hand. 'Shut up a minute, can't you?' She put her hand to her forehead. 'That'd be Dan Rochford's son's child, or his child maybe.' She fumbled in her handbag. 'I've two thrupenny bits. Here, take one of these in your hand. It has to be silver. Put it in the baby's hand and say what I say: "Hold your hansel, long life and the height of good luck to you." Come on.'

I tried to speak but the tears were choking me. I thought she would give me one of the thrupenny bits anyway. It was like a blow in the face to me, and I'd done nothing on her but walked nice and easy down the street when she leaned on my head, and went over and got the snuff.

She looked down at me, and I put the thrupenny bit into the pram, and turned my heart, and—cheeks and eyes all full of tears—ran through the hall and out into the street.

My mother only laughed and said it didn't mean that Mrs Murphy fancied the baby more than she did me. It could have been any new baby. It was the thing to do, and I a big fellow that had run out of two schools to be jealous of a little baby that couldn't even talk.

She brought me into Mrs Murphy, and the two of them talked and laughed about it while I didn't look at them but sat in the corner playing with Minnie Murphy who, if she was vicious enough to scrawb you if she thought she'd get away with it, didn't make you feel such a fool. When my mother went I wanted to go too but my mother said Mrs Murphy was sick and I could mind her till she came back.

Mrs Murphy called me to the bedside and gave me a pinch of snuff, and had one herself, and the new baby went out of our heads.

The doctor came and said she'd have to go to the Refuge of the Dying. He told her that years ago.

Mrs Murphy didn't know whether she'd go or not. I hoped she would. I heard them talk about it before and knew you went in a cab, miles over the city and to the southside. I was always afraid that they might have got me into another school before she'd go for, no matter how well you run out of them or kick the legs of the teacher, you have to go sometime.

She said she'd go and my granny said she'd order a cab from the Roto to be there in the morning.

We all got into the cab. Mrs Murphy was all wrapped up in blankets. She didn't lean on my head, but was helped by the jarvey, and off we went.

Going past a pub on the corner of Eccles Street, she said she didn't like to pass it, for old times' sake. My granny and Long Byrne and Lizzie MacCann all said they'd be the better of a rozziner. And the jarvey came in with the rest of us. On the banks of the other canal we went in and had another couple. We stopped there for a long time and my granny told the jarvey she'd make it up to him.

Glasses of malt she ordered, and Mrs Murphy called on Long Byrne for a bar of a song.

The man in the pub said that it wasn't a singing house, but Mrs Murphy said she was going into the Refuge and it was a kind of a wake.

So Long Byrne sang, 'When the Cock, Cock Robin, comes hop, hop, hoppin' along,' and *On Mother Kelly's Doorstep*, and for an hour it was great and you'd wish it could go on forever, but we had to go or the Refuge would be shut.

We left in Mrs Murphy and waited in the hall. Long Byrne said you get the smell of death in it.

'It's the wax on the floors,' said my granny.

'It's a very hard-featured class of a smell, whatever it is,' said Lizzie MacCann.

'We'll never see her again now, till we come up to collect her in the box,' said Long Byrne.

'For God's sake, whisht up out of that, you,' said my granny, 'people's not bad enough.' She fumbled with her handkerchief.

'All the same, Christina,' said Lizzie MacCann, 'you'd feel bad about leaving the poor devil in a place like this.'

The jarvey was trying to smoke without being caught. 'It's a very holy place,' he said, but not looking too sure about it.

'Maybe it's that we're not that holy ourselves,' said Lizzie MacCann. 'We might sooner die medium holy, like.'

'It's not the kind of place I'd like to leave a neighbour or a neighbour's child,' said Long Byrne.

'Oh, whisht your mouth,' said my granny, 'you'd make me feel like an ... an informer or something. We only do the best we can.'

A very severe looking lady in a white coat came out and stood in front of us. The jarvey stuck the pipe in his pocket and straightened his cap.

'Whars in charge of the peeshent?' she says in a very severe tongue.

My granny stood up as well as she could. 'I am, with these other women here. She's a neighbour of ours.'

'There are no admissions here after five o'clock. The patient arrived here in an intoxicated condition.'

'She means poor old Murphy was drunk,' says Long Byrne.

'The poor old creature had only about six halves, the couple of glasses of malt we had to finish up, and a few bottles we had over in Eccles Street,' said Lizzie MacCann, counting on her fingers, 'God forgive them that'd tell a lie of an old woman, that she was the worse for drink.'

'And I get a distinct smell of whiskey here in this very hall,' said the woman in the white coat.

'How well you'd know it from the smell of gin, rum or brandy,' said Long Byrne, 'Ah well, I suppose practice makes perfect.'

The woman in the white coat's face got that severe that if she fell on it she'd have cut herself.

'Out,' she put up her hand, pointing to the door, 'Out, at once.'

There was a shuffling in the back of the hall, and Mrs Murphy came out, supported by two nurses.

'I wouldn't stop where my friends aren't welcome,' said Mrs Murphy.

'Come on so,' says my granny. When they got back to Jimmy the Sports, they had a few and brought some more over to Mrs Murphy's while they put her to bed.

Long Byrne said herself and Lizzie MacCann would look after her between them.

My granny liked laziness better than she did money and said she'd bunce in a half a bar towards their trouble.

'And it won't break you,' says Long Byrne, 'damn it all, she's not Methuselah.'

MAEVE BINCHY

Maeve Binchy's Dublin 4

DUBLIN ❧ WARD RIVER ❧ 1982

Carmel waited until the end of the Gay Byrne show. During the Living Word she put on her coat and took out her shopping basket on wheels. She never liked to miss Gay; once she had been able to give him a small cooker for a one-parent family. She hadn't spoken to him himself but the girl on the show had been very nice, and they had sent a nice girl to collect it, or else she was from the organisation which had asked for it. It had never been made quite clear. Carmel had sent in one or two entries for the mystery voice competition too, but she had never been called on to guess it. She didn't like to leave the house before the Living Word. It seemed rude to God, to walk out just when the few short minutes of religion were on.

She knew she should really listen to programmes like Day by Day which followed it, they would make her informed, but somehow she always felt her mind wandering and she never quite understood why people go so hot under the collar about things. Once she had said to Sheila that it would be nice to have someone sitting beside you to tell you what was going on in life, and Sheila told her to shut up, otherwise everyone would say they had learned nothing after all those years with the Loreto nuns ... She thought that Sheila had been upset that day but she couldn't be sure.

It was bright and sunny out, a nice autumn day. She pushed her tartan shopping bag on wheels in front of her, remembering when it had been a pram that she pushed. She used to know many more people in those days. She was always stopping and talking to people, wasn't she? Or was that memory playing tricks, like thinking that the summers were always hot when she was young and that they had spent their whole time on Killiney beach? That wasn't true, her younger brother Charlie said that they only went twice or three times a summer; perhaps the other memory wasn't true either. Perhaps she didn't stop at the bottom of Eglinton Road when she pointed out to the girls where the buses went to sleep in the bus home, perhaps there had been nobody much around then either.

She looked at the prices of wine in the off-licence and wrote down the names of some of them so that she could make her list and selection later on. She then spent a happy hour looking at books in the big book shop. She copied down recipe after recipe in her little jotter. From time to time she got a look from one of the assistants, but she looked respectable and was causing no trouble so nobody said anything. Seared in her mind was a remark that Ethel had once made about a house where she had dined. 'The woman has no imagination. I can't understand why you ask people round for prawn cocktail and roast beef ... I mean, why not tell them to eat at home and come round later for drinks?' Carmel loved prawn cocktail, and had little glass dishes which it would look very well in. They used to have trifle in them when she was young. She had kept them after things had been divided up between herself and Charlie but she had never used them. They stood gathering dust, eight of them, at the back of the cupboard in the scullery. She would make another kind of starter, not prawn cocktail, and she would use those selfsame glasses for it, whatever it was. She rejected grapefruit segments and worked it out methodically. You couldn't have paté, that would have to be on a plate, or soup, that couldn't be in a glass, or any kind of fish of course ... no, it had to be something cold you ate with a spoon.

She would find it eventually, she had all day, she had twenty-nine more days ... there was no rush. She must not get fussed. She found it. Orange Vinaigrette. Ethel couldn't say that that was unimaginative ... you cut up oranges and black olives and onions and fresh mint ... sounded terrific, you poured a vinaigrette sauce over it ... it would be perfect. Carmel smiled happily. She knew she was doing the right thing. All she had to do was go at it slowly.

She would go home now and rest; tomorrow she would come out and find a main course, and then a dessert. She had work to do at home too. Joe had said that if he was going to come and help her he would need co-operation. She mustn't have turned into a dowdy middle-aged old frump, she must look smart and glamorous and well turned out. She had thirty afternoons to organise that.

WILLIAM CARLETON

*The Clarionet, The Dead Boxer
and Barney Branagan*

LONDON ❧ ROUTLEDGE & CO. ❧ 1850
FIRST PUBLISHED *DUBLIN UNIVERSITY MAGAZINE*, 1848

Barney, having nothing else to do for the remainder of the day, inquired his way to the butter market, not only that he might pass the time, but also to see how the wind blew, touching the prices. Until he reached that busy and classical spot, the adventures of the day seemed to him like a dream. Not a man looked at him that he did not suspect to be a blackleg, robber, or cut-throat. He had always heard awful accounts of the numerous strangers that had been robbed, kidnapped, or murdered in Dublin; and it is not, indeed, surprising, if we consider what he had encountered since his arrival in it— a space of only a few hours—that his apprehensions should have been excited until they were little short of actual terror.

The butter market, however—heavens! the great Dublin butter market—which he was in a few minutes to see, gave a complete *supersedeas* to every such sensation. His whole soul was in a tumult of high-wrought expectation and prophetic enjoyment; but never did man suffer more from allowing his imagination to run riot when he saw the poor, paltry, shabby, miserable, contemptible exhibition that it was—he groaned at heart and in spirit. He felt chap-fallen, annoyed, grieved. 'Here,' said he, 'have I thravelled above four score miles to see the great Dublin butter market, and may I never bite an auger, but I have seen more butter of a market day in the town of Kilscaddaun than comes here at this rate for a month. Mavrone, oh—but I am the unfortunate boy every way! Chiernah yeelish! Sich a market! May God send me safe home wid my life and health, and I'll be continted!' For an hour or two he amused himself by sauntering about, piercing one cask, tasting another, guessing the weight of that cool, and examining with great vigilance and sagacity all the local tricks, strange usages, and technical phrases that prevailed. In a little time he forgot himself, and became better pleased. He had added something to his experience as a butter merchant, ascertained the market prices, and was every way prepared for the sale of his own to-morrow.

Never did any human being pass a night of such terror and distress as did Barney on that. His throat was cut successfully several times; he was robbed of the proceeds of his butter; he was stripped naked and narrowly escaped with his life. But above all that he felt, in the groaning and spasmodic horror of sleep, were the paralyzing agonies which he suffered from the associations connected with the sack-'em-ups. The grin of the corpse was in his soul. The white eyelids, the flattened nose, and the hideous mouth were before his spirit, exaggerated by terror and imagination into all that was frightful. Sometimes the dead body was astride of him, poking his ribs with his own butter auger. Sometimes he thought it was one of the magistrates who wore a queue, that was laying on him with that luckless appendage as if he had been pushing him for the Derby stakes; and though last, not least, came the old mendicant with his bitter sneer and glittering eye looking into his very soul, and attempting to suffocate him into the bargain, with the clouted patches of his old great coat. When to all this is added, that he never yet could sleep soundly in a strange bed, and had a most pitiable fear of ghosts, the reader may give a pretty correct guess as to the nature of the repose he enjoyed on that night.

It had been arranged during the evening between him and the mendicant, whom he had reason to look upon as his guardian angel, that they should both go to the butter market together. Without this promise from his friend, Barney would not indeed have considered himself safe; but as it was, on reaching the market, he went through it with the air of a man confident in his own sagacity, and up to all the tricks and manoeuvres of the place. In the course of a very short time he disposed of his butter, saw it tasted, weighed, marked, and, what was still better, received in good Bank of Ireland notes, such a sum of money as, allowing for the contingency of his reaching home safely, caused him to feel quite satisfied that he had made the trip in question to the metropolis.

Nothing now prevented him from leaving Dublin but the purchase of several things for his wife and children which he could get neither so good nor so cheap near home, and which he had promised them. The old mendicant, after giving him every necessary advice and caution against the tricks and traps that might be laid for him, said he could stay no longer; but now that the principal danger was over—his butter well sold and the money for it in his fob—in good notes, too—he thought there could be no such very great danger, provided he looked well to his pockets, did not drink with anyone, and entered into no intercourse with strangers. 'But you must not leave town today. The danger here is past, because *I* am with you; but go out of town by yourself, and the danger is before you and over you. I must now go, but I will see you in the evening.'

'Stop,' said Barney, 'you have been a friend to me when I wanted one—ay, an' a good friend, too—I won't ax questions, but you know I promised you the price of a betther coat than that.'

The old fellow looked at the coat and then at Barney, and the eye as before glittered.

'Well,' said he, 'a better coat—maybe not: a newer, a decenter, a more fashionable coat you might easily get me—but I tell you I wouldn't part with this coat for all the coats in the shop of the wealthiest tailor in Dublin. It's an old friend and an old companion, and is more valuable to me than it looks: so you see I don't like to throw it away yet. At the same time I'll take, thankfully, any present you may give me. I will not deny but I deserve something at your hands.'

'Then,' said Barney, 'here's two pound ten—a thirty-shilling note and a pound note—get some better duds than thim—for betune you and me your dress is open to objection. If you think that's not enough I'll put more to it.'

The old man looked at him, and seemed to calculate, if one could judge by the keen cold expression of his eye, to what extent the benevolence of the other might carry him; but, as if upon further consideration, he appeared to change his purpose.

'Why,' said he, 'you might make it—eh? let me see—you might—no, no—you have done the generous thing—I'll take—take no more—no, I'll take no more, not a penny.'

'Well, get the feathers, for you want them.'

'Would you wish,' said the old fellow, after having slipped the notes into his pocket, 'to ruin my trade? No, no—these clothes must do me for the rest of my life. But thank you, thank you,—take care of yourself, and I'll convoy you some miles out of town when you're going home.'

They then separated, Barney to the White Horse, in order to get a youngster acquainted with the town to show him the streets and particular houses in which he wished to make his purchases; the old fellow adjourned to his usual seat upon the park-road. The only person about the inn who could be afforded to him as a guide was a slipshod tattered girl about nineteen years of age; but as she knew the places to which he was going, and had her honesty solemnly vouched for by her mistress, Barney was fain to accompany her, being anxious to lose as little time as possible in a city which he felt to be a series of pitfalls, into some one of which every step he took was likely to tumble him.

Three or four hours elapsed in this shopping expedition, and Barney, with his tattered guide walking loaded with his purchases before him—for on no possible account would he let her for a moment out of his sight— was on his return home through Little Britain Street, when the girl was stopped by an acquaintance of her own sex, who shook hands with and appeared very glad to see her. Barney, who was himself burdened pretty heavily, being determined not to let the wench get behind him, was obliged to stand, and of course had an opportunity of hearing their conversation. This consisted of the usual gradations by which such casual recontres between individuals of the sex are marked, viz., first, warm inquiries as to the personal welfare of the parties; secondly, of their absent friends; and thirdly, a discussion upon sweethearts and love.

'And how is your mother, Biddy?'

'Bedad, sportin', as light as a cobweb. Where are you livin' now Judy?'

'At the White Horse, up in Stoney Batther.'

'Oh, I know; sure my cousin Mary lived there before she tuck to the bad, poor girl. Is Pat Rorke there still?'

'Lord, Biddy, but you're full o' your mock modesty. Maybe you don't know who he is?'

'Bad luck to the hair I care whether he is or not—he's but a poor crature. Are you in a hurry? Well, divle cares, wait a minute. You know Peggy Halpenny, from Stockin' Alley below, her mother keeps half a sheet an' a stool o' tay at the Egg Market. Sure, my dear, who does I meet but her an' a soger from the barricks above, that she's doing it heavy wid—he's to bring her to the Straw Market on Tuesday night, no less. Well, my dear, she was biddin' him good by when I came up; an' my dear, says she to me, "sure I have news for you, Bid."

'"I hope it's good, Peggy" says I, "an' be on your guard, my dear, becase you know what sogers is," says I, givin' her a bit o' good advice at the time.'

'"My dear," says she, "that's all settled; a red coat's his Majesty's livery, Bid; an' on Tuesday night, my dear, we are to be spliced at de Market—I'm not ashamed of it—an' so I tould them at home. I'll follow him to de world's end," says I, "an farther, if he goes it—so yez may make your minds aisy", says I, "I'm not the girl to desart the boy that's true to me"—so seein' how I tuck afther him, they said no more. Well, but the news—I must tell you that—sure, Judy—but first, when did you see Mickey Gallaher?'

'Not these three weeks—Sunday night three weeks at the dance in Grange Gorman.'

'Well, my dear, it's a friend would tell you this—he's as great a scamp as Pat Rorke himself. Sure, no longer ago than last Sunday, he had Nancy Moran at de Strawberry Beds—he an' some schamin cadey out o' place traited her an' a girl from Boot Lane at de Beds, and had half a pint of punch on their way home, at the Hole in the Wall.'

'Well, my dear, who cares? Mickey Gallaher was never more than any other boy to me, whatever he might be to others.'

This was accompanied by a short toss of the head, which showed, however, that she felt it. 'I wish them joy of him that gets him. Where are you goin' now Bid?'

'To the Post Office, wid a note from poor Mr Cassidy—oh, but *you* never seen him—it was before your time when he used to be at the White Horse. Sorra the fut I'll stop in that house; they're a gallis pack that comes about it. There's poor Mr Cassidy—oh, Judy, if you'd see him now, he can't live four an' twenty hours—there he's lyin' in my aunt's, down on Boot Lane, half mad, I believe, an' half dead, too.'

'I know your aunt's.'

'Bad luck to the whole crew o' them—there he's dying be inches, and they know it at the White Horse very well—but not one o' the blackguard crew ever comes next or near him.'

Barney had been for some time impatient, and would ere now have made the girl move on, were it not that he felt a kind of curiosity in the communications which they made to each other. His patience, however, was on the very point of yielding, when the mention of Cassidy's name not only arrested his attention, but if we may use the expression, actually caused his very ears to erect themselves with the interest he felt at it. Nor was this the sole cause of the excitement which began to absorb his feelings. The very bad character given by this girl to the White Horse Inn, astounded and alarmed him. Could it be possible, after all, that he was in danger *there*? The old mendicant certainly proved himself his friend, but yet even he was surrounded by mystery, and appeared to know the movements of half the swindlers and blacklegs in the city. One thing would relieve him, and that was an interview with Cassidy, if he were the same person? From him he could expect the truth as far at least as he knew it. He could advise him also how to act, and perhaps throw light upon circumstances which to him were at the present time unaccountable. But above all, he himself might be able to soothe the death-bed of his old friend if he were dying, or if not, to afford him such assistance as his health and circumstances then required.

'Poor fellow,' said kind-hearted Barney, with a sigh; 'who knows but I might be able yet to send him to his friends. If he can bear the journey he won't want the needful to pay his passage, and keep him comfortable till he gets to them.'

Little he knew what was to befall himself when his sterling heart conceived the benevolent sentiments he then uttered.

'Come, girsha,' said he to the girl—'get an, get an—you don't intind to stop here the whole day.'

'Good-by, Bid—will you be at the dance in Church-street on Sunday evenin'?'

'If I can,' replied Biddy. 'Give my love to Pat Rorke—ha, ha, ha—the poor rap!'

'Now,' continued he, addressing Judy, when the other passed on, 'I'll give you a shillin' to yurself over an' above what I'll pay you for this trip, if you'll bring me in an hour or two to the man named Cassidy that your acquaintance spoke of. An' see, girsha, say nothin' about it to any one.'

'Very well,' said the girl, 'I'll be goin' out on a message as far as Mary's Abbey, anyhow—a shillin' mind.'

'Ay, a shillin', an' if you can keep your mouth shut may be another.'

'Devil a one about the place I'd think worth tellin' it to,' she replied. 'Keep your eye on me in the evenin': an' when I'm goin' out I'll look to you, and pin my shawl this way, then you can slip afther me, and no one will notice us.'

It was so arranged.

BRIAN CLEEVE

Cry of Morning

LONDON ❧ MICHAEL JOSEPH ❧ 1971

At the end of 1956 the Cecil Gandons returned to Europe, and to Dublin. They bought a pleasant eighteenth-century house in Merrion Square, perfect for small intimate dinner parties of a dozen or so, to which she was determined none of Cecil's dull and horrid family would ever be invited; and for visits to London the lease of a mews cottage in Knightsbridge. It was when they were moving some furniture into the Mews that they saw Felicity O'Connor's play. As a play it meant nothing to Lady Honoria. If she thought anything about it she thought that it was very lower class and very vulgar. But Lord John Somerville had recommended them to see it, and Lady Featherstonhaugh was so hysterical with laughter trying to describe the sausage scene that she was in tears for half of a dinner party, and Anne Bench the society portrait painter was actually painting the girl who wrote the play and calling her 'Fil', so that there was no doubt that one had to go to it. She contrived to meet the girl at Anne Bench's house in Chelsea, met the Lennoxes at the same party, and asked everyone back to the Mews. She was still not acting consciously, working consciously towards anything. She was simply like a kitten trying to rake sunbeams towards itself with lazy, playful paws. If it was warm and bright it must be hers to play with, that was the way life was. Since she had come back to Europe one beautiful thing after another had dropped into her small, joyful grasp, and in a delightfully different way to South Africa.

There, there was always Cousin Julius disapproving of things and talking about politics and the family's responsibilities and what so-and-so would think. And people had always thought of her as one of 'the family'. But here in lovely, lovely London, and darling Dublin, she was simply herself, Lady Honoria, young and beautiful and rich and unique. Some of the stuffy older people in Dublin also talked about 'the family' and said some of the dreary things that Cousin Julius used to say, but somehow it was easier to escape from them, laugh at Lord Alfred and blow him a kiss and go off to the races or fly over to London to get her hair done, or to Paris to buy a dress, or just sit in Jammet's Bar while people whispered, 'That's Lady Honoria, isn't she a peach?'

And gradually, out of this warm and gorgeous happiness there was growing the ambition to be more than just a peach; to establish her uniqueness on rocklike foundations; to achieve the queenship she had daydreamed about in South Africa when some millionairess with diamonds like headlamps had outjewelled her at a party. The Queen of Dublin Society.

For nearly half a century Dublin had had nothing that could really be called society. The Viceroy and his Court had gone, and the Marty Mullins and their like had come. The well-bred, both Protestant and Catholic, had shuddered and fled to London, or stayed in their desolate country houses, if the Shinners hadn't burned them down. The great families, people like the Gandons and the Gardiners, the Beauchamps and the De Rigos, had become part of English society, regarding Ireland simply as the place where they had their businesses, or their estates, or their shooting-lodges and racing-stables. The Gandons more than most had kept some kind of roots in Ireland, and made a quiet display of the fact that they had kept them, but in their hearts their London houses were their real homes, and secretly they regarded their Irish houses and estates as being in a kind of rebellious colony. They had sound working relation-ships with the new rulers of the place (still 'new' after ten, and twenty, and thirty years) but they were purely working relations and it would not have occurred to any of the Gandons, any more than to the Beauchamps or the De Rigos, that there could be any *Society* in Ireland. In Ireland, one worked, or shot, or fished, or hunted, or joyfully met one's friends at the Horse Show. But for Society, if one bothered with that kind of thing, one went to London. It was so axiomatic that one never thought about it.

It would be an exaggeration to say that Lady Honoria thought about it herself. She simply felt it. That like South Africa, London was too big. But Dublin was within her reach. Why shouldn't Dublin have a Society, and why shouldn't she be Queen of it? She imagined herself surrounded by all the Beautiful People whose pictures she saw in the glossy maga-zines. Or people like them. Well bred and rich and clever and talented and adoring her. Some of them of course not quite so rich, so that she could help them. Indeed some of them, particularly the talented ones, might be quite poor, so that she could guide their careers towards tremen-dous successes, and afterwards everyone would say, 'Without Lady

Honoria so-and-so would be absolutely nowhere. She *made* him, my dear, absolutely made him.'

Again it was instinct rather than any conscious plan. It was obvious that Dublin Society would have to be different to London's, centred not so much on wealth, or even birth, where in any event she was not really in favour of strong competition, but on some quality or qualities that she could influence. She could not make people rich. She could not confer titles of nobility or start an Order of Chivalry. But she could patronise talent. Young, handsome, well-behaved talent that would be adoringly grateful. Poets, painters, scholars, young lawyers whom she would encourage to become judges, architects whom she would nurse towards creating splendid skyscrapers and wonderful country houses. At some stage in her childhood an elderly French acquaintance of the Earl's had told her about Madame de Staël and the great French salons, and fractured remnants of the stories had stuck in her subconscious. A lovely woman lying on a beautiful, elegant couch; young men in satin coats on their knees beside her, reciting poetry and witticisms—the witticisms making fun of other, far less attractive women. As a small, angry child with a courtesy title and no shoes she had clutched that image to her bony little chest like a beautiful doll, until it became part of her being. To be rich, to be adored, to be admired and flattered and looked up to. As black Marcia's voice screeched after her in the scented Jamaican dusk, threatening her with woeful punishments, for whatever she had most recently done or not done, she dreamed of queenship, of being forever beyond the necessity of having to wash her father's shirt, or scrub out the hut, or go down to the post office in Falmouth to see if the remittance had come.

To be Queen of Dublin. It was surely possible. As the young and beautiful wife of the heir presumptive of the Gandons the title was almost hers for the asking. The Gandons had laid the foundations of their fortune at the beginning of the eighteenth century, speculating in land, buying up estates from Catholics who could not keep them without abjuring, and jobbing government contracts for timber and building stone. By the 1760s they were so rich they could afford to be half honest, and began to yearn for prestige. They were among the first and the greatest of the Dublin developers, leasing enormous tracts of land from the Crown on the south side of the Liffey, and trying to rival the Gardiners and Fitzwilliams in laying out streets and squares of handsome Georgian houses that would make Dublin one of the finest cities in Europe.

By the end of the century they were so rich they could even afford patriotism and instructed the six members of the Dublin Parliament who owed their seats to Gandon influence to vote against the Act of Union. Two betrayed them for English pensions. One died of apoplexy at cards the night before the vote. The other three did what they had been ordered to do, and the Gandons were enshrined in Dublin legend as 'a fine family, the rale thing, rale old gintry'. And to do them justice they kept faith with their city. What they had built and laid out they protected. And even when the Gandon Estates and properties in Dublin became very much a secondary matter for the family, and their main financial interests lay in London and South Africa, they saw to it that no unscrupulous lease-holder spoiled or exploited their part of Dublin. No one could alter or build or rebuild or demolish anything without their Estate Offices' care-fully considered permission, and every leaseholder was bound by severe penalty to maintain his property in good condition.

Dublin owed a great deal to the Gandon family and ever after a generation of 'Independence' resentment of the Gandons as Anglo-Irish snobs and West-British God-Save-the-Kings was balanced by a vague recognition, a half-remembrance, that they had done something for the city. But if Dublin's recognition of what the Gandons stood for in Irish history was vague and shadowy, Lady Honoria's was non-existent, and it was purely accident that she stumbled on 'Evictions' as a Cause, a means to her end of becoming Dublin's Madame de Staël. During a long and atrociously boring dinner party she was obliged to sit beside an elderly architect who insisted on telling her about Aram Court, and the abom-inable sins of the Dublin Developers who were obviously going to destroy it, along with the rest of eighteenth-century Dublin.

By the end of the dinner she would happily have burned Aram Court to the ground with her own hands. It was only afterwards, telling the story of the dinner party and all the boring details to which she had been forced to listen to some artistically minded friends, as a sample of the kind of thing she had to suffer from the Gandons' idea of social life, that she realized, from their unexpected reaction, that here was indeed a Cause, and that these particular friends, who hadn't yet grasped the point of her story, were electing her its leader. 'Darling Honoria, how brilliant of you to know so much about it all. Those poor, poor people! Where will they go? What will they do? I mean, they'll be put out into the street. If only the Gandons could stop these awful Developers?'

It took her barely a second to change the point of her story from resigned boredom to passionate Queenly indignation. 'The Gandons?' she said. '*I shall stop them.*' The Society of the Friends of Aram Court was born half an hour later. And did indeed deserve to be born.

The two houses in the courtyard were truly unique; the last remaining pair in Dublin of Dutch Billy houses, built at the end of the seventeenth century, with cross-ridged roofs, leaded windows, overhanging first and second storeys, and a third storey in the attics, lit by small, square-leaded windows tucked into the shallow triangles of their gables. The Georgian developers of the middle and late eighteenth and early nineteenth centuries, who had swept away most of Tudor and Jacobean Dublin to make room for their own neo-classical ideal of a city, had overlooked them, or not been able to buy them up, and had built round them, hiding them behind the mid-Georgian façades of Oxman Street.

Because of their discreetly hidden position they had been bought in 1759 by a wealthy Dublin Catholic and used as both a Convent for French nuns and a Mass house. After the Catholic Emancipation of 1829 they had been willed to the Catholic Archbishop of Dublin as homes for indigent clergy and had been kept for that use until 1903, when they had been sold to a Solicitor. The Solicitor's hand-painted sign, *Scrivener & Attorney*, still hung in one of the windows. His grandson had been interested in the theatre, and from 1931 until 1958 the two houses had been used to store costumes, to rehearse homeless plays, and sometimes to shelter homeless actors and hangers-on of the theatre.

Now, emptied of most of the costumes and occupied only casually and occasionally by some 'fit-up' players whose travelling lorry and caravan were parked in the courtyard, the houses were for sale by public auction, the auctioneers being Messrs Moberley & Gunn.

And but for the accident of that dinner party and two of her friends misunderstanding the point of Lady Honoria's rather long story and where her actual indignation lay the auction would have gone off as quietly as everyone else had intended it to, and the two Dutch Billy houses would have changed hands for a few hundred pounds apiece. As things turned out, they were to become one of the *causes célèbres* of Dublin, and would make auctioneering history as well.

'Those poor, helpless little people,' Lady Honoria cried, genuinely moved by her own fineness of spirit. 'They'll lose their homes over my dead body!' Or at least over Cecil's overdraft. Because as even she had realised from what the elderly architect had told her, the two houses in Aram Court were right in the middle of the Developers' planned new building. Without them their whole scheme would be paralysed. And she would paralyse it. She would simply buy the houses in Aram Court herself.

ANTHONY CRONIN

The Life of Reilly

LONDON ❧ SECKER & WARBURG ❧ 1964

I returned to Dublin to find things greatly changed. Sir Mortlake had come into an unexpected legacy and returned to England, and The Warrens was no more. Eunice had departed to Paris, saying, apparently, that it could hardly be worse than Dublin. The closing of The Warrens had indeed been a great blow. Gone was my broom-cupboard and my undulant mattress. Never again in that tiny space would I solace myself with the sages of the New World Bible. I faced now for the first time the problems of homelessness, but let me gloss over them; let me instead describe my next home, my next haven, which was to be mine until I was flung by chance or circumstance or the stars into the big world once more, as editor of a monthly magazine known as *The Trumpet*: though when I describe this home as mine I do so with the reservation that in its physical being it belonged to someone else, and that when I occupied it I was plagued a good deal by guests.

This new home soon came to be called 'The Gurriers', from the number of people of that ilk whom it accommodated. Gurrier is a Dublin word I find it rather difficult to define. Not that it is not a word of precise application, in the sense that the justness or otherwise of that application is not immediately apparent, but that the gurrier elements in a personality can crop up in widely differing contexts. Thus, for instance, a Cabinet Minister can be, and frequently is, justly described as a gurrier; at least half the population of O'Turk's could be, and were, so described. An element of shiftiness is implied, and perhaps an element of braggadocio. A certain lack of respectability is almost certainly imputed, but with some unsuc-cessfully worn trappings of respectability: a double breasted suit, slightly wrong about the shoulders and slightly frayed at the rather wide trouser ends, would be more likely to be the uniform of a gurrier than the polo-neck and corduroys, though the latter certainly could be, and frequently were, also. On the other hand one could be completely disreputable and still not qualify for the appellation. An element of shabbiness of style,

ready to degenerate at any moment into complete shamelessness of
manoeuvre or approach, is certainly to be conveyed, but the word must
on no account be confused with the word gutty, which simply means a
low, loud-mouthed fellow from the slums. It would be hard to qualify for
the appellation if one were genuinely and unmistakably remarkable: a
person of extreme depravity or genius; on the other hand your ordinary,
run-of-the-mill fellow in a pub would scarcely qualify either, unless by
ordinary were meant ordinary, run-of-the-mill gurrier, for some, however
slight, eccentricity or oddity of character, betraying an unusual if of course
completely inaccurate view of the world, is implicit in the description
also. Conscious knavery is not a necessary part of the meaning of the
term, and a scrupulously honest gurrier is certainly conceivable; yet at the
same time a scrupulously honest gurrier would certainly be a surprise.
Most, if not all, of the O'Turk's beggars were gurriers.

'The Gurriers' was a shed of sorts, but it was a shed whose original
function or *raison d'être* it would have been extremely hard to decide. It
stood at the bottom of one of those long, overgrown gardens behind
Baggot Street, which suggests, if I may hazard a joke, that it was a shed of
the common, or garden variety, but it was by no means that. For one
thing it was made of concrete, though with a corrugated iron roof, and it
stood on its own, with four walls, being no sort of a lean-to. It had a door
in the middle of one wall, and to one side of that door was a window
which resembled an ordinary window except that no part of it was made
to open. Thus, with its four concrete walls, its door and its window, 'The
Gurriers' was in a way more like a little house than a shed, and yet it was
quite definitely not a little house either, for the interior was entirely bare
and there was no fireplace, nor chimney, nor outlet for smoke; neither
was there recess or cupboard or protuberance or angle, but simply the
four concrete walls, the door, the fixed window, the corrugated iron roof
and a concrete floor. There was nothing, that is to say, structural apart
from these, for there was some furniture. The most outstanding article
was a curious double decker iron bedstead, a perfectly plain, ordinary,
old-fashioned bedstead, with tubular black structure and brass knobs,
except that the structure was partly duplicated, like a freak of nature, and
the brass knobs were consequently high in the air near the roof.

I acquired 'The Gurriers' through the agency of a friend of mine who
had recently, for want of anything better to do, set up in a small way as a
contractor; hired some men from O'Turk's who had learned or purported
to have learned carpentry and other minor arts in various gaols; and

proceeded to outbid other, more orthodox and more established contractors for some sort of renovating job on the house to which the garden and
shed were attached. He explained that he would gladly have let me sleep
in the house while the renovating job proceeded, but that the activities of
himself and his men would undoubtedly have been a disturbance to me, at
least in the unseasonable hours of the morning, while I might possibly
have been an impediment to them, to say nothing of the fact that the
owner's representative might occasionally take it into his head to visit the
house at night to see how the work was proceeding, and while I on my
palliasse might conceivably have been explained away as a night-
watchman, the explanation might not be found convincing. In the
meantime he certainly hoped that the job—they were breaking the house
up into plywood boxes, to be let at extravagant rents—would be
protracted, and he was prepared to let me have the shed at the merely
nominal rent of five shillings per week.

'The Gurriers' curious resemblance to a little house, albeit a little
house without light, water, recesses or openable aperture for the egress of
smoke or the ingress of oxygen, pleased me very much. I felt, for a short
while at least, that I had a home, almost, as I say, a house, of my own.
Access to 'The Gurriers' in the daytime was through the big house,
merrily resounding with hammerings, blasphemies and complaints. At
night the big house was unfortunately locked up, I think to prevent the
workmen sleeping or junketing on the premises, for fear, as I said, that the
owner or his representative might drop in as they were passing. Then
entrance and exit had to be effected over the garden wall, a feat not physi-
cally difficult for one could hoist oneself with the help of a wire guy that
supported a telephone pole and various footholds in the wall, and descend
by the roof of the shed and some boxes that I soon arranged. The only
drawback about that was that it looked rather odd in daylight or the early
hours of the evening, and quite suspicious if one should happen to be
observed later in the night, nor was it easy to explain to the police the
circumstances in which one lived. However, after a certain hour the lane
was not very populous, being like most of the carriage lanes behind those
broad Dublin streets, occupied mostly by little workshops and garages
which closed reasonably early.

I am afraid, though, however houselike it was, that 'The Gurriers'
had certain very definite disadvantages as a home; and that I tended to
regard it as a poetic concept, something to be nested in the heart rather
than very much frequented. I slept there at nights, certainly, but

somehow, once one had emerged in search of one's morning cup of tea, there was an inclination not to go back until the possibilities of the day or the evening were absolutely exhausted. On a summer morning one could lie on, listening to the birds singing in the garden, looking at the roofs of the mews and the blue sky; but once out, you were out in the world, there was little doubt about it. It was nice to know one had a place, and a place that so much resembled an odd little house, but there was a tendency to try to get the day filled up without actually spending much time there. There was something just a little off-putting about the lack of the appurtenances of home, the gas-ring, the tap, the fire or anyway heater, which the miniature house-like charm of the place did not quite compensate for, at least circumstantially, though I thought of its existence often and gratefully during the day, and it much pleased me to think that I had as it were a secret, invisible house in the middle of the city.

TERENCE DE VERE WHITE

The March Hare

LONDON ❧ VICTOR GOLLANCZ LTD ❧ 1970

Milly's rate of pay with Mr Mantovani was three pence for small statues and five shillings for life-size ones. She came to work at ten o'clock, getting off the tram at the Ballast Office and walking up the Quays to Usher's Island, where her employer's premises were, in a yard at the back. If there was enough work she sometimes stayed until after lunch and then walked slowly along the Quays, looking into the second-hand shops at furniture, books and pictures. Everything interested her. Then at four o'clock she went to the college in Stephen's Green where there were always a few backward pupils ready to pay for coaching. Sometimes she worked until seven o'clock.

At the end of the week she gave Carrie a pound; but kept her counsel as to what she was earning 'in that dreadful place with that dreadful man', as Carrie put it.

Milly's employment shocked her mother. She saw it as only one degree above a nursemaid's, and two, if that, above prostitution. It was never mentioned. On no account was Lady Kelly to hear of it. She had never recovered from the ingratitude of Milly's refusal to act as governess to the French consul's children, and concealed her curiosity under a fine show of indifference. 'Milly is well, I hope.'

'I don't know how you can do it, Milly,' Dolly told her after she had accompanied her mother on a surprise visit to Milly's studio. Milly was angry; but Carrie stood her ground. It was her duty to see the circumstances in which her daughter was working; it was also essential that the dreadful Italian should be appraised of the fact that Milly had a mother, and a mother of a kind to be reckoned with. They arrived unexpected, and stood in the yard looking like hibernating birds that had just landed and not yet found their bearings. Carrie, smaller than Dolly, stood her ground better. Dolly wavered and hovered, five feet seven of apology. Carrie, nose in air, looked round. Milly saw them come in, was surprised, annoyed, and in no hurry to disclose her hiding-place. Mr Mantovani's workshop was what met you when you came into the yard. He was covered in plaster; but he put down the mould on which he was working and came out politely to attend to his callers.

'Good-morning,' Carrie said. Dolly smiled and swayed.

'Buon giorno,' said Mr Mantovani, looking past Carrie at Dolly and deciding she was a virgin.

'I want to see Miss Preston, my daughter. I happened to be passing. Are you her employer?'

Mr Mantovani had never had time to master the language, but he had gathered that this was Milly's mother and, presumably, her sister. He had always been surprised that Milly wanted to work for him, and he assumed that her family were calling to take her away. She was turning out statues at a prodigious rate; and if this was a deputation to demand better terms he was ready to capitulate. His conscience was easy. He had treated Milly with the respect due to the Madonna even if she was beginning to interfere with his concentration.

'Miss Preston,' he said, pointing to a ladder. 'Miss Preston up there.' He was in a dilemma induced by natural politeness. His respect for all three ladies left nothing to be desired; but Milly's force of character had always subdued him and he hesitated to call her down. At the same time it was wrong to send her mother up a ladder after her. He decided to lead the way.

'We can manage,' Carrie said. 'Hold the ladder, Dolly.'

At this point Milly emerged. The studio was once a hay loft over stables. Dolly got up in two bounds; but her mother, holding her skirts appropriately, took longer. She looked round, contracting her nostrils, exuding disapproval. Dolly's interest was more cheerfully expressed. The loft was crowded with white figures, standing in rows, like a Greek chorus; on a trestle table there were scores of smaller ones; Milly's paints were on a smaller table at a north window. She was finishing the sandals on a life-sized St Anthony.

Carrie shivered. 'You will get your death of cold here.'

'There's a fire in the grate,' Dolly said, earning a frown from her mother for her pains.

'I'm not cold,' Milly said.

'We were shopping at McBirney's, looking for blankets for the spare bed. We thought you might like us to pay you a visit,' Carrie said.

Milly said nothing.

Carrie looked round disapprovingly. 'What happens,' she said at length, echoing the thought in Dolly's mind, 'when you want to go to the WC?'

'I go across to the hotel. In an emergency the Mantovanis have a place in the yard.' Carrie shivered and Dolly blushed.

'It's primitive, but it's clean. They have the sweetest little children, tons of them. I've lost count. I wish you had told me you were coming. I'd have warned them. Mr Mantovani would have put on his best trousers.'

Dolly blushed again. She had noticed Mr Mantovani's trousers.

'I brought you some fruit. It's good for you,' Carrie said. 'Dolly we had better be on the move. I have an appointment with Prost for twelve o'clock.'

'There's nothing very much to see,' Milly said, 'unless you would like to meet Mrs Mantovani. I'm sure they would like you to admire the family.'

'I haven't sweets for them or anything,' Carrie said helplessly. She had a feeling of defeat, of having walked up to the walls of a fortress, and then retreated without giving battle. Milly was too much for her, and Dolly as effective an ally as a blade of grass.

But Milly was right. Mr Mantovani had gone indoors, and when the ladies came down the ladder they found Mrs Mantovani in an advanced state of pregnancy at the foot surrounded by a flock of black-haired, white-faced, black-eyed little Mantovanis, chattering like sparrows. Mrs Mantovani, like her husband, had no proficiency in English; but she was eloquent in her Neapolitan greetings to the mother and sister of the hen that was laying eggs of gold. Carrie and Dolly were wafted indoors. Coffee was magically produced and sweet biscuits. One little Mantovani threw up. Another disgraced himself. Mr Mantovani was equally delighted by both.

'It's a frightful come-down. I don't know how she can do it.'

Carrie, returned from her visit to Prost's, was sitting with Dolly over their luncheon—brown bread, butter, a slice of ham each, and coffee; with coffee, as a treat, they had Marie biscuits.

'I suppose she's making lots of money,' Dolly replied, defending her sister and tremulously envious. It was depressing never to have any. It made you feel so completely powerless and at the mercy of anyone who chose to pay.

'She never tells me a thing. I might be a stranger, instead of her mother.'

DERMOT DEVITT

1884 A Novel

DUBLIN ❧ FOILSEACHAIN NAISIUNTA TEO 1984 ❧ 1984

Perused the advertisements dealing with advancing of money and cut out a couple: 'Money advanced on the deposit of every description of valuable property by James J. Cunningham, Pawnbroker, 10 and 11 Lombard Street, Westland Row,' and 'Advances for £5 and upwards to Householders, Dairymen, Farmers etc. in any part of Ireland on note of hand only, at moderate interest, repayments to suit borrowers.' My pockets are suffering from a severe dose of colic and I really must do something to ease the pecuniary pain. The income from my newspaper pieces and the allowance from Father are being gobbled up by the cormorant-like appetite of the landlady and the need to eat, drink and generally indulge that which philosophers are pleased to call existence.

I also cut out the following advertisement: 'Mountjoy Square: a tutor in French is sought for a schoolboy in that area: Current rates paid.' I'll reply to that; why not? My French, although a little brown-red with the rust of disuse, is surely competent to keep one page ahead of any Dublin school boy; Mountjoy Square is convenient, a mere six minutes' brisk walk from my address in Lower Gardiner Street; and then, of course, I need the money. Perhaps the fees are not gargantuan but the difference between financial sufficiency and financial embarrassment is often a mere handful of shining shillings. Putting aside deterring thoughts of the inconvenience caused by being tied to a couple of pre-appointed hours, and the possibly nerve-shredding effect of being in close and continuous proximity to a boisterous boy, I replied to the advertisement. I was not depreciatory in the assessment of my qualifications and ability.

I also cut out another advertisement, this time from the miscellaneous column: 'Would young lady, dressed in black, who travelled by evening train from Longford to Clonhugh on Saturday last send her address and she will benefit by it.'

Went to McBirney's. Bought a blue worsted suit for thirty-five shillings. Saw a nice Irish-tweed suit for forty-five shillings which I might consider if my finances improve. Collected my made-to-measure shirt at Taaffe and Caldwell's in Grafton Street. It cost me five shillings and sixpence. I looked at the pianos in Pigott's of Suffolk Street. If my fingers could pick out a tune on the ivories they would pick out a melancholy one. Even after putting on my new clothes I was not able to shake off the forlorn feeling. I have been in cahoots with the God of Gloominess all day.

The morning brought the dawn standing tip-toe on the Hell-Fire Club—and a missive summoning me to Mountjoy Square.

I am beginning to look upon Mountjoy Square as being a sort of prison and Number 36 as a cell where I have to endure my punishment for the crime of being almost poor.

Eleven-year-old Aubrey Fitzharris is my cell-mate and tacit tormentor.

'Il y a quatre chaises dans la chambre.'

This was the beginning of the Il y a iliad.

'Il y a une table dans la chambre.'

Aubrey's inability to pronounce chambre in any way other than the English equivalent prompted me to think longingly of emptying the contents of the vessel usually associated with that particular room over his head. Even Homer would have nodded off if he had to endure an hour of this. But then Mrs. Charlotte Fitzharris entered the *chambre*, bearing with her *une tasse de thé pour moi*.

Spent an hour tutoring Aubrey Fitzharris in French. Mountjoy Square resounded with the sounds of mispronounced *Français*. How to tell my pupil that the Gallic tongue is nothing like the Queen's English, that the difference is akin to that between Gorgonzola and Cheddar, and that they must be treated accordingly?

'*Suis,*' I said, making the second 's' as silent as a parasite's curse.

Aubrey's pronunciation recalled the resplendent mediaeval uniforms worn by the Pope's guards in the Eternal City.

'Swiss.'

I tried again.

A similar result.

I looked at the ceiling. Its stuccoed simplicity hinted that Michaelangelo had not been consulted in its design. Whatever about the Sistine Chapel and the uniforms of the Swiss Guard.

Eventually I compromised and settled for 'swish', as in cat-o'-nine-tails.

'*Je* swish *Aubrey Fitzharris. Je* swish *un garçon.*'

'No, *Je m'appelle Aubrey Fitzharris; je* swish *un garçon.*'

To grasp the concept of a book on a table is a relatively simple one. To encourage an eleven-year-old Dublin schoolboy, who in all probability will need no more French than 'D'Olier' in his lifetime, and who seems to have the precocity to recognise that fact and the disinterest to bolster that recognition, to express that simple concept in basic French can be a difficult proposition.

'Book' is an object which the medical profession does not normally connect with the condition of cirrhosis, but that was the disease which seemed to affect the following sentence:

'*Le* liver *est sur la table.*'

'*La table.* Lah, lah, lah as in lah-di-dah. Yah, say that now.'

When Mrs. Charlotte Fitzharris came in with the tea and biscuits I watched her as she turned to lay the tray on the sideboard, and paid particular attention to her *quartier dernier*.

Maria Edgeworth

Ennui Vol. VI The Absentee
The Last of the Tales of Fashionable Life

LONDON ❧ J. JOHNSON ❧ 1812

The tide did not permit the packet to reach the Pigeon-House, and the impatient Lord Colambre stepped into a boat, and was rowed across the Bay of Dublin. It was a fine summer morning. The sun shone bright on the Wicklow mountains. He admired, he exulted in the beauty of the prospect; and all the early associations of his childhood, and the patriotic hopes of his riper years, swelled his heart as he approached the shores of his native land. But scarcely had he touched his mother earth, when the whole course of his ideas was changed; and if his heart swelled, it swelled no more with pleasurable sensations, for instantly he found himself surrounded and attacked by a swarm of beggars and harpies, with strange figures and stranger tones: some craving his charity, some snatching away his luggage, and at the same time bidding him 'never trouble himself', and 'never fear.' A scramble in the boat and on shore for bags and parcels began, and an amphibious fight betwixt men, who had one foot on sea and one on land, was seen; and long and loud the battle of trunks and portmanteaus raged! The vanquished departed, clinching their empty hands at their opponents, and swearing inextinguishable hatred; while the smiling victors stood at ease, each grasping his booty—bag, basket, parcel, or portmanteau: 'And, your honour, where *will* these go?—Where *will* we carry 'em all to for your honour?' was now the question. Without waiting for an answer, most of the goods were carried at the discretion of the porters to the custom-house, where, to his lordship's astonishment, after this scene of confusion, he found that he had lost nothing but his patience; all his goods were safe, and a few *tinpennies* made his officious porters happy men and boys; blessings were showered upon his honour, and he was left in peace at an excellent hotel, in —— Street, Dublin. He rested, refreshed himself, recovered his good-humour, and walked into the coffee-house, where he found several officers, English, Irish, and Scotch. One English officer, a very gentlemanlike, sensible-looking man, of middle age, was sitting reading a little pamphlet, when Lord Colambre entered; he looked up from time to time, and in a few minutes rose and joined the conversation; it turned upon the beauties and defects of the city of Dublin. Sir James Brooke (for that was the name of the gentleman) showed one of his brother officers the book which he had been reading observing that, in his opinion, it contained one of the best views of Dublin which he had ever seen, evidently drawn by the hand of a master, though in a slight, playful, and ironical style: it was 'An Intercepted Letter from China.' The conversation extended from Dublin to various parts of Ireland, with all which Sir James Brooke showed that he was well acquainted. Observing that this conversation was particularly interesting to Lord Colambre, and quickly perceiving that he was speaking to one not ignorant of books, Sir James spoke of different representations and misrepresentations of Ireland. In answer to Lord Colambre's inquiries, he named the works which had afforded him the most satisfaction; and with discriminative, not superficial celerity, touched on all ancient and modern authors on this subject, from Spenser and Davies to Young and Beaufort. Lord Colambre became anxious to cultivate the acquaintance of a gentleman who appeared so able and willing to afford him information. Sir James Brooke, on his part, was flattered by this eagerness of attention, and pleased by our hero's manners and conversation; so that, to their mutual satisfaction, they spent much of their time together whilst they were at this hotel; and, meeting frequently in society in Dublin, their acquaintance every day increased and grew into intimacy; an intimacy which was highly advantageous to Lord Colambre's views of obtaining a just idea of the state of manners in Ireland. Sir James Brooke had at different periods been quartered in various parts of the country—had resided long enough in each to become familiar with the people, and had varied his residence sufficiently to form comparisons between different counties, their habits, and characteristics. Hence he had it in his power to direct the attention of our young observer at once to the points most worthy of his examination, and to save him from the common error of travellers—the deducing general conclusions from a few particular cases, or arguing from exceptions as if they were rules. Lord Colambre, from his family connections, had of course immediate introduction into the best society in Dublin, or rather into all the good society of Dublin. In Dublin there is positively good company, and positively bad; but not, as in London, many degrees of comparison: not innumerable luminaries of the polite world, moving in different orbits of fashion; but all the bright planets of note and name move and revolve in the same narrow limits. Lord Colambre did not find that either his father's or his mother's representations of society resembled the reality which he now beheld. Lady Clonbrony had, in terms of detestation, described Dublin such as it appeared to her soon after the Union; Lord Clonbrony had painted it with convivial enthusiasm, such as he saw it long and long before the Union, when *first* he drank claret at the fashionable clubs. This picture, unchanged in his memory, and unchangeable by his imagination, had remained, and ever would remain, the same. The hospitality of which the father boasted, the son found in all its warmth, but meliorated and refined; less convivial, more social; the fashion of hospitality had improved. To make the stranger eat or drink to excess, to set before him old wine and old plate, was no longer the sum of good breeding. The guest now escaped the pomp of grand entertainments; was allowed to enjoy ease and conversation, and to taste some of that feast of reason and that flow of soul so often talked of, and so seldom enjoyed. Lord Colambre found a spirit of improvement, a desire for knowledge, and a taste for science and literature, in most companies, particularly among gentlemen belonging to the Irish bar: nor did he in Dublin society see any of that confusion of ranks or predominance of vulgarity, of which his mother had complained. Lady Clonbrony had assured him, that, the last time she had been at the drawing-room at the Castle, a lady, whom she afterwards found to be a grocer's wife, had turned angrily when her ladyship had accidentally trodden on her train, and had exclaimed with a strong brogue, 'I'll thank you, ma'am, for the rest of my tail.'

Sir James Brooke, to whom Lord Colambre, without *giving up his authority*, mentioned the fact, declared that he had no doubt the thing had happened precisely as it was stated; but that this was one of the extraordinary cases which ought not to pass into a general rule—that it was a slight instance of that influence of temporary causes, from which no conclusions, as to national manners, should be drawn.

'I happened,' continued Sir James, 'to be quartered in Dublin soon after the Union took place; and I remember the great but transient change that appeared from the removal of both houses of Parliament: most of the nobility and many of the principal families among the Irish commoners, either hurried in high hopes to London, or retired disgusted and in despair to their houses in the country. Immediately, in Dublin, commerce rose into the vacated seats of rank; wealth rose into the place of birth. New faces and new equipages appeared: people, who had never been heard of before, started into notice, pushed themselves forward, not scrupling to elbow their way even at the Castle; and they were presented to my Lord-Lieutenant and to my Lady-Lieutenant; for their excellencies might have played their viceregal parts to empty benches, had they not admitted such persons for the moment to fill their court. Those of former times, of hereditary pretensions and high-bred minds and manners, were scandalized at all this; and they complained with justice, that the whole *tone* of society was altered; that the decorum, elegance, polish, and charm of society was gone. And I, among the rest,' said Sir James 'felt and deplored their change. But, now it's all over, we may acknowledge, that, perhaps, even those things which we felt most disagreeable at the time were productive of eventual benefit.'

'Formerly, a few families had set the fashion. From time immemorial everything had, in Dublin, been submitted to their hereditary authority; and conversation, though it had been rendered polite by their example, was, at the same time, limited within narrow bounds. Young people, educated upon a more enlarged plan, in time grew up; and, no authority or fashion forbidding it, necessarily rose to their just place, and enjoyed their due influence in society. The want of manners, joined to the want of knowledge, in the *nouveaux riches*, created universal disgust: they were compelled, some by ridicule, some by bankruptcies, to fall back into their former places, from which they could never more emerge. In the meantime, some of the Irish nobility and gentry, who had been living at an unusual expense in London—an expense beyond their incomes—were glad to return home to refit; and they brought with them a new stock of ideas, and some taste for science and literature, which, within these latter years, have become fashionable, indeed indispensable, in London. That part of the Irish aristocracy, who, immediately upon the first incursions of the vulgarians, had fled in despair to their fastnesses in the country, hearing of the improvements which had gradually taken place in society, and assured of the final expulsion of the barbarians, ventured from their retreats, and returned to their posts in town. So that now,' concluded Sir James, 'you find a society in Dublin composed of a most agreeable and salutary mixture of birth and education, gentility and knowledge, manner and matter; and you see pervading the whole new life and energy, new talent, new ambition, a desire and a determination to improve and be improved—a perception that higher distinction can now be obtained in almost all company, by genius and merit, than by airs and address ... So much for the higher order. Now, among the class of tradesmen and shopkeepers, you may amuse yourself, my lord, with marking the difference between them and persons of the same rank in London.'

Lord Colambre had several commissions to execute for his English friends, and he made it his amusement in every shop to observe the manners and habits of the people. He remarked that there are in Dublin two classes of tradespeople: one, who go into business with intent to make it their occupation for life, and as a slow but sure means of providing for themselves and their families; another class, who take up trade merely as a temporary resource, to which they condescend for a few years; trusting that they shall, in that time, make a fortune, retire, and commence or recommence gentlemen. The Irish regular men of business are like all other men of business—punctual, frugal, careful, and so forth; with the addition of more intelligence, invention, and enterprise, than are usually found in English men of the same rank. But the Dublin tradesmen *pro tempore* are a class by themselves: they begin without capital, buy stock upon credit, in hopes of making large profits, and, in the same hopes, sell upon credit.

Now, if the credit they can obtain is longer than that which they are forced to give, they go on and prosper; if not, they break, turn bankrupts, and sometimes, as bankrupts, thrive. By such men, of course, every *short cut* to fortune is followed: whilst every habit, which requires time to prove its advantage, is disregarded; nor, with such views, can a character for *punctuality* have its just value. In the head of a man, who intends to be a tradesman today, and a gentleman tomorrow, the ideas of the honesty and the duties of a tradesman, and of the honour and the accomplishments of a gentleman, are oddly jumbled together, and the characteristics of both are lost in the compound.

He will *oblige* you, but he will not obey you; he will do you a favour, but he will not do you *justice*; he will do *anything to serve you*, but the particular thing you order he neglects; he asks your pardon, for he would not, for all the goods in his warehouse, *disoblige* you; not for the sake of your custom, but he has a particular regard for your family. Economy, in the eyes of such a tradesman, is, if not a mean vice, at least a shabby virtue, of which he is too polite to suspect his customers, and to which he is proud of proving himself superior. Many London tradesmen, after making their thousands and their tens of thousands, feel pride in still continuing to live like plain men of business; but from the moment a Dublin tradesman of this style has made a few hundreds, he sets up his gig, and then his head is in his carriage, and not in his business; and when he has made a few thousands, he buys or builds a country-house—and then, and thenceforward, his head, heart, and soul, are in his country-house, and only his body in the shop with his customers.

NORAH HOULT

Holy Ireland

LONDON ❧ HEINEMANN ❧ 1935

Glancing forward, the tall column of Nelson's Pillar came into his view, and recalled him to his errand. It was like a grey shadow on his heart; his lips came together, his steps slackened. He took out his watch; he should turn off for the Pro-Cathedral—if he was going.

Of course he was going. But he needed time to collect his thoughts. He'd been in a sort of dream walking along, whatever it was had got him that way. He went on towards the junction of Earle Street. Now gutter Dublin was all about him: the fruit sellers round the Pillar were yelling, 'Oranges, fower a pen-ny, oranges fower a pen-ny,' with abandon and frenzy; by the curb an old woman, her grey locks tattered about her, was whining out a 'Come-all-ye' ballad; past her a man in an overcoat reaching down to his ankles, and a bowler hat tipped down over a short red-nosed cunning face was playing *The Croppy Boy*. A beggar ran at his heels, 'For the love of God, mister, for the love of God.' The respectable poor dragged up and down behind prams and laden with parcels, looking wistfully into windows, comparing prices. The poor who disdained respectability, and were there to make a real Saturday night, whined and howled, and cringed and cursed, or swayed backwards and forwards overcome with mirth at some shared jest. Beyond the Pillar Corporation officials, standing with note-books and watches in their hands, sent off the trams for the South Side on journeys which were still new enough to carry the glamour of an adventurous quest.

Charlie, his face now set, turned from it all into Marlborough Street, and found the steps of the Pro-Cathedral teeming with dirty barefooted small boys, often dressed in the queerest assortment of garments, who advanced on each newcomer to the chapel to endeavour to extort a

ha'penny. Some of them proffered medals in exchange. 'Buy the Blessed
Saint Anthony, gentleman, and gi' us a ha'penny, and I'll pray for you,'
one clamoured, pulling at Charlie's coat tails. He lifted his stick. 'Go to
hell out o' that.'

The church was crowded; the smell of unwashed human bodies,
mixed with a fainter odour of incense and oil, cut sharply at his nostrils.
It's a human stable, no less, he thought, as a filthy old man, his bare chest
showing under his coat, his beard dishevelled, hobbled past him muttering
to himself. People knelt on the stone floor and in front of the pews, their
eyes fixed unseeingly in front of them, their lips murmuring. He moved
to the right, going up the side of the church. Every confession box had its
rows of waiting penitents: his mind sought for the name of the deaf
priest—wasn't it O'Mara? Each side of the church was in half gloom, and
it was difficult for him to see the names on the boxes without going close;
he side-stepped, and peered ... Rev. A Farrell, C.C., Canon Duffy ... not
here. Rev. Peter Fleming ... his heart felt sick with anticipation, and to
give himself breathing space he knelt at the back of one section, and
blessed himself mechanically.

He'd been foolish to come into a strange church, and think of going
to a strange priest with his confession. If he didn't find Father O'Mara,
there was no telling what sort of queer fellow he might get. It might be all
right; weren't there heaps of men as young as himself after confessing the
same sin? But supposing it was one that ate the head off him?

A young woman was coming out of the box, another woman hastily
rose and slipped in. Sure, they'd have no time to be questioning everyone
to-night. They wouldn't be through till close on midnight. The young
lady who'd come out seemed comfortable enough; she had joined a
friend, and they knelt side by side whispering to each other with smiling
faces. The priest might be easy so!

But what would bits of things like them have to tell? He might as
well just cross to the other side, and see if Father O'Mara was in it. He
might see someone that looked friendly, and ask. As he rose from his
knees, he caught the murmur of the priest's voice, and the sound sent a
faint shudder of recoil through him; he passed swiftly around, and up the
far aisle, staring with eyes whose pupils were dilated at the worshippers
and at the penitents, at the white candles with their tiny flickering lights,
every light an intention, a prayer and an aspiration. The strangeness of the
packed church, the unfamiliar faces, the hot close smell, the shadows in
corners weighed on his spirit impeding it, even while he told himself he

was acting like a bloody gom. He tried to square his shoulders, explaining to himself that his hesitation was due to the number of people; had he time to wait? He wouldn't have time. But it seemed as if his soul stood mutely away from this answer, watching him with cold eyes, accusing him of sin even at that moment in that he was looking for a deaf priest whose ears would not hear his confession, and who therefore could not give him true absolution.

A hand touched his arm. He turned with a queer fright in him, and was looking into the face of Denis Lalor. Denis had been at school with him; it was Denis he liked best of the few he'd kept up with. He felt him his superior because he was in his father's office studying law. It was a surprise seeing him, for you didn't think of Denis in connection with chapels. Not that he was a Protestant, but he boasted that he wasn't religious and didn't give a god-damn whether his soul was saved or not. They stood together, whispering:

'What are you up to, Charlie?'

'I was after looking for a priest named O'Mara. Have you been yourself?'

'Who do you think I am? Sitting up with the shawls on a Saturday night. I've got enough already to buy a tin of flea killer.' He scratched the back of his shoulders. 'No, there's a mott I want to lead astray comes here.'

'It's like that, is it?'

'Come on out; we can't talk here.'

'Well, but ...'

'They'll keep you all night. Honest to God they will. Look round you. Sure, it'll keep, won't it?'

'I see Father O'Mara's over beyond, and ...'

'For Christ's sake will you come? We'll have to take a disinfectant for our throats.'

He was following Denis. After all, wouldn't it wait? He was going to let on to be as holy as all that. He didn't feel in the mood that night. His nerves were upset ... deep inside him a faint voice whispered desperately, God, forgive me putting it off. Sure, I'll be back. You know I'll be back. And tell everything. I promise I will. Sure, I will ...

They sat in a public-house, crowded, as every public-house in the city at that time was crowded. But Denis had whispered to the barman, and they were in a special snug reserved for the favourites. Charlie looked at Denis's dark handsome face with admiration. A year and a bit more ago, and Denis had been only a school-boy. In a year he'd learnt the ins and outs; there were lines under his eyes; you'd take him for twenty.

'What took you to go to Marlborough Street, in the name of God?'

'Ah, just a change.'

'Tell me, do you go every week?'

'I haven't been for a month.'

'I haven't been for six months. So that beats you, old boy.'

JAMES JOYCE

A Portrait of the Artist as a Young Man

LONDON ✸ JONATHAN CAPE ✸ ILLUSTRATED EDITION
1956 ✸ FIRST PUBLISHED 1916

He was sitting in the midst of a children's party at Harold's Cross. His silent watchful manner had grown upon him and he took little part in the games. The children, wearing the spoils of their crackers, danced and romped noisily and, though he tried to share their merriment, he felt himself a gloomy figure amid the gay cocked hats and sunbonnets.

But when he had sung his song and withdrawn into a snug corner of the room he began to taste the joy of his loneliness. The mirth, which in the beginning of the evening had seemed to him false and trivial, was like a soothing air to him, passing gaily by his senses, hiding from other eyes the feverish agitation of his blood while through the circling of the dancers and amid the music and laughter her glance travelled to his corner, flattering, taunting, searching, exciting his heart.

In the hall the children who had stayed latest were putting on their things; the party was over. She had thrown a shawl about her and, as they went together towards the tram, sprays of her fresh warm breath flew gaily above her cowled head and her shoes tapped blithely on the glassy road.

It was the last tram. The lank brown horses knew it and shook their bells to the clear night in admonition. The conductor talked with the driver, both nodding often in the green light of the lamp. On the empty seats of the tram were scattered a few coloured tickets. No sound of foot-steps came up or down the road. No sound broke the peace of the night save when the lank brown horses rubbed their noses together and shook their bells.

They seemed to listen, he on the upper step and she on the lower. She came up to his step many times and went down to hers again between their phrases and once or twice stood close beside him for some moments on the upper step, forgetting to go down, and then went down. His heart danced upon her movements like a cork upon a tide. He heard what her eyes said to him from beneath their cowl and knew that in some dim past, whether in life or revery, he had heard their tale before. He saw her urge her vanities, her fine dress and sash and long black stockings, and knew that he had yielded to them a thousand times. Yet a voice within him spoke above the noise of his dancing heart, asking him would he take her gift to which he had only to stretch out his hand. And he remembered the day when he and Eileen had stood looking into the hotel grounds, watching the waiters running up a trail of bunting on the flagstaff and the fox terrier scampering to and fro on the sunny lawn and how, all of a sudden, she had broken out into a peal of laughter and had run down the sloping curve of the path. Now, as then, he stood listlessly in his place, seemingly a tranquil watcher of the scene before him.—She too wants me to catch hold of her, he thought. That's why she came with me to the tram. I could easily catch hold of her when she comes up to my step: nobody is looking. I could hold her and kiss her.

But he did neither: and, when he was sitting alone in the deserted tram, he tore his ticket into shreds and stared gloomily at the corrugated footboard.

SEAN O'FAOLAIN

Foreign Affairs

LONDON ❧ CONSTABLE ❧ 1976

T he Major galloped downstairs, rang for a taxi, drove to his old Guest House on Leeson Street. They were delighted to see him. But there was no room in the inn. Oh! A foreign lady, they slyly said, had been asking after him only an hour ago. Phew! Being without his address book he drove on to External Affairs, on

Saint Stephen's Green, to collect a few friendly telephone numbers from the usual solitary Casabianca holding the Saturday fort. He had barely time to shout 'Full speed ahead' to the cabby before she bounded like a dripping mermaid from the portico down to the pavement to shriek in Walloon after him. He remembered an old Irish army friend who had a base on Earlsfort Terrace, around the corner from the Green. Terror poured its adrenaline all over his kidneys at the sight of her black, spearlike figure under the spotlight of that portico too. 'Down the Hatch!' he roared, and with whistling tires down the Hatch they went. Were there ten of her? He must think. He must have a drink. He must eat. Round the Green to the Unicorn. Or had he by chance spoken to her of that estimable restaurant as a haunt of his legendary student days? He evidently had. Peeping from his knees on the floor of the taxi, he saw her against the restaurant's lighted, curtained window. He surrendered. Back to the Club! There for the first time in his life he was relieved to find the bar empty. It took him half an hour and three brandies to clarify the situation.

What were the simple facts? He shook his head wildly. Damnation! What WERE the simple facts? He had been lonely. Right? She had been lonely. Right? What more natural than he should want to comfort her, be kind to her? Right? And if he ever had gone beyond that whose business was it but his own? Anyway everybody knew that half the international population of Brussels was living in sin—except the cage Irish. It would all have been hunkydory if the cow hadn't pulled the teat out of the baby's bottle. Chasing him over here in broad daylight! And God knows what she had been saying to whatever junior she had found across the Green in External Affairs! And, no doubt, she would be back there on Monday morning screaming fit for a French farce. Right? No! Yes!!!

He was a ruined man.

A third brandy was needed to give him the courage to ring for the firing squad.

'Miriam! It is me. I'm simply dying to see you.'

'George!'

She sounded sad. Could she be shy? How dicey was this going to be? He tried to make his own voice sound neither soft nor hard. It came out as hoarse as an old hinge.

'I needn't tell you, Miriam, that I'd have rung you at once if it hadn't been for this wretched cold.'

'Your poor cold! Caught, I presume, racing around Dublin from that woman.'

His stomach fell a foot.

'How soon can I see you Miriam?'

'I am afraid not tonight, George. Nor tomorrow. Ever since your housekeeper arrived in Dublin she has been telephoning me every half hour. You must have confided greatly in her, she is so accurately informed about this city. Have you been telling her all about your golden youth? Also you left your address book behind you. For all I know she may have rung the Secretary. Even the Minister. Perhaps the entire Cabinet? Some little while ago she took up her position on the pavement opposite my flat, parading up and down under the rain between two lamp-posts like an unemployed whore. After watching her through my curtains for half an hour I brought her in. Soaked to the skin, poor slut! I gave her a stiff drink, let her pour some of her European despair over me, gave her some dry clothes and sent her to soak in a hot bath where she is wallowing at this moment. When she emerges I suppose I shall have to listen to a few more lurid revelations about our man in Bruxelles before I park her in some modest guest house where she can prepare herself for her interview with the Secretary on Monday morning.'

'But the woman is daft, Miriam! You can't, nobody can believe a word she says!'

'It is not only what she says, it is what she sees. She says you have a mole in the small of your back. Have you, George?'

'She makes shirts for me!'

'How intimate! And that you have a scar on the inside of your right thigh.'

'I must have mentioned it to her.'

'She has a letter you wrote to her from Paris two months ago. It almost made me blush.' Her voice became soft and sad again. 'I am sorry, George. You ought to have stayed in Trinity and become a tutor in Ancient Greek. I realise now that what you are is a man so afraid of the lonely, little Irish boy in you that you have grown fold after fold of foreign fat to keep him in. Just as this poor woman may well have had an exuberant Peter Paul Rubens goddess bursting to get out of her skinny body ever since the day she was born. O dear! I sometimes wonder how many Ariels were imprisoned in Caliban. And how many Calibans were imprisoned in Ariel? It is a thought that makes one feel sorry for the whole human race.'

'Well!' he blustered, 'since you are so damned sorry for the whole human race would you kindly tell me what I had best do now?'

'That is quite simple. You have only two alternatives. The first is to resign and return. You would have to accept a spot of demotion. But, never fear, we will find a cosy berth for you somewhere. A consulate in South America? In Africa? Say in Uganda? We won't let you starve. The other possibility you must surely have gathered from my letter. If you should still wish me to announce that we have been privately engaged for the past six months you can blow the whole business out like a candle. But you must decide at once so that I may ring up the Secretary, or the Minister, and a gossipy friend or two, and have it published in Monday's *Irish Times,* and break it gently to the poor slut upstairs, and drive her to the airport tomorrow. You could then break off our engagement at your convenience. Only, in that case, George, please do, I beg you, return my letter. It puts me completely in your power as a woman.'

She knew the flattery of that last bit would be irresistible.

'You mean ... I mean ... You mean you meant all that in your letter?'

'George! Do you not realise how attractive you are to women?'

He answered her without hesitation in the voice of a small boy saying, 'Mummy! May I go to the pictures?':-

'Miriam! Let us be married at once.'

'I hear her bath water running out. At once cannot be too soon, George. I must hurry. Get on a plane for Brussels *il più presto.* If you don't she will strip our flat naked and then set fire to it. Goodnight, darling. Ring me from Brussels.'

For a long time he looked with a dazed smile into the mouth of the receiver. He carried the same smile to his mirror. Attractive to women? Well! He brushed his graying wings, chucked his lapels, arranged his lolling peony handkerchief, smilingly went downstairs to dinner. What a woman! Such tact, ability, foresight! He would have ample time for dinner before catching the last plane for London. His concierge in Brussels would do the rest. Touching his empty *boutonnière* at the turn of the stairs his descent was halted by a memory: her story of the rash Egyptologist whose frail flower wilted at the sight of day.

She, hit at that precise moment by a memory of a different sort, hastily concluded a swift goodnight to her most gossipy gossip -

'Happy? I remember what happened to poor Pygmalion. He had worked for years on a statue of the perfect woman and found himself left with a chatterbox of a wife. I think of all the years I have devoted to my chatterbox.' She laughed philosophically. 'Never mind. I am really very fond of poor old George. I always have been. And he needs me. I must fly. Tell the world!'

As she replaced the receiver she turned in her chair to watch the china handle of the door slowly turning. When it was thrown wide open her eyes stared at her dark visitor staring at her, wearing the long, soft, white, woollen shawl, interwoven with gold thread, always kept in tissue in her tallboy, the gold torque that had so diverted George, three bracelets from her dressing table on each scraggy arm, and a red rose in the black mat of her hair. For one statuesque second the door became a beveled mirror asking, 'And who is who, now?' Then, resolutely conquering her weakness, she rose and advanced with her arms wide open.

'Virginia!'

They sat side by side on the cozy sofa beside the fire. There, speaking ever so gently, but firmly, she tenderly, gradually, almost absentmindedly, woman to woman, stripped her guest of her dreams and her plumes. From both a few tears, a shrug, a hug and, in three or four languages, 'Men!'

Conal O'Riordan

Adam of Dublin

LONDON ❧ W. COLLINS, SONS AND CO. LTD ❧ 1920

I n the capital of what is believed by many to be the fairest, if not the most extensive kingdom of Europe, and it may not be concealed from the reader, is Ireland, there lived not so long ago a tailor called Macfadden. He enjoyed the distinction of being perhaps the tallest and almost certainly the thirstiest of his trade in Dublin; but it is doubtful if he were one of the best. His profits, had he devoted them to that end (which he did not), were barely sufficient to provide for himself, his wife, and a son with whom he had been, somewhat unexpectedly, blessed. This son was duly christened, at the Pro-Cathedral, that architectural hybrid of Athens and Rome, which is dedicated to St Mary of the Immaculate Conception, and is the commanding feature in the decorative scheme of Marlborough Street and the adjacent stews. He was given the names of Adam Byron O'Toole Dudley Wyndham and Innocent, to add to that of Macfadden. His godfather, Mr Byron O'Toole, an acquaintance of Mrs Macfadden's, boasting ancient if obscure descent, had linked with his own name those of one or two Englishmen of blood, whose intimacy he had enjoyed when, as an extra waiter, he had frequented the Castle. His godmother, Miss or Mrs Robinson, an acquaintance of Mr O'Toole's (Mrs Macfadden having no lady friend worthy of the name) had suggested that he be called Innocent, after her spiritual adviser, Father Innocent Feeley; and Mr Macfadden insisted on the precedence of his own choice, Adam.

Adam was the name of one of Mr Macfadden's, scandal said, too famous brothers; who, having gone to Africa as a private in the army, to be heard of by his relatives no more, was believed by Mr Malachy Macfadden, the tailor, to have amassed a large fortune. 'If the truth was known now,' he would say, 'I wouldn't wonder now if my brother Adam wasn't Dr Jim or Eckstein, or it might be old Rhodes itself ... D'ye mind that million pounds, or whatever it was now, that Rhodes gave Parnell for the Party? That was my brother Adam all over. He was always a ...' and here followed a rough and ready estimate of his brother's intellect.

The Macfaddens, as will be understood, were pious people; and they lived under the shadow of the sacred fane where their son had made his first appearance in Irish society. Mr O'Toole dwelt in the immediate neighbourhood: previous to the birth of our hero he had been the tenant of a cosy corner in the apartment of the Macfaddens': thence he moved to a house where dwelt the infant's godmother. It would not advantage the reader to indicate more precisely the spot, as the names of these streets are, by the whim of contending authorities, frequently changed, and you may go to bed in Orange Street to wake up in Green. Let us say that the Macfadden domain lay in an alley off the commercial artery called by some such name as Count Street, where a great business was done by the trams carrying people anxious to get away from it; while more to the north and east lay Mr O'Toole and Miss or Mrs Robinson, in one of the group of houses to which we may give the name of Mountjoy Court. Mr O'Toole preferred Mountjoy Court to Count Street; partly because it was more grandiosely planned, if in worse repair, and partly because it had once been the residence of a nobleman, and was actually still occasionally visited by members of the aristocracy.

Despite the piety of his parents, who were not so mean spirited as to spoil their child by a parsimonious administration of the porter bottle that served them for a rod, young Adam B.O'T.D.W.I. Macfadden had not turned out a credit to them. He had the aspect of one who, from the beginning, had been neglected by his mother and altogether escaped the notice, the favourable notice, of his father. Even by the standard of Marlborough Street, he was a dirty child: though it would be unjust to suggest that Mr Macfadden used upon his own person that share of soap and water due to his son: nor did Mrs Macfadden's comparative cleanliness throw any lustre on her reputation in Count Street, where that quality was regarded as remote from, or even perhaps hostile to Godliness.

It was not Adam's bituminous colouring that troubled the hearts of his parents: it was his dissolute and untrustworthy character. When he had passed the age of seven years, at which it is reasonable for a young man to support his parents, he was barely able to more than keep his father in tobacco and provide for his own expensive maintenance, by the profits from the sale of extinct evening papers to those too charitable, to phlegmatic, or too slow of foot, to resent effectively the transaction. His father more particularly was aggrieved that the boy seldom accounted at home for a larger sum of money than was represented by the face value of the articles he had sold. Returning one evening, with a bottle of porter from his club, he took him severely to task: 'Now I seen you myself with my own eyes, so there's no mistake now, there in O'Connell Street it was now, outside the Gresham Hotel I saw you, with my own eyes, selling the *Telegram* ...'

'*Telegraph*,' interjected the young hopeful, foolishly desirous of a precision hateful to his elder's soul.

'Telemiyelbo,' returned Macfadden fierily: 'will you tell me I didn't see it with my own eyes?'

'What the hell did you see?' inquired Mrs Macfadden, who sometimes betrayed impatience in the home circle.

'I seen him sell a *Telegram* to Father Muldoon himself. And you needn't tell me now that a grand man like that, the head of the Jesuits he is, and a friend of Murphy's, would give you no more than a halfpenny for the love of God.'

'He gave me nothing at all', said Adam.

Indignation carried Mr Macfadden's voice an octave upwards: 'Will you tell me that the holy man would go and cheat an innocent child for the sake of a copper or two?' ... As Adam contumaciously held his opinion on this subject to himself, his elder roared: 'Now didn't I see you put the paper in his holy hand?'

'He gave it back to me,' was the child's perplexing answer.

But Mr Macfadden seldom allowed himself to be perplexed: 'I thought it was your own fault,' he snorted, 'letting him see what it was before he paid you for it.'

'Did his reverence make no excuse for not buying it after he'd asked for it?' Mrs Macfadden inquired searchingly.

'No,' said Adam. 'He just told me to run home and tell me parents not to send me out swindling people any more.'

'Impident old scut!' cried Mr Macfadden, and emptied the porter bottle. 'If I ever catch you selling him anything again, I warn you now I'll cut your back. Bringing disgrace on us all with your foolishness, I call it.'

Mrs Macfadden eyed her husband without respect: 'Sure, how could his reverence tell where the lad came from?'

The tailor rounded on her: 'And now why couldn't he tell as well as I could or any one else? You'd think that just because he was a holy father with a tall hat on him, he was too grand to know anything .... Now what d'ye think he's there and paid for if it isn't to give his money to them that deserves it? ... And there he goes now behaving like and worse than any old Prodestan that never heard the name of Christian charity.'... He turned to Adam: 'Did you ever know a Prodestan itself to do the like of that?'

'I never gave them the chance,' said Adam, with a reckless air; but his mother noticed his gray face tinge with ruddy brick.

'There, there,' said she, 'don't you be putting ideas into the boy's head, or we'll be having him prostutelised on us one of these fine days.'

'Don't provoke me, woman,' shouted Mr Macfadden, clutching the porter bottle, 'with your letting on to think that a son of mine would ever go and be a bloody turncoat.'

'I never said he was a son of yours,' returned Mrs Macfadden, and the conversation took a direction in which Adam Byron O'Toole Dudley Wyndham Innocent was not called upon to follow it.

He willingly retired into that corner of the room once tenanted by his godfather, where now lay the cunning arrangement of old sacks, disused garments, and refuse from his own and his father's stock-in-trade, which served him, as it might a pig, for a bed. There he lay and fitfully slumbered while the controversy between his parents raged high and low. He was used to these debates and had lost interest in them even when he himself furnished the basis of discussion. He knew that his mother, despite her shortness of temper, had certain amiable qualities which would ensure her an eventual peace without crushing defeat, or even with moral victory.

And tonight as always within his experience, he heard Mr and Mrs Macfadden finish their conversation cosily in bed. 'It's all very well for you, my love,' said she, 'to laugh at me for being silly. But I'd die of shame if he was got hold of by Lady Bland. Father Innocent told Emily Robinson that she was the worst woman in Dublin.'

'Lady Blandmiyelbo!' returned Mr Macfadden, with homely affability, and the report of a hearty kiss signalled to Adam that the family equilibrium was for the moment restored. So, like the good little Catholic he had learned to proclaim himself to a musical accompaniment every Sunday in the Pro-Cathedral, he said a short prayer to the Blessed Virgin, to protect him that night and for ever after from the machinations of the unspeakable Lady Bland.

He then went to sleep and dreamed that her ladyship was something between a unicorn and a road-roller, with several tails, to each of which was tied a flaming sardine-tin, and as many heads, crowned by helmets of that fashion affected by the Dublin Metropolitan Police. Her ladyship had run him down in Mountjoy Court, and, obsequiously assisted by Mr O'Toole, was about to put him into one, or perhaps more, of the sardine tins, when he woke with a scream, was soundly chastised by Mr Macfadden with the fortunately convenient porter bottle; and, after he had recovered from the shock, fell into a peaceful and refreshing slumber.

So far, he had an easy conscience; but already he knew that not it, nor even the intercession of Holy Mary ever Virgin, could protect him from evil dreams. And again he had dreams he deemed sublime, though he knew not that word nor, waking, could recall what were these wonderful things he dreamed.

JOHN D. SHERIDAN

Paradise Alley

DUBLIN ❧ TALBOT PRESS ❧ 1945

H e gathered the roll books into the press and locked away for the last time the sloping attendance marks that were like tombstones to the dead days. The monthly return lay on the table in front of him. It was the last one he would ever fill in. From now on it would be Sullivan's job to collect the signatures of the other teachers, see that all absences were duly entered, and bring the completed form down to the Archdeacon. But the Archdeacon, God help him, hadn't so many monthly returns to sign either. He too, like Anthony himself, and the old school, was nearing the end of his tether. They were all finishing up together.

St John's National School, Paradise Alley, Dublin.

Roll No. 14567.

Anthony Domican, Principal.

As he stood up from the table a great, unwieldly seagull lobbed on to the window-sill. Behind it he could see the nodding masts of the little sailing boats that were anchored outside the school, and behind them the low grey line of the Bull Wall and the misty outline of Howth Head. That was the best way to look from Paradise Alley—to lift your eyes and stare into the distance. If you looked straight down you saw the low sea wall, the muddy foreshore that the tide was so slow in covering, and the yellow cloud that rose from the chugging outflow pipe of the manure factory.

The seagull was late, and the lunch-time crumbs had been scooped up long since by his more punctual fellows. Perhaps, Anthony thought, it had as bad a time sense as he had himself. Until now he had never realised that he was growing old. Every summer, when the last year's Infants had marched in from the convent next door, clutching their little slips of age and identity tightly, he had given time a post-dated cheque. And now, when he had, as the rules and regulations put it, reached 'the end of the quarter in which he attains his sixty-fifth birthday' (it seemed incongruous to think of the staid Department taking any notice of a man's birthday), the cheques had come in together and his store of youth was withered and shrunken.

He felt old.

It would be more fitting, he thought as he went out into the street, if he could lock the door behind him to symbolise his passing, but Mrs Malone would lock the door. There was no statutory retiring age for Mrs Malone. She would go on brushing and scrubbing until she dropped.

He crossed the railway bridge and the canal, but instead of calling on the Archdeacon, as he had intended, he kept straight on past the new school and out on to the quays. He would bring the monthly return down to the Archdeacon after tea and drop it into the Education Office on his way home. There was no hurry. There would never again be any hurry. His time was his own.

Men touched their hats to him: men loading ships, men driving lorries, men standing outside public-houses. They were all his old pupils. Some of them were the sons of old pupils. Was he as old as all that?

He fell to thinking then of the new school, with its eighteen class-rooms, an assembly hall, a playground as big as a barrack square, and *mirabile dictu*, a teachers' room. All he had ever had in Paradise Alley was five rooms and two crazy, concrete-floored, unheated, death-trap, overflow sheds. The magnificence would all be Sullivan's. A good chap, Sullivan, though a little excitable. The capitation money would be useful to him.

It had taken a long time to get the new school out of the Canon. Donkey's years. The Canon had hated the thought of gathering money from his poor parish, bargaining with architects and contractors, coaxing the Education Department to put its hand deep in its pocket. Ten years before—and he had been an old man even then—he had pleaded that it was a job for his successor. If he started it it would kill him. But it was finished now and the Canon was still at the wicket. (He was an Archdeacon now, of course, but Paradise Alley called him 'the Canon' as often as not).

A man of God, the Canon, if ever there was one; crotchety and kind by turns, but in love with his people; gentle with sinners but merciless where plain chant was concerned. 'The little la-la' he called it,—'ad-or-e-e-moos—moos, not muss.'

'If the children are taught to sing their hymns properly,' the Canon used to say, 'they won't have Dublin accents.'

Anthony could laugh at it all now, but it had been different in the old days.

'They *must* have Dublin accents,' he had told the Canon time and time again. 'Surely you don't expect them to have Cahirciveen accents?'

'There you go again,' the Canon would say. 'Trying to be funny.'

He had never let anything go with the Canon. That was the way to get on with him. They had argued for forty years, and looking back on it neither of them would have had it otherwise.

The Canon was sorry to see him go. He knew that. And the Canon was as proud as Punch of his new school, though at times he seemed to forget that only for the nagging of Anthony Domican it wouldn't have been started yet. But to do the Canon justice, he had made a good job of it—a palace of green and white, with wide, rubberoid-floored corridors, and red EXIT signs in the assembly hall. The Canon was tickled at the EXIT signs. 'As good as a picture house,' he had said.

And the Canon, gangrened foot or no gangrened foot, would preside at his presentation and make a whale of a speech. Sullivan would be sending an account of it to the newspapers, no doubt, and he knew the kind of account Sullivan would write.

'A very pleasant function took place in the Regal Hotel, Dublin, on Thursday, ... when Mr Anthony Domican, N.T., was entertained at a banquet given by some of his colleagues, friends, and grateful ex-pupils, and presented with a substantial cheque to mark his retirement from the principalship of St John's National School, Paradise Alley, Dublin, where he laboured with such success for forty years....

'The presentation was made by the Very Rev. Archdeacon Dunphy, P.P., who, in an eloquent and graceful valedictory oration, paid well-deserved compliments to the guest of the evening....'

God help us!

'Senator M. Logue said it was a signal honour for him to propose the health of his friend and kinsman....'

You've come along way, Mandy, since we knocked out the captain of the *Ayr Maid* on the quay at Milford—a long, long way.

'Mr Edward Bolger, T.D., speaking on behalf of the ex-pupils, associated himself cordially with the remarks of the previous speakers. It was a long time since he had first made the acquaintance of Mr Domican....'

The divil of a long time, Nedser, and yet not so long. I remember the cow's lick that straggled down over your bumpy forehead. I remember your red and white face and your button nose. You were like a ventriloquist's doll.

'Mr Adrian O'Sullivan recounted the sterling qualities of his predecessor....'

Adrian was a great respecter of traditions. All the old, moth-eaten phrases would roll off his tongue in a cascade of rich Kerry vowels.

'... taught for some time in his native Donegal before coming to Paradise Alley in 1903 ... appointed Principal in 1936 ... zeal and conscientiousness ... enduring work for God and Ireland.... A man of culture and scholarship ... many of his pupils occupy prominent positions in Church and State. The large and representative gathering testifies in no small measure to the esteem and affection in which he was held by everyone with whom he came into contact.'

Maybe he was anticipating a little. That was a bit of the funeral notice—'large and representative cortege.' The funeral stuff would come later. But in one sense part of the funeral was over already, for it was like dying a little to leave Paradise Alley: the place had become part of him. The send-off would be like a shovel of clay on his coffin. 'Many of his pupils now occupy prominent positions in Church and State.' Flapdoodle. One was a curate in Toowoomba, another a missioner in the Philippines. He had turned out a dozen postmen, and two or three civil servants who had risen from boy clerkships to heights only a little more dizzy. But these were the exceptions. The lucky ones got trades: the unlucky became public-house porters, private soldiers, billiard markers.

Precious little he had done for them ... taught them to sign their names, to add and subtract.... Battle of Clontarf, 1014 ... Derby and Nottingham coalfield ... 'like signs give plus, unlike signs give minus.' It wasn't his fault. He couldn't have fed them and dressed them. He couldn't have taken them out of their two-pair backs and given them decent houses. He couldn't have paid for them in secondary schools and put them on for medicine or apprenticed them to accountancy.

The children of the poor were unintelligent. They inherited dullness from their parents. So the intelligence-testers said, the research education-ists, the new psychologists. A fat lot they knew. The children of the poor were as intelligent as anyone else, but they didn't get a dog's chance. They didn't get food, or living space, or proper rest. They didn't get woolly vests, or seaside holidays, or cod liver oil, or bedtime stories. They became men and women before their time, so that their mental develop-ment was telescoped and stunted. Intelligence was a function of the soul, but its proper development depended on physical factors. His own experi-ence had proved it. He had seen, every six years or so, batches of bright, normal children march in from Sister Ita, and he had seen them grow dull and listless as they grew old. They couldn't attend. They couldn't concen-trate. They got no chance. Their environment in Paradise Alley was one huge barrier to development—mental, physical, and moral. It made poverty and misery an almost inescapable inheritance.

'Many of his pupils occupy prominent positions in Church and State.' Aye, indeed. One was second sacristan in St Stephen's. Another had been hanged in Pentonville.

A man could do a lot of harm in forty years.

It was a long time, and he had a few weeks now to remember, a few weeks in which to get the picture of his life into focus—before Sullivan and the others distorted it with high praise.

JAMES STEPHENS

Here Are Ladies

LONDON ❧ MACMILLAN AND CO. LTD ❧ 1913

Between impartial sips at his own and my liquor the old gentleman perused the small volume which he had taken from my pocket. After he had read it, he buttoned the book in his own pouch and addressed me with great kindness -

'In some respects,' said he, 'poets differ materially from other animals. For instance, they seldom marry, and when they do it is only under extreme compulsion—This is the more singular when we remember that poets are almost continually singing about love. When they do marry, they instantly cease to make poetry and turn to labour like the rest of the community.

'It has been finely said that the poet is born and not made, but I fancy that this might be postulated of the rest of creation.

'Many people believe that all poets arise from their beds in the middle of the night, and that they walk ten miles until they come to a hillside, where they remain until the dawn whistling to the little birds; but this, while it is true in some instances, is not invariably true. A proper poet would not walk ten miles for any one except a publisher.

'The art of writing poetry is very difficult at first, but it becomes easy by practice. The best way for a beginner is to take a line from another poem; then he should construct a line to fit it; then, having won his start, he should strike out the first line (which, of course, does not belong to him) and go ahead. When the poet has written three verses of four lines each he should run out and find a girl somewhere and read it to her. Girls are always delighted when this is done. They usually clasp their hands together as though in pain, roll their eyes in an ecstasy, and shout, "How perfectly perfect!" Then the poet will grip both her hands very tightly and say he loves her but will not marry her, and, in an agony of inspiration, he will tear himself away and stand drinks to himself until he is put out. This is, of course, only one way of being a poet. If he perseveres he will ulti-mately write lyrics for the music halls and make a fortune. He will then wear a fur coat that died of the mange, he will support a carnation in his buttonhole, wear eighteen rings on his right hand and one hundred and twenty-seven on his left. He will also be entitled to wear two breast-pins at once and yellow boots. He will live in England when he is at home, and be very friendly with duchesses.

'Poetry is the oldest of the arts. Indeed, it may be called the parent of the arts. Poetry, music, and dancing are the only relics which have come down to us from those ancient times which are termed impartially the Golden or the Arboreal Ages. In ancient Ireland the part played by the poet was very important. Not alone was he the singer of songs, he was treated with a dignity which he has since refused to forget. When a poet made a song in public, it was customary that the king and the nobility should divest themselves of their jewels, gold chains, and rings, and give this light plunder to him. They also bestowed on him goblets of gold and silver, herds of cattle, farms, and maidservants. The poets are not at all happy in these constricted times, and will proclaim their astonishment and repugnance in the roundest language.

'A few days ago I was speaking in Grafton Street to a poet of great eminence, and, with tears in his voice, he told me that he had never been offered as much as a bracelet by any lady. Times have changed; but for the person who still wishes to enter this decayed profession there is still every opportunity, for poetry is only the art of cutting sentences into equal lengths, and then getting these sentences printed by a publisher. It is in the latter part of this formula that the real art consists.

'There are a great many poets in Ireland, particularly in Dublin. In an evening's walk one may meet at least a dozen of this peculiar people. They may be known by the fact that they wear large soft hats, and that the breast-pockets of their coats have a more than noticeable bulge, due to their habit of carrying therein the twenty-seven masterpieces which they have just written. They are very ethereal creatures, composed largely of soul and thirst. Soul is a far-away, eerie thing, generally produced by eating fish.'

The old gentleman borrowed the price of a tram home; but as he instantly stood himself a drink from it, I was forced to relend him the money when we got outside.

THOMAS BODKIN

Hugh Lane and his Pictures

DUBLIN ❧ PUBLISHED BY THE STATIONERY OFFICE FOR
AN CHOMHAIRLE EALAION (THE ARTS COUNCIL) ❧ 1956

Soon after the close of the Royal Hibernian Academy Exhibition of Old Masters in 1903, the President of the Academy, Sir Thomas Drew, spurred on by Lane to strike while the iron was hot, wrote, on 22 January 1903, a letter to the papers, in which he claimed from the Government a new Charter, an increased endowment and more suitable buildings in which to maintain the Academy and to establish a gallery of modern art. 'Art,' he declared 'is in the air in Dublin just now. Mr Lane's enterprise has given an Exhibition so charming and surprising, as to attract for a few weeks to the old Hibernian Academy house in Lower Abbey Street all that is best in cultured society in Ireland. It has, with its pleasant social intercourse, formed a collective enthusiasm about Art in Ireland.... An Academy House in the educational centre of Dublin, with the grouped Art Institutions for passing exhibitions of Living Art, and a permanent gallery of modern and living artists' works, as advocated by him, are the least that Dublin, among English and Irish cities, should now stand for.'

This was the first definite intimation of Lane's project for the establishment in Dublin of a gallery of modern art. Within a fortnight, the President and a number of artists went on a deputation to the Lord Mayor and Corporation of Dublin to sue for their support. The Lord Mayor, in reply to their address, made the usual official speech and averred that the Academy's project 'had the entire sympathy of the Corporation, who had long engaged their earnest attention to the problem of forming such a gallery in Dublin.' He pointed out that there 'were difficulties in the way of their providing funds' ... and that 'they would join a committee or deputation to the Chief Secretary, or Lord Lieutenant, praying them to form such an institution.'

On 1 July following, a Special Commission of the House of Commons was appointed, with the Hon. Arthur Elliott in the chair, 'to consider a proposal that a portion of the site allocated for the College of Science should be transferred to the Royal Hibernian Academy, who would establish thereon a Gallery of Modern Art.' Lane and Sir Thomas Drew were called as witnesses; and Lane stated that many of the greatest living artists, among them Whistler, were interested in the scheme and had promised to give a representative example of their work to form the nucleus of such a collection. He also told the Commission that he had secured promises from several collectors to contribute pictures, and from a number of public-spirited friends to contribute substantial sums of money upon condition that such a site was granted. Here, again, the reply was of the official kind, full of vague goodwill. The chairman in summing up the evidence, declared that 'the desirability of such an Institution had been clearly shown, but that without excluding some of the Public Offices no room could be found on this spot. He, however, encouraged the idea of any new proposal.'

It soon became evident to Lane that the Royal Hibernian Academy were not wholly satisfactory allies. Many of the Academicians were aged men and indifferent artists, reluctant to be drawn into any public agitation and critical of his dashing ways. They did not always share his enthusiasms for their advanced contemporaries. He quickly grew to feel that their passive support was the most he could hope for, and that the brunt of the fight would have to be borne by himself. The bulk of his followers already showed signs of slipping back again into lethargy. Some fresh enterprise was needed to revivify their recently-awakened interest in pictorial art. He looked about him for an opening, and found it, as he thought, in the forthcoming International Exhibition at St Louis, where he proposed to organise a great show of Irish paintings.

Under the British Government, the Department of Agriculture and Technical Instruction for Ireland were responsible, absurdly, for the administration of official art activities. He obtained their blessing for his project, and started at once to build up the requisite collection of pictures.

Unversed in Civil Service ways and, indeed, somewhat contemptuous of them, he omitted to comply with the preliminary formalities which custom ordained. His work was well advanced before he learned that the Department were not prepared to add sound financial to their nebulous moral support. They declined to be responsible for the insurance of the borrowed pictures.

Negotiations broke down and Lane, who felt he had been badly treated, was left with his scheme in seeming chaos. He refused to accept defeat. It occurred to him that the collection which he had brought together with much trouble might be shown, perhaps to even better advantage, nearer home. For some years past the annual exhibitions held in the Guildhall Gallery of London, under the direction of Sir A.G. Temple, had proved highly successful. Lane offered to undertake the organisation there of an exhibition of Irish pictures, to be opened in the spring of 1904, and his offer was accepted.

In the meantime the impetus provided by his Winter Exhibition in the Royal Hibernian Academy carried that body onward into further effort. They held an exhibition in the winter of 1903 of the works of Walter Frederick Osborne, one of their most distinguished members, who had died prematurely in the spring of that year. I well remember visiting it in Lane's company, and marking his anxiety to obtain for permanent exhibition in Dublin some of Osborne's chief works. He succeeded in doing so. He bought the painter's masterpiece: 'A View of the Old Fish Market in Patrick Street' showing the picturesque slum, long since demolished to make room for the Iveagh Buildings, a large, unfinished study entitled 'Tea in the Garden', and an exquisite small picture of a 'Mother and Child'. All three are now to be seen in the Dublin Municipal Gallery of Modern Art.

Lane's public services were shortly afterwards officially recognised for the first time when he was appointed by the Lord Lieutenant to be a Governor and Guardian of the National Gallery of Ireland, on 1 January, 1904.

The 'Exhibition of a Selection of Works by Irish Painters' was duly opened in the Guildhall, in the following May. It comprised four hundred and sixty-five exhibits, gathered by Lane from all imaginable quarters. Some of the artists there represented had never claimed, or even adverted to, their Irish nationality. Others, such as Mr Charles Shannon, RA, had the slenderest qualifications on that ground: in his case, a single Irish grandfather. Yet, on the whole, the exhibition was a genuine revelation to those critics who had concluded that Ireland's contribution to pictorial art was negligible: and during the eight weeks in which it remained open eighty thousand people paid for admission.

Lane, as honorary director, contributed an introduction to a well-produced and illustrated catalogue. It was a plea for the establishment of a gallery of modern art in Dublin, and must be quoted at some length as the first formal pronouncement of his aim. He wrote:

'There are so many painters of Irish birth or Irish blood in the first rank at this moment, that extreme interest is being taken in this bringing together of sufficient specimens of their work to enable students of art to discover what common or race qualities appear through it. There is something of common race instinct in the work of all original Irish writers to-day, and it can hardly be absent in the sister art.

'We have in the Dublin National Gallery a collection of the works of the Old Masters which it would be hard to match in the United Kingdom outside London. But there is not in Ireland one single accessible collection or masterpiece of modern or contemporary art....

'A gallery of Irish and modern art in Dublin would create a standard of taste, and a feeling of the relative importance of painters. This would encourage the purchase of pictures, for people will not purchase where they do not know.

'Such a gallery would be as necessary to the student if we are to have a distinct school of painting in Ireland, for it is one's contemporaries that teach one the most. They are busy with the same problems of expression as oneself, for almost every artist expresses the soul of his own age.

'I think anyone who looks at the collection at the Guildhall will admit that we have artistic capacity, and that with the same opportunities, not only of other European countries, but of such cities as Glasgow, Liverpool and Manchester, we should develop a beautiful and original artistic expression.

'I feel that even if our students are expected to work without ever seeing or being stimulated by the sight of a Corot, a Watts, a Whistler, or a Sargent, yet to allow the pictures of men who belong to us by birth or blood to be hung everywhere but in Ireland, is an injustice that we must do away with.

'I and my friends look forward to having in Dublin, sooner or later, a gallery where such works, and, if possible, the works of all great contemporaries may be hung. We have had promises of a picture from many of the painters exhibiting at the Guildhall. The finding of a site and of a building in Dublin should be the lesser part of our task.'

During the course of the Guildhall Exhibition, Lane got in touch with the executors of Mr J. Staats Forbes, who were then engaged in the difficult task of realising to the best advantage the enormous collection of pictures, mainly of the modern French school, which that voracious collector had accumulated. Hitherto, Lane's interest in modern Continental painting had been slight, and his knowledge of the subject slighter still. But the sight of the Corots in the Staats Forbes collection awoke a new enthusiasm, and he realised at once the urgent desirability of representing Continental art adequately in his projected collection of modern art for Ireland.

He immediately planned another exhibition, to be held in the forthcoming winter, in the galleries of the Royal Hibernian Academy. It was composed of about one hundred and sixty pictures and drawings which he persuaded the Staats Forbes executors to send to Dublin, and which they offered to sell on special terms to any public body; thirty or forty other modern Continental pictures which he borrowed from Messrs. Durant-Ruel, and about a hundred pictures and drawings and a couple of pieces of sculpture which he himself and various artists and friends offered to present to Dublin.

This exhibition was duly opened in November 1904, under the patronage of a committee consisting of the Earl of Drogheda, the Earl of Mayo, KP, Sir Thomas Drew, PRHA, Lieut.-Col. Sir Hutcheson Poë, CB, and T. Harrington, Esq., MP (ex-Lord Mayor), Lane himself acting as Honorary Secretary. It was entitled: 'An Exhibition of Pictures presented to the City of Dublin to form the nucleus of a Gallery of Modern Art, also pictures lent by the executors of the late Mr J Staats Forbes and others.'

Lane contributed an 'Explanation' to preface the catalogue, in which he said:

'We have here the nucleus for a Gallery of Modern and Contemporary Art. Such an institution is especially necessary to the Art student if we are to have a distinct school of painting in Ireland; for it is our contemporaries that teach us most. At this time we in Ireland possess the unique position of being the country that cannot boast of a Gallery of Modern Art. There is hardly any great modern city (either capital or provincial), which has not such a Gallery. The distinct "schools" that have sprung up as a result of the founding of such institutions at Glasgow, Liverpool, Birmingham and Manchester, are proof, if any is needed, of the value and importance of such a collection in our midst ... it now depends on the inhabitants of Dublin and on all artistic Irishmen to support the project in a practical manner, and bring it to a successful issue.... The Corporation of Dublin has in every way shown its sympathy with the scheme; and it is greatly to be hoped that they will now help it in a practical manner by granting a small annual sum, which will enable us to have the collection open free to the public—by day and in the evening. On this will also depend many of the most valuable gifts ... the small collection that I have formed myself will only be presented on the condition that certain steps are taken to place the "Gallery" on a sound basis.'

This exhibition was also a success, though not such a striking one as Lane's earlier venture with the Old Masters. He worked hard to stimulate the public interest and arranged for lectures in the evening, to be given by Sir Walter Armstrong, then Director of the National Gallery; by Mr J.B. Yeats, RHA.; by George W. Russell, D.Litt., better known as "AE"; and by Mr George Moore. Mr George Moore's lecture, the only lecture, I believe, which he has ever delivered, was subsequently reprinted, with a preface, under the title "Reminiscences of the Impressionist Painters", and published as No.3 of the Tower Press Booklets, by Messrs Maunsell of Dublin, in 1906. Dr D.S. MacColl also rallied to Lane's aid and spoke with enthusiasm of his plans, though I cannot now recall whether his remarks were uttered in Dublin or in London.

There were some cavillers: the usual jealous detractors, out-of-date and incompetent painters and anxious citizens who feared a further charge upon the rates. Some of these were even base enough to attempt to spread a rumour that Lane, himself a dealer, was seeking to sell Dublin the Staats Forbes pictures in order to gain a secret commission. In every community there are always a few to whom altruism and generosity are incomprehensible. But their whines and innuendoes were drowned in Dublin's well-nigh universal chorus of applause.

The Dublin Municipal Collection of Modern Art had been well and truly created. Though its subsequent career was destined to be chequered, Lane had achieved a great and lasting service to his countrymen. He was just twenty-nine years of age at the time.

WILLIAM SMITH CLARK

The Early Irish Stage

OXFORD ❧ CLARENDON PRESS ❧ 1955

The commencement of the Georgian era found Dublin, now a city with close to 100,000 inhabitants, more affluent, more spacious, and more urbane than ever in spite of persistent English legislation to repress Ireland's prosperity. The capital's elegance in manners and taste steadily advanced because of the growing number of titled residents—particularly country gentry who, like Sir Jowler Kennel in *Irish Hospitality* (1717), came up to town at the Michaelmas and Easter terms—and of the wealthy merchant families who, like the Sevilles in *The Sham Prince* (1719), aped the aristocracy. The patterns of fashionable activity were not changed but intensified. Public entertainments became more frequent and lavish: the all-day anniversary festivals, the state concerts at the Castle, the Lord Mayor's 'feasts' at the Tholsel, the municipal processions known as 'the riding of the franchises'. Of this last ceremony Lady Homebred in a contemporary play speaks with especial pleasure: 'When the Corporations ride the Fringes, I carry [my Girls] to a Relations of mine in Castle-Street, where they take their Bellies full of the Show'. As for private diversions,

> Visiting and Ombre so intoxes,
> The Ladies quite forget to fill our Boxes,

lamented a Dublin prologue speaker in 1716. Servants and coaches multiplied. Parading in stylish finery increased at the seaside to the north of the Liffey's mouth and at the circular drive in Phoenix Park. One pert young lady of the smart set quipped on the local stage:

> To flaunt it on the Strand, or in the Ring,
> Oh! Equipage is a delightful thing.

The world of fashion most abundantly exhibited itself outdoors at St Stephen's Green, the heart of the rising exclusive district. In fair weather, coaches, with their occupants ogling one another through the glass windows, streamed around the mile-long circuit of the park. Many beaux and belles preferred, however, to walk the Stephen's mall and garden paths, while their coaches waited by Dawson Street or some other thoroughfare adjoining the Green. Sir Bullet Airy, the fat spark in a Dublin comedy of the day, follows the prevailing mode when in mid-morning he calls by coach on Mr Trueman, a young citizen of fortune, and urges him, before dinner at a tavern, to take the air: 'But come, are you for Stephen's-Green, 'tis a fine Morning, and there will be a great deal of Company.'

For this polite society the playhouse in Smock Alley, though decidedly inelegant, still served as the indoor equivalent of St Stephen's Green. At the playhouse, however, 'the quality' increasingly had to rub shoulders with the general populace. In the pit city baronets, squires, army officers, and 'wits' sat alongside of bucks, law clerks, collegians, and 'extravagant male citizens', as one prim reporter termed those bourgeois bachelors who were enjoying a merry evening at the theatre. In the box circle behind the pit *nouveaux riches* social climbers infiltrated among the people of rank and distinction. Such 'impudence' on the part of the female sex was encouraged by the now well-established custom of 'government nights'. On these occasions the boxes were thrown open to all ladies who dressed in full regalia. The official invitations to a free performance met with enthusiastic feminine response, well illustrated by Lady Homebred, the genteel matron in *The Sham Prince*. She 'hate[s] all publick Places, and all publick Diversions', and keeps her two daughters as well as herself pretty much at home, but she takes care that 'when the Government invites, they always see the Play'.

In Smock Alley's middle gallery the masked coquettes and ladies of pleasure mingled with business and professional men, their wives and daughters. Numerous beaux also invaded this precinct to carry on heavy flirtations. '"Nymph" is never said to anything but a Vizard in the Middle Gallery', observes a wise young belle to an over-zealous admirer in *The Sham Prince*. More ardent love-making occurred in the 'lattices', the two boxes in line with the middle gallery on either side of the stage above the doors. The greater privacy of the lattices made them the favourite resort of the courtesans and the rakehells. 'My Lord talk'd a great deal to me in the Lattice last Play Night; I know he likes my Colour, and he prais'd my

Hand and Neck'—so runs a strumpet's letter in *The Hasty Wedding* (1716).

The more foppish gallants, taking their cue from London, were beginning the practice of locating themselves upon Smock Alley's stage and of strutting about there like peacocks during the programme intervals. A Dublin epilogue of the time refers disparagingly to

> One of these Fops who crowd behind our Scenes,
> To shew their ill–shap'd Legs, and awkward Meins;
> Their want of Sense to the whole Pit expose,
> To charm the Boxes with embroider'd Cloaths.

In the upper gallery the plebeians held complete sway. Here soldiers, apprentices, journeymen, lackeys, housemaids and yokels of all sorts formed the most rowdy, but also the most enraptured, group in the whole theatre.

Thus the Smock Alley audience, though it continued to be dominated by the titled and fashionable coterie to an extent no longer true in London, was slowly taking on a metropolitan character. To cater to its more varied attitudes and interests proved difficult for the entertainers, as one epilogue of the period plaintively demonstrates:

> Now, 'tis observ'd, our Friends two Story high
> Do always Laugh, when other People Cry,
> And murdering Scenes to them are Comedy.
> The middle Region seldom mind the Plot,
> But with a Vizard chat of *You know what,*
> And are not better'd by the Play one Jot
> But you great Judges of the Pit, who come,
> In order to be sent with Pleasure Home,
> Are like the Waterman, that looks Two Ways,
> You first observe the Ladies, then our Plays.

Another epilogue points out in even sharper detail the disturbing range of taste:

> Ladies will smile, if Scenes are modest writ,
> Whilst your *double Entendres* please the Pit.
> There's not a Vizard sweating in the Gallery,
> But likes a smart Intrigue, a Rake, and Raillery.
> And were we to consult our Friends above,
> A pert and witty Footman 'tis they love;

And now and then such Language as their own,
As, *Damn the Dog, You lie,* and *Knock him down.*
Consider, then, how hard it is to show
Things that will do Above, and please Below.

Despite the increasingly mixed patronage the approbation of the ladies of high station, 'the bright Nymphs, who in the Circle sit,/And with a Look can govern all the pit', still possessed a far larger importance to the stage in the Irish capital than in the English. Charles Shadwell, Dublin's leading playwright of the moment, recognised their decisive influence in local theatrical matters by dedicating in 1720 his collected plays to the Right Honourable Lady Newton and asserting that 'the Countenance You have shewn, and the Persons of Quality You have brought with You [to the Theatre], are convincing Demonstrations how much the Spirit and Gaiety of Dublin center in Your Ladyship.'

The spirit and gaiety to which Shadwell paid homage failed to bring about at the Theatre Royal any marked changes or renovations in celebration of the beginning of George I's reign. As for some years past, the doors opened between four and five o'clock so that the ladies and, much more rarely, the gentlemen could send their servants early to keep good seats in the boxes. Performances in general started at six o'clock and took place twice a week, usually Monday and Thursday. The curtain hour may have shifted a little with the time of year, as in London. The weekly schedule varied, of course, whenever a special occasion demanded a production on other than the conventional days. A new play, if warmly applauded at its première, was repeated again and again so long as the first enthusiasm lasted. The playwright did not look upon his work as a success until it had reached at least the third night of performance, the night set aside for the author's 'benefit'. Only then, remarked Shadwell to his Smock Alley audience in the prologue to *The Hasty Wedding,* could he feel assured that his creation had achieved a kind of permanency in the current stage repertory:

For if two Nights we can your Persons see,
'Tis well: a Play becomes a Wife in Three.

The Theatre Royal's supply of customers and scenery remained very limited and tawdry. Additions to the threadbare wardrobe still chiefly depended upon the generosity of the Dublin playgoers, and fresh donations often incited a public acknowledgment from the stage. A prologue of 1717 was expressly designed to permit a young actress to exhibit 'a new Suit of Cloaths' which a group of solicitous ladies had bestowed upon her. The charming Mary Lyddal enters all decked out and is pursued by Thomas Griffith, Smock Alley's star comedian. To his exclamation, 'You'r[e] finely drest to Day, and why all this?', she makes the perfect retort: 'Your Play-House Cloaths gains no Lovers.' Then Griffith proceeds to tease her about her present splendour:

> Full oft, I've seen You act in Tragick Love,
> With a bedraggled Tail, and dirty Glove,
> Representing then, some beauteous Goddess,
> With a poor wretched Head, and ill Shap'd Boddice.
> But so Transformed, you will surprize the Town,
> I fear some cully, child, has lay'd thee down—
> That Head, that Hoop, that Petticoat, that Gown!

With surprising frankness this little skit thus ridicules the mean appearance of the customary stage dress at Smock Alley in early Georgian times.

The condition of the scenery was little better. Current stock sets, such as 'The Field', 'A Parlour', 'A Prison', 'The Street', had been used repeatedly and were refurbished only when worn out. Stock pieces were put together now and again in various combinations with the hope that the reshuffling of parts would give some freshness to a too familiar stage background. For example, the 'Windmill Scene', a back flat, was framed by a pair of wing flats from the scene of 'the Wood' to depict a rural landscape in *Irish Hospitality*. Strictly localised sets which were not often employed had lasted for decades. The set of 'St Stephen's Green' probably saw its first use in 1699 and then reappeared twenty years later in *The Sham Prince*. Infrequently a new scene had to be built to fit a peculiar and specific setting. 'Dermott's Cabbin' in *Irish Hospitality* may well have required 'getting up', since the representation of anything other than an Irish tenant cottage would surely have seemed absurd to the Smock Alley spectators.

The ageing Theatre Royal might have undergone to its considerable advantage a few renovations in observance of its fiftieth season and its first under the new monarch. Its ageing manager, Joseph Ashbury, who had just completed forty years in that post, stood in no such need. At seventy-six he still presided over the playhouse affairs with vigour and still performed regularly. By now he had moved across the river at some distance from Smock Alley and lived in the attractive Bowling Green House, Oxmantown, a place with which he had enjoyed almost half a century of association. On its grounds he had played bowls with the fashionable in the days of Charles II. A young Englishman, William Rufus Chetwood, who assisted Ashbury around the theatre in 1714-15, long afterwards recalled the manager's Oxmantown residence as 'the finest spot of its kind in the whole Universe'. Chetwood also preserved a lively impression of the distinguished Smock Alley leader:

> His Person was of an advantageous Height, well-proportioned and manly; and, notwithstanding his great Age, erect; a Countenance that demanded a reverential Awe, a full and meaning Eye, piercing, tho' not in its full Lustre; ... a sweet-sounding manly Voice, without any Symptoms of his Age in his Speech.

Ashbury's pre-eminence as a teacher of acting continued to draw aspirants from Britain. In the early fall of 1714 Thomas Elrington's younger brother Francis arrived from London to serve his apprenticeship at Smock Alley. At the same time a twenty-one-year-old Englishwoman, Mrs Eliza Fowler Haywood, who later became a well-known dramatist and novelist of London, put herself under Ashbury's tutelage. Recently abandoned by her husband, she had decided to try the stage as a means of livelihood. In December 1714 Robert Wilks, now an outstanding figure on the current London stage and an Ashbury product, sent his nephew William over to Dublin for training with the declaration that 'no one ... is able to give him so just a Notion of the Business as Mr Ashbury.'

Mary E. Daly

The Deposed Capital 1860–1914

CORK ❧ CORK UNIVERSITY PRESS ❧ 1984

The Housing of Dublin's Working Class

The question of working class housing involves virtually all aspects of the city's economic and social structure. Housing was related to income and employment, to the geographical organisation of the city, and to matters of health and sanitation. It proved to be a major preoccupation of public health authorities from the 1880s until the 1940s and it is a matter of grave concern at the present time.

Unlike other Irish or English cities, the typical Dublin working class family lived in a tenement—a large house in multi-family occupancy. This was a characteristic which they shared with Scottish and continental cities. The limited evidence available would suggest that such tenements were consistently overcrowded, perhaps to a greater degree than in the later nineteenth century. In 1798 Rev. Joseph Whitelaw, rector of a city centre parish surveyed the south city Liberties.

> With the exception of St James and St Thomas St and a few others the streets in this part of the city are generally narrow, houses crowded together in the reres of backyards of very small extent, and some without accommodation of the kind. A few streets are residences of shopkeepers and others engaged in trade but a far greater proportion of them with their numerous lanes and alleys, are occupied by working manufacturers, by petty shop-keepers, and the labouring poor and beggars crowded together to a degree distressing to humanity. A single apartment in one of these truly wretched habitations, rates from 1–2/- per week; and to lighten this rent two, three or four families become joint tenants, hence at an early hour we may find 10–16 persons of all ages and sexes in a room of not fifteen feet square stretched on a wad of filthy straw and without any covering save the wretched rags that constitute their wearing apparel.

One street, Plunkett Street contained a total of 917 inhabitants in 32 houses, or an average of 28.7 per house. The average for the Liberties in 1798 was said to be 12–16 per house.

It is impossible to obtain exact knowledge of the city's housing until the 1841 Census which gave information on the quality of houses and of accommodation.

The figures confirm the impression of multi-family house occupancy as the norm. Only 8.5% of the city's housing stock in 1881 consisted of small cottages of 2–4 rooms, and only 1,876 families, or 3.4% of the total lived in such cottages on their own. In fact, only 14,334 families, 26% of the population had exclusive occupancy of a house or cottage. This figure had risen to almost 40% in 1901 as a result of the extension of city boundaries. Not all housing in multi-family occupancy can be regarded as a slum, correspondingly many third class houses were, particularly those erected in courts and yards to the rear of larger houses, which lacked air light and sanitation.

The location of slum property, according to H.J. Dyos, was determined by the supply and demand for houses: 'slums were the residue'. Slums were created by the blighting effect of docks, canals, a railway line, gasworks or dairies, 'slumness confirmed a builder's mistake'. This general description is broadly applicable to Dublin. By the late eighteenth-century the fashionable areas had been established as the north-west quadrant, including Sackville St, Dominick St and the south-east quadrant of Merrion and Fitzwilliam Squares. The south-western area, which contained the traditional city industries was almost exclusively working class, where the extreme north-eastern belt was not heavily populated, and much of it was unfashionable because it was low-lying and subject to flooding and because of its proximity to an army barracks.

The status of the north-western quadrant declined to a marked extent during the nineteenth century. Street directories trace the gradual decline of various addresses. Upper Dominick St contained four tenements in 1861, by 1871 this had risen to ten, while the doctors and solicitors had disappeared. By 1881 much of the street had passed into the hands of the Artisans Dwelling Co. Lower Dominick Street was a more respectable address which still clung to some status. Decaying house property gradually gave way to a national school and Carmelite seminary. The number of resident lawyers had been thirty-eight in 1851; by 1861 this had fallen by ten; in 1871 a further seven had left and by 1881 they had fallen by a dramatic seventeen. One of the most dramatic social reversals took place in Henrietta St, formerly the home of judges and bishops. In 1847 although nearby Henrietta Lane contained three tenements, Henrietta St retained much of its status. The former aristocratic residents had largely disappeared; of seven residences, three were vacant, but Lady Harriet Daly remained. Most of the remainder provided legal offices for lawyers attracted by proximity to the courts and Kings's Inns. By 1879 most of the street consisted of tenements and property valuations had fallen from £2,280 in 1854 to £1,040. The declining status of north city streets reflects the shift of fashion towards south city residences. Tenement housing was found in the south-east quadrant, mainly in streets bounded by the railway lines and gas works.

In many cases tenements were the former homes of the upper classes, which failed to find alternative tenants. Their decline into tenement status reflects the relative absence of major rebuilding schemes in nineteenth-century Dublin, a reflection of economic decline. With the exception of schools and religious institutions few alternative uses present themselves for the deserted mansions of previous generations. Yet not all tenements fell into this category. Those in the south-west quadrant of the city, such as the Coombe and High St were simply the traditional houses of the city's tradesmen. By mid nineteenth-century many were perhaps over a hundred years old and in urgent need of replacement but few private building schemes emerged. Such houses had traditionally been over-crowded and insanitary. Structural conditions had deteriorated, while contemporary standards of appropriate housing had risen to a point where these traditional houses were no longer acceptable. The final category of slum housing consisted of properties of more recent construction erected in courts and lanes at the rear of streets and houses. They were generally smaller than the older tenements, but no less overcrowded and insanitary. In 1888, G. Glorney of Kane's Court requested a change of name to Glorney's buildings, reflecting his construction of 'property for superior artisans and tenants'. By 1914 Dublin Corporation could report that 589 inhabitants of Glorney's buildings had been dispossessed, the buildings demolished and a total of £39,600 spent on erecting new housing on the site. The registrar-general was of the opinion that the worst housing was to be found in the courts and lanes.

Most of the new housing built in the city in the late nineteenth-century consisted of properties of four to six rooms suitable for lower middle class, or occasionally skilled working class occupancy. Most cheaper property, with the exception of Artisans Dwelling Co. schemes, seems to have been overcrowded and insanitary. The provision of working class housing by private companies was uncommon, reflecting the lack of large industrial concerns, the existence of a captive labour market and a general weakness in philanthropy. In 1854 the Quaker textile firm of Pim built cottages for employees at Harold's Cross. The only firms to follow suit were Guinness's and Watkins' breweries and the railway and tram companies. In 1914 these amounted in total to a mere 569 dwellings, mostly built in the suburbs. The absence of alternatives, and financial constraints forced the majority of the working class to live in tenements.

Housing was among the major preoccupations of public health reformers. The history of municipal public health in mid-nineteenth century England is a litany of the suppression of back-to-back housing, cellar dwellings and the introduction of water and sanitation and regular applications of white-wash. Dublin lacked any back-to-back houses and in the 1860s the small number of cellars which had been used as dwellings were closed. More active intervention against tenement housing was slow to emerge. In 1862 a corporation sub-committee directed the inspector of nuisances to draw up lists of tenement houses together with names of owners, number of occupants and sanitary condition. There is no evidence that this was implemented, and almost fifty years later the exist-ence of a tenement register remained in doubt. In 1866 bye-laws were introduced providing for a minimum of 300 cubic feet per person, regular inspection, water and sanitary accommodation and regular cleaning. Breaches of the regulations were to lead to fines. When these measures were proposed they inevitably led to a protest from a group entitled the 'anti-political ratepayers society' who threatened to close their tenement houses rather than comply and it would appear that Dublin Corporation relented. Many of the 1866 regulations were still being regularly breached in 1914.

PAGE L. DICKINSON

Dublin of Yesterday

LONDON ❧ METHUEN & CO. LTD ❧ 1929

About 1906 a small group of people in Dublin came to a decision that there was room for a club which should bring together those interested in Art—using the word 'art' in a wide sense. In actual fact the main spirits in this venture were not artists. The most energetic element was the James Duncans. Mrs Duncan was a fine pianist and at the same time practised the writing of rather precious essays and critical articles. She wrote cleverly of pictures, but without much knowledge. The jargon was hers, but study she had had little. James Duncan, one of the kindest and most charming souls that ever breathed, knew nothing of art. He was, however, rather unusually well-read in the literature of England and France. Few subjects had failed to yield secrets to him: a more delightful companion it would be impossible to find. As a philosopher, a metaphysician and a logician he was quite outstanding. As a writer of terse English, when his subject interested him, he was unsurpassed among amateurs of his generation.

These two, then, and a few other spirits, decided that they would, as it were, crystallize the renaissance movement then going on in Dublin. The Arts Club was formed—Yeats was in it, the Markieviczs, the Orpens, George Russell (AE), and a host of minor lights, many of whom are now more or less well known in their various spheres. Maurice Joy—now a second-rate but popular poet in the US—Patrick Colum, good writer as he was, now, alas! little heard of, and numerous other literary folk all came in.

One or two good musicians were among the original members. P.J. O'Hara, a writer of songs, who will be heard of in the future, although little known in the jazz world of the moment, contributed his quota. After all these people, with many hangers-on, many titled would-be artistic folk among them, had been got together the club was started. Modest premises were taken, with Mrs Duncan installed as secretary in a flat overhead.

The early phase of the Arts Club was somewhat self-conscious. A simple lunch and dinner were provided, and ten or twenty people used to turn up for these meals and talk of important matters while they ate; and afterwards over coffee in the smoking-room. Most of these people were middle-aged and not too exciting. Their talk was the rippling of a breeze over still, dark waters, and resulted in a froth that piled up against the weir-gates of the minds of us youngsters who had become involved in the current.

Soon, however, matters took a different course, and the Arts Club developed a social activity and an influence which was noticeable and, as I think, important; not only in the local life of the time, but as a factor in the provincial centres in England and, indirectly, in London.

After some three or four years of rather precarious financial and social existence, during a time when an energetic young barrister with artistic tendencies held the post of treasurer, it was decided to move into more ambitious surroundings, and to take a house in St Stephen's Green—the centre of Dublin Clubland. The deed was done, and a dinner was held on moving into the new premises. The following song, written by Frank Sparrow—an architect by trade but a light-verse writer of genius by nature—was sung during the course of the evening:

THE ARTS CLUB CIRCULAR

If you long for things artistic,
If you revel in the nebulous and mystic,
If your hair's too long
And your tie's all wrong
And your speech is symbolistic;
If your tastes are democratic
And your mode of life's essentially erratic;
If you seek success
From no fixed address,
But you sleep in someone's attic,
     Join the Arts Club, join the Arts Club,
     Where the souls do congregate,
     Where observance of convention
     Arouses fierce dissension:
     In the Arts Club, in the Arts Club,
     You may sit and dissertate,
     If your trousers bag and your coat-tails sag,
     You'll probably be hailed as great.

Now although the Club's exclusive,
The hereditary element's elusive,
But the presence at the helm
Of a peer of the realm
To a high tone's found conducive.
There are clever folk who lecture,
There are several who live by architecture,
While the club is rife
With folk whose life
Is a matter of conjecture
     In the Arts Club, etc.

If you feel a fool, don't show it,
And don't ever let a single person know it,
But join the Club
And pay your sub,
And you'll find yourself a poet;
Don't be a base secessionist—
If a painter, you are bound to be progressionist;
So though it hurts,
Forswear boiled shirts,
And become a Post-Impressionist:
     Join the Arts Club, etc.

If your talents are not patent,
But your taste for domesticity is latent;
If you think aloud
In the presence of a crowd
And your voice is fairly blatant;
If you're moved to thoughts symbolical
By proximity to liquids alcoholical,
If a pint of beer
Makes you a seer
Of visions apostolical:
     Join the Arts Club, etc.

If for Art you've no utility,
If your mind is somewhat lacking in agility,
You can still have tea,
From half-past three,

In complete respectability;
Don't imagine that you need be boisterous—
There's a regular department for the roisterous—
They pursue their horrid revels,
Down at subterranean levels,
In a dungeon damp and cloisterous,
    In the Arts Club, etc.

During these years a pleasant comradeship had grown up; constant dining together, the everyday lunch-hour, and occasional cheerful evenings had developed a sort of unity among a large group of members, not perhaps unique in its harmony, but certainly unique in its striving towards a defined social goal. All sorts of people had been drawn in. The time was ripe for a rich cohesion of ideals. Literature, Art, the Theatre and political adventure were in the air. The Arts Club group gave an outlet to all who were interested in life and its obvious and obscure reflections. Indeed, by this time, two or three years after its commencement, the club stood for a wide intellectual outlook. Everything was represented. William Yeats was a prominent member; Jack Yeats played his part; Percy French, great Irish gentleman and gifted song-writer, and painter of the scenes of our romantic dreams of landscape, was there whenever his work allowed. There were numerous lesser lights. Betty Duncan, now well known in a certain English county as a charming and capable hostess, Conor O'Brien, artist, writer, mountaineer and celebrated sailor; Frank Sparrow, best of all-round men, and one of the great wits of Ireland of the time, are only a few names that come to the memory. It was a gathering of the talents which will never be beaten, will never be replaced: at least, not in Ireland. I quote two stories to illustrate the atmosphere.

One night at dinner, when there were present Markievicz, Sparrow, Conor O'Brien, and someone whose name and personality have escaped my memory, the talk turned on one Carrie, then a sculptor, now an actor well known in certain parts in London. Carrie's name cropped up. A hasty verse was written to which, I think, every one contributed. Carrie, it must be mentioned, was a particularly abstemious man:

We had to carry Carrie to the ferry;
    The ferry carried Carrie to the shore.
The reason that we couldn't carry Carrie
    Was—Carrie couldn't carry any more.

Impromptu verse-making was brought to rather a fine art, and after the club dinners amazingly clever verses were often produced on current topics. Every one had their chance; there was no jealousy or no scar turn. One entertainment consisted of a song 'Vive la Compagnie', in which the rapid making of rhymes, with no time for reflection, was the point. It depended, of course, for its success on the nimbleness of wit of the people taking part. This song was in full blast one night when Yeats happened to be present. After ten or twelve verses of rather high standard had been reeled off, Yeats turned round and said, 'It's marvellous—wonderful. I never heard such rhyming in my life.' One member of the party was subsequently heard to say that this was the only moment in his career in which he took himself seriously as a poet.

Yeats was, in an intellectual sense, the father of the Arts Club. He attended its dinners and discussions pretty regularly when in Dublin. He was extremely good-natured and kind to folk less gifted than himself, and indeed often cast his pearls before swine in an open-handed and haphazard way.

He was very absent-minded, and I remember one night he came to dinner rather late, and sat down at the table with Sparrow, myself and one or two more, at the concluding stage of dinner. Yeats was full of some subject or another, I have no recollection what, and started talking, regardless of our conversation. He was in very good form that night, and in a short time we were all absorbed in listening to him. As he talked he ate, and finally caught us up at dessert.

Then came a lull in the flow of his talk and he sat up and took notice—he had reached the climax of his argument. He turned round and said, 'Have I dined, or have I not? I have been so absorbed that I don't know.' For a joke, I said, 'No, you haven't dined; you must be hungry.' He turned to the waitress and asked for dinner, which was duly brought, and he went right through the menu a second time. He was tired, I think, and although he talked well (he always does), the second dinner failed to produce the amazing eloquence of the first. I remember, among many episodes concerning Yeats, another rather amusing one. Sparrow and I were sitting having a drink after the theatre in the Arts Club smoking-room, when Yeats entered. He was obviously dying to talk to someone, and he asked us round to the hotel where he lived (at that time he had no house), and, indeed, insisted on our going. He said, 'I think there is some whisky; and I know there is some wine.' We went, very flattered, and sat in his room till three or four in the morning, while he talked. Such a flow of talk I have never heard before or since. We made an occasional remark, but conversation it was not. It was a series of brilliant lectures on all sorts of abstractions, mainly of a metaphysical nature. I remember no word of what was said, but I do not think I have ever been so enthralled.

Yeats was at his best at such moments, I think. He is (it is rather absurd to say so) a wonderful lecturer and speaker—few men of modern times have such control over ideas and words—but it is when he is in the company of a few congenial people that he reaches his heights. He talked books away that night for the benefit of his own mind and that of two not particularly well-educated young men.

TONY FARMAR

The Legendary Lofty Clattery Café: Bewley's of Ireland

DUBLIN ❧ RIVERSEND LTD ❧ 1988

For three generations Bewley's Oriental Cafés have had a special place in the hearts of Dubliners. Shoppers and gossipers, actors, poets, students, politicians, lovers and business people, townees and country people, tramps and tourists all make time in their day for half an hour or so on the famous red plush benches. People come to Bewley's to see and be seen; to savour a moment's leisure, or a little sugared luxury, in the unique mix of private and public space provided by the high ceilings and cloistered booths, in a nostalgic atmosphere of open fires and mahogany.

They come for a leisurely breakfast with the newspapers; for lunch with friends; for business meetings or deep conversation over sticky buns and tea; or simply for a refreshing cuppa, amid the friendly clatter of crockery, and the fierce smell of roasting coffee that spills into Dublin's central shopping streets.

Bewley's is the Irish counterpart of those great cafés that spread through Europe after the first introduction of coffee in the seventeenth century. In serious-minded England coffee houses developed into financial institutions such as Lloyds and the stock exchange, or became places for political intrigue. In Venice, Florian's in the Piazza di San Marco, and

in Paris, Procope's, were the rendezvous of the idle, of gossips, conversa-
tionalists, wits and beautiful people. Everywhere the cafés became centres
of social life—clubs without an entrance fee that generated an extraordinary affection and loyalty among their patrons.

Since Bewley's first café opened in a busy Dublin street nearly a
hundred years ago, the famous and the infamous have enjoyed this atmosphere: James Joyce discussed the setting up of Ireland's first cinema in
Bewley's, and Arthur Griffith, Paddy Kavanagh, Maud Gonne, Jimmy
O'Dea, Micheal MacLiammoir, Mary Lavin, Terry Wogan and Ludwig
Wittgenstein, to name only a few, all visited the cafés regularly. Up from
the country for shopping? An essential part of the treat was a visit to
Bewley's for tea. Books were talked out of existence, political plots
dissected, business plans hatched, tea-time treats dispensed, gossip
exchanged *('Well! as I said at the time …')*.

Bewley's now run five cafés, seven shops, and several franchising
units, serving some 45,000 customers a week. Over 200 staff contribute to
a turnover of £10 million, deriving from the cafes, from wholesale
supplies of coffee and tea, and from retail sales of a range of products from
jam to wine, but particularly their own famous bakery goods. These pages
describe how the company developed from quite small beginnings in the
China tea business, to an institution that Garret FitzGerald, when he was
Taoiseach, described as *'an integral and vital part of Dublin's essential character
and atmosphere'*.

The cornerstone of all Bewley's business is the Irish appetite for the
products of two exotic shrubs originally found only in China and Africa:
Camellin sinensis and *Coffea arabica*. Tea and coffee are so much part of our
way of life now, that it is impossible to imagine Ireland without them.
Yet a mere 150 years ago they were virtually unknown to ordinary
people, being drunk only by the gentry. The companies run by the
Bewley family, of which Bewley's Cafés are the only survivors, were inti-
mately involved in developing the Irish taste for tea and later for coffee.

The Bewley family is French in origin; they moved from France to the
north of England in the middle ages, first to Yorkshire and then to
Cumberland, where they were in the fourteenth century. During the religious turmoil of the seventeenth century some members of the family
became 'by convincement' members of the Society of Friends (Quakers)
under the influence of the fiery George Fox.

What differentiated Quakers from other radical sects of the day was
the doctrine of the *Inner Light*. Fox described this as the *'mystical, but*

Divine, light in the hearts of men; a light which would, if followed honestly and steadily, infallibly lead to God: and that without the aid of either the Bible or any ordinances'. Every act, grave or trivial, was to be judged according to this light of truth. The stubbornly maintained assertion that a person's inward truth should have more weight than the Bible or the statements of the Church often got members of the new sect into trouble with the authorities.

In 1700 Mungo Bewley, the first of the family to live in Ireland, came to the midlands at the age of 23, to practise his religion and seek a living in a more tolerant and less strictly policed atmosphere. The family thrived, specialising in the wool and other clothing trades. By 1780 Mungo II (grandson of the first Mungo) had a linen factory in Mountrath employing as many as 150 people. His brother, John Bewley, had a textile printing works near Blessington in County Wicklow, and a third brother, Samuel, had set himself up in Dublin as a silk merchant, importing silk from Italy, the Levant and London.

Samuel was born in 1764, the son of Thomas Bewley and his wife Susanna Pim. She was a member of the great Pim family that was to become powerful throughout the nineteenth century in Dublin financial and business circles. As we shall see, Samuel was frequently to be joined with his Pim cousins in financial ventures.

By the 1820s Samuel was a great man in Dublin commercial circles. He was a ship-owner; he was Treasurer of the Chamber of Commerce; he was a major shareholder (with Joseph R. Pim) in the Mining Company of Ireland (capital £500,000); he was a leading founder and honorary auditor of the National Assurance Company (capital £1 million), which was among other things for twenty years the only Irish company under-taking marine insurance; he inaugurated the Dublin Savings Bank, which by 1838 had three branches in the city; he was a major investor in a Quaker-owned brewery (the temperance lines were not then so strictly drawn). He was also the prime influence in the establishment of the Retreat at Bloomfield in Donnybrook, the first asylum in Ireland to insist on the gentle treatment of the insane.

Many of Samuel's business contacts and partners were Quakers, and the ideals of the Society of Friends have been a significant influence in the development of the firm ever since. In 1820 there were no more than 700 Quakers in Dublin, out of a total city population of 224,000. They came from some 130 families, who were in general well-off and closely connected to each other, a connection they took pains to preserve.

Children were expected to marry within the fold, on pain of expulsion from the Society. A closely-knit series of family and business alliances grew up, of which the Pims and the Bewleys were among the most prominent.

Following the implications of the doctrine of inward truth, Quakers became famous for providing in all their commercial dealings fair measure, reasonable prices and good quality. The Quakers were also well-known in business circles for their attitude to bankruptcy, of which they strongly disapproved. Because the banking and company law systems were so underdeveloped, businesses at this time were run by a web of interlocking personal credit and loans. If one merchant house got into trouble, it frequently brought others down as well, by breaking the chain of owing and paying. Although this might have happened without any personal fault, Quakers held that not to pay one's debts was an offence against truth, and expelled members from the Society if they failed in business.

To prevent this, if it was discovered that one of their number was in difficulties, certain Friends, selected for their sensitivity and knowledge of commercial procedures, would be appointed to help him. A report on the case would be brought in to the next monthly meeting. This would describe the general outlines of the case, and unless there was any flagrant transgression of the customary laws of the Society the visitors would be encouraged to continue their 'care' of the transgressor and report back to a further meeting and so on for a number of months. The object of the procedure was to ensure that the transgressor would act according to the demands of the Quaker view of justice in the payment of debts. Samuel Bewley frequently acted as advisor on these occasions.

Despite Samuel Bewley's success in other areas, his silk business was not prospering. Fashions had changed after the French Revolution, so that men no longer wore silk stockings; and economic changes after the Act of Union meant that more and more Irish trade was being taken by London merchants. Samuel spread his wings, and began trading in other goods, particularly from the Mediterranean. In November 1824 he advertised for sale in the *Dublin Mercantile Advertiser* the following goods: gum arabic, opium (for medicinal purposes), galls, liquorice paste, Gallipoli oil, silkworm gut and Turkey carpets. As an afterthought he mentioned that he had in stock 1,500 drums of new Turkey figs, and 60 tons of valonia.

Samuel had been pushing the Chamber of Commerce for some time to encourage the direct importation of goods into Dublin, no doubt conscious that failure to do this had been a major cause of the silk industry's collapse. In 1835 his enterprising son Charles (who died young) engineered the great coup of importing 2,099 chests of tea on the *Hellas*, which was said to be the first ship ever freighted directly from Canton to Dublin; a few months later the *Mandarin* loaded a further 8,623 chests. These two consignments between them probably accounted for 40 per cent of the annual Irish consumption of tea at that time (though of course some of it may have been intended for export to England).

This activity, as a contemporary in the tea-trade put it, *'caused a complete revolution in the old-fashioned style of business in that article ...'*. At this time all tea was grown in China, and until recently every ounce had been sold in the East India Company's auction rooms in the City of London. In 1833 the statutory monopoly of the East India Company was broken; merchants could make their own arrangements, and tea suddenly began to be imported direct into Dublin, Liverpool, Belfast and Cork. Tea was to remain Bewley's key product for years, only to be overtaken by coffee in the new century.

There were various grades of tea, distinguished by exotic names which have now fallen out of use: gunpowder, caper, bohea, congou, singlo, twankay. At this time the Irish consumed a mere half a pound of tea a head per year, and, if we can judge from the contents of that first shipment in the *Hellas*, drank mainly the better-quality congous and pekoes—only 15 per cent of the consignment was the low-grade bohea.

The one thing all teas had in common was their expense. The duty on a pound of congou was 2s 2d, effectively 125 per cent. Like alcohol today, tea was a major contributor to government revenues. The duty on tea paid for nearly two-thirds of the whole of the (admittedly small) British civil service establishment, including the expenses of the Crown.

Samuel Bewley died in 1837, leaving seven of his thirteen children alive after him. Youngest of these was Joshua, the direct founder of the business we know today as Bewley's, who was only eighteen. By this time the Bewleys had built up a network of related businesses in Dublin. Samuel's brother Henry ran an apothecary and chemist establishment in Sackville (O'Connell) Street called Bewley and Evans; Joshua's brother James was a tea and wine merchant in Dun Laoghaire, and the eldest son Joseph ran Samuel Bewley and Sons, an importing merchant, from William Street.

It is likely that Joshua began his commercial career with Joseph, who soon became prominent in organising help for victims of the Famine. In November 1846 a group of Friends, led by Jonathan Pim and Joseph

Bewley, formed the Central Relief Committee, which pioneered the organisation of soup kitchens and food shipments to areas badly hit by the potato blight. The dedicated work of this committee in developing famine relief services was one of the few bright spots in those dark days. Close connections with American and British Friends were very important in this effort. American Quakers, for instance, provided nearly two-thirds of all Quaker relief supplies during the Famine period.

Joshua set up his own business as a tea merchant some time in the 1840s. A decade later he worked from 19 and 20 Sycamore Alley, where were based his China Tea Company, the store-room of Samuel Bewley & Sons, and a depot for his uncle Henry's other business Bewley, Fisher & Co. Sycamore Alley (now Sycamore Street) runs down from Dame Street, near the Olympia Theatre, to Essex Street.

Then as now, that area of Dublin is more remarkable for traders, bankers and administrators than shops and retailing. Sycamore Alley itself was not at all grand: at number 1 (from the Dame Street end) lived Charles Keenan, a dealer in leeches for medical use, and eight of the houses were in tenements and a further four in ruins. The new business was however significantly near to the handsome Quaker meeting house in Eustace Street, which Samuel Bewley had been instrumental in developing.

Joshua was reasonably prosperous by 1850: apart from his tea merchanting he also did some business as an actuary, and owned a fine house in 20 Pembroke Road, only two doors away from the Director of the Irish Geological Survey. His brothers, who appear to have been considerably better off, had houses in the comfortable suburbs of south Dublin, in Sandford Hill, Ranelagh (now occupied by Gonzaga College), in Rockville, Blackrock and in Rathfarnham.

Unfortunately no records have survived to reveal the scale of Joshua's tea business, or indeed how his business was run. His will of 1866 mentions a stable of horses in Coghill's court, between Eustace Street and Sycamore Alley, which opened under an arch into Dame Street. He was certainly in at the beginning of a growing market. Between 1840 and 1890 the Irish diet changed radically. In particular the tea-drinking habit, combined with a taste for sugar and white bread, spread rapidly westward throughout the country after the Famine. Annual tea consumption grew from 4.1 million lbs in 1840 to 35 million lbs in 1890.

For generations before this the Irish diet had been much as Sir William Petty described it in 1672; *the diet of the people is milk, sweet and sour, thick and thin ... their food is bread in cakes, potatoes from August til May, eggs and butter.*' Two hundred years later, An tAthair Peadar ˙Ó Laoghaire recalled '*the oatmeal bread and the wheaten bread from the mill, hen-eggs and duck-eggs, sweet milk and thick milk and buttermilk, the potatoes and butter taken fresh from the churn, the bit of bacon now and again*' that he used to eat as a young man on holidays from Maynooth in the 1860s.

But change was in the air. The failure of the potato crops during the Famine had introduced new dietary habits into the country, in particular the much-disliked maize. This was eaten as stirabout, a form of porridge made by boiling it in water to the consistency of a soft pudding and then mixing with sugar and milk. A government enquiry in 1864 found that sugar was used by 80 per cent of the population (usually with maize and therefore not in the potato season), tea by only 57 per cent. Tea was, so a witness reported, '*used very generally in towns, and sometimes to a large extent, whilst in some of the country places its use is almost unknown.*'

Gradually the habit took on throughout the country. Many people no doubt picked up the taste for tea while working as servants in the houses of the gentry. An early example of this comes from the diary of Elizabeth Smith of Baltiboys, Co Wicklow, who records having tremendous trouble with a newly-recruited servant. At the bottom of it was, as she wrote crossly in her diary, '*the wish to have tea for her breakfast like the other maids! She, who has often and often had but one meal a day and that dry potatoes.*'

One contributory cause to the spread of tea was the temperance movement, itself allied to a general spread of refinement throughout the century that made such rougher traditions as Donnybrook Fair, faction fights and the drunken revelling described by both Jonah Barrington and Humphrey O'Sullivan no longer acceptable. Strong drink was also held by many nationalists to have contributed to the failure of the risings in 1798.

As a result of all those forces, Irish tea consumption began to rise very markedly. Between 1840 and 1860 it went up three-fold to just under 2 lbs per head per annum; by 1900 it had risen to 7·5 lbs per head, not far away from the present figure. The steady reduction in tax over this period, from 2s 2d per pound in 1850 to 4d per pound in 1880 was no doubt a considerable help.

By 1870 Joshua's business occupied five houses, nos 15–19 Sycamore Alley, and his brothers and cousins had similarly extended themselves into a considerable range of businesses. His brother Thomas ran a sugar refinery in Brunswick (now Pearse) Street, and *his* son, also Thomas, ran the shipbuilders Bewley, Webb & Co. Joshua's brother William was running Fawcett & Co., 18–20 Henry Street, which by the 1880s was renamed Bewley, Sons & Co. and was the biggest wine and whiskey retailer in Dublin. Joshua himself had moved twelve miles out of town to the fashionable resort of Bray, where he lived in a comfortable house under the shadow of Bray Head.

JOHN GAMBLE

Sketches of History, Politics and Manners in Dublin and the North of Ireland in 1810

LONDON ∾ BALDWIN, CRADDOCK AND JOY ∾ 1826

Style of living in Dublin—Society—Professional men—Barristers—Progress of luxury—Hospitality—Inference from the number of beggars

Dublin

I am come here at an unlucky period—visiting Dublin in August is as bad as going to the country at Christmas—the town is as bare of company now as the trees are then of leaves, or the earth is of verdure. Fashion has prodigious influence in this metropolis; and the gentry, merchants, and tradesmen, think it incumbent on them to pass the summer out of town, because the fashionables of London go at that season to watering places. Notwithstanding the gaiety of Dublin, I do not think a stranger would find it a pleasant residence after its novelty has subsided;—there is, no doubt, much hospitality, and, on slight introduction, he may get many dinners; but, as ostentation mingles in its full proportion with kindness of heart in these invitations, this hospitality is rather a holiday suit (if I may so speak) than a plain jacket; it is drawn forth on state occasions, but is too costly for every day's wear. The usages of Dublin make it necessary to give dinners, often beyond the income of the entertainer; who, in his ordinary mode of living, probably pays the penalty of his occasional profusion. He never wishes, therefore, to be taken unawares, or to expose himself to the chance of being caught at his humble meal of mutton and whiskey punch by the man who a few days before had feasted with him on venison and claret: a stranger, therefore, does not find his hospitality a resource at the time he wants it most—in the hour of langour and lassitude, when it would be so agreeable to have a house to step into on the footing of unreserved intercourse.

Nor does the public life perform what the private denies: the *savoir vivre* is but moderately advanced in Dublin: there are none of those comfortable eating-houses in which London so much abounds, where one often meets rational and agreeable society, and has a good dinner at a reasonable price; without being obliged to swallow a quantity of sloe-juice, which the courtesy of England denominates wine. The taverns in Dublin are either so miserably low that a respectable person cannot be seen going into them, or are equally extravagant with the most expensive London ones. The lodging-houses, with some exceptions, and I have been lucky enough to get into one, are liable to the same objection: they are either barracks, which the mop seems never to have visited, or beyond all reason extravagant. In all these and various other conveniences, London abounds to a degree that makes it, of all other places, the most agreeable residence for a man of small fortune: nor is there, perhaps, a town in the world, where a man, who hangs loosely by society, can glide more gently down the stream of time, or where, if he cannot greatly enjoy, he can *endure* life better. Dublin has another great disadvantage: paradoxical as it may appear, it is too small for retirement; a stranger can never long remain so; curiosity busies itself about his profession, his fortune, and manner of living, until every thing about him becomes known: he may be said, therefore, to be too much on his good behaviour. This, as far as morality is concerned, is perhaps an advantage; but in various minor matters of economy it is attended with many evils: a man, watched by eyes more numerous and wakeful than those of Argus, can neither eat, drink, nor dress, as he likes; he cannot live for himself, but for the world. Places of amusement are not numerous here—until lately there was but one theatre; and even that resource will not continue many days longer, as it shortly closes for the summer: drinking will then be the only amusement; and it is not half so good a summer as a winter one. The weather just now is insufferably warm, and wine is by no means so agreeable a beverage as water: I shall, therefore, leave this in a day or two, to breathe the cooler air of the northern mountains, where excessive heat is as rare as adultery. A traveller can no more quit a town, however, than he can turn off a servant, without giving it a character—like an epilogue, after a new play, it is always expected of him.—In conformity, therefore, to immemorial usage, I shall say a few words of the general state of society and manners in Dublin; though, when I speak, I had better perhaps remain silent; when I seem to move, I may make little progress; and when I flatter myself with giving a group, I may only sketch a few individuals.

There are few resident nobility in Dublin. Irish Nobility is a sickly and delicate plant: like the myrtle, it does not do in this northern climate: it thrives only in the sunshine of court favour: it is not a non-substantive kind of greatness; it cannot stand by itself; it leans for support on the minister, who often finds the propping-up of this tender vine an embarrassing and expensive species of gardening. People of large landed property are equally rare: these gentry, like swallows, take an annual flight to England, where they hop about from London to Weymouth, from Bath to Cheltenham, till their purses are as empty as their heads; when they return to wring further sums from the hard hands of their wretched tenants, who seldom see them but on such occasions. The learned professions may be therefore said to form the aristocracy of Dublin—law, physic, and gospel, take the lead here, and give the ton in manners, as well as in morals and literature. These three professions go hand-in-hand; though haud passibus aequis: law is always the foremost. A physician can be but a knight, or, at the best, physician to the Lord Lieutenant: a lawyer may be Lord Chancellor, and rule the Lord Lieutenant himself:—the wool-sack is a very comfortable seat, far softer than the bench of a bishop, and therefore much higher in public estimation.

The Irish bar contains many men of shining abilities: the eloquence of Mr Curran is well known and generally admired; Mr Bushe, the Solicitor-general, is considered an able reasoner and sound lawyer; and Mr Plunkett, the late Attorney-general, is an admirable public speaker, either at the bar or in parliament. The style of the Irish bar is different from that of the English. It is less solemn and decorous, but more lively and animated, more glowing and figurative, more witty and sarcastic; it reasons less, it instructs less, it convinces less, but it amuses more; it is more ornamented, more dramatic; it rises to the sublime, it sinks to the humorous, it attempts the pathetic—but in all this there is too much of the tricks of a juggler. I do not say that an Irish advocate thinks less of his client than an English one, but he appears to think less; he appears to think most of himself—of his own reputation, of the approbation of his brethren, the applause of the spectators, and the admiration of the court. I dare say I should be most gratified by specimens of eloquence taken at the Irish bar, but were either my life or my fortune at stake, I should like to be defended at an English one.

In society the Irish lawyer is equally amusing; there is a mixture of gentlemanly manners and professional acuteness; of gay repartee and classic allusion, which makes him often an instructive, and always an agreeable companion. Yet even here it is easy to remark the traces of the defects I have mentioned: a rage to shine, and disposition to dazzle; his wit cloys by repetition, and his allusions are often forced and far-fetched—difficultly found, and not worth the trouble of seeking: he is too fond of antithesis, likewise, and says smart, rather than sensible things; specious rather than solid things. This disposition, however, to be witty rather than wise, is not confined to the gentlemen of the bar, but is universal through the city. In ever party I have been in, talkers were many, and listeners were few; and wit, or what was meant to be such, was bandied about with the bottle, or the cards. As many of these would-be wits had little pretensions to it, we had often to laugh when there was no joke, and much merriment when there was little reason for it. They are great punners, and to do them justice, I heard some excellent ones. I should recommend the editor of a fashionable print, who seems so partial to this species of humour, to import a quantity for the use of his paper, as the stock on hand is of the vilest kind. I am not clear, however, but that this constant effort after wit produces beneficial effects in Dublin society. It animates the man and sharpens his faculties, and makes him alive to the approbation of those about him;—he is the complete reverse, therefore, of the lazy, lounging man of fashion in London; who holds it the essence of ton to be haughty, silent, supercilious, and indifferent; who, unlike Falstaff, is not only not witty himself, but a damper of it in others; who sits by the side of genius without a wish to be instructed by it, by the side of venerable old age without a desire to contribute to its comforts, and by the side of beauty, which he surveys with the scrutinising look of a jockey at a horse-fair, without the smallest effort to make himself agreeable.

The lower classes of the inhabitants of this city have afforded abundant materials to the dramatist, as well as to the tourist. They are represented as a wrong-headed and a warm-hearted, a whimsical and eccentric kind of people; who get drunk and make bulls, and who cannot open their mouths that something funny and witty does not come tumbling out, like pearls, every time she spoke, from the lips of the fair princess Parizade, in the Arabian Nights' Entertainments. I do not deny that there may be some foundation for this character; but if I am to judge from what I have seen myself, it is greatly exaggerated. A Dublin shoe-black, like a London one, may sometimes utter a quaint or witty saying, which the uncouthness of his appearance, and the singularity of his accent, may render more striking; but I should suppose most of the stories told of him are without any foundation; and that their authors give as recollec-tion, what is only invention.

Luxury has made as great progress among people in business here, as in any other place I have ever visited. A shopkeeper gives splendid entertainments, and his wife elegant routs, in which her own manner and appearance, that of the females she invites, and the costliness and embellishments of her furniture, would bear comparison with persons of a much higher rank; nor does her husband acquit himself with less propriety at the foot of his table, or in the drawing-room. In this respect the Dublin shopkeeper has infinite advantage over the London one: in morals he is not, I believe, inferior, but in manners he is decidedly superior; he is cheerful and easy, frank and unembarrassed; in conversation he is lively and pleasing—he may not have much to say, but the manner is excellent; his ideas, from the nature of his profession, are not numerous; but, like the goods in his shop, he possesses the art of showing them off to advantage. The universal prevalence of good-breeding, among all descriptions of respectable people in Dublin, must strike the most unobservant spectator: to assign a plausible reason for it would not be easy. I should attribute it in a great measure to vanity; to a slavish imitation, and servile admiration of fashion and rank, which lead them to adopt their prejudices, to echo their opinions, to copy their manners, and to boast of their acquaintance. Vanity, indeed, seems the prominent feature of every inhabitant of Dublin: he is vain of himself, vain of his city, of its beauty, of the splendour of its public buildings, and of its vast superiority over London. In this respect, doubtless, he is deserving of praise, which he would get more readily, if he did not demand it so imperiously. The difference between a citizen of London and Dublin seems to be this: the latter is vain, and the former is proud; he has a lofty opinion of his country and of himself; he never dreams that this can be disputed; and, satisfied with it himself, is indifferent even if it should: the latter is not so assured of a ready acquiescence to his claims, either for his city or for himself; perhaps he is not so well assured of them himself; nor if he were, could he exist so well on his own resources. His advantages and superiority must be reflected from the eyes, the tongue, and consideration of others, to make them truly valuable to himself. In this observation, however, I do not deny but that I may be refining too much, and that Dublin vanity only strikes me more, because I am accustomed to it less. In the account I have just been giving, I beg leave to be understood I only comprise the Protestants; I have not seen a sufficient number of Catholics to form a decided opinion of their character; though I have seen enough to be convinced that there is a considerable difference between them and the Protestants.—In their air and manner, in their ready acquiescence, and smiling civility, I think I perceive the traces of the thraldom in which they have so long been held; while in the erect and upright step of the Protestant we recognize the freeman. We recognize something more—we perceive the lofty bearing of an individual of a cherished caste, situated in the midst of a rejected one. We may imagine an Englishman in the East Indies, or a Creole in the West; or if we wish to be further fanciful, we may try to imagine a Norman knight about two centuries after the Conquest, when he was beginning to regard those around him as his countrymen.

The citizens of Dublin (Catholics I believe as well as Protestants) are hospitable: how much of this is benevolence, how much ostentation, is an ungracious point for a man who has benefited by it to decide; nor does it admit of easy decision. I shall be tempted, however, to give them credit for a considerable portion of the former: if some alloy mixes with the gold, if the statue is partly brass, and partly clay, it is the same, perhaps, with most of our virtues, and most of our actions. This hospitality, however, compared to what it was in former times, is much on the decline:—writers like me, who cheerfully eat their dinners, and allow them no credit for giving them, may have some share in this; but the increasing pressure of the times, which makes it every year more difficult to support a family, is probably the great reason: along with this, hospitality is seldom to be met in excess in any town, when it comes to a certain magnitude, or in any community, at a certain point of civilisation. But if hospitality has diminished, charity remains: were the faults of the inhabitant of Dublin ten times greater than I have described his foibles, he has charity enough to cover them all; his foibles he has in common with others, his charity is peculiarly his own. I know of no spot in existence, of the size of the city of Dublin, where there is such unbounded munificence: in London, no doubt, there are many valuable institutions for the relief of distress,—and God forbid I should undervalue them,—but still it must be remembered, that much is compulsory, and not meritorious; much the mere consequence of boundless wealth: the man who rolls on guineas may well bestow farthings on the poor. But the charity of Dublin is not strained: it is not founded on acts of parliament; it is not weighed and measured by the standard of law; nor is it the gilded offering, the filleted and garlanded sacrifice of wealth. It gives not on compulsion, it gives not from a hoard. The waters of the Liffey do not bear, like the waves of the Thames, the riches of the two hemispheres; the inhabitants of its banks have no Eastern mines of gold; but they have what is better still—they have humane and benevolent hearts.

The number of beggars in Dublin is remarked by all travellers, and is said to prove its poverty. Admirable reasoners, who see nothing but on one side!—Does it not prove its charity likewise? There are few beggars in London: what is the reason?—there is little poverty, perhaps, will be the answer:—Is that so?—is that indeed so?—is there really little poverty in London?—Alas! there is much; much suffering, much sorrow, much want in every quarter, in every lane, and in every street—but there are few beggars—if there were many they would *starve*.

J.D. HERBERT

Irish Varieties for the Last Fifty Years

LONDON ❧ WILLIAM JOY ❧ 1836

THE PINKING DINDIES

It is now upwards of fifty years since Dublin was infested by an organised body of dissolute characters, composed of persons;— some were sons of respectable parents, who permitted them to get up to man's estate in idle habits, without adequate means of support; others were professional students, who, having tasted the alluring fruits of dissipation, abandoned their studies and took a shorter road to gain supplies, by means no matter how fraudulent. They were of imposing appearance; being handsome and well made in general; so that, individually, you could not suspect them: it was by their acts only you could convict them, and they commonly pursued their schemes in parties, and by night; and they were so well prepared for battle that the 'ancient and quiet watchmen,' the only protectors of the citizens of Dublin at that period, were worsted in almost every attempt made to subdue them; so that they were permitted to assail passengers in the streets, to levy contributions, or, perhaps, take a lady from her protector; and *many* females were destroyed by that lawless banditti. Another vile plan they had of providing supplies, by exacting from unfortunate girls, at houses of ill-fame, their share of what they deemed booty; and for this boon each had his wife, as he called her, and, if necessary, would assist her as bully, to awe, or compel, a flat to come down handsomely. Another source of gain they sought at a low gambling-house, in Essex Street; and when unsuccessful, they sallied forth, enraged at their losses, and repaired them, by robbing the first eligible subject they met in the streets.

Dress, at that time, was indispensable. No gentleman was seen without a sword: if in undress, a *cuteau de chasse*; if full dressed, a small sword;—and the use of the sword was well understood.

The pinking dindies made a rule to be well-dressed, and, to a man, they were skilful swordsmen.

Their plan of attack was thus:- Two of them, walking arm-in-arm, jostled the victim they meant for prey; then, with their swords in their scabbards, chapeless, so that the point just protruded, they pricked him in various parts, and if he did not throw down his watch and money, two others came and took it by force; whilst two more in reserve were on the watch to give alarm if any persons approached. In that case they disappeared, and had their hiding-places adjacent, doors open; so, that if the punctured man was willing to pursue, he knew not where to go, but was glad to get away, bleeding and terrified. It appears incredible that such a practice should be endured for years without any effort to check it effectually, and Dublin had all her nobles, gentry, citizens, mayor, aldermen, sheriffs, peers, and a garrison of soldiers—no small number. The only way I can account for it, is that the Pinks never attacked swordsmen, nor any but single men and citizens, who neither wore fine clothes nor swords; so that gentlemen never felt the pointed evil, as it did not point at them. The last achievement I recollect of one of these redoubted champions, was a robbery he committed, at eleven o'clock at night, in Fleet Street, on a merchant, who had reached home, but had not knocked at his door. The robber presented a pistol at him, the merchant delivered his watch and money, and the freebooter escaped; but the merchant recognised him as a person with whom he had been well acquainted, having been at the same school with him. The next morning he had him arrested and committed to prison. He prosecuted him. When brought to trial, counsellor Curran defended, and exercised his wit on the occasion. The merchant swore positively to the man, and gave satisfactory evidence, which Curran, in cross-examination, attempted to invalidate. He drew from him that he had dined with a friend, and had partaken freely of the bottle; that he was returning home at nine o'clock, when he was induced to enter a tavern, and had supper of nine poached eggs and three or four tumblers of whiskey punch. Then Curran said,—'Now, sir, you have sworn positively to this man. Pray, how can you, after the confession I have heard from your lips of so many bottles—*two, at least* of wine; then, at night, a strata of poached eggs, and three or four tumblers of punch? Pray, do you not think your judgment might have been a little under the yoke?' This set the court in a roar of laughter, but though sport to them, it was death to the delinquent. The jury pronounced him guilty. However, his character had not been so very depraved as many of his fellows; his manner was always kind and civil, prepossessing; he was as fine a figure and as handsome a man as could be seen: he had many friends, from his redeeming qualities, and the respectability of his family. It was his first known offence, and the jury recommended him strongly. The judge refused the recommendation. This drew forth a host of influential persons, and the case was sent to the lord-lieutenant. For some time the unfortunate fellow hung in doubt, *but no more,*—there was no execution; nay, such interest was made for him, that he was allowed to transport himself for life. I saw him a few days before he took shipping for America. I had known him, and he stopped to speak to me; he appeared truly ashamed, and with great candour acknowledged his good fortune, so much beyond his hopes or his deserts.

My readers may think me a strange character for acknowledging such a person, but I knew him before his fall, and I owed my life to him once, in a case where I was attacked by ruffians, who use little ceremony when enraged. The prosecution of that pink struck terror through the whole fraternity, for many of them were as liable to punishment, and could easily have been identified: several went to London, and became expert at gaming-tables; two of them were enabled to obtain admission to clubs in St James's Street, and I have often seen them walking and conversing familiarly with high fashionables. But the party of pinking dindies were never finally extirpated until the police was established. That useful institution, though decried by many, was more salutary, and timely to the city of Dublin, than any plan that has since been devised, coercive or otherwise, yet so capricious and unthinking are many, they condemn an establishment without proving its inefficacy; and though they suffered by the want of civil protection, and have been since, and are at present, in a state of tranquillity and security, many are insensible of the acquisition they possess in a well-regulated police establishment.

RICHARD M. KAIN

*Dublin in the Age of William Butler Yeats
and James Joyce*

NORMAN, OKLAHOMA, USA
UNIVERSITY OF OKLAHOMA PRESS ❧ 1962

From the time of Barrington to that of Brendan Behan, Dublin has cherished personality. The city is small enough for individuals to be known as individuals. People are news, and the only thing worse than being talked about is not being talked about. Everyone worth knowing is sure to turn up in the course of the day, at the theatre or the library or the newspaper offices and pubs. In Irish novels and reminiscences they are to be found, those eccentric dons from Trinity, the ready-witted advocates, the worldly scholars, the poetic medical students. Long after they are gone their words are remembered and their presence felt. There was the eighteenth-century don, Jacky Barrett, whose antics are still relished. Although an outstanding Orientalist, he was such an extraordinary hermit that he reached middle age before he knew what sheep looked like. His expression of delight at seeing 'live mutton' was equaled only by his appreciation of the sea, which he described as 'a broad flat superficies, like Euclid's definition of a line expanding itself into a surface.' He once made the practical suggestion that Trinity College dispose of some rubbish by digging a hole in which to bury it. When asked what was to be done with the earth taken out of the hole, he came up with the idea of digging another hole for it!

Visitors to Dublin in the early years of this century were quick to notice the charm of the people they met. H.W. Nevinson wrote of the 'varied and lovable' men and women 'who have given a grace and poignant interest to Dublin life such as I have found in no other city.' Nevinson's descriptions of his visits in 1900 and 1903, with their brief vignettes of Dr Sigerson, AE, O'Leary, and others, are among the most rewarding pages of his autobiographical *Changes and Chances* (1923). He tells of Maud Gonne, 'lovely beyond compare', and of Yeats, 'very much the poet', who 'talked well and incessantly, moving his hands a good deal, and sometimes falling into a natural chant'.

In *Dublin Explorations, by an Englishman* (1917), Douglas Goldring gave a more detailed and more critical account of Dublin's intellectual life. Political discussion was free and unprejudiced, a refreshing change from the timidity and conventionality of English conversation. On literary and artistic matters, however, 'the value of the opinions expressed' seemed to him rather limited and commonplace, 'rarely on a level with the authority and brilliance with which they were delivered'. He found his tour of the National Portrait Gallery less an artistic experience than a delightful visit with interesting people: 'All the Irish great seem to have been men who were spendthrift of their personalities, giving most generously to the social life of their time all that they possessed of wit, of creative energy, intelligence, fantasy, or charm.'

Seldom have personalities played so important a role in literature as in the Ireland of Yeats. One thinks of George Moore's reminiscences and of Joyce's *Ulysses*; but no Irish writer hesitated to use himself, his friends, or his enemies, as copy. The Dubliner's gift of phrase made these verbal portraits as memorable as the familiar oil paintings and drawings of celebrities, many of them gifts by Hugh Lane, the art connoisseur and nephew of Lady Gregory.

A sensationally successful art dealer, Lane was a center of controversy in death as in life. He was suspected of selfish motives when he urged Dublin to buy masterpieces, and even when he offered his own collection to the city provided a suitable gallery be built. Obviously the best-qualified candidate for the curatorship of the National Museum, he was passed over in favour of the Papal Count George Plunkett, thereby provoking the first of Yeats's topical satiric poems, 'An Appointment', published in 1909. The ironies of history decreed that Plunkett's son was to be among the martyrs of the Easter Rising, and that the Count himself was to serve a prison sentence as a patriot and to become the first Sinn Fein candidate to win a parliamentary seat, early in 1917. Lane died in the sinking of the Lusitania in 1915, and thenceforth his unwitnessed codicil, bequeathing thirty-nine paintings to the Dublin National Portrait Gallery, was disputed. The London National Gallery, to which the pictures were first given in the will, kept them until, in 1960, a reciprocal loan plan was instituted. The last years of Lady Gregory's life were saddened by her failure to gain the pictures for Ireland.

Even without the disputed pictures, Lane's benefactions were impressive, including more than sixty paintings of the traditional schools. Among them were canvasses by Bordone, Strozzi, and Poussin which provided images for Yeats's poetry. In addition, Lane, inspired by Lady Gregory's enthusiasm, commissioned John Butler Yeats, William Orpen, and others to paint portraits of Irish celebrities. These pictures reveal strong features, in which vigor and sensibility are blended. Seeing them, one understands the impact of these writers, actors, and political leaders on Irish culture, and senses the distinctively Irish and Anglo-Irish flavour of their personalities. In the eager gaze of AE as he peers through his spectacles Count Markievicz creates an impression of this famed host who was as keen to hear the views of others as he was to express his own. J.B. Yeats caught in the relaxed figure of Synge, arms crossed, a faintly perceptible smile on his lips, the earthy humour and tragedy of his plays. Epstein's bold head of Lady Gregory conveys her matronly strength. In the pencil sketch by J.B. Yeats the young poet Padraic Colum is wistfully meditative. Mancini's bold use of chiaroscuro was admired by Synge, who, Yeats tells us in his poem on the Municipal Gallery, thought the Lady Gregory portrait the finest since Rembrandt. Even better is his monumental canvas depicting the sensitive and aristocratic figure of Lane himself.

Portraits of the Fay brothers of Maire Ni Shiublaigh and Moira O'Neill, as well as Robert Gregory's striking depiction of Arthur Sinclair in cavalier costume, from the Abbey Theatre collection, remind us of the important role played by the actor in the development of the Irish revival. The tradition continues. The work of Hilton Edwards and Michael MacLiammoir in the Gate Theatre has been memorable, and the current tour de force of MacLiammoir, the most gifted of living Irish actors, in his one-man recreation of Wilde's life and times, has deserved the plaudits it has won in Europe, South America, and the United States. For more than two hours he holds his audiences as he recreates the personality of the most famed of Dublin wits and summarises his meteoric rise and even more sensational nemesis.

At every stage of his long career William Butler Yeats looked the part he was playing, from the youthful aesthete his father painted in 1900, in dark jacket, with unruly forelock, pince-nez, and flowing tie, to the mocking old man in the 1934 portrait by Augustus John, in shirt sleeves with open collar, his white hair blowing in the wind.

In these Dublin collections—the Municipal Gallery, the National Portrait Gallery, and the Abbey Theatre portraits—are to be found the true images of Yeats's Dublin. No one, however, seems to have been able to capture the statuesque beauty of Maud Gonne, the inspiration of a dozen immortal poems. Sir William Orpen's striking portrait of Captain

John Shawe-Taylor, in scarlet coat, conveys the same impression as did Yeats in his essay on this gallant man. His handsome appearance was not an idle consideration, Yeats wrote, for in some men 'good looks are an image of their faculty.' Like the commanders whose features were admired by ancient historians, such men have the power of sudden decision, like hawk or leopard, 'as if their whole body were their brain.'

The exaltation of the personal carries over into the realms of thought. The lack of any central cultural tradition in Ireland prompted a free play of individuality and a refreshing originality, but its perils can be seen in the constant tendency toward the subjective and the esoteric.

Yet however far the artist's quest leads into the irrational and the occult, it seems eventually to return to the world of men. AE describes his visions in paintings and poems, but he finds these visions applicable to his other careers of economist and molder of public opinion. Yeats transmutes his cabalistic speculations into concrete symbols of sword and fire and golden bird, and the world's poetry is thereby enriched. One striking exception is the later work of Joyce, whose contrapuntal, polylinguistic *Finnegans Wake* demands a dozen pages of exegesis for each page of text.

Writers were saved from the dangers of private delusion by the practical affairs in which they participated, and by the constant interplay of personalities in Dublin. The popular 'at-homes' provided both sounding boards and testing grounds. Seldom have there been such gatherings of talent, at least since the days of Johnson's Club. The quality of these evenings can never be retrieved, but something of their atmosphere has been preserved. Most brilliant of all Dublin talkers seems to have been the journalist and self-taught classicist Stephen MacKenna. The astonishing variety of his conversation is still remembered, ranging in subject from poetry to politics—he had reported the abortive Russian Revolution of 1904-5—and in tone from the splendour and dignity of Yeats to the gay fantasy of James Stephens.

As famous as the MacKenna Saturday evenings were the Sundays at AE's and the Mondays at the home of Yeats. Most spectacular of all were the monthly parties held by the venerable Sarah Purser in the grand ballroom of her Georgian mansion. Although she was Shaw's senior by almost twenty years and had seemed old to Yeats as a boy, she outlived Yeats and maintained to the time of her death at the age of ninety-five the reputation of being the wittiest woman in Dublin as well as one of its most distinguished artists. Her sensitive portraits of the major literary figures are comparable to those by John Butler Yeats.

In *As I Was Going Down Sackville Street,* Gogarty describes one of his own Fridays at the time of the Civil War. Ignoring the machine-gun fire in the street, AE expostulated imperturbably, holding the attention of the stalwart military hero of the Free State, Michael Collins, who had been tracked by spies to the very doorstep. Although subject to ambush at any moment—he was murdered a few weeks later—Collins maintained his cool gallantry, even reaching for a pad to take a note. But AE's mystic speculations were beyond the General's ken. Collins' voice rang out in direct question: 'Your point, Mr Russell?' The mood was shattered. In his multiple roles as host, proud friend of Collins, and *littérateur,* Gogarty was, for the moment, almost thrown off balance. But he recovered sufficiently to let Collins depart for a place of hiding, to urge AE that the group was still avid for astral wisdom, and, at the end of the evening, to apologise to the American college girls who were among the guests, explaining that though his home was ever open to patriots and to friends, it was, above all, 'a house for artists and not for lecturers, readers, preachers, teachers or people with points.' As an artist, AE communicated himself, not points.

The value of Monk Gibbon's recent memoir of Yeats may arise largely from the resentment which it expresses, for none of the biographical studies of the poet convey the unfavourable impression he sometimes created in Dublin during his life. On his return home from his teaching post abroad, Gibbon always found it 'an intoxicating experience to come back to Dublin and its great talkers.' Himself Irish, Gibbon was not content to listen. He felt impelled to question, and to contradict. And he sensed, perhaps wrongly, that Yeats would entertain no opposition, speaking ex cathedra on all issues, and showing no interest in contrary views. T. Sturge Moore once made a distinction between the 'provocative truculence' of the public Yeats and his 'seductive delicacy' in private. If this be true, Gibbon seems to have seen only the public man. The dramatic frankness of Gibbon's account somewhat alleviates its bitterness, but the slurs which the young man suffered, or imagined, have apparently rankled for years. He suppresses neither his personal resentment nor his respect for Yeats, and one puts down the book with a vivid picture of both the greatness and the smallness of Yeats—his mastery of words and ideas, his occasional lack of mastery of his own vanity.

For Gibbon, evenings at AE's were entirely different, since 'one never went away with the feeling that one had talked too much, for everyone there talked too much.' The crowded Sunday evenings were lively and democratic. Olivia Robertson recalls how the poet 'shed over those who knew him the beautiful atmosphere of blue and gold tranquillity that one finds in his paintings'. His friend and neighbour Constantine Curran has written that 'the variety of his conversation was a Dublin proverb, ranging over philosophy, economics and the arts.' John Eglinton quoted a visitor's impression of 'this big bearded man' who, surrounded one evening by sophisticated talkers, 'remained silent and ruminative, only occasionally interrupting to state in simple quiet words so wise that in a moment they annihilated the brilliant twaddle'. As he said goodby to this 'kindly, humorous, wise man, of enormous tact and great toleration', the visitor 'could not but feel as he took my hand that I had for some few hours been in the presence of a man of noble mind and strange, disturbing genius'. Ernest Boyd has described the 'great rhythmic torrent' of AE's conversation, with its emotional depths and spiritual overtones.

AE had an incredible memory, and at one time was reputed able to recite not only all his own verse but everything that his friend Yeats had written. We must not let the image of the seer blind us to the fact that he was a man of affairs. For twenty-five years his was the most articulate voice of the national conscience. His periodicals, *The Irish Homestead* and later *The Irish Statesman*, constantly measured current political events against his own high standards. He answered Kipling's inflammatory attack on Irish Catholicism. When the newspaper owner William Murphy was breaking the Dublin transport strike of 1913, AE's 'Open Letter to the Masters of Dublin' arraigned the capitalist with the vehemence of a Hebrew prophet:

> You may succeed in your policy and ensure your own damnation by your victory. The men whose manhood you have broken will loathe you, and will always be brooding and scheming to strike a fresh blow.

Three years later he traced the tragic Easter Rising to the ill will of employers during the Great Strike: 'It was Labour supplied the passional element in the revolt.'

Like Yeats, he could accept the 'terrible beauty' that was born in Easter week, although he felt that the Devil was loose in Ireland during the Civil War, with 'crazy Gaeldom' uncontrolled. As the new country seemed to develop the same old politicians, he was finding it more and more difficult to remain loyal. Left alone by his wife's death and his son's moving to America, however, at last he decided it was time 'to break the mould of mind in which I was decaying.' Even so, he parted with his paintings and his books and left home and friends in a characteristic mood of optimism and indignation: 'I think the change will reinvigorate me, and it will be a relief to get away from Ireland in its present mood, which is one of smugness.'

Throughout his life, AE enjoyed an almost universal love and respect. George Moore even forgot himself—*mirabile dictu*—long enough to make AE the most attractive figure in his *Hail and Farewell* (1911-14). To Moore, he seemed a man from fabled Arcady, with 'the mind of Corot in verse and prose', whose pastels conveyed 'a spiritual seeing of the world'. Arch-mocker and egotist as he was, Moore could not ridicule a man whose 'gray pantheistic eyes ... looked so often into my soul with such a kindly gaze'. The kindly gaze embraced younger writers too. It was AE who opened his journals as well as his home to new talent, and who published lyrics by Padraic Colum, Eva Gore-Booth, Susan Mitchell, and others in his anthology *New Songs*. Joyce's disappointment at not being included is apparent in the discussion of the book in *Ulysses*, but again it was AE who first published Joyce's fiction, three of the *Dubliners* stories appearing in *The Irish Homestead* in the latter half of 1904.

Yeats and Moore gibed at AE's protégés with such expressions as 'Russell's poultry-yard' or his 'canaries'. Yeats was honest enough to admit his jealousy of the personal popularity of his former schoolmate and fellow poet. He suspected AE's salon to be the main source of opposition to his control of the Abbey Theatre, even though it was the 'chief centre of literary life in Dublin'. A shrewd appraisal of this rivalry by Mrs Yeats is probably correct. Yeats himself quoted it in a letter to Dorothy Wellesley: 'My wife said the other night, "AE was the nearest to a saint you or I will ever meet. You are a better poet but no saint. I suppose one has to choose."'

As ugly political realities began to tarnish ideal visions of Ireland, AE's reputation started to wane, and later visitors were not so much entranced by the evenings on Rathgar Avenue. They could note the little drama of preparation before the oracle spoke. They accused him of loving to hold the floor, a charge to which few Dubliners could plead innocent. O'Casey, for one, was immune to AE's charm. To him the aging seer was 'Dublin's Glittering Guy'. In his two visits O'Casey had heard nothing but a 'spate of blather'. AE was as much a humbug in his monotonous and vague poetry as in his romantic and amateurish paintings. O'Casey made no attempt to be fair in his judgment, and one can scarcely imagine a greater disparity than that between O'Casey and his target—in background, character, or outlook.

The salons of Yeats and AE constituted rival camps. The history of literary affinities and antipathies in Dublin has the complexity of Balkan politics. Alliances could be charted by noting the roles of the major figures. Throughout his life Yeats remained faithful to Synge and Lady Gregory, citing them in his Nobel Prize acceptance speech:

> When your King gave me my medal and diploma, two forms should have stood, one at either side of me, an old woman sinking into the infirmity of age and a young man's ghost. I think when Lady Gregory's name and John Synge's name are spoken by future generations, my name, if remembered, will come up in the talk, and that if my name is spoken first their names will come in their turn because of the years we worked together.

Compiled by

BENEDICT KIELY

Compilation, Introduction and Editorial Matter
DONAGH MACDONAGH
LOUIS MACNEICE
PATRICK KAVANAGH

DUBLIN ❧ OXFORD AND NEW YORK
OXFORD UNIVERSITY PRESS ❧ 1983 ❧ THREE POETS ON DUBLIN

I group together three poets, and their varied tributes to this city. First of all I listen to Donagh MacDonagh whose father also was a poet. Thomas MacDonagh was one of the signatories of the 1916 declaration of the Irish republic and, for that reason, died before a British firing-squad. Of P.H. Pearse and Thomas MacDonagh, W.B. Yeats wrote:

This man had kept a school
And rode our wingèd horse;
The other his helper and friend
Was coming into his force:
He might have won fame in the end,
So sensitive his nature seemed,
So daring and sweet his thought.

from 'Easter 1916'

The fame he won was to be of another and more tragic kind.

The father's memories and affections of place were of the rich land of Tipperary: Norman country. The son grew up in Dublin and, also, very much under the shadow of the event that had ended his father's life. He could talk most movingly, even disturbingly, of what it had felt like to appear on public platforms as the orphaned son of a patriot father.

This poem makes clear his allegiance to and love for the Dublin streets:

DUBLIN MADE ME
Dublin made me and no little town
With the country closing in on its streets
The cattle walking proudly on its pavements
The jobbers, the gombeenmen and the cheats,

Devouring the fair-day between them
A public-house to half a hundred men
And the teacher, the solicitor and the bank-clerk
In the hotel bar drinking for ten.

Dublin made me, not the secret poteen still,
The raw and hungry hills of the West
The bare road flung over profitless bog
Where only a snipe could nest.

Where the sea takes its tithe of every boat.
Bawneen and currach have no allegiance of mine,
Nor the cute, self-deceiving talkers of the South
Who look to the East for a sign.

The soft and dreary midlands with their tame canals
Wallow between sea and sea, remote from adventure,
And Northward a far and fortified province
Crouches under the lash of arid censure.

I disclaim all fertile meadows, all tilled land
The evil that grows from it and the good,
But the Dublin of old statutes, this arrogant city,
Stirs proudly and secretly in my blood.

An Ulsterman and the son of a bishop of the Church of Ireland, an Oxford classical scholar, a teacher in England, a producer with the BBC, Louis MacNeice when he thought of home may have thought of Carrickfergus in County Antrim about which he wrote a fine poem. But equally well he wrote of 'the laughter of the Galway sea/Juggling with spars and bones irresponsibly'.

That last was in a poem called 'Train to Dublin', and in another fine poem he defined to perfection the historic character of the city, and, as he then saw it, its contemporary appearance:

DUBLIN

Grey brick upon brick,
Declamatory bronze
On sombre pedestals—
O'Connell, Grattan, Moore—
And the brewery tugs and the swans
On the balustraded stream
And the bare bones of a fanlight
Over a hungry door
And the air soft on the cheek
And porter running from the taps
With a head of yellow cream
And Nelson on his pillar
Watching his world collapse.

This was never my town,
I was not born nor bred
Nor schooled here and she will not
Have me alive or dead
But yet she holds my mind

With her seedy elegance,
With her gentle veils of rain
And all her ghosts that walk
And all that hide behind
Her Georgian facades –
The catcalls and the pain,
The glamour of her squalor,
The bravado of her talk.

The lights jig in the river
With a concertina movement
And the sun comes up in the morning
Like barley-sugar on the water
And the mist on the Wicklow hills
Is close, as close
As the peasantry were to the landlord,
As the Irish to the Anglo-Irish,
As the killer is close one moment
To the man he kills,
Or as the moment itself
Is close to the next moment.

She is not an Irish town
And she is not English,
Historic with guns and vermin
And the cold renown
Of a fragment of Church Latin,
Or an oratorical phrase.
But O the days are soft,
Soft enough to forget
The lesson bitter learnt,
The bullet on the wet
Streets, the crooked deal,
The steel behind the laugh,
The Four Courts burnt.

Fort of the Dane,
Garrison of the Saxon,
Augustan capital
Of a Gaelic nation,

Appropriating all
The alien brought,
You give me time for thought
And by a juggler's trick
You poise the toppling hour –
O greyness run to flower,
Grey stone, grey water
And brick upon grey brick.

Also from Ulster, from the County Monaghan, came the poet Patrick
Kavanagh, walking, as William Carleton the novelist had done a century
or so previously, to make his own of the capital city.

For Kavanagh, Baggot Street constituted his village or small town. At
one end the Fairgreen: the splendid park of St Stephen's Green. At the
other end the bridge below the town: the bridge over the Grand Canal.
That street he made particularly his own and it is quite possible that his
ghost may still walk there. Or so he is prepared to tell us:

If ever you go to Dublin town
In a hundred years or so
Inquire for me in Baggot Street
And what I was like to know.
O he was a queer one
Fol dol the di do,
He was a queer one
I tell you.

My great-grandmother knew him well,
He asked her to come and call
On him in his flat and she giggled at the thought
Of a young girl's lovely fall.
O he was dangerous
Fol dol the di do,
He was dangerous
I tell you.

On Pembroke Road look out for my ghost
Dishevelled with shoes untied,
Playing through the railings with little children
Whose children have long since died.

O he was a nice man
Fol dol the di do,
He was a nice man
I tell you.

Go into a pub and listen well
If my voice still echoes there,
Ask the men what their grandsires thought
And tell them to answer fair.
O he was eccentric
Fol dol the di do,
He was eccentric
I tell you.

He had the knack of making men feel
As small as they really were
Which meant as great as God had made them
But as males they disliked his air.
O he was a proud one
Fol dol the di do,
He was a proud one
I tell you.

If ever you go to Dublin town
In a hundred years or so
Sniff for my personality
Is it vanity's vapour now?
O he was a vain one
Fol dol the di do,
He was a vain one
I tell you.

I saw his name with a hundred others
In a book in the library
He said he had never achieved
His potentiality.
O he was slothful
Fol dol the di do,
He was slothful
I tell you.

He knew that posterity has no use
For anything but the soul,
The lines that speak the passionate heart,
The spirit that lives alone.
O he was a lone one
Fol dol the di do
Yet he lived happily
I tell you.

CONSTANTIA MAXWELL

Dublin Under the Georges 1714–1830

LONDON ❧ GEORGE G. HARRAP AND CO. LTD ❧ 1936

Apart from visits to friends, those who lived in Dublin and the neighbourhood were kept amused by a constant round of gaiety. Miss Herbert, sister of Henry Herbert, afterwards Earl of Carnarvon, wrote to Lady Louisa Stuart on 11 April 1782, 'Nothing can be so gay as Dublin is—the Castle twice a week, the opera twice a week, with plays, assemblies, and suppers to fill up the time.' The parties given at the Castle were naturally on the grandest scale. Here is an account by Mrs Delany of a ball that took place there in the spring of 1732:

The ball was in the old beef-eater's hall, a room that holds seven hundred people seated; it was well it did, for never did I behold a greater crowd. We were all placed in rows one above another, so much raised that the last row almost *touched the ceiling*! The gentlemen say we looked very handsome, and compared us to Cupid's Paradise in the puppet-show. At 11 o'clock minuets were finished, and the Duchess went to the basset table. After an hour's playing the Duke, Duchess, and nobility, marched into the supper room, which was the council chamber. In the midst of the room was placed a holly tree, illuminated by a hundred wax tapers; round it was placed all sorts of meat, fruit and sweetmeats; servants waited next, and were encompassed round by a table, to which the company came by turns to take what they wanted. When the doors were *first* opened the hurly-burly is not to be described; squawking, shrieking, all sorts of noises; some ladies lost their lappets, others were trod upon.... I and my company were more discreet than to go with the torrent; we staid till people had satisfied their curiosity and hunger, and then took a quiet view of the famous tree which occasioned more rout than it was worth.

Towards the end of the century the most magnificent entertainments were given by the Duke and Duchess of Rutland, who had brought over with them from England complete services of gold and silver plate, and who were so lavish in their hospitality that it was commonly remarked that they might well have been sovereigns of a rich and independent kingdom.

The Duke of Leinster also entertained on a large scale; so did the Marquis of Ely and other members of the Irish aristocracy. In the *Anthologia Hibernica* for April 1794 is a description of a grand ballet which had just taken place at Antrim House. This is worth quoting as a typical entertainment of the period:

The day fe'nnight the Marchioness of Antrim gave a most superb rout, ball and supper, at her ladyship's house in Merrion Square, to a most brilliant and extremely numerous assemblage of the first rank and fashion. His Excellency the Lord Lieutenant and most of the nobility of the town were present. The Grand Scot's ballet, which has been of so much expectation in the circles of fashion, was on this occasion performed by the following Ladies, with the universal and unbounded applause of the whole assembly: Countess of Antrim, Lady Letitia Macdonald, Lady Isabella Beresford, Lady Anne Butler [here follow the names of ten others].... The ladies who danced the ballet were in uniform dresses of white muslin, trimmed with blue ribbands; with sashes and petticoats trimmed with silver fringe: head dresses—white turbans spangled with silver, and blue feathers. The music which was all in the Scots' style, was compiled for the occasion. The ballet commenced with a Strathspey in slow time, and the figures of the dance varied with the tunes, which had a most admirable effect. The ballet, on its commencement, excited so much admiration as to draw the whole company crowding to the ball-room which scarcely left the charming performers room to move. But by the polite and persuasive interference of the noble marchioness, the room was tolerably well cleared, and the press of the company restrained by barriers of ribband, held by noblemen.... Dancing commenced at 11 o'clock, and at one the company were summoned to the supper rooms, where elegance and plenty seemed to vie in the decoration of the festive board—while wit, beauty and all the gaiety and splendour of fashion enlivened the enchanting scene. Dancing was resumed after supper, and the company separated with reluctance at 6 o'clock in the morning.

The masked ball was especially popular in Dublin under the Georges, and people dressed in the most fantastic characters. Here are a few descriptions from newspapers of the time to bear out this statement: 'a grand Turk very superb who drank wine most irreligiously'; 'a jolly tinker who had something to say to every person'; 'a Pan well-dressed playing on his pipes with great judgment and ease'; 'a Spaniard of amazing size'; 'a Methodist preacher, characteristical and masked with judgment'; 'a Sultana most splendidly dressed'; 'a half-abbé and half-officer, a very laughable figure'; 'a side-board of plate'; 'a representation of the Devil'. It is no wonder that we hear complaints of the rude pressure of the mob who gathered round the doors to see guests arrive and were 'vastly incommodious' when the night's entertainment was done by crowding around and impeding the return to the carriages. Not that people of fashion were unpopular, for there was a general idea that all forms of luxury gave employment to the poor. And the rich, especially during the time of the non-importation agreements, made a point of wearing stuffs of pure 'Irish manufacture'— 'even to the shoes and petticoats of the ladies.'

Campbell, the North of Ireland clergyman who made a tour of his country in 1777, thought Dublin streets depressing to those who knew London, 'so rich and full of business'; still, he admitted that all kinds of social pleasures in the Irish capital were easier to obtain. 'Every night in the winter,' wrote Arthur Young, 'there is a ball or a party,' but the English farmer remarks that many Dublin houses to which he was invited were not nearly large enough for the numerous company that was squeezed into them. This was also the opinion of De Latocnaye, a young French émigré who was in Dublin a little later (1796–7). De Latocnaye was present at one rout where every room from the street door to the garret was full of handsome, well-dresssed women so closely packed together that they could hardly stir and were forced to speak through their fans. The Frenchman was fond of feminine society, but thought that on this occasion he would have enjoyed it better had he been able to find a more secluded place to converse than the staircase.

In the highest circles Irish ladies were distinguished for their intelligence, wit, and repartee, but Lady Morgan's mother about the time of the Union told her that much of this had been so coarse in the middle of the century that it would not then be mentionable to polite ears. The women of the middle class were praised by strangers as a pleasing mixture of modesty and vivacity, but they were as often criticised for frivolity and lack of interest in things intellectual. Edward Melville, an American citizen who visited Ireland between 1805 and 1807, contrasted them unfavourably in this respect with French women. They seemed to him to be thinking more of the dinners that they gave their guests than the nature of their discourse. Conversation in Ireland, however, has often disconcerted or puzzled the Anglo-Saxon. 'In England conversation is a game of chess,' explains Lady Morgan—'the result of judgment, memory and deliberation—with us it is a game of battledore, and our ideas like our shuttlecocks are thrown lightly one to the other, bounding and rebounding—played more for amusement than conquest, and leaving the players equally animated by the game, and careless of its results.' Yet Irish wit when exported across the Channel had a certain value. 'Ireland, which one did not suspect,' wrote Horace Walpole in 1756, 'is become the staple of wit, and I find coins *bons-mots* for our greatest men.'

Apart from racial considerations, one may explain the sprightliness of Irish conversation by 'the mixture of ranks' which then distinguished Dublin Society. Politicians, soldiers, divines, and lawyers all rubbed shoulders together in the great houses. The barristers were an especially lively element. They were famous for their eloquence and wit, and had more time for social pleasures than London lawyers. As in London, the public places of entertainment were open to all except the poorest. Chief of these was the Rotunda Gardens and Assembly Rooms (an imitation of Vauxhall and Ranelagh combined), which were opened in support of the Lying-In Hospital. Here concerts, masquerades, card-parties, and balls were held, the entertainments given during the winter being described by Malton as 'the most elegant amusements of Dublin'. In the Gardens in summer one could get tea, ices, and other light refreshments. There were walks and shrubberies, a spacious bowling-green, and a grand terrace upon which an orchestra played. The most fashionable time to visit the Rotunda was on Sunday evenings, when, we learn, the Rooms and Garden were 'prodigiously crowded'. De Latocnaye when in Dublin in 1796 visited one of these promenades. He happened to be alone, and went round quizzing the company. The interesting remarks that he makes in his journal (omitted from the English translation) are characteristic of his nation.

G. Ivan Morris

In Dublin's Fair City

LONDON ❧ HOME & VAN THAL LTD ❧ 1947

D ublin is a city of cafés, ranging from glorified snack bars to expensive and exclusive restaurants, where a dinner and wine, with tips, will cost about £2.

Everyone of note visits Jammet's, and the new Frascati's is drawing many distinguished patrons who like to take their ease over a magnificent meal to the accompaniment of sweet, soft music. The 'arty' crowd and writers are usually to be seen in numbers, doing themselves well at the Unicorn, where a Viennese atmosphere has been captured with considerable success.

Before the war there were two Indian restaurants noted for their curries, but they closed when rice and curries went off the market during the Emergency. It is remarkable that, with its large floating population of foreigners, Dublin has none of those really foreign cafés so common in Soho district in London. A few Italian ice-cream and fish and chip saloons flourish, and the 'Country Shop' in Stephen's Green makes a great effort to catch a typically Irish atmosphere, with its sugaun chairs and scrubbed kitchen tables; but, apart from these, no provision is made to give foreigners the food peculiar to their own country.

For the person whose purse is not overflowing, and for the tight fisted strangers from the North-eastern part of Britain, there are dozens of cafés giving good luncheons and high teas from 2/6 to 3/6. Unfortunately, as in London, flies and chipped tableware are frequently an important part of the meal. However, an English visitor struck the right note when he remarked: 'These are only details. It's the grub that counts.'

There is little or no spam in Dublin, and rabbits do not form part of the restaurants' menus. There are no powdered eggs and the milk and cream are the genuine articles. Ice-cream abounds, and is generally of the variety that does not kick back.

Ice-cream has a great attraction for English 'fair, fat and forties' who, with reckless abandon and a total disregard for their already expanding waist-line, gorge themselves on this luscious dessert. And it is good in Dublin, for the principal manufacturers use only the best ingredients, and they use them liberally.

Children, spotted with pimples from the sudden change-over to rich diet, are encouraged to aggravate their indigestion with cornets, wafers, sliders or fruit ices, and they respond with amazing alacrity to the encouragement.

Even rugged Englishmen, fresh from the fighting forces on the battle fronts of the world, are seen making determined attempts to recapture their pre-war youth by sucking, licking and otherwise manipulating a creamy ice-cream 'tub'.

'Never mind,' they say, 'in a week or two we'll be back to rations.'

Strangely enough, there is a shortage of bacon in Eire. The government controlled the industry during the war, and the result is that a severe shortage has been achieved. Irish country kitchens are now lonely places since the little piglets no longer roam about the floor. Gone are the days when the following incident could have happened. An English tourist called at a cottage for a drink of buttermilk. The woman of the house asked him in while she went to fetch the drink. During her absence in the dairy the little pig in the kitchen rubbed himself affectionately, like a cat, against the visitor's legs. With true English diplomacy he addressed the good woman when she returned with the bowl of buttermilk.

'Your little pig has taken quite a fancy to me,' he remarked. 'He seems to know me.'

'It's not you he knows at all, sir,' she replied. 'It's his little bowl.'

Fussy visitors have often asked why the people allow pigs into the kitchen (which, of course, they don't), and their question has been answered for ever by the Cork farmer who said:

'Well, the pigs help to pay the rent, and they are entitled to the use of the property.'

Despite the shortage, however, one may sit down to breakfast in the better-class Dublin hotels and confidently expect to be served with a plate of delicious bacon and eggs, and to inhale, as in pre-war days, the old-fashioned aroma of the morning as it rises from the dish.

Queues for restaurants are almost non-existent except in the height of the holiday season, when thousands of visitors make heavy demands on the accommodation available, but the service is perhaps a little more leisurely than in the busy cities of England. Holiday-makers will not mind that, for they have plenty of time to spare for the important business of eating. An occasional impatient customer may grumble about the obviously inefficient waiting in some of the cafés and may compare the service unfavourably with his own particular haunt at home, but this is usually an indication that he has been in Ireland for a fortnight, and is getting so accustomed to the good food that he can afford to growl. In the main, one does not have to wait too long, and there is really no serious ground for complaint.

Café proprietors are fond of unusual names for their cafes, or 'eating houses', as the country folk call them. Among these are the Green Rooster, the Chicken Inn, the Singing Kettle, the Mad Hatter, the Green Tree, the Cabin, and so on. Typically Irish names are uncommon, possibly because it is felt that patrons prefer something glamorous, and are more impressed by the unusual and clever than anything so common as the Leprechaun's Kitchen, the Banshee's Pantry or the Finn MacCool Dining Rooms.

A. PETER

Dublin Fragments Social and Historic

DUBLIN HODGES FIGGIS & CO. LONDON JOHN MURRAY 1927

COST OF LIVING IN DUBLIN ONE HUNDRED YEARS AGO

At the present time, when the price of food and the cost of living generally is uppermost in the minds of all households, it is of interest to look back a century and see what our ancestors were paying then for the ordinary commodities of life.

From an account-book kept by a citizen of Dublin, in which each item is entered carefully every day, we are enabled to form some comparisons. The gentleman in question occupied a respectable position, and had an official salary and some private means. He had three children, so that, together with his wife and three servants (two maids and a manservant), a family of eight had to be catered for.

Dealing with the year 1816, we notice that in the month of August fresh butter was 1s 4d a lb, and the same price in December. Eggs varied from 9d to 1s 2d a dozen, a turkey could be got for 5s, and a goose for 3s 4d. Potatoes, 10d a stone. Mutton was 6½d a lb, a hare cost 2s 2d, and a dozen 'oisters' 1s 6d. Bacon was 10d a lb, and a large piece of beef weighing over 27 lbs seems to have been obtained at the low price of 5d a lb. Bread was expensive, the lowest amount paid on any day being 1s 11d, apparently for two loaves. There are, however, other entries showing loaves obtained were 5d each. Beer for the week came to 3s 6d. A week at Bray in November 1818 ran away with close on a ten-pound note, during which time the servants were allowed 30s for board wages. In the accounts for each month there is an entry: 'James (evidently the manservant), tea money, 5s.' This would be the price of 1 lb of tea. The laundry account varied from 20s to 30s per month. A cow that cost £9 7s supplied the family with ample milk. A pair of chickens cost 2s 8d and a calf's head 1s 8d. This seems reasonable enough, as also two soles for 2s 1d, and a York ham was only 1s 1d a lb. When milk had to be bought it was 4d a quart. Eels cost 8d each, and a lobster could be had for 1s. Vegetables, such as cabbages or cauliflowers, were sold at much the same price as at present, but 'cellery' was apparently dear, as it figures frequently at 1s 8d, but the quantity is not stated. Quarter of a stone of 'flower' cost also 1s 8d.

Servants' wages were low compared with today—the cook got ten guineas a year and the housemaid the same, which was to include tea money; but the nurse received £12 as wages and was also found in tea and sugar. James, the man, got a present of £3 when leaving, having also received a pair of strong shoes which cost 9s 9d, and a new coat, vest, and breeches during his term of service, which cost £4.

Twopence-worth of turf was occasionally bought, and the sweeping of the kitchen chimney cost 20d, but a load of turf was got for 4s 2d. A stone of oatmeal was 1s 8d, and a lb of mould candles 1s. Four John Doreys figure in the account for 8d, while six whiting were 10d. A supply of rush lights came to 1s. Wine and spirits for the year came to £34, coal and candles for the same period mounting to £31. It cannot be said that there was extravagance in newspapers, for the amount mentioned weekly is only 1s 1d. The hire of a coach cost 1s 8d, and a visit to the playhouse ran to 22s 9d! So human nature was in those olden times not very different from what it is today with regard to the creature comforts of life, but our fathers were fortunate in respect of such items as gas, and telephones, motors, and telegraphs, and the thousand other things now regarded as indispensable.

Two letters from

SISTER M. SELIO

Sisters of Charity, Gardiner Street, Dublin

1 OCTOBER 1911

Dearest Sis,

T hank you very much for your letter. I suppose as I got yours you will get mine. The city is in the most awful state with strikes. I suppose you know that ever so many of the bakers are out and consequently it is almost impossible to get bread. Those that are not on strike refuse to supply any but their own customers with bread. Fortunately we have a cook who makes very good yeast bread. The poor little children are really the sufferers. You know, we give breakfast to nearly 300 every day. So far we have been able to make bread for the breakfast but they can't get any for their lunch or to bring home. Some of the babies took to crying piteously for bread in the middle of the day, so ever so many of the big and better off girls sacrificed their lunches for them. We can't take any more patients into Vincent's because we have no bread for them. Today I hear the army bakers, under military protection, are going to take possession of all the Bakeries on strike.

Tell Johnny when you write that the Dublin people think Jim Larkin, the leader of all the strikes in Dublin, is either Antichrist or in the pay of the Tories to prevent us getting Home Rule.

OCTOBER 23 1913

My dear Johnny,

My opinion on this article from *Times* you sent me is that the statements made therein are absolutely *true*. I know nothing about the sanitation of the North Dublin [*sic*], but I do know from personal observation that the tenement houses in Dublin are simple dens of poverty and dirt, that numbers of families live in simple tenement rooms. I have before my mind a family of eleven children father and mother in one room and though you may hardly credit it possible a 'sanitary officer' told me she had come across an old dining hall in Henrietta Street where *11 families* were sleeping at night.

The description given by your writer of 'the one-roomed tenements of two kinds' is perfectly correct though I must say the 'hovels in fetid courts' are being knocked down by degrees and the underground cellars have in most places been condemned. The criticism of the Slum landlord is also quite true. Though undoubtedly the authorities are much to be blamed for this state of affairs I am firmly convinced that no one or nothing will ever succeed in making the Dublin Poor clean; they *love dirt*. No one but an eyewitness could believe that human beings could exist in the wretched holes they live in. I have become so used to see it, it has ceased to cause me any wonder.

Jim Larkin has I think at last overstepped his mark. The people are wild at the kidnapping of the children. The last description I got of him is that he is the devil in human flesh. The women hate him, the men on the whole so far worship him. Must stop.

Your very loving
(May) Sr. M. Selio

Please send me some money for the children really they are in an awful way.

JOHN EDWARD WALSH

Ireland Sixty Years Ago

DUBLIN ❧ JAMES MCGLASHAN ❧ 1847
ORIGINALLY PUBLISHED IN *DUBLIN UNIVERSITY MAGAZINE*

CHAPTER V

Drunkenness—Notions of Conviviality

The habit of intemperate drinking had grown to such an excess in Ireland, that it was gravely asserted there was something in the people's constitution congenial to the excitement of ardent spirits. The propensity for intoxication among the people had been remarked from the earliest times. Sir W. Petty, who wrote in the year 1682, when Dublin contained but 6,025 houses, states 1,200 of them were public-houses, where intoxicating liquors were sold. In 1798, in Thomas Street, nearly every third house was a public-house. The street contained 190 houses, and of these fifty-two were licensed to sell spirits. Among the upper classes the great consumption was claret, and so extensive was its importation, that in the year 1763 it amounted to 8,000 tuns, and the bottles alone were estimated at the value of £67,000. This fact is detailed by honest Rutty, the Quaker historian of the county of Dublin. Such were the convivial habits of the day, and so absorbed were the people in the indulgence, that the doctor recommended that port should be substituted in its place—'because,' said he, with quaint simplicity, 'it would not admit so long a sitting—a great advantage to wise men in saving a great deal of their precious time.' In fact, the great end and aim of life in the upper classes seemed to be convivial indulgence to excess. The rule of drinking was, that no man was allowed to leave the company till he was unable to *stand*, and then he might depart, if he could *walk*.

If on any occasion a guest left the room, bits of paper were dropped into his glass, intimating the number of rounds the bottle had gone, and on his return he was obliged to swallow a glass for each, under the penalty of so many glasses of salt and water. It was the practice of some to have

decanters with round bottoms, like a modern soda-water bottle, the only
contrivance in which they could stand being at the head of the table,
before the host; stopping the bottle was thus rendered impossible, and
everyone was obliged to fill his glass at once, and pass the bottle to his
neighbour, on peril of upsetting the contents on the table. A still more
common practice was, to knock the stems off the glasses with a knife, so
that they must be emptied as fast as they were filled, as they could not
stand. Sometimes the guests, as they sat down, put off their shoes, which
were taken out of the room, and the emptied bottles were broken outside
of the door, so that no one could pass out till the carouse was over.

Such orgies were not occasional, but often continued every night,
and all night long. A usual exhortation from a father to his son was 'make
your head, boy, while you're young;' and certain knots of seasoned
drinkers who had succeeded in this insane attempt, were called 'the
heads,' from their impenetrability to the effect of liquor. It was said that,
'no man who drank ever died, but many died learning to drink'; and the
number of victims who fell in acting on this principle was an appalling
proof of the extent of the practice—most families could point to some
victim in this premature indulgence.

An elderly clergyman of our acquaintance, on leaving home, to enter
college, stopped, on his way, at the hospitable mansion of a friend of his
father for a few days. The whole time he was engaged with drinking
parties every night, and assiduously plied with bumpers, till he sank under
the table. In the morning he was, of course, deadly sick, but his host
prescribed 'a hair of the old dog', that is, a glass of raw spirits. On one
night he contrived to steal through a back window. As soon as he was
missed, the cry of 'stole away' was raised, and he was pursued, but effected
his escape into the park. Here he found an Italian artist, who had also
been of the company, but, unused to such scenes, had likewise fled from
the orgies. They concealed themselves by lying down among the deer,
and so passed the night. Towards morning they returned to the house, and
were witnesses of an extraordinary procession. Such of the company as
were still able to walk, had procured a flat back car, on which they heaped
the bodies of those who were insensible—then throwing a sheet over
them, and illuminating them with candles, like an Irish wake, some taking
the shafts of the car before, and others pushing behind, and all setting up
the Irish cry, the *sensible* survivors left their departed insensible friends at
their respective homes. The consequences of this debauch were several
duels between the active and passive performers on the following day.

No class of society, even the gravest, was exempt from this indulgence. Even judges on the bench were seen inebriated, without much shame, and with little censure. One, well known, was noted for the maudling sensibility with which he passed sentence. It was remarked of him by Curran, that, 'though he did not weep, he certainly had a drop in his eye.' The indulgence was so universal, that pursuits of business never interfered with it. An attorney (Howard), writing in 1776, complaining of the want of reform in the law, and the evils of his profession, thus speaks:-

'This leads me to mention an evil, which I would feign have thrown a veil over, but for the great degree of excess to which it has arrived in this kingdom, above all others, and even among the professors of the law, a profession which requires the clearest, coolest head a man can possibly have. Can we complain of being censured of dishonesty, if we undertake the management of a man's affairs and render ourselves incapable of conducting them? and is not this the case with every man who has filled himself with strong wines, unless he has such an uncommon capacity as not one in a thousand is ever blessed with? The observation of Englishmen of business is, that they could not conceive how men in this kingdom transacted any business, for they seemed to do nothing but *walk the courts the whole morning, and devote the whole evening to the bottle.*'

Innumerable are the anecdotes which might be collected to illustrate the excessive indulgence in drink, now fortunately wholly exploded from all classes. Sir Jonah Barrington has recorded some, in which he was an actor, which are so highly characteristic, that we cite two of them, though, perhaps, already known to most of our readers. Near to the kennel of his father's hounds was built a small lodge; to this was rolled a hogshead of claret, a carcase of beef was hung up against the wall, a kind of ante-room was filled with straw, as a kennel for the company, when inclined to sleep, and all the windows were closed, to shut out the light of day. Here nine gentlemen, who excelled in various convivial qualities, were enclosed on a frosty St Stephen's day, accompanied by two pipers and a fiddler, with two couple of hounds, to join in the chorus raised by the guests. Among the sports introduced was a cock-fight, in which twelve game cocks were thrown on the floor, who fought together till only one remained alive, who was declared the victor. Thus, for seven days, the party were shut in, till the cow was declared cut up, and the claret on the stoop, when the last gallon was mulled with spices, and drank in tumblers to their next merry meeting. The same writer describes a party given in an unfinished room, the walls of which were recently plastered, and the mortar soft. At ten, on the following morning, some friends entered to pay a visit, and they found the company fast asleep, in various positions, some on chairs, and some on the floor among empty bottles, broken plates and dishes, bones and fragments of meat floated in claret, with a kennel of dogs devouring them. On the floor lay the piper, on his back, apparently dead, with the table-cloth thrown over him for a shroud, and six candles placed round him, burned down to the sockets. Two of the company had fallen asleep, with their heads close to the soft wall; the heat and light of the room, after eighteen hours' carousal, had caused the plaster to set and harden, so that the heads of the men were firmly incorporated with it. It was necessary, with considerable difficulty, to punch out the mass with an oyster-knife, giving much pain to the parties, by the loss of half their hair and a part of the scalp. Allowing all licence for the author's colouring, in what other country on the face of the earth could anything like such scenes have occurred?

J. WHITELAW

History of the City of Dublin

LONDON ❧ T. CADELL AND W. DAVIES, IN THE STRAND ❧ 1818

A s we advance westward however, a gradual declension both in streets and houses is perceptible; the former less spacious, and the latter, though comfortable and in good repair, yet, with the exception of Dame-street, and perhaps Parliament-street, which are of modern erection, wearing the marks of antiquity. As we still continue to the westward, the scene continues to become more and more unpleasing to the spectator, until it terminates in that neglected portion of the metropolis usually denominated the *Liberty*, from its being independent of the jurisdiction of the lord mayor, to which the other parts of Dublin are subject. Even here, however, there are some streets spacious, though irregular and inelegant, such as the great western avenue comprehending St James's and St Thomas' streets, with a few others; but with these exceptions, the streets in this part of the city are generally narrow, the houses crowded together, the reres, or backyards, of very small extent, and some without any accommodation of the kind. Of these streets a few are the residence of shop-keepers or others engaged in trade, but a far greater proportion of them, with their numerous lanes, and alleys, are occupied by working manufacturers, by petty shop-keepers, the labouring poor, and beggars, crowded together, to a degree distressing to humanity. A single apartment in one of those truly wretched habitations, rates from one to two shillings per week; and to lighten this rent two, three and even four families, become joint tenants: hence, at an early hour, we may find from ten to sixteen persons, of all ages and sexes, in a room not fifteen feet square, stretched on a wad of filthy straw, swarming with vermin, and without any covering, save the wretched rags that constitute their wearing apparel. Under such circumstances it is not extraordinary that from thirty to fifty individuals may be frequently found in one house; and it is a certain fact, that No. 6 in Braithwait-street, contained a few years since, one hundred and eight souls. From a careful survey twice taken of Plunket-street in 1798, it appeared that thirty-two contiguous houses contained 917 inhabitants, which gives an average of 28.7 to a house, and the entire liberty averages from about 12 to 16 persons to each house. This is certainly a dense population: the best informed inhabitants, however, assert, that it was much greater a few years since, and to this opinion we willingly accede: we do not, however, affirm, that the houses at present in existence contained more inhabitants at any former period, though such probably was the fact; but it is certain, that in the *Liberty* a great number of houses, that once teemed with population, are no longer to be found. These were situate in narrow back courts and lanes, off the principal streets, and their ichnography is distinctly expressed in Roque's four-sheet map of Dublin, which was generally found minutely exact. With this map search was made for these courts: some had totally disappeared, and their entrances had been built up; the greater part, however, were found, but their houses were mostly in ruins, or converted into warehouses or work-shops, now perfectly useless; and the few that remained were in a state of rapid decline.

This crowded population, wherever it obtains, is almost universally accompanied by a very serious evil—a degree of filth and stench inconceivable, except by such as have visited those scenes of wretchedness. There are few or no necessaries, and, of course, into the backyard of each house, frequently not ten feet deep, is flung, from the windows of each apartment, the ordure and other filth of its numerous inhabitants; from whence it is so seldom removed, that it may be seen nearly on a level with the windows of the first floor; and the moisture that after heavy rains, ouzes from this heap, having no sewer to carry it off, runs into the street, by the entry leading to the staircase, for, strange as it may appear, it is a fact that there is not one covered sewer in that populous portion of the Liberty south of the street called the Coombe.

How far it is the duty of the magistrate to interfere in the removal and prevention of such dreadful nuisances, or how far he is enabled to do so by the existing laws, we shall not presume to determine: we are certain however, that every friend to decency and cleanliness, every person who is anxious to promote the comforts of the poor, will unite with us in opinion that a police that attends to our streets and lanes only, and that but partially, while it never bestows a thought on the back-yards of the poor, performs only half its duty: the more essential part is neglected: the stench of filth in an open street may be dissipated by an unobstructed current of air; but that arising from human excrement, in narrow yards enclosed by lofty buildings, must operate with unchecked malignity.

Why slaughter-houses, soap-manufactories, carrion-houses, distil-leries, glass-houses, lime-kilns, dairies, &c.. are suffered to exist in the midst of this crowded population, we shall not presume to enquire: their deleterious effects are abundantly known, and we trust will be remedied. On the subject of dram-shops, however, the most alarming of all nuisances, we will take the liberty of stating one simple but authentic fact: Thomas-street, the termination of the great southern and western roads, and the link of connection between the disaffected of country and city, contains 190 houses; and of these, in 1798, and probably at this day, no less than fifty-two were licensed to vend raw spirits; a poison, productive of vice, riot, and disease; hostile to all habits of decency, honesty, and industry; and, in short, destructive to the souls and bodies of our fellow-creatures. These houses, open at all hours, by day and by night, are scenes of unceasing profaneness and intemperance, which even the sanctity of the Sabbath cannot suspend; and it is an undoubted fact, that, on that day, sacred among Christians to piety and peace, more deeds of profaneness, immorality, and disorder, are perpetrated in this vicinity, than in the other six. Intemperance, idleness, and irreligion, afford excellent materials for the designing and disaffected to work on; and, accordingly, here was found the focus of rebellion. That, in northern climates, a moderate quantity of spirits may be necessary to the labouring poor, to counteract the effects of cold and damp, is admitted: but the abuse of it has become, not only distressing to humanity, but frightful to reflection; and every good man must, with an aching heart, lament that necessity, which obliges a Christian government to derive a revenue from the temporal and eternal misery of thousands of its subjects.

It is a circumstance, perhaps, not generally known, that not one house of ill-fame exists in the Liberty: this circumstance we wish we could attribute to its superior virtue, not its poverty: but where intoxication is almost universal, chastity cannot exist; and we found on inquiry, that, of the nocturnal street-walkers that infest the more opulent parts of the city, a very large proportion issues from this quarter.

THOMAS WILLIS

Facts Connected with the Social and Sanitary Conditions of the Working Classes in the City of Dublin

DUBLIN ❧ T. O'GORMAN, 35 UPPER ORMOND QUAY ❧ 1845

A mong the interesting collection of medical facts to be found in the Annual Reports of the Physicians of Cork-street Fever Hospital, few are of more practical interest than the statements made with reference to the condition of the dwellings of the poor. Many suggestions have been made as to the causes of the origin and propagation of disease, but throughout the entire series of the reports no one cause is so repeatedly referred to, or so prominently put forward, as being an important agent in the generation and extension of disease, as the state of the dwellings of the wretched poor. These reports extend from the opening of the hospital, in 1804, to the present time, and teem with the most valuable and varied information.

It was remarked by Dr Short, who wrote in 1750, 'That sickly years are more fatal in Dublin than in London'; and Dr Rutty, in 1772, observes, 'That those who know the situation of the poor here can be at no great loss to account for the frequency and the mortality, especially in fevers, several families being in one house, and not infrequently in one room, which must undoubtedly contribute not only to the propagation, but also to the malignity, of these diseases.'

Hawkins, in his *Medical Statistics*, states, 'That Dublin appears to have suffered more continually from epidemic fever than any other great city in

Europe. The causes of this calamitous state are attributed by the resident physicians to want of employment, poverty, and sometimes to famine amongst the lower classes; and (if we continue to use the strong language of one of the eye witnesses) to circumstances unhappily deeply laid in the frame of society, and arising from manners and habits generated by ages of civil and moral degradation, which has checked the natural progress of civilisation, exhibiting a population increasing, but not improving.'

Sir William Petty, in 1672, states, 'That six of eight of all the Irish live in wretched nasty cabins, with neither chimney, door, stairs, nor window.' From this up to the present time the same miserable hut described by Petty is still the residence of 42·53 per cent. of the entire population; and as a consequence we have had frequent visitations of epidemics, unequalled in duration and virulence by any known; and we have a moral certainty that as long as these huts are used as residences for the people, so long will every, the slightest epidemic, degenerate into contagious fever. Other countries are visited by occasional epidemics, but here we have at all times a plague at our very doors. Why is this so?—It is because no care has ever been continuously extended to the comforts of the poor. Occasionally, as when the fearful ravages of cholera spread terror and alarm among the comfortable classes, or when the extent and malignity of epidemic fever so crowd the hospitals that the dependants of the wealthy can find no place within these establishments, active, but only *temporary*, efforts have been made to produce greater cleanliness in the localities occupied by the poor. Boards of health have then been formed; parochial officers, inspectors, and visitants nominated, who day after day, during the continuance of the alarm, visited the back courts and streets, caused the yards to be cleaned, the cess-pools emptied, &c.: but a few weeks, and all were again as before the terror had arisen—the boards were dissolved, and the wretched localities of the poor relapsed into their wonted filth.

To very many, the facts herein set forth, as regards the actual condition of a large proportion of the working classes in the city of Dublin, will appear scarcely credible. It may naturally be said, that these facts cannot apply to a state of society in the present age, but must have reference to some period when a moral and physical pestilence existed, and when neither the dictates of humanity, the promptings of benevolence, nor the light of science could be fairly exercised; but that in the present day, with a universal peace existing for upwards of a quarter of a century, with abundance of means and the power of creating wealth amongst us, with benevolent societies for charitable and humane objects, and with efforts daily making for the improvement of our social condition, it is impossible that our working classes, the manufacturers of our wealth, and the materials of the real strength and importance of a state, can be in a condition from which the brute creation is exempt. Let such persons, however, take the trouble of inquiring for themselves; and they will find that the facts before mentioned, are not only not highly coloured, but the contrary— that they convey a very imperfect sketch of the actual condition of a great proportion of our fellowmen.

After detailing such a state of things, it may be fairly asked, what remedies I would suggest for its amelioration. I confess the subject has occupied much of my attention, and although my opinions may not be much valued, I still think it my duty to make them public, did they produce no other benefit than that of inducing those who possess the power and the means of remedying those evils, to devote themselves to the consideration of the best means of so doing.

In this hope I would suggest, that in cities and large towns there should be some legislative enactment, under which officers of health, or something of a medical police, could be formed, with power to compel the owners of all houses let to lodgers or weekly tenants, to have them thoroughly lime-washed, from cellar to garret, at least every six months, or oftener in cases of contagious epidemics; to have a privy, communicating with a sewer when practicable; with dustbin; to have the yard of house paved, with a sufficient fall to privy pit; and to have the water conveyed into each house; and the cellars paved, flagged, or bricked. The under story of all houses might be used for any purpose, such as kitchen, business store, etc. but *in no instance should an underground room be used as a sleeping room*; pigs, asses, poultry, should not be allowed within the dwellings; and if room-keepers will have dogs, they should be subject to some small police tax. The officers of health should have the power of enforcing some such regulations as these, under a penalty recoverable in the most summary manner.

Public privies and urinaries should be erected in such a manner as to secure some approach to decency. This could be done by having them in the immediate neighbourhood of each police station. They ought to be of sufficient size, with door at each end, thoroughly ventilated, and seats separated by divisions. These could be got up as a kind of water closet; and if properly erected, would be quite free from smell. A metal pan, with neck of sufficient length inserted, and delivering into a tank of water, would answer these purposes; and could be had at very little more expense than the common open privy. In the immediate vicinage of such structures should be large fountains, with the water constantly on, and deliveries of sufficiently large bore to allow of free use for rinsing, washing, etc. The waste water would be considerable, and should fall into the privy tank, which tank should be connected with the main sewer. I do not presume to put forward the above plan as perfect; I merely suggest it for the consideration of those whose business makes them conversant with the erection of such buildings.

Public pumps would also be a source of great comfort; pure spring water would be estimated by all classes. Rutty, in his time, enumerates beyond thirty public pumps or wells within the city; I do not know of the existence of one at present.

Police stations should have large fires at all times: if these fires could be made available to warm water, to be given freely to the poor, it would tend much to cleanliness.

As public opinion has nearly abolished interments within the city, good care should be taken that the old burying grounds be not built upon. I would suggest their inclosure with iron railing, even at the public expense; and would leave the ground inside to be improved, according to the taste of the parishioners. By these means, what is at present an unsightly nuisance, might become in a very short time an ornament in each parish.

These suggestions may be allowed to pass unheeded by those in comfortable circumstances, as things in which they have no personal concern; but it might be very easily shown, that their interest is more involved in the state of things which they are intended to remedy, than appears at first view—that disease, generated in these abodes of rags, and oil, and misery, not unfrequently stalks within the threshold of the wealthy and the proud, and that, when it does, its attackers are often accompanied with a virulence that sets all human aid at nought.

BRIAN BEHAN

Mother of All The Behans

LONDON ❧ ARENA: ARROW BOOKS LTD ❧ 1984

The Grannie always said that, when she died, she wanted fine fat-arsed black horses to take her to the cemetery, not skinny old knackers. 'Let them have great black plumes leaping and rearing out of their heads,' she used to say—and we saw to it that she got them. Funerals then were grand occasions. The body would be laid to rest at the chapel for a couple of days, then the procession would take the body twice round the area, passing the house twice, and ending up at the graveyard. Everyone saved for their funeral then—not like today—so it was a great party for all the neighbourhood. The processions were all the same. First you would get the best carriages, then the poorer ones, then people on bicycles, and last of all people walking—them that couldn't afford either a carriage or a bicycle. They would stop at every pub on the way, and by the time they reached the graveyard they were fairly staggering. And it was so for the Grannie. She might have taken money all her life from the people in her houses, but in death she all but gave it back again. Still, I couldn't help thinking that she'd have to answer to God for taking the money off poor people that hadn't any.

After she was dead I found out all her secrets. First there were the whiskey bottles behind the bed. I told you that she used to pour the whiskey out of a china teapot so that the neighbours wouldn't know. Then, while sorting her things, I found a letter from the Corporation. It surprised me because it said that most of the houses were condemned—and that meant she wasn't entitled to charge a penny rent. She was kind to us, but for the tenants, she'd take the eyes out of their heads and come back for the lashes.

Still, now her property wasn't our business anyway. Having quarrelled so badly with Stephen, she left all the money to Paddy—and he wouldn't let us have a penny of it. He was so mean—even if he were a ghost he wouldn't give you a fright. Stephen was very bitter—but he had refused to see her before she died, even though she had asked for him.

The Grannie left £3,000, which was an awful lot of money in 1935. Would you believe that Paddy drank the lot in nine months—him and his two old aunts, Maggie and Jack? It killed him, too. No wonder Stephen felt he was hard done by.

Almost immediately we moved out. I'd been on at Stephen for years to move away from Russell Street, but he had always hated the idea. We could have taken a purchase house: you could buy them for just shillings a week, and they were yours after twenty years. A friend of mine took one about the same time as we moved—a lovely house just off the Clonliffe Road, far nicer than the one we went to. But Stephen wouldn't have it, because a purchase house would be fifteen shillings a week—ten went towards buying it. So for us it was off to Kildare Road, Crumlin. It seemed like a thousand miles from the city and the people we loved, where everyone was ready to help everyone else, and where there were plenty of pubs nearby so that we could always meet our friends and have a bit of a sing-song and a laugh. When he first heard about Crumlin Da was horrified. 'My God, Kathleen', says he, 'sure they eat their dead out there.'

We had gone down, year in, year out, to the Housing Department of the Corporation. We should have had a house years before that, with nine of us living in two rooms. But there were people even worse off than us, and the ones who got houses first were the ones with TB. Well, one day I went down, and Mr Marks in the office told me, 'Good news, Mrs Behan. You have a house if you want it. Do you?'

'Would a duck swim?' say I, grabbing the key.

I dragged Da out to look at the house on the Sunday before we moved. We had the trams that time—they ran out to Dolphin's Barn and then you walked. It was miles away. Sacred Heart of God, I nearly died. I thought we were going to Siberia. Crumlin, you know, is right out of the city, on the slopes of the Dublin Mountains. It would put your heart crossways, just looking at miles and miles of new roads. No lights. It was like the Wild West. Da cursed and swore about leaving his dirty old pub and being miles away from his work, but I didn't care. *He* didn't have to put up with one lavatory used by seven families, because he spent most of his time in that pub, so Russell Street suited him. The wind would take the skin off your bones that day. What with Da stumbling here and there he almost fell down a ditch. It was no joke, I can tell you.

At last we reached Kildare Road. The little house was lovely—it's still there today. It has a plaque over the door now, put up by locals to honour Brendan. (It was made by a famous Dublin sculptor, John Behan—no relation, but as good to me as any son). Anyway, I wouldn't call the queen my aunt just to be there in that house. Is there anything better than the smell of fresh paint? I was delighted. Tiny it was, with a little front parlour and two little bedrooms, but that was still better than all of us stuck in two rooms.

Even then Da didn't want to take it, making up all sorts of excuses. 'There's no buses,' says he. 'No trams, no schools, no pubs, no nothing. Only miles of these houses stretching away into nowhere.' Well, I went for him. I told him move we would—Hell or high water. And we did.

I knew that previous to this Da had refused another offer of a house in Emmet Road. I told Rory and he said, 'Don't ask *him* to sign for anything, because he will stay in Russell Street for ever and it's getting worse.' Well, it was then that the Grannie died. A Mr Best acted as her agent and tried to look for the rent, but no one would pay him, and naturally the houses fell into rack and ruin. Rory said, 'Don't tell Da. *You* sign for the key.' I hired Mrs Farrell the coalman's cart—she sold coal either by the stone for fourpence or by the bag for two shillings and sixpence. She was another one that brought the oul ass up into her room to keep him warm.

Well, we threw our bits and pieces up on the cart and set off. We were just going to Jemmy Gill's pub when Da ran out, shouting, 'You're not going to Crumlin now, are yez?' We just kept on going all the way, and went up a place called the Dark Lanes in Crumlin. It was dark—no street lamps, as I've said—but Rory found some candles. We had to peer into gardens over mountains of clay until we found number seventy.

PATRICK BYRNE

The Wildes of Merrion Square

LONDON ❧ STAPLES PRESS ❧ 1953

I t was a September day in the year 1845 and the autumn sunshine gave an added graciousness to the Georgian squares and streets in the centre of Dublin; there was a great concourse of people in the streets. The occasion, however, was not a festive one: it was a funeral, and Dublin has always been a city of gigantic funerals.

While the crowd was thickest a young lady emerged from her apartment in a house in Leeson Street, adjacent to St Stephen's Green. Her appearance invited attention. She was aged about twenty and tall and stately of bearing. She was carefully, indeed elegantly, dressed, and there was even a hint of ostentation. Her countenance, pale in colouring, was too large and broad for true feminine beauty, but the features were regular. The wide mouth had a suggestion of sensuality or carelessness and under the bonnet there was an abundant mass of hair arranged delightfully in the current fashion of ringlets, black as the proverbial raven's wing, but with the fugitive glint of blue which gives this raven hair its peculiar beauty. Altogether, one would conclude, an attractive young lady, and the more so now when her face was petulant and her brows knitted in annoyance. She had come out to take her morning stroll through the Green; she lived with her widowed mother, and life for one of her temperament was not always serene and easy; she relied on this outing in the September sunshine to undo the domestic vexations of the past few days. She would have a stroll through the Green, then a little leisurely shopping and gossip in Grafton Street and return to an overpowering mid-Victorian dinner.

On this particular day her annoyance was intense. She was jostled and pushed by the crowds, her morning walk was spoiled and in the end she had to run and take shelter in a shop. The whole town, she thought, bore a dismal aspect appropriate to the occasion. She had become rather tired of these great cortèges for she recalled vaguely that this was the second or third within the past year. Well, she reflected, as there was a funeral she might as well find out the details. The great procession had by this time gone by, colourful and impressive, the music of the bands died away and the people stood about looking half-dazed. Her observant eyes could detect that the grief was deep and genuine. Strange that she had heard nothing about this death. In the circles in which she moved there had been no mention that a prominent personage had died and the pomp could hardly have been greater if it were the Lord-Lieutenant himself. She turned to a mourning bystander and asked the simple question: 'Who is dead?' He seemed surprised but in deference to the well-dressed and imposing girl, whom he took to be an English visitor, he answered simply: 'Thomas Davis.'

She pondered the name Davis; she could not recall having heard it mentioned either in her home environment or at the Castle assemblies or among the gossips. 'Thomas Davis,' she repeated. 'Who was he?' The answer was equally simple. 'He was a poet, ma'am.' 'A poet!' she exclaimed in surprise. 'Yes, ma'am, a young poet.'

Jane inquired at the booksellers about the poems of Thomas Davis. She was informed that he had published no volumes, that his poems had not been collected; but she was recommended to buy a little volume called *The Spirit of the Nation*, which, said the bookseller, contained most, if not all, of the poems she sought. She glanced through it curiously. It was evidently a patriotic production, with a green cover adorned with a device and the contents were mainly political and propagandist ballads. It is indeed a remarkable little volume, for it was first published in 1843 and has run into thirty-five editions, the last of which appeared in 1936.

Jane noted that the poems were all taken from a current newspaper, *The Nation*. This paper had a feature named the Poet's Corner, and if the truth is to be told, the published collection never rose above the level which we usually associate with a 'Poet's Corner', and the modern reader would probably regard it with a combination of tolerance and amusement. Jane, however, was not in any sense amused. On the contrary, she was highly appreciative. It happened that a wave of ballad-making had swept over the country, and *The Nation* gave ready hospitality to all the young men and women who felt the call to write verse. There was a repetition of sentiment, a sameness of rhyme which is almost unbearable, but a girl who had read most of Macphearson and had herself dabbled in verse-making took these verses seriously and she was deeply moved. The ballads, almost without exception, were taken up with a sentiment termed 'Nationality'. They personified the motherland, there was much reference to the 'Dear Land' and the 'glories of long ago'. Disregarding historical accuracy they threw a heroic glamour over events, some of them of quite recent date. Thomas Davis himself had a strident ballad about a raid by Algerian pirates on the village of Baltimore in County Cork, although such a raid had never taken place. He had another in which he eulogised 'the Geraldines' as patriots although none of them was ever identified as such until Lord Edward FitzGerald in 1798 and *he* was a disciple of Tom Paine. Occasionally the verses went further and sounded a call to action with many references to the 'Sword' and the 'closing of the ranks'.

The following day it seemed to Jane Francesca that she had awakened from a great sleep. She felt a certain irritation. Here she was in the midst of life with great events happening all round, while all the time she slumbered. She resolved to remedy the position at once. The petty social round which formed the background of her life seemed unbearably silly. There were the assemblies at the Castle, there was always the inane talk of those beardless young officers, there was the gossip of a small set of

Anglo-Irish matrons. But now she found, or believed that she had found, that outside and beyond this paltry existence was the country, the old motherland, and, above all, the Nation.

PATRICK CAMPBELL

My Life and Easy Times

LONDON ❧ ANTHONY BLOND ❧ 1967 ❧ PRODUCED BY VIVIENNE KNIGHT

My mother said to me on the telephone from Dublin, 'I don't want to talk too loudly because I think he can hear me, but you'd better come over. He had a bad night and he's very feeble.'

I said I'd come at once.

I found I was neither shocked nor sad, but only excited. My father, Lord Glenavy, was going to die. It would be an event of some importance in Dublin and I, as the inheritor of the title, would be playing a leading part in it.

At this moment it wasn't possible to guess what the effect of his death would be. Death to me was an unknown quantity.

My sister had been killed by a flying bomb towards the end of the war in London, but we hadn't seen one another for a long time. The only emotion I could remember was a disgruntled feeling of waste. Her husband was killed at the same time and they hadn't been married long enough to have any children, so that one of the things I wasn't going to be was an uncle. But behind this familiar selfishness was the grey melancholy of knowing I'd never see my sister again.

I supposed I'd feel the same sort of thing about the Lord if, indeed, he was going to die. He'd already made, at the age of seventy-eight, an astonishing recovery from a major abdominal operation and when I'd last seen him a couple of months ago he'd been talking about playing golf again and buying a small boat.

No one ever spoke of the reason for the operation. The Lord himself called it, with a cheerful good-humour that didn't look faked, 'Just straightening out the guts'. Perhaps he really didn't know, but everyone else could only believe that it was cancer. The Old Lord had died of it, too, although he was eighty-eight.

They were always known in the family, and to the few close friends who ventured into it, as the Lord and the Old Lord. My mother, however, referred to my father as Gordon and his sister called him Charlie, while my brother and I spoke to him as Lordship. His infrequent letters to us were signed in the same way.

I know, for my part, that this use of 'the Lord' and 'Lordship' in place of 'my father' or 'Daddy' was to relieve us of an intimacy that would have been embarrassing to both. The Lord liked to keep everyone at a safe distance from him and particularly those that he didn't know well. Whenever I brought new friends to the house he'd refer to them for months afterwards as 'the Paul' or 'the David', de-personalising them for curious reasons of his own. Once the 'the' was dropped they were in.

And now it seemed that he was dying, and I was going to have to face the fact of his death. But all that I had at this moment was the feeling of excitement, of much to be done, of taking over the leadership of the family.

I rang the traffic manager of Aer Lingus in Regent Street, with whom I'd had dealings in the past, and told him my father was dying and that I had to get over to Dublin as quickly as possible. The feeling of excitement and importance had risen to a warm glow.

The traffic manager seemed to share it. He said he would ring their people at London Airport and tell them to do everything they could to help me. It wasn't the best time, he said, with the August Bank Holiday and the Dublin Horse Show coming up, but he was sure they could find me a seat.

The Aer Lingus representative at the airport got me one on the very next plane although, as he told me, 'There's ninety-three people standing by.' It was not unpleasant to be the Hon. Patrick Campbell, receiving VIP treatment on the way to the bedside of his dying father, Lord Glenavy.

A hired car, sent by my mother, was waiting for me at the airport in Dublin. It was a large and derelict Dodge which must have been used that morning for a wedding because the back seat was full of confetti and the smell of stout. It was strange to think that two people had got married while my father was dying, but then they'd probably never heard of either of us.

The battery of the Dodge was almost flat, but the engine fired on its last dying revolution. I hoped the driver wouldn't stall it, because I was suddenly sure that the Lord would die while we were stuck in one of the side streets around Ringsend Basin.

He stalled it on the hill up to the traffic lights in Blackrock, a couple of miles away from home. The only way we could get it going was to push it back down the hill in reverse, but there was a queue of cars behind us. I jumped out to wave them past and found I knew at least one of the people in each of the first three cars. They were pleased and amused to see me. As I pushed the old Dodge back down the hill one of them called out, 'Give you a grand bit for the *Sunday Times*, Paddy, what?' Several more car loads gave me a cheer as they went past. When the engine fired and I got into the back again I found I no longer believed that my father was dying. People lived for ever in Dublin. The informality, the easy laughter, the complete lack of pressure kept everyone going until they were ninety.

I remembered my mother had told me on the phone that the Lord had taken her and her sister, Marjorie, to dinner in the Royal Irish Yacht Club only a week ago, and that he'd driven the car himself.

He, too, would live to be ninety and we'd be playing golf together again soon. He'd had relapses before, but he was made of leather. No one ever died in careless, irresponsible Dublin.

We turned off the sea road in Sandycove into the horribly named Ballygehin Avenue, and there was the house, looking small and ordinary in the sunshine.

For fifteen years or so my father and mother had lived in Rockbrook, a large house in the Dublin mountains. If the weather was very clear you could see the whole city laid out beneath you, and the shadow of the Mountains of Mourne eighty miles away to the north.

A brown mountain stream ran through the grounds in a series of natural waterfalls. My father had planted hundreds of trees and shrubs around the swimming pool, which he'd had blasted out of solid rock that sparkled with quartz. On a summer's day it was a magic place, a thousand miles away from the uproar of cities and people. But in the winter, when the wind and the rain howled down from the ruins of the Hell Fire Club above, it was peculiarly lonely and desolate, and full of dying.

The news of my sister's death came to Rockbrook, and of the death of Ralph Brereton Barry, my mother's inseparable friend. Two favourite dogs had died there and a few miles farther up in the mountains was the Military Road with its lonely crosses, marking the places where men had been shot during the Civil War. In the winter it was too far from Dublin, and too close to death. My father sold it and bought this much smaller house, called Rockall, on the sea road in Sandycove, on the outskirts of Dun Laoghaire.

There was a tiny croquet court at the back, overlooked by terraced houses, but in the front only the garden and the sea road separated it from Dublin Bay.

My mother's taste and highly developed capacity for home-making had, at least, made it comfortable and original inside, even if the back of the house was the only part that got the sun.

The sun was shining now as the derelict Dodge left me outside the gate. The door was open and the house seemed to be empty. I called out several times, 'Anyone there?' but there was no reply.

I was sure that my father had had another of his miraculous recoveries and that he and my mother and Marjorie had gone out for a drive in the sunshine. Just to make sure I went upstairs to my father's room and opened the door and saw the most frightening thing I'd ever seen.

A shrivelled little old man was propped up against a lot of pillows in my father's bed. The face was yellow, and the bones were protruding through it. The right forearm was resting on top of the head in the position of someone trying to think of something, when the thought won't come. The figure was motionless, as still as death.

I was staring at it, paralysed, when a pretty little blonde girl in a white coat came round the end of the bed. I saw she must be the nurse, and that she was as startled as I had been.

I said, 'I'm Paddy—his son.' She said, confusedly, 'I knew you would be.' Then I found myself sitting on the chair beside him. I took his hand. It was very small and bony and cold. I said, not knowing what I was saying, 'You're a great man. You're a great man.'

His eyes were opaque, completely unseeing.

The little nurse bent down and spoke clearly and precisely into his ear. 'It's Mr. Paddy. It's your son.'

My father stayed absolutely motionless. He seemed not even to be breathing. 'It's me,' I said. 'Paddy. How are you?'

The little nurse spoke to him again. 'Just squeeze his hand,' she said. 'Tell him you know he's here.'

The cold, bony little hand lay lifelessly in mine.

'I think he knows,' the nurse said to me. Then she spoke to him again. 'Just move your finger,' she said. 'Tell him.'

I believe I felt the faintest little flutter.

The little nurse looked down at him with a gentleness which seemed to come from more than just a familiarity with death. 'He knows you're here,' she said. Then she said suddenly, 'He was a lovely man. We had the grandest laughs.'

I realised then for the first time that I'd never talk to my father again. 'He *was* a lovely man.' Very soon now he would be wholly dead.

I said, 'I'd better go.' I didn't have the courage to wait to see it happening. I said to the nurse, 'Is my mother in?' She said she thought she was in the garden.

WINSTON SPENCER CHURCHILL

My Early Life

LONDON ❧ ODHAMS PRESS ❧ 1947 ❧ FIRST PUBLISHED 1930

When does one first begin to remember? When do the waving lights and shadows of dawning consciousness cast their print upon the mind of a child? My earliest memories are Ireland. I can recall scenes and events in Ireland quite well, and sometimes dimly, even people. Yet I was born on 30 November, 1874, and I left Ireland early in the year 1879. My father had gone to Ireland as secretary to his father, the Duke of Marlborough, appointed Lord-Lieutenant by Mr Disraeli in 1876. We lived in a house called 'The Little Lodge,' about a stone's throw from the Viceregal. Here I spent nearly three years of childhood. I have clear and vivid impressions of some events. I remember my grandfather, the Viceroy, unveiling the Lord Gough statue in 1878. A great black crowd, scarlet soldiers on horseback, strings pulling away a brown shiny sheet, the old Duke, the formidable grandpapa, talking loudly to the crowd. I recall even a phrase he used: 'and with a withering volley he shattered the enemy's line'. I quite understood that he was speaking about war and fighting and that a 'volley' meant what the black-coated soldiers (Riflemen) used to do with loud bangs so often in the Phoenix Park where I was taken for my morning walks. This, I think, is my first coherent memory.

Other events stand out more distinctly. We were to go to a pantomime. There was great excitement about it. The long-looked-for afternoon arrived. We started from the Viceregal and drove to the Castle where other children were no doubt to be picked up. Inside the Castle was a great square space with small oblong stones. It rained. It nearly always rained—just as it does now. People came out of the doors of the Castle, and there seemed to be much stir. Then we were told we could not go to the pantomime because the theatre had been burned down. All that was found of the manager was the keys that had been in his pocket. We were promised as a consolation for not going to the pantomime to go next day and see the ruins of the building. I wanted very much to see the keys, but this request does not seem to have been well received.

In one of these years we paid a visit to Emo Park, the seat of Lord Portarlington, who was explained to me as a sort of uncle. Of this place I can give very clear descriptions, though I have never been there since I was four or four and a half. The central point in my memory is a tall white stone tower which we reached after a considerable drive. I was told it had been blown up by Oliver Cromwell. I understood definitely that he had blown up all sorts of things and was therefore a very great man.

My nurse, Mrs Everest, was nervous about the Fenians. I gathered these were wicked people and there was no end to what they would do if they had their way. On one occasion when I was out riding on my donkey, we thought we saw a long dark procession of Fenians approaching. I am sure now it must have been the Rifle Brigade out for a route march. But we were all very much alarmed, particularly the donkey, who expressed his anxiety by kicking. I was thrown off and had concussion of the brain. This was my first introduction to Irish politics!

In the Phoenix Park there was a great round clump of trees with a house inside it. In this house there lived a personage styled the Chief Secretary or the Under Secretary, I am not clear which. But at any rate from this house there came a man called Mr Burke. He gave me a drum. I cannot remember what he looked like, but I remember the drum. Two years afterwards when we were back in England, they told me he had been murdered by the Fenians in this same Phoenix Park we used to walk about in every day. Everyone round me seemed much upset about it, and I thought how lucky it was the Fenians had not got me when I fell off the donkey.

It was at 'The Little Lodge' I was first menaced with Education. The approach of a sinister figure described as 'the Governess' was announced. Her arrival was fixed for a certain day. In order to prepare for this day Mrs Everest produced a book called *Reading without Tears*. It certainly did not justify its title in my case. I was made aware that before the Governess arrived I must be able to read without tears. We toiled each day. My nurse pointed with a pen at the different letters. I thought it all very tiresome. Our preparations were by no means completed when the fateful hour struck and the Governess was due to arrive. I did what so many oppressed peoples have done in similar circumstances: I took to the woods. I hid in the extensive shrubberies—forests they seemed—which surrounded 'The Little Lodge'. Hours passed before I was retrieved and handed over to 'the Governess'. We continued to toil every day, not only at letters but at words, and also at what was much worse, figures. Letters after all had only got to be known, and when they stood together in a certain way one recognised their formation and that it meant a certain sound or word which one uttered when pressed sufficiently. But the figures were tied into all sorts of tangles and did things to one another which it was extremely difficult to forecast with complete accuracy. You had to say what they did each time they were tied up together, and the Governess apparently attached enormous importance to the answer being exact. If it was not right it was wrong. It was not any use being 'nearly right'. In some cases these figures got into debt with one another: you had to borrow one or carry one, and afterwards you had to pay back the one you had borrowed. These complications cast a steadily gathering shadow over my daily life. They took one away from all the interesting things one wanted to do in the nursery or in the garden. They made increasing inroads upon one's leisure. One could hardly get time to do any of the things one wanted to do. They became a general worry and preoccupation. More especially was this true when we descended into a dismal bog called 'sums'. There appeared to be no limit to these. When one sum was done, there was always another. Just as soon as I managed to tackle a particular class of these afflictions, some other much more variegated type was thrust upon me.

My mother took no part in these impositions, but she gave me to understand that she approved of them and she sided with the Governess almost always. My picture of her in Ireland is in a riding habit, fitting like a skin and often beautifully spotted with mud. She and my father hunted continually on their large horses; and sometimes there were great scares because one or the other did not come back for many hours after they were expected.

My mother always seemed to me a fairy princess: a radiant being possessed of limitless riches and power. Lord D'Abernon has described her as she was in these Irish days in words for which I am grateful.

...'I have the clearest recollection of seeing her for the first time. It was at the Vice-Regal Lodge at Dublin. She stood on one side to the left of the entrance. The Viceroy was on a dais at the farther end of the room surrounded by a brilliant staff, but eyes were not turned on him or on his consort, but on a dark, lithe figure, standing somewhat apart and appearing to be of another texture to those around her, radiant, translucent, intense. A diamond star in her hair, her favourite ornament—its lustre dimmed by the flashing glory of her eyes. More of the panther than of the woman in her look, but with a cultivated intelligence unknown to the jungle. Her courage not less great than that of her husband—fit mother for descendants of the great Duke. With all these attributes of brilliancy, such kindliness and high spirits that she was universally popular. Her desire to please, her delight in life, and the genuine wish that all should share her joyous faith in it, made her the centre of a devoted circle.'

PADDY CROSBIE

Your Dinner's Poured Out

DUBLIN • THE O'BRIEN PRESS LTD • 1981

Our entire district had a strong agricultural air about it during my boyhood. Unlike boys from the other parts of Dublin, we were in daily touch with the people from the farms of Meath, Kildare and County Dublin. The Haymarket was held twice weekly and farmers with hay loads as high as fifteen feet were arriving in Smithfield and Haymarket Street itself from early morning.

The men from the hay factors were always 'on the stones', that is, out on the roadway, to meet them. The men I remember were Jim and Matty McAuley from 7 Haymarket, Mr Keane of Dodds, Larry O'Neill and Larry Cuffe from Smithfield, men from Wilkinsons and Cartons, plus one or other of the principals of McKeown and McKeogh. Larry O'Neill was Lord Mayor of Dublin at this period.

Queues of haycarts formed at the six weigh-houses and Tony, Kevin and myself loved to wander up and down through these long corridors of yellow hay. Horses and farmers were very patient and the selling of the crop was done at a leisurely pace. Later in the day, when all of the hay had disappeared, some of the empty carts were left at the sides of both streets. The horses from these carts were being fed in different yards around the place. The owners made their way to one of the many aytin' houses for a meal. Church Street and Benburb Street had an abundance of these aytin' houses. The most popular one was that of Conroy's in Benburb Street. The smell of rashers and eggs from this place would make you hungry, even if you were just after a good meal. This was after the war of course, from 1919 on. There was another well-known aytin' house at the north end of Smithfield named Doggets.

With the farmers out of sight we children took over the empty carts. They made ideal see-saws, as the protruding prongs at the rear were about half the length of the shafts. Tony, Kevin, Philip and myself, perched at the four corners of one cart, see-sawed the happy hours away until the return of the owners. Sometimes the farmers returned, not from a meal, but from one of the pubs, St John's, Minogues or Keogh's. 'Look out! Here's the man!'

To cater for the farmers and their horses there were forges, coach-builders, saddlers, wheelwrights, seed shops, butchers, poultry shops and shops with farming implements. Scanlan's, the saddler in Haymarket was a very popular place and we loved to look in and watch Mr Scanlan working on a harness. The smell of leather always attracted us; it was such a clean smell.

The forges fascinated us. The two Byrne brothers had their forge over by Stable Lane. I thought then that the blacksmith was the greatest man on earth. Only a great man could take up the hind-leg of a young horse and slice and rub and prepare the hoof for the coming shoe. Tom Byrne often allowed us into the forge and on one occasion he let me pump the bellows. I have never forgotten that.

Tom Byrne picked a long strip of iron, put the end of it into the furnace, then broke off the required amount for a shoe. Next with a tongs he put the cut piece into the furnace again, and then he and his brother shaped out the shoe on the anvil with the hammer. The smell of burning hoof made me cough, and I always looked at the horse to see if he felt the hot steel.

The flying sparks as the hammer struck the red-hot metal turned the forge into a fairy-land. Then when the shoe was finished, it was shoved into a huge tub of water, making a sizzling sound, of which I was reminded, when I heard the hiss of a snake for the first time. The forge in the Haymarket was owned by Bill Walsh; afterwards a Tom O'Loughlin took over.

Church Street, King Street, Stoneybatter and Arbour Hill and many other streets had back-yard farms. Pigs were reared and fattened in all of these places. Float cars were a common sight in the streets as boys or young men went from house to house looking for slop for the pigs. 'Slop! Any slop! Slop!'

Mr McAuley of the Haymarket, the hay factor, also kept pigs in a yard in our lane. These were tended by a young man named Matty Brazil, a fresh-faced, good-humoured, young man, who always whistled at his work. The other boys, Tony, Kevin, Philip and I often watched him cleaning out the byres; they were always spotless, and particularly so after Matty had given the walls a coat of white-wash, which was often.

There was a coach builder at the corner of Haymarket, the north-west corner. The name over the gates was James Doyle & Son, Coach Factory. The building stretched half way up the Haymarket and all kinds of horse-drawn coaches were made there. The Doyles and Bourkes supplied the 'Long Cars' for the many outings of the Queen Street community. These took place on Sundays or Bank Holidays and all the adults seemed to go on the trips. Another well-known coach builder was Moore of Brunswick Street.

The outings were to the Strawberry Beds usually, and on one occasion to the Scalp, near Enniskerry. The day (we heard afterwards) was spent drinking and singing and dancing. The excitement and bustle in Queen Street on the morning before departure was infectious. Now and then, a giddy horse caused a commotion with a sudden move forward. The few not travelling, stood at the hall-doors, or arm-folded themselves at the windows: 'Mind yourselves now! Don't do what Francy did! Watch that Jemser coming home. Keep him up straight or he'll spill some'. Poverty was forgotten. Sure wasn't 'Uncle' there with the three brass balls? What about the Trouble? What Trouble? Haven't we troubles of our own? No matter how late they returned some insisted on dancing on the street. Up the Rebels!!

In all of the Dublin parishes in the Twenties a house to house collection was made by special collectors. The collector for Arran Quay was an ex-altar boy named John Hanway. John was a tall, fresh-complexioned fair-haired boy from Stoneybatter. His area was Queen Street and on many occasions I went with him to help. A rap at each door brought one of the occupants of the room quickly enough to find out who was there.

Over the shoulder was shouted 'It's the Arran Quay man.' 'There's a penny on the cabinet under the tumbler. Give it to him.' The frying-pan was heard from some rooms, while the smell of pig's head and cabbage came from others. The former were the late risers, the latter the early ones. The collection was made about 10.30 a.m. or 11 o'clock. I helped on those occasions, when I wasn't scheduled to serve Masses.

The shouts and noises of the tenements were very O'Casey-like in one way, but I never once heard the people of Queen Street use the flowery poetic language used in *Juno* or *The Shadow*.

The doors of most tenement houses were left open all night. The stairs were areas of pitch darkness. In many of the King Street and Queen Street houses there was only one flush toilet for the entire house and this was sited in the yard. The houses were Georgian-style with basements. In Blackhall Street the houses were four-storeyed over basement.

LOUIS HYMAN

The Jews of Ireland

SHANNON-IRELAND ❧ IRISH UNIVERSITY PRESS ❧ 1972

SOME ASPECTS OF THE JEWISH BACKGROUNDS OF *ULYSSES*

On 7 October 1904, James Joyce left Dublin for good (returning only in 1909 and 1912 for brief visits), a voluntary exile, as Yeats wrote of him in 1923, 'in flight from the objects of his hatred, bearing in mind always in minute detail, even to the names over the shops, the Dublin that he hated but would not forget'. His novel *Ulysses*, begun in 1914, was published in Paris in 1922 by a young American, Sylvia Beach. Everyone now knows that it records events in the lives of three main characters on an average day in Dublin, 16 June 1904: that it succeeds in its pervasive symbolism in presenting an exhaustive critique of contemporary society as reflected in the doings of the Irish capital on that day; that the chief figures in it, Leopold Bloom, the middle-aged Irish-Jewish advertising canvasser, his voluptuous wife, Molly, the young writer, Stephen Dedalus, correspond to the Homeric trio, Ulysses, Penelope, and Telemachus. The novel puts Dublin in a conspicuous charting on the map of contemporary world literature.

Apart from that of Bloom, the baptised Irish Jew, the names of authentic members of the Dublin Jewish community who lived on the south side of the city in St Kevin's Parade, Lombard Street West, and in and about Lower Clanbrassil Street appear in the novel. In the *Circe* episode, when Bella Cohen, the 'madam' of the brothel which Dedalus visited, threatens Bloom and commands that he should sign his will, die, and be buried in the shrubbery jakes, he bursts into tears:

> *(Bloom, broken, closely veiled for the sacrifice, sobs, his face to the earth. The passing bell is heard. Darkshawled figures of the circumcised, in sackcloth and ashes, stand by the wailing wall. M. Shulomowitz, Joseph Goldwater, Moses Herzog, Harris Rosenberg, M. Moisel, J. Citron, Minnie Watchman, O. Mastiansky, the Reverend Leopold Abramovitz, Chazen. With swaying arms they wail in pneuma over the recreant Bloom).*

THE CIRCUMCISED: (In a dark guttural chant as they cast dead sea fruit upon him, no flowers.) Shema Israel Adonai Elohenu Adonai Echad.

Bella Cohen, who appears in the records simply as Mrs Cohen, was a real person, occupant in 1890 of 82 Mecklenburg Street, in the heart of Dublin's then 'red-light' district, and in 1904 still living at the same address, which by then was officially called 82 Tyrone Street. The one-eyed Moses Herzog fits into the *Cyclops* episode and the name of Citron appealed to Joyce because it spoke for the traditional fruit of the Jewish festival of Tabernacles, commemorating the wanderings of the Israelites in the desert, and thus a symbol of the Wandering Jew. Bloom's tailor, George Robert Mesias, of 5 Eden Quay, was a native of Russia and appears in a parade of false messiahs in the *Circe* episode. In the Census of Ireland, 1901, he is listed as a widower of the Jewish persuasion, aged 36, lodging at the home of Hoseas Weiner in Clontarf West. A tall and handsome man, he married Elsie Watson as his second wife, on 5 November 1901 at Clontarf Presbyterian Church. The names of the other Dublin Jews, of whom one at least was made a friend of Leopold Bloom in his youth, were taken from *Thom's Directory* for 1905, a source book of *Ulysses*, because their names suited the Jewish themes in the novel and were introduced into the narrative to show that they comprised a part of Dublin's contemporary population, for one aspect of *Ulysses*, and a major one at that, is the presentation of the city in 1904.

One English Jew appears in *Ulysses* in the person of Dr Hy Franks, a quack doctor who had posters stuck up in greenhouses and urinals offering treatment for venereal diseases. 'All kinds of places are good for ads' is Bloom's observation on Franks' promotional activities. In the *Circe* episode Lipoti Virag, Blooms's grandfather, unscrews his ibis-head which is carried out crying 'Quack' of the pox doctor advertised on the fly bill. Henry Jacob Franks, born in Manchester in 1852, arrived in Dublin in 1903 after deserting his Turkish-born wife Miriam (née Mandil) and their four children.

Several persons, some Dubliners, others Italian, Greek and Hungarian, helped Joyce to complete his hero; Joyce was rarely content to fasten a major character to a single individual. The first of the Dublin models for Bloom was a tall, dark-complexioned clerk named Alfred H. Hunter, who was rumoured a cuckold. Richard Ellman was misled by Stanislaus Joyce into believing that Hunter was a Jew. The son of William H. Hunter, shoe-maker, Alfred, lodging at the home of a Mrs Ryan, of 2 Oxford Road, Rathmines, was married in the Catholic Church of Our Immaculate Lady of Refuge, Rathmines, on 1 February 1898 to Margaret Cummins, stationer, of 32 Castlewood Avenue, Rathmines, a few doors away from No. 23 where James Joyce lived from 1884 to 1887. After their marriage, the Hunters lived at Clonliffe Road near Ballybough Road. In 1899 Hunter had an office at 1 Clare Street in the building occupied by W.A. Gilbey, wine merchant, and A. Leslie and Co., house and land agents and surveyors, and next door to Marcus J. Bloom, dentist, and father of Joseph Bloom, also dentist of 2 Clare Street, an authentic character in *Ulysses*. Hunter's name appears in the *Freeman's Journal* of 14 July 1904 in a list of mourners attending the funeral of Matthew Kane, a friend of James Joyce's father and a model for Martin Cunningham in the novel. Joyce had met Hunter only twice and on 3 December 1906 asked his brother Stanislaus, and afterwards his aunt, Josephine Murray, to obtain all the details about him that they could. He had intended writing a short story for *Dubliners* called 'Ulysses', describing the day's wanderings of Hunter about Dublin, but on 6 February 1907 he wrote that 'Ulysses never got any forrader than the title.' On the night of 22 June 1904, Joyce was involved in an incident which he adapted in *Ulysses* and after which Hunter played a notable part. Joyce was badly beaten up by a young man to whose girlfriend he had made overtures, apparently unaware that the young woman had an official escort. He was left in the street with 'black eye, sprained wrist, sprained ankle, cut chin, cut hand' and was rescued by Hunter, who took him home and, as Joyce makes Leopold Bloom minister to Stephen Dedalus in the *Eumaeus* episode after he had rescued him from Nighttown, 'bucked him up generally in orthodox Samaritan fashion'.

The figure of the cuckolded Jew occupied Joyce's mind for the next 14 years. On one of his visits to Dublin, in 1909 or 1912, he may have been intrigued by the story of an Irish Jew whose wife had been unfaithful to him during his absence in foreign parts. On 8 November 1889, Joseph Blum (*sic*), draper, of 20 Oakfield Place, Dublin, son of Jonas Blum, dealer, of the same address, was married by certificate at the Registrar's Office, Cork, to Sarah Levy, born in or about 1870, of 68 Hibernian Buildings, daughter of Joseph Levy (1838–1936), a great wit, beadle of the Cork synagogue, Councillor of the Cork Chovevei Zion (Lovers of Zion) Tent in 1893 and, as a native of Tavrig, among the first Lithuanian Jewish settlers in that city. After a stay of four years at 64 Hibernian Buildings where two daughters, Bertha in 1891 and Dora in 1892, were born, Blum, now spelling his name Bloom, returned to Dublin and lived in a cottage at 3 Blackpits, off Lower Clanbrassil Street. There his wife gave birth to three sons: Myer in 1894, Eli in 1895 and Solomon in 1898. In the birth certificate of his son Eli he is described as an agent. In or about 1900, Bloom decided to seek his fortune in South Africa and, like the enigmatic sailor from Carrigaloe, in Queenstown (now Cobh), in the County of Cork, mentioned in the *Eumaeus* episode, and Joyce's Leopold Bloom, left his wife a grass widow. Sarah, completely assimilated in Irish mannerisms and speech, is reputed to have become the mistress of a Jewish lodger, by whom she had a daughter. One can imagine Sarah saying to herself as Molly did in the *Penelope* episode, musing about her adultery with Blazes Boylan, 'anyhow its done now once and for all with all the talk in the world about it people make'. Deserted by her husband, alienated from her parents and ostracised by the community, Sarah, who is remembered by her contemporaries for her good looks, was hard put to it to maintain her family on her own and moved to a tenement house in 3 Bishop Street, opposite Jacob's Biscuit Factory, to whose girl workers she sold drapery on the weekly payments system. Dora was sent in 1900 to her grandparents' home in Cork and emigrated to America in 1908. On board ship she met and married a fellow-emigrant, a Liverpool musician. After two years her two younger brothers, Eli and Solomon, followed her to the United States. Living in very straitened circumstances, Sarah and her eldest teenage daughter are reputed to have turned to prostitution. An old lady, a native of Dublin, recalls, some months before her marriage on 20 February 1907, seeing Sarah and her daughter apparently soliciting at the corner of Earl Street, near Nelson's Pillar. Laurence Elyan, a native of Cork and a retired Irish civil servant, now (1971) resident in Jerusalem, recollects, as a boy, reading for old Joseph Levy, in 1914, a letter from Sarah of 3 Bishop Street, Dublin, appealing for money. It is believed that Bertha who, like fairhaired, slimsandalled Milly Bloom, is described by a contemporary as tall and fair-haired and who, in 1911, worked as an assistant in a stationer's shop, was befriended by and taken care of by the Salvation Army at whose rallies she is reported to have sung. Her brother Myer worked first as a library clerk and later as a book-seller at Eason's. It may be mentioned that Solomon Levy (died *circa* 1910), Sarah's brother, was a great lover of light operas which he used to hum continually. The five children of May (Michele), her sister, were all musically inclined and organised themselves into a private band which played at family functions. About 1920, Sarah, after a short stay in Belfast, is said to have emigrated to America together with her daughter Bertha and son Myer. Joyce was anxious to know from A.J. Leventhal, then a young graduate of Trinity College, Dublin, who visited him in Paris in 1921, whether the Blooms still lived in the South Circular Road district, although he did not mention any particular person of that name. Leventhal recalls that Joyce's interest in the Blooms was more than casual and that he was relieved to hear that they had died or left the city.

Joseph Blooms's sister, Bassa (1870–1941), blue-lipped, of plumpish build and highly rubicund complexion, was usually clad in a one-piece dress and a shabby brown coat; of dubious repute, dishevelled and invariably carrying an umbrella, she used to roam the Jewish district mumbling maledictions. Her father Jonas or Jone, popularly known as Yonah, moved in 1892 to 38 Lombard Street West, Leopold Bloom's address in 1893–4, until his death in 1912. A kindly and witty man with a gentle smile, neatly groomed with a trimmed red beard, he wore a frock-like coat and a silk hat of the period. Mrs Rebecca Ita Isaacson (1889–1970), while visiting her grandfather Nisan Moisel of 20 Arbutus Place, a character in *Ulysses*, recalls, as a schoolgirl in 1902 or 1903, seeing Jonas Bloom with saddened eyes and hands folded behind his back, following his pregnant spinster daughter as she walked slowly up and down Oakfield Place, a cul-de-sac opposite their home.

A son or nephew of Jonas was Jacob Bloom, dealer, of 1 St Michael's Terrace, Blackpits, who, on 30 May 1899, married Matilda, sister of Rudolph Burack, a witness at the marriage and a brother-in-law of the Louis Wine of 33 Wellington Quay. It was Wine's antique shop that

Leopold Bloom, in the *Sirens* episode, passes on his way to the Ormond bar, bearing the volume *Sweets of Sin* which he had purchased for Molly in the bookshop in the cubbyhole partitioned from the main shop of 26 Wellington Quay rented by a Dublin Jew, Aaron Figatner of 6 Seapoint Terrace, Irishtown. Leopold Bloom, passing the jeweller's shop, read Figatner's name and asked himself why he always thought his name was Figather: 'Bloom whose dark eye read Aaron Figatner's name. Why do I always think Figather? Gathering figs I think'. Lionel Marks, a brother-in-law of John Michael Higgins, was the second witness at Jacob Bloom's marriage and kept the antique shop at 16 Upper Ormond Quay where Leopold Bloom in the *Sirens* episode sees in the window a picture of Robert Emmet, the Irish rebel, whose dying words, which have a carminative effect on him, he tries to recall. Jacob Bloom, whose occupation is given in his children's birth certificates as a brass-finisher, worked as a plumber. He had five children: Bertha Jenny, born at John Street, Sligo, in 1900, Sarah at 59 Lombard Street West, Dublin, in 1901, Fanny, at No. 77 in 1903, Mayer William at 4 Brainboro', off Greenville Terrace, in 1905, and Rachel at the same address in 1907. One of his children is said to have married out of the faith and the family emigrated to America after the First World War.

Another member of the Bloom clan who lived in Dublin contemporaneously with Joyce was Isaac Blum (*sic*), leather merchant, of 3 Desmond Street, off Lombard Street West, whose wife Daisy, née Liknaitzky, gave birth to a daughter Gladys Margaret on 23 December 1903. Daisy, who converted to Catholicism, was a music teacher in Dublin in 1909. It is possible that Joyce knew of her and derived some of the characterisation of Molly from her.

BILL KELLY

Me Darlin' Dublin's Dead and Gone

DUBLIN ❧ WARD RIVER PRESS ❧ 1983

You always knew it was Friday. Every Friday a little man in a dust coat and cloth cap stood outside Bill Bushe's pub at the corner of Gardiner Street and rendered 'Roses of Picardy' on a cornet—the musical type, not the ice-cream. He carried a collecting box which pleaded, 'Help an ex-Serviceman', but the help he could expect from the denizens of Dorset Street in the early 'twenties was meagre, because the people who might have contributed—the other British ex-servicemen—had as much as he had, which was sweet nothing. And the others, the ones who hadn't gone away to fight for the King and Empire, wouldn't have helped him even if they had it. For some of them had fought against the King and his Empire in the vicious bitter bloody Tan War, and they wouldn't help. And others, those who had fought neither for nor against His Britannic Majesty wouldn't have helped him on principle (the principle of self-interest, which is what Irish people generally mean when they talk of 'principle'), that they had managed to walk the tightrope of neutrality and they weren't about to rock the boat at this stage.

You always knew it was Friday, too, because dinner on Fridays was a saucer of rice, and for dessert, a ha'penny chocolate biscuit: a Lucullan feast for a six-year-old slum dweller.

You always knew it was Friday in the tenements, because every Friday each woman scrubbed her own landing and flight of stairs and the whole place reeked of Jeyeses Fluid.

Dorset Street was as far in spirit as it was geographically from that lovely country in England from which it took its name. It was a long wide street, stretching from Granby Row to Binn's Bridge across the canal, which divided semi-suburban Drumcondra from the slums. Apart from the shops, which were mainly on the right-hand side of the street as you headed north, towards Swords and, at the outer limits of the imagination, Belfast, the Georgian houses in Dorset Street, which had once accommodated the petite bourgeoisie and traders, had long since given up the pretence of being the relics of oul' dacency, and sadly and resignedly accepted their tenement status.

They've all been levelled now, but the people who lived in them, those who survived the consumption long enough to escape, will never forget them. For you can never forget the feel of a tenement. More, you never quite get the smell of a tenement out of your nostrils. It's a smell of damp and decay, of deep-rooted dust and poverty, of urine and red raddle, and above all of hopelessness. Hopelessness, just fringing on despair, but not quite despair, because every room in the house, each one occupied by a different family, kept the 'colzoil' lamp with the red shade burning in front of the ubiquitous picture or statue of the Sacred Heart. And that kept flickering hope just barely alive.

On Fridays, the dealers brought out their wooden barrows from which they sold fresh-Howth-herrins-a-ha'penny-each or Dubalin-bay-mack'rel-only-a-penny. The dealers also obliged their tenement neighbours with a loan of a shilling or two, or half-a-crown, to be paid back on Saturday, from the man's wages, if he was lucky enough to be working, and if it weren't paid on Saturday, 'shure it'd be alright, only it's two shillins or four shillins or five shillins next week'. A number of them became quite wealthy from the dealing and the money-lending and there's more than one doctor or lawyer or professional man today who doesn't want to trace the family tree back to his grandmother.

The Jewman and the landlord usually came on Friday, and there was some substance to the rumour that these gentry occasionally collected the rent or the loan repayment in kind, and indeed, I remember one coalman—at that time the bellman went his rounds with the coal in his horse-drawn dray and he measured out the stones of coal at the side of the path—very clearly calling out 'coal for cash'. It didn't mean anything to me as a snotty kid of six or seven, but in after years, like the eighty-years old gent sweeping the floor in the county home who flung down the sweeping brush and said: 'blast it, now I know what she meant', it dawned on me.

The dark suspicions and rumours anent the Jewman and landlord erupted in the full glare of public interest when two of the oul wans, at odds with each other and overburdened with the frustration of existing in what is now described as a deprived environment, would decide to settle their differences in a manly way. But first there was the slanging match in which each wan's ancestry was called into question and then the argumentum descended into ad hominem, or wominem to be more accurate, with banshee-like screeches of 'Y'oul hairbater, yeh'll keep away from my childher, y'oul trollop ... y'hoorsmelt.' 'Hoorsmelt is it? I was always clean an' dacent, not like some I know when their poor husbands were out at the front fightin'. I never dropped a bastard anyway ...'

At that stage, the feathers hit the fan, and like two she-elephants disputing a bull in must, they collided in mid-fight, claws grabbing for hair, eyes, or clothes, as the neighbours tried to separate them, and the word spread along the street like wildfire—'Ruggy Up'—and the crowds poured in from nowhere and we kids scurried from the corners and the backyards and the cellars, to join in the excitement. It was cheap enter-tainment for the masses, really, and apart from a few tufts of hair missing, neither of the antagonists was injured, though the neighbours would file in their memories for future reference the more outrageous of the accusa-tions cast in the pre-fight ceremonies.

On the Saturday night, however, all was forgiven, at least temporarily and the gladiatoresses could be found in the snug of Bill Bushe's, sipping gills of porter and backbiting.

Five tenements, 83 to 87, housed some fifty families, probably about two hundred people and it was a close-knit community, though the resi-dents of 83 were a cut above buttermilk because they had a shut hall-door, the outward and visible sign of near-respectability. They could have a shut hall-door because there was only four or five kids in the house alto-gether, most of the tenants being lonely elderly couples.

In each of the other four houses, there were nine families and hordes of kids, so they couldn't have shut hall-doors. There was one toilet, a noisome white-washed shed, and one cold water tap in the backyard of each house, and water had to be carried bucket by bucket to each room. Those nearer the top had the tougher job in ferrying water.

Only during the day was the toilet used by the kids, and even the grown-ups trained their bowels to function mainly during the hours of daylight. At night, The Bucket, which stood in The Corner, a recess in each room, served as emergency toilet for the whole family, and only babies were washed in the zinc bath, and that once a week, on Saturday nights, with water heated on the fire, because to heat on the gas would cost too much.

I can't remember for the first eight years of my life, using the backyard toilet at night. Like all the other kids in the house, I was afraid. You see, the Mad Oul Wan lived in the basement, a stone-flagged room under street level, whose window looked out into the area. I suppose in the days when the tenements were occupied by the petite bourgeoisie or traders, this was the kitchen. Up six flights of stairs and six lobbies—the more genteel called them landings—were the front and back top, presumably the skivvies' quarters in the good old days, and, in between, at street level, were the parlour and back parlour. Then the two per front and back, and then the top. I still don't know if it's 'per' or 'pair' or maybe it was originally a French word sounding something like it.

We were terrified of the Mad Oul Wan. She lived alone in the basement, and though she looked the acme of respectability when she went out in the street, dressed in a dark grey serge costume with a black blouse and one of those little round hats Chinamen always wore in the comics, she frequently made forays from the nether regions, lashing out at us kids with a sweeping brush handle as we dashed hell for leather through the hall and up the first two flights of stairs. We never knew the reason. One day, just as I was going out through the hall, she came in, and I nearly fainted with fright as she stopped in front of me, but she just glared and passed by. When she wasn't terrifying us, she could be heard singing hymns in the fastness of her basement fortress.

The rooms were lit by gas, and when the St Vincent de Paul men were doing their rounds—and God love and bless them, they were sorely needed with their half-dollar food dockets—the gas light was extinguished and the fire doused, and a butt of a candle put flickering on the mantelpiece. Times were so bad that the SVDP men had to look on the ability to put a penny in the gas meter as comparative affluence and most of the families in the block needed their beneficence, though there were the prouder ones who would sooner starve than take their charity. They did.

Looking back, weren't they depriving the SVDP of the chance of performing one of the corporal works of mercy? And if nobody accepted charity, that would be one of the corporal works made redundant.

The older women wore shawls, and were looked down on by the younger married women who felt that only dealers should wear shawls, and it was de rigueur to have a hat and coat for important occasions like going to Mass, or funerals, or Visiting. Visiting meant going at least to the house next door and sitting for a gossip for a couple of hours. You didn't visit the people in the same tenement—usually there was a feud with at least one of them at any given time—and you only 'dropped in' on them.

O'Casey lived around the corner in the North Circular Road, and I've often thought he got his characters from Dorset Street. In the house where he lived there was a Captain Moore of the IRA who once escaped a raid by the British by climbing out the back window and crossing the network of back walls until he reached Sinnott Place. In 87 Dorset Street, there was a Mrs Burgess, whose husband had been fighting 'at the front', as taking part in the first Great War was always called, and who herself had worked in a munitions factory in Arklow during that disturbance. Though her name wasn't Bessie, she was certainly no Shinner.

My impression of Fluther and Joxer was formed by a living person in No. 85: Diddler, he was called, and he never had a permanent job, though indeed he wasn't unique in that, but always was engaged in some kind of handyman's jobs. He was low-sized, had a brush moustache and always wore a cap and a black muffler, crossed across his chest over a collarless shirt with a bright stud. Apart from F.J. McCormack, the one who came nearest to my mental vision of Fluther was Phillip O'Flynn, despite the difference in stature.

There were a couple of Rosies, described in sotto voce, as 'goin' with Sailors', and Mollsers were a dime a dozen, though nobody mentioned the dread word consumption, almost as if it could be contracted by verbal association. It was always a weakness or a decline, but the galloping consumption showed no pity for many with blue eyes and flaxen hair and took them within a matter of weeks.

There was a popular song in the forties that bemoaned Saturday night as the loneliest night of the week. But in Dorset Street in the twenties, Saturday night was the liveliest night in the week, looked forward to as the highlight of the week's entertainment by those who had gallery seats in their tenement windows.

As regularly as clockwork, when at closing time Bushe's pub at the corner of Gardiner Street and McAuley's at the corner of the North Circular Road disgorged their respective clientele through the swing doors, there was one, who, filled with porter and indignation at countless unrighted wrongs, dashed into the middle of the tramlines, flung down his tattered coat, and offered to fight the best man in Dorset Street.

Sometimes his choice would be restricted to a Free-stater; at other times it would be an ex-serviceman who took the shillin'; still more rarely, and only if he happened to have been at the front, he'd want a murdherin' bastard of an IRA man who shot dacent men in the back while they were out fightin' at the Front. But mostly it was just a general invitation.

There was always the real danger, if he invited a murdherin' IRA bastard, that there might happen to be one available, and he just might happen to have a gun and the whole complexion of the sport would be altered drastically.

The challenge was usually taken up and most often it would end with a pas de deux of shadow-boxing, coat-throwing on the ground, and verbal threats, after which, honour satisfied, the antagonists and their multifarious seconds would drift homewards. Occasionally, however, the matter came to blows, but the peculiar chivalry of the age didn't allow the use of weapons or boots. If an opponent fell or was knocked down, he prudently stayed prone until the victor was taken away by friends, or the arrival of two burly DMP men, massive in their darkened night helmets, encumbering capes and fearsome batons in leather sheaths from either Mountjoy or Fitzgibbon Street depending on the location of the ruggy, cleared the street as if by magic.

While the menfolk were in the pub sipping their six-penny pints, the women had the coddle on the hob, simmering away. Only old women went into the snugs: a respectable woman couldn't, except for a funeral, when she could coyly consent to have a glass of port wine. When the ruggy was over and peace had descended on the street and the men had reached home, the coddle, a recipe peculiar to Dublin—a pound of bacon pieces, (6d), a half pound of sausages, (3d), a bit of onion and a few potatoes simmered for hours—was eaten. And then it was bed, for there was no television, no wireless, and damn few gramophones, and the gas had to be saved, and the coal had to be stretched, and anyway, it was warmer in bed.

SHANE LESLIE

The Skull of Swift

LONDON ❧ CHATTO AND WINDUS ❧ 1928

I n the year of Grace 1835 some graceless ghouls excavated a pair of skulls in the Cathedral Church of Saint Patrick the Apostle of Ireland within the Metropolitan City of Dublin. One skull was that of a woman, frail tabernacle of the frail, in which the late Sir William Wilde, an Irish physician and antiquary of repute, discerned 'perfect model of symmetry and beauty' and added that 'the teeth were perhaps the most perfect ever witnessed in a skull.' The inscribed stone testified the mortal name of Mrs Hester Johnson, but gave no clue whether she was really wife, widow or maid. But among the immortals she appeared to bear another name, as it were in Homer, who attributed characters with both earthly and divine names. Mrs Johnson to men, to the gods she was apparently known as STELLA.

In close proximity lay the skull of an old man, which Sir William Wilde diagnosed as resembling 'in a most extraordinary manner those skulls of the so-called Celtic aborigines of North-Western Europe'. According to effigy and epitaph it pertained to a Dean of the Cathedral, who there had eventually sought rest for bone and oblivion for heart. The passing stranger might read further and feel surprised that a Minister of the Sanctuary and a Professor of Christian retirement and benevolence should leave arresting and racking words upon a tomb:

'UBI SAEVA INDIGNATIO ULTERIUS COR LACERARE NEQUIT'

Why this savage indignation and what lacerations? Surely from ordained and established priests of settled conviction and settled income this was a hard saying and disturbing words to carve in black marble. Surely the lives of Christian Deans, protected from the cares, which afflict poor curates, and the responsibilities, which depress Bishops, should be the glorified impersonation of peace and good will upon earth. But this was a Dean, who sought beyond the grave a place where the savagery of his indignation should no longer lacerate his heart. This was a Dean, who was no gentle shepherd even to his sheep; and, dividing humanity into wolves and sheep, it would have been difficult to say whether the cords of his tongue fell fiercest on flock or foe. This was a Dean, who finding no rest himself, was unwilling to allow rest to others. This was a Dean, who was fretted by the ungodly. This was one, who left no record for theology when he lived, and who emptied no episcopal throne when he died. This was the writer whom mortals called Jonathan Swift but whom the gods, should he have travelled into their far country, must call Lemuel Gulliver, for, though his bones were fashioned after the manner of mortal bones, his mind befitted the godlike, full of anger and power, and raining fury upon the righteous and unrighteous alike, fiercely pitiful and condescendingly faithful unto those whom he loved, but loving them as the gods love, and bringing those who loved him to their death. His was a mind not without vain ambitions, which he allowed to destroy themselves, not without desires, which he compelled to die within. A mind not without many affections and affectations, but a mind, which pierced and broke the glass of illusions and tore the imagery and rent the clothing which swathed the minds of those about him. A thwarted, frenzied and disappointed mind, which might have disappeared into the void like bitter fume, had it not been tempered with the rare gift of irony. Men that are mortal and born of women write and utter themselves in satire. The gods are ironical in silence. This Dean had brought the irony of the gods with him to earth and used it to the dread and diversion of his fellow-men. Before he died, the irony had entered his soul also, and he asked only to suffer no further laceration by the acts of unwise men or by his own wounding thoughts.

The skull of Dean Swift was brought to the Phrenologists, who were camped at that time in the middle ground between Science and Fashion. This Phrenological Art enabled them to decipher 'amativeness large and wit small' between the sutures of his dead brain. With this sapient finding let Phrenology at least rest content. The 'Prince Posterity' to whom the Dean offered the most remarkable of his works, might be amused or puzzled by the attribution of 'amativeness large and wit small' to a dean, whose flashing wit was only small in comparison to the thunder-clouds of wrath from which it was derived; and whose amativeness was only the dancing shadow of passions as terrible as his hate. 'Amativeness' is insufficient to describe that passion by which the gods destroy those whom they cause to love themselves. Otherwise the Post-Mortem exposition of this skull was unrevealing. The great gifts had passed with the ghost. The Phrenologists were condemned to conduct the autopsy of the hen which laid the golden eggs. 'Amativeness large and wit small'!—and with that verdict both skulls were returned to sepulchral peace.

DR GEORGE A. LITTLE

Malachi Horan Remembers

DUBLIN ❧ MERCIER PRESS ❧ 1943

'Just past the door here, where the bohereen joins the mountain, was a great place for dancing of a summer Sunday long ago. Kitty Shea, the blind fiddler, would be there; and her daughter would be singing with her and keeping time on the tambourine. A man would be made leader for the evening. He would be holding a tin plate in his hand, and in it he would auction the music. Every man would bid for his choice to please his partner, and he who bidded most put his money on the plate and called the tune.—Ay, "He who pays the piper calls the tune."—What was collected went to the fiddler. It was all jigs and horn-pipes we danced. Ah, it was jolly! Jolly it was. It was wonderful how the music and the dancing, the songs and the laughing, brightened up the hill.

'But, of course, what we would have here was nothing to the dancing at Rathfarnham Fair. It was held on 10 June each year. The Sunday previous to the fair was called "Walking Sunday", as it was on that day that the people who lived at a distance commenced walking their stock. Well, the fun of the fair started on Walking Sunday and went on till the fair was over.

'There were all kinds of side-shows in the streets. We would have trick-o-the-loop men, wrestlers, strong men, pipers, ballad-singers, and the rest. But the cream of the milk was the dancing. Lads, the best dancers in Ireland, would not fail to attend. Every inn in the town would have a floor in its yard. The best of them were in the Yellow House, O'Connor's and Curtis's. There were all kinds of musicianers, but blind Kitty Shea and her daughter were as good as the best. They did well enough out of it, too, for the music was auctioned there the same as here in Killenarden. We would be selling all day and dancing all night. Them were the days!

'This was chiefly a horse and sheep fair. (The cattle fair was held earlier in the year on "The Strand", off Butterfield Lane). This June Fair was first-rate for horses. Great prices were paid by city firms for van-horses, and this was the sort chiefly on offer. Good luck to the old times, says I.

'You know the old forge facing up the Tallaght street? It was there that up to fifty years ago they held the Hirage Fair. It would be held a few days before 15 August. The men would come in from as far as Baltinglass. Some would be hired on the road before they reached the fair. The leavings of them would gather themselves about the forge. Each man would stick his pipe in the band of his hat as a badge that he was free for service. When he was hired he would put it in his pocket. It was the small "Dutch" pipe they smoked. They were made of rough, hard clay, mortal coarse on the lip or gum. My father, God care him, and many another would slip the big end of a goose-quill on the stem for a mouthpiece. They shaped them the very same way as old Hughes, the hedge school-master, would be making the pens. Gor-a-war, he used loam sand to dry his writing. *All* the time the men would be carrying a pipe-readier in the hatband—it was handier than to be forever rooting out a thraneen for to free the shank. Every man of them would be wearing his whetstone in a pouch on his belt, and often enough a high-crowned rush hat on his head. They were a great breed of men and civil spoken. Some could reap an acre a day. I could myself one time. Ay, the street would be full; what with farmers looking for help and men anxious for work. And when all was over there would be laughing and talking and a bit of a dance or the wrestling. The ballad-singer would be doing a great trade, nor were the fiddlers idle. Maybe they are better off these days, but I wonder are they as happy at just being men?

On 15 August the farmers met and struck the rate of wages for the year. It would be about half-a-crown a day. Of course, if a man was getting his keep it would be less—maybe a shilling. Some would be lodging in the town, but others might be getting the use of an old barn. It would be late in the season and the day shortening when they would be meeting of an evening. That was the time for the songs and the stories. It comes to my mind that it is not what a man gets but what he buys with it that crops him "prasshac" or corn.

'Oh! about the inns.

'Of course, as you would be knowing, sir, the inns in Rathfarnham were great places, surely; real stylish, anybody could go to them. Different entirely they were to the little mountain places that used to be around here. Tantiutherums we called them. Eh? A tantiutherum was a public-house and it wanting a licence. Oh, I know well that in other parts of the country they are called sheebeens, but around here we call them nothing but tantiutherums. 'Tis a real old name. Malachi Sheridan of Ballinascorney, made a ballad about one of them they called "The New Mountain Inn",—Oh, him? He was a great poet, a mountain man, a "hash" man to hurt, but a good friend. We called him Black Malachi of the Hills. He was tall and black-advised, thin and strong as a mountain ash. He could (and would) do anything, from poaching a "patheridge" to building a house.

'Oh, ay, Mr Fitzgerald, about the tantiutherum, "The New Mountain Inn". There was a young farmer. His name was Paul O'Neill, and he had his farm at the Commons of Ballinascorney. This was about seventy years ago. Times were hard with him—harvest bad with blight; a cow died, and the agent raised his rent because he always had his ready. As a woman up there said at the time: "It is as dangerous to pay as not to pay." Well, with him in debt and in danger, he had to do something. He took a chance and opened his place as a tantiutherum. He called it "The New Mountain Inn".

'As mad as a bag full of cats in a bed of briars was Lanky Tom Callaghan when he heard the news. Knowing Paul O'Neills's trouble, you see, he had his eye on Paul's farm. "Lanky Tom Callaghan of the Hurley Foot" was the name they had on him. What with one thing and another he was a great wrestler. He used to use the hurley-foot as a hook to trip his man.

'Howsomever, at first all went well with Paul O'Neill. He was well liked by the neighbours, so they did what they could to give him a hand. And why wouldn't they? Had he not always the open hand, a joke and a smile (or a song, maybe) for everyone?

'Then one fine day Lanky Tom Callaghan up and informed on him to the police. It looked like that there was to be a mart of trouble for Paul. But the neighbours, *rich and poor*, were at the back of O'Neill, so that the upshot was that instead of gaol they got a licence for him. After that, all went well—for a while.

'But Lanky Tom was not bet yet. He was a sore man. He went on with his working against O'Neill. He made it his business to see that every mischief about the place was blamed on The New Mountain Inn. He saw to it, too, that Fr Buckley, the parish priest of Tallaght at the time, would hear the bitter end of it. Then when he had the ground prepared, as you might say, he informed again. This time, what with the police and the clergy against it, the place was closed for good.

'He did, indeed! Callaghan got the place, but that was all the good it did him. He died in it after, without ever knowing a day's luck. The ruins of the inn are there yet on the Commons of Ballinascorney.

'Malachi Sheridan wrote a ballad about the Land League, and how they took and hanged the Kearneys. Innocent men they were. A father and two sons. Not a father or son in the whole country but knew them innocent. And all this, for what? For the murder of an *agent*. Mick (*sic*) Kinlan was the name he owned to. Did you ever hear tell of the Kearneys?'

'Yes,' I assured him. I remembered reading the following in Handcock's *History of Tallaght*: "A strange scene took place near this, in the year 1816, when thousands of the country people were assembled on the banks of the River Dodder, to witness the execution of three men named Kearney, a father and two sons, Peter, Joe, and Billy Kearney. They were hung for conspiracy to murder John Kinlan, a steward of Ponsonby Shaw, of Friarstown. The body of Kinlan never was found, and it was said at the time that it had been burned to ashes; however, I have heard that the country people knew right well where it was buried. The evidence was purely circumstantial; the Kearneys were heard to say that they would finish Kinlan whenever they got the chance; and there was a hatchet found with blood on it, and hair that resembled Kinlan's. In those days this was sufficient to criminate the men; and Lundy Foot, a justice of the peace, then living at Orlagh or Footmouth, pressed on the prosecution to conviction. I believe it was one of the first convictions under the then new "Conspiracy to Murder Act". The three Kearneys were brought from Newgate to Kilmainham, surrounded by a troop of dragoons, as in the sketch taken at the time by an eye-witness. When the procession was passing Bushy Park, the seat of Sir Robert Shaw, they requested the carriage to be stopped, and there knelt down in the vehicle, and solemnly cursed the Shaw family through all their generations. Having thus relieved their feelings, they went cheerfully on their way, and arrived at a field on the side of the river, just above a house then owned by a Mr Wildridge, a builder, who built several of the houses in Harcourt Street. In this field were three gallows erected; the dragoons were drawn up all around, and in a brief time the wretched men were launched into eternity, amid the screams of the women, and the execrations of the men." (Kinlan's body was found at the opening of a new sand pit in Tallaght in 1933.)

'It was the only bad thing' remarked Malachi, 'that Dan O'Connell ever did. You know Ponsonby Shaw and Lundy Foot of Orlagh—the brother of the snuff-man beyond in Westmoreland Street—were hand in glove. They used to have Dan in to eat his dinner with them in Orlagh. They asked him his advice about having the Kearneys arrested under the new Act. Dan told them they were entitled to have the poor men arrested under this law. The country round here never forgot and never forgave Dan O'Connell for that—the only bad thing he ever did.

EAMONN MACTHOMAIS

Gur Cakes and Coal Blocks

DUBLIN ❧ O'BRIEN PRESS LTD ❧ 1976

We were more afraid of the Glimmer Man than we were of the war or a German or British invasion. Not even when Lord Haw-Haw, the German radio announcer, said that Ireland, which was the land of saints and scholars, would soon be the land of the skulls and crossbones, did we pay any attention to him. Sure, weren't we all ready and organised, right left and centre: gas masks, sand buckets, water hoses, the ARP, the LSF and the LDF, the 26th Battalion and the Construction Corps.

Every second girl was a Red Cross nurse and the big boys were ARP messengers with real steel helmets and an arm-band. Oh, we joked about 'Ireland's only hope', but, be jaysus, we were ready. The gas masks were well and truly tested as we stuck our heads down all the street shores. The hoses were used for watering the flowers in the garden and the buckets came in very handy for collecting horse manure around the roads.

A man told us one day that it was the only way we could make money—by following the horses. A bucketful of fresh manure would fetch fourpence from any true gardener. Now and again we ran into a little bit of trouble, when the ARP suddenly called a fire-drill display or exercise and we might have to run from house to house.

'Have ye the bucket, missus?' 'No, missus, no. The RED bucket, the WAR bucket, the bloody ARP bucket...' The hose and pump were nearly as bad. It was always lost or lent to someone who forgot who he gave it to. There was the ARP all ready to go into service and we couldn't find the hose and pump. One man came to his door to ask us: 'Did yiz know there's a war on?' He told us not to be codding ourselves with buckets and hoses. 'If the Jerries drop a bomb here,' he said, 'it's not first-aid, but last aid of holy water and rosary beads yiz will be needing'.

We weren't official ARP messengers: we were too young, but we always moved into the action without being asked. I suppose we were more of a hindrance than a help, but we did manage to find the bucket, hose and pump and believed that we were doing our bit.

I tried to join the ARP messengers but the man sent me home: 'You're too small and skinny and you can't even use a telephone' he said. During the test I put the speaking part to my ear and the hearing part to my mouth. My brother was a messenger and every night he went to bed with his helmet and armband hanging on the bed-post in case of emergency. When I was sure he was asleep I used to get out of bed and put on the steel helmet and armband, look at myself in the wardrobe mirror and then sit at the bedroom window, waiting for German planes to drop bombs. When, however, the bombs fell in the Phoenix Park, the South Circular Road and the North Strand, I was fast asleep in bed.

'Diya know there's a war on?' became the familiar saying as ration books, black bread and a half-ounce of tea per person per week were all you got. The rich people could buy a lot on the black market, but the poor people had to soldier on, on rations. The shop in the Coombe sold a pound of tea for a Pound Note. That was a lot of money to pay in those days and whenever I was sent for it by the lady in the big house, she always gave me sixpence for myself. When I said to the woman in the shop one day: 'It's very dear,' she said: 'Diya know there's a war on, and I had to go to India meself for it!'

Everything was scarce or rationed. The shortage of petrol brought out horses, donkeys, mules, jinnets and bikes of every description. Some motor vans were run on charcoal and others on gas balloons. The bike or the horse became the safest and surest way of travelling as the charcoal or gas motors were liable to break down without notice. In winter-time, the forge in Dolphin's Barn did a roaring trade, putting frost nails on the horses' hooves. Cigarettes were another problem and the 'No cigarettes' sign appeared on many shop counters or windows. 'Get them from under the counter' we'd roar, and run out of the shop banging the door.

Two of the best places for giving out cigarettes to everyone were Brendan Hyland, of Suir Road, and Carthy's, of Errigal Road, Drimnagh.

People came from all over Dublin to these two shops to stand in the queue and get their rations on Fridays and Saturdays. Foreign cigarettes began to appear, with all sorts of names: *Yanks, Lucky Strike, State Express, 333* or *555*. Sailors coming into Dublin Port also brought their supply of black Russian, French and Dutch cigarettes, but none were a patch on the old coffin nail *Woodbines*—ten for fourpence or five for twopence. Instead of putting up the price of the tuppeny packet, Wills made a smaller packet and now it was four for twopence; the five packet disappeared. The five Players packet for threepence-ha'penny also disappeared and *Sweet Afton* coupons were no longer free, but cost a ha'penny each and of course cigarette pictures vanished like the snow before the sun.

Air raid shelters were built all over the city. These were long stone huts which later came in handy for courting until they were turned into dry toilets and finally torn down. Newspapers were confined to one page and if anything unusual happened the stop press newspaper appeared. Everyone bought the stop press, but I can't remember any of the reports carried. The ARP issued booklets on how to make your own air raid shelter in the back garden and what to do if an air raid took place. I suppose the rich had their own ones built, but we were told the safest place was in the coal hole under the stairs.

Nearly everyone had a vegetable plot, even the Polo Ground in the Phoenix Park was turned into plots and other parts of the Park were used for coal and turf dumps. Every Sunday, volunteers went to the mountains to cut hard-won turf. The slogan 'Don't close down: switch off' also became a familiar one and the *Dublin Opinion* magazine commented that Radio Eireann should switch off and close down. Gas was also rationed, only to be used at certain peak hours and people were warned not to use the glimmer. The glimmer was a very small jet of gas that came through the pipes during the switch-off period. It would take the glimmer nearly an hour or more to boil a kettle of water. Sure, God love the poor women, dying for a hot cup of *Shell Cocoa, Bovril, Oxo* cube or tea, if they were lucky enough to have it, and so the Gas Company sent out inspectors to ensure that the gas was not being used during the off-period. These inspectors became known as the Glimmer Men. It was easy at first to spot them, as they all rode Gas Company bikes which were painted orange. You'd see the bikes a mile away. The billy (warning) would go from street to street and road to road—'Look out, Missus, here's the Glimmer Man.' Buckets of water, wet towels and even the ice and snow in the back garden would be placed on the gas jets to banish the heat, as the Glimmer Men tested the jets by putting their hands on them to see if they felt warm. There must have been many Glimmer Men with burnt hands in Inchicore, Goldenbridge, Kilmainham and other parts of Dublin. Many's the day I kept nix (look-out) for the Glimmer Man. Those who could afford it built little brick fires in their back gardens to boil their kettles and pots, but the vast majority used the glimmer.

One day I was told to stand at the front gate and if I saw the Glimmer Man to rattle the gate latch. After an hour or so a man on a black bike stopped at the gate. 'Where's Anner Road?' he asked. I told him it was the second turn on the right. As he was about to cycle away, he asked me who I was waiting on. I told him I was keeping nix and that if I saw the Glimmer Man I was to rattle the gate latch.

'Well, you can rattle away,' said he, 'because I'm the Glimmer Man.' Just imagine, disguising the bloody bike, painting the orange colour black!

JOHN MITCHEL

Jail Journal

27 May 1848

DUBLIN ❧ M.H. GILL AND SON LTD

REPRINTED FROM *THE CITIZEN*, MITCHEL'S FIRST NEW YORK
NEWSPAPER, 14 JANUARY–19 AUGUST 1854 ❧ BOUND COPY

27 MAY 1848

On this day, about four o'clock in the afternoon, I, John Mitchel, was kidnapped, and carried off from Dublin, in chains, as a convicted 'Felon'.

I had been in the Newgate prison for a fortnight. An apparent *trial* had been enacted before twelve of the castle jurors in ordinary—much legal palaver, and a 'conviction' (as if there were *law, order, government* or *justice* in Ireland). Sentence had been pronounced, with much gravity, by that ancient Purple Brunswicker, Baron Lefroy— *fourteen years' transportation*; and I had returned to my cell and taken leave of my wife and two poor boys. A few minutes after they had left me a gaoler came in with a suit of coarse grey clothes in his hand. 'You are to put on these,' said he, 'directly.' I put them on directly. A voice then shouted from the foot of the stairs, 'Let him be removed in his own clothes'; so I was ordered to change again, which I did. I asked to what place I was to be removed. 'Can't tell,' said the man. 'Make haste.' There was a travelling bag of mine in the cell, containing a change of clothes; and I asked whether I might take it with me. 'No; make haste.' 'I am ready then'; and I followed him down the stairs.

When we came into the small paved court, some constables and gaolers were there. One of them had in his hand a pair of iron fetters; and they all appeared in a hurry, as if they had some very critical neck-or-nothing business in hand; but they might as well have taken their time and done the business with their usual unconcerned and sullen dignity of demeanour.

I was ordered to put my foot upon a stone seat that was by the wall; and a constable fastened one of the bolts upon my ankle. But the other people hurried him so much that he said quickly, 'Here, take the other in your hand, and come along.' I took it, and held up the chain which connected the two, to keep it from dragging along the pavement, as I followed through the hall of the prison (where a good many persons had gathered to see the vindication of the 'law') and so on to the outer door. I stood on the steps for one moment, and gazed round: the black police-omnibus—a strong force of the city constabulary occupying the street on either side; outside of them dark crowds of people, standing in perfect silence; parties of cavalry drawn up at the openings of the streets hard by. I walked down the steps; and amidst all that multitude the clanking of my chain was the loudest sound. The moment I stepped into the carriage the door was dashed to with a bang. Someone shouted, 'To the North Wall!' and instantly the horses set forward at a gallop. The dragoons, with drawn sabres, closed both in front and rear and on both sides; and in this style we dashed along, but not by the shortest, or the usual way to the North Wall, as I could see through a slit in the panel. The carriage was full of police-constables. Two of them, in plain clothes, seemed to have special charge of me, as they sat close by me, on right and left, one of them holding a pistol with a cap on the nipple. After a long and furious drive along the North Circular road, I could perceive that we were coming near the river. The machine suddenly stopped, and I was ushered to the quay-wall between two ranks of carbineers, with naked swords. A Government steamer, the *Shearwater*, lay in the river, with steam up, and a large man-of-war's boat, filled with men armed to the teeth, was alongside the wall. I descended the ladder with some difficulty, owing to the chain, took my seat beside a naval officer, who sat in the stern, and a dozen pulls brought us to the steamer's side. A good many people who stood on the quay and in two or three vessels close by, looked on in silence. One man bade God bless me; a police inspector roared out to him that he had better make no disturbance.

As soon as we came on board, the naval officer who had brought me off, a short, dark man of five-and-forty or thereabouts, conducted me to the cabin, ordered my fetters to be removed, called for sherry and water to be placed before us, and began to talk. He told me I was to be brought to Spike Island, a convict prison in Cork Harbour, in the first place; that he himself, however, was only going as far as Kingstown, where his own ship lay; that he was Captain Hall, of the *Dragon* steam-frigate; and that he dared to say I had heard of the unfortunate *Nemesis*. 'Then,' quoth I, 'you are the Captain Hall who was in China lately, and wrote a book.' He said he was, and seemed quite pleased. If he had a copy of his work there, he said he should be most happy to present it to me. Then he appeared apprehensive that I might confound him with Captain Basil Hall. So he told me that he was not Basil Hall, who in fact was dead; but that though not actually Basil Hall, he had sailed with Basil Hall, as a youngster, on board the *Lyra*. 'I presume,' he said, 'you have read his voyage to the Loo Choo Islands.' I said I had, and also another book of his which I liked far better: his 'Account of the Chilian and Peruvian Revolutions,' and of that splendid fellow, San Martin. Captain Hall laughed. 'Your mind,' said he, 'has been running upon revolutions.' 'Yes, very much—almost exclusively.' 'Ah, sir!' quoth he, 'dangerous things, these revolutions.' Whereto I replied, 'You may say that.' We were now near Kingstown Pier, and my friend, looking at his watch, said he should still be in time for dinner; that he was to dine with the Lord Lieutenant; that he had been at a review in the Park this morning, and was suddenly ordered off to escort me with a boat's crew from the *Dragon*; further, that he was sorry to have to perform such a service; and that he had been credibly informed my father was a very good man. I answered I know not what. He invited me to go with him upon deck, where his crew were preparing to man the boat; they were all dressed like seamen, but well armed. I pointed to them, and asked, 'Are those fellows marines?' He looked at me with a peculiar smile—'Well, come now, they *are* marines.' He was evidently amazed at my penetration in detecting marines without their uniform (I had asked the question in mere ignorance and absence of mind); 'but,' he quickly added, 'our marines are all seamen.' 'I suppose so,' quoth I.

Captain Hall, of the *Dragon*, now bade me good evening, saying he should just have time to dress for dinner. I wished him a good appetite, and he went off to his ship. No doubt he thought me an amazingly cool character; but God knoweth the heart. There was a huge lump in my throat all the time of this bald chat, and my thoughts were far enough away from both Peru and Loo Choo. At Charlemont Bridge, in Dublin, this evening, there is a desolate house—my mother and sisters, who came up to town to see me (for the last time in case of the worst)—five little children, very dear to me; none of them old enough to understand the cruel blow that has fallen on them this day, and above all—above all—my wife.

What will they do? What is to become of them? By this time, undoubtedly, my office, my newspaper, types, books, all that I had, are seized on by the Government burglar. And then they will have to accept that public 'tribute'—the thought of which I abhor. And did I not know this? And knowing it, did I not run all the risk? Yes; and I did well. The possible sacrifice indeed was terrible; but the enterprise was great, and was needful. And, moreover, that sacrifice shall not have been made in vain. And I know that my wife and little ones shall not want. He that feedeth the young ravens—but then, indeed, as I remember, young ravens and other carrion-birds have been better fed in Ireland than the Christians, these latter years.

After all, for what has this sacrifice been made? *Why* was it needful? What did I hope to gain by this struggle with the enemy's 'Government', if successful? What, if unsuccessful? What *have* I gained? Questions truly which it behoves me to ask and answer on this evening of my last day (it may be) of civil existence. Dublin City, with its bay and pleasant villas—city of bellowing slaves—villas of genteel dastards—lies now behind us, and the sun has set behind the peaks of Wicklow, as we steam past Bray Head, where the Vale of Shanganagh, sloping softly from the Golden Spears, sends its bright river murmuring to the sea. And I am on the first stage of my way, faring to what regions of unknown horror? And may never, never—never more, O, Ireland?—my mother and queen!—see vale, or hill, or murmuring stream of thine. And *why*? What is gained?

GEORGE MOORE

Hail and Farewell

LONDON ❧ WILLIAM HEINEMANN ❧ 1911

One of Ireland's many tricks is to fade away to a little speck down on the horizon of our lives, and then to return suddenly in tremendous bulk, frightening us. My words were: 'In another ten years it will be time enough to think of Ireland again.' But Ireland rarely stays away so long. As well as I can reckon, it was about five years after my meditation in the Temple that W.B. Yeats, the Irish poet, came to see me in my flat in Victoria Street, followed by Edward. My surprise was great at seeing them arrive together, not knowing that they even knew each other; and while staring at them I remembered they had met in my rooms in King's Beach Walk. But how often had Edward met my friends and liked them, in a way, yet not sufficiently to compel him to hook himself on to them by a letter or a visit? He is one of those self-sufficing men who drift easily into the solitude of a pipe or a book; yet he is cheerful, talkative, and forthcoming when one goes to see him. Our fellowship began in boyhood, and there is affection on his side as well as mine, I am sure of that; all the same he has contributed few visits to the maintenance of our friendship. It is I that go to him, and it was this knowledge of the indolence of his character that caused me to wonder at seeing him arrive with Yeats.

Perhaps seeing them together stirred some fugitive jealousy in me, which passed away when the servant brought in the lamp, for, with the light behind them, my visitors appeared a twain as fantastic as anything ever seen in Japanese prints—Edward great in girth as an owl (he is nearly as neckless), blinking behind his glasses, and Yeats lank as a rook, a-dream in black silhouette on the flowered wall-paper.

But rooks and owls do not roost together, nor have they a habit or an instinct in common. 'A mere doorstep casualty', I said, and began to prepare a conversation suitable to both, which was, however, checked by the fateful appearance they presented, sitting side by side, anxious to speak, yet afraid. They had clearly come to me on some great business! But about what, about what? I waited for the servant to leave the room, and as soon as the door was closed, they broke forth, telling together that they had decided to found a Literary Theatre in Dublin; so I sat like one confounded, saying to myself: 'Of course they know nothing of Independent Theatres', and, in view of my own difficulties in gathering sufficient audience for two or three performances, pity began to stir in me for their forlorn project. A forlorn thing it was surely to bring literary plays to Dublin!... Dublin of all cities in the world!

'It is Yeats', I said, 'who has persuaded dear Edward', and looking from one to the other, I thought how the cunning rook had enticed the profound owl from his belfry—an owl that has stayed out too late, and is nervous lest he should not be able to find his way back; perplexed, too, by other considerations, lest the Dean and Chapter, having read of the strange company he is keeping, may have, during his absence, bricked up the entrance to his roost.

As I was thinking these things, Yeats tilted his chair in such dangerous fashion that I had to ask him to desist, and I was sorry to have to do that, so much like a rook did he seem when the chair was on its hind legs. But if ever there was a moment for seriousness, this was one, so I treated them to a full account of the Independent Theatre, begging them not to waste their plays upon Dublin.

'It would give me no pleasure whatever to produce my plays in London', Edward said. 'I have done with London'.

'Martyn would prefer the applause of our own people,' murmured Yeats, and he began to speak of the by-streets, and the lanes, and the alleys, and how one feels at home when one is among one's own people.

'Ninety-nine is the beginning of the Celtic Renaissance', said Edward.

'I am glad to hear it: the Celt wants a renaissance, and badly; he has been going down in the world for the last two thousand years'.

'We are thinking', said Yeats, 'of putting a dialogue in Irish before our play ..."Usheen and Patrick".'

'Irish spoken on the stage in Dublin! You are not –'

Interrupting me, Edward began to blurt out that a change had come, that Dublin was no longer a city of barristers, judges, and officials pursuing a round of mean interests and trivial amusements, but the capital of the Celtic Renaissance.

'With all the arts for crown—a new Florence', I said, looking at Edward incredulously, scornfully perhaps, for to give a Literary Theatre to Dublin seemed to me like giving a mule a holiday, and when he pressed me to say if I were with them, I answered with reluctance that I was not; whereupon, and without further entreaty, the twain took up their hats and staves, and they were by the open door before I could beg them not to march away like that, but to give me time to digest what they had been saying to me, and for a moment I walked to and forth, troubled by the temptation, for I am naturally propense to thrust my finger into every literary pie-dish. Something was going on in Ireland for sure, and remembering the literary tone that had crept into a certain Dublin newspaper— somebody sent me the *Express* on Saturdays—I said, 'I'm with you, but only platonically. You must promise not to ask me to rehearse your plays'. I spoke again about the Independent Theatre, and of the misery I had escaped from when I cut the painter.

'But you'll come to Ireland to see our plays', said Edward.

'Come to Ireland'! and I looked at Edward suspiciously; a still more suspicious glance fell upon Yeats. 'Come to Ireland! Ireland and I have ever been strangers, without an idea in common. It never does an Irishman any good to return to Ireland ... and we know it'.

'One of the oldest of our stories', Yeats began. Whenever he spoke these words a thrill came over me; I knew they would lead me through accounts of strange rites and prophecies, and at that time I believed that Yeats, by some power of divination, or of ancestral memory, understood the hidden meaning of the legends, and whenever he began to tell them I became impatient of interruption. But it was now myself that interrupted, for, however great the legend he was about to tell, and however subtle his interpretation, it would be impossible for me to give him my attention until I had been told how he had met Edward, and all the circumstances of the meeting, and how they had arrived at an agreement to found an Irish Literary Theatre. The story was disappointingly short and simple. When Yeats had said that he had spent the summer at Coole with Lady Gregory I saw it all; Coole is but three miles from Tillyra: Edward is often at Coole; Lady Gregory and Yeats are often at Tillyra; Yeats and Edward had written plays—the drama brings strange fowls to roost.

'So an owl and a rook have agreed to build in Dublin. A strange nest indeed they will put together, one bringing sticks, and the other—with what materials does the owl build'? My thoughts hurried on, impatient to speculate on what would happen when the shells began to chip. Would the young owls cast out the young rooks, or would the young rooks cast out the young owls, and what view would the beholders take of this wondrous hatching? And what view would the Church?

'So it was in Galway the nest was builded, and Lady Gregory elected to the secretaryship', I said. The introduction of Lady Gregory's name gave me pause ... 'And you have come over to find actors, and rehearse your plays. Wonderful, Edward, wonderful! I admire you both, and am with you, but on my conditions. You will remember them? And now tell

me, do you think you'll find an audience in Dublin capable of appreci-
ating *The Heather Field*'?

'Ideas are only appreciated in Ireland,' Edward answered, somewhat
defiantly.

I begged them to stay to dinner, for I wanted to hear about Ireland,
but they went away, speaking of an appointment with Miss Vernon—that
name or some other name—a lady who was helping them to collect a cast.

SIR WILLIAM ORPEN

Stories of Old Ireland and Myself

LONDON ❧ WILLIAMS AND NORTHGATE LTD ❧ 1924

The following little stories may help to illustrate what I feel
about 'criticism' in Dublin at that time, or the feeling of superiority its citizens had for all the outside world. 'Ourselves
Alone!' Alas! the thought brought lots of its best people to
nothing in the end.

There was a young man there then who showed promise as a
sculptor, and some of the great 'intellectuals' of the city took him up and
'ran him'—in fact, they ran him so hard that they got a subscription up,
and it rose to the enormous amount of something like £80! This was to
enable the young man to leave his wife and children and go to France,
Italy, and Greece for a year or so and study the great masterpieces of the
world in sculpture! I was in Dublin one August when this happened, and
the young man left on this great adventure. On returning to Dublin in
October I was surprised to meet him. Said I, 'What on earth are you
doing here?' To which he answered, in a tone which showed he thought
the question extremely foolish, 'And where else would I be?' 'But,' said I,
'I thought you had gone off to France, Italy, and Greece?'

'Oh, I did,' said he; 'but I only got as far as Paris and saw the Louvre,
and as I did not see anything there I couldn't do a damned sight better
myself, I came back to Dublin again!' Poor old Paris in this case was an
utter failure!

But the most amusing thing in Dublin then, in the picture line, was the work of a poet—a poet who was also an 'organiser', and I am told he had an excellent brain for the organising job; but I have also been told he was an excellent poet and also an excellent painter. But it is only with the latter that I dare to deal, and I have great admiration for his pictures if not taken too seriously. When I first knew him he was, as I have mentioned, 'organising' all the week—that is, all those parts of the week that the fairies left him alone; for they apparently appeared to him often enough to give him two fine subjects to be painted on each Sunday—one in the morning after eggs and bacon, and the other after a heavy midday dinner. These fairies, at least as he represented them, used to worry me. They were exactly like very badly drawn figures by Blake, and I used to wonder if fairies were the same all the world over—Celt fairies, Sassenach fairies, and all the lot, to far-off Honolulu. It would be so dull, if one saw fairies, to travel all over the world and find them the same, even were they as beautiful as those Blake depicted! Then a terrible thing happened to this artist and the fairies. Hugh Lane brought the French pictures to Dublin. Hi! presto! the fairies disappeared. Now, each Sunday produced two rather slimy canvases by a 'would-be' Jean François Millet. Yes, the heaviness of the earth, the men and women of toil, the sadness of everything— they were all attempted. Two each Sunday came regularly, and the people of Dublin bowed their heads and muttered, 'How wonderful!' Yes, J.F.M. had a good innings, but in the end he got played out.

Monticelli had a short time, and with him the poor fairies nearly got back to their own again. Then Renoir had an innings, and scored eight or nine runs (Sundays) freely. But the shade of Daumier came up and gave him a clip on the jaw, and he was 'outed', and we had numerous little Daumiers all playing about at some unascertainable game. After this I lost interest and count; but I suspect the list is still growing bigger and bigger; perhaps by now Winterhalter is at the wicket. I only knew one other painter who plied his trade by such means, but he was a Scotchman and he left the fairies alone. But this Irishman's work was taken quite seriously then by Dubliners, who would say at the same moment, 'Manet! Shure, he couldn't draw, far less paint, and he had no imagination at all! Manet a colourist? You're codding! Shure the man had no idea of colouring at all.'

Yet at that time there were, among the young of Ireland, men and women with the real gift and love of nature, together with the wish and energy to try to express their love both in line and colour—James Slater, Margaret Crilly, Bertie Power, Kathleen Fox, John Keating and young Touey, a lad with one hand, and I was told by a good artist lately that he is doing the best work in Dublin at the present time.

But don't imagine for one moment that they could sell their works in

Dublin then. No, the Dubliners preferred a £5 mock J.F. Millet any day. I hope all this is changed now, and that the people I have mentioned above are receiving some praise and money for their labours of love. We had some great years of hope and promise there, then the war came and we were all knocked apart, and Hugh Lane was drowned when the *Lusitania* was sunk. And impossible people began to rule art in Ireland once more, but now I hope all is changed for good once again.

Apart from the young artists of Ireland that I have already named, there was one who stood out alone—Beatrice Elvery, a young lady with many gifts, much temperament, and great ability. Her only fault was that the transmission of her thoughts from her brain to paper or canvas, clay or stained glass, became so easy to her that all was said in a few hours. Nothing on earth could make her go on and try to improve on her first translation of her thought. The thing was impossible; she was bored at the very idea. I remember some twenty years ago meeting an artist in London who told me he liked to start his pictures all wrong so that he could later give them the quality of correction. This is of course going a bit far; at the same time, if Beatrice Elvery had the art of criticising her own work and correcting the mistakes, I believe she would be a very considerable artist indeed. At present she is engaged in bringing up fine children for a good husband. I cannot believe she got as bored with them after their birth as with her thoughts. I remember meeting her in Dublin one morning and asking her to lunch with me. She said, 'Yes, but make it half-past one, will you? I have to do a large window this morning.' I called to take her out to lunch, and during those three hours or so she had designed a huge stained-glass window, three enormous 'panels' or whatever they call them; a hundred figures or so were in the design. I saw this window finished in glass some time later, and there was no particle of change from what she had put on paper that first morning in a few hours. It was an extremely good window, but with some glaring mistakes which would have been perfectly simple to set right. But that 'setting right' never did exist in her 'make up', bless her heart!

Then there were the Morrows, endless Morrows, all good fellows, especially poor Norman, who died. Also the three Gifford girls. Not forgetting for one moment Count Marcovitch, 'Cassie'. A certain world in Dublin centred round Cassie—an enormous man, but as gentle in body and mind as a child. He painted, wrote plays, kept his front door open all night in case any stray person might want food, drink, and a sleep. Oh, Cassie was a great fellow, a magnificent great man! Had he not won the Paris–Bordeaux bicycle race two years, and on one of the occasions with no tyre on one wheel for the last hundred miles? A formidable man to be up against. I only saw him have a 'little bit of bother' one night; but indeed it seemed to bother him not at all. It was one evening when the Christmas Pantomime was on at the Gaiety Theatre. Cassie and I were dining at Gogartys', and the conversation got on the subject of what one saw behind the scenes in a theatre. I was very interested, so Cassie took me about half-past ten to the theatre, and we went behind. I realised that the English manager of the company objected to our being there, but I thought nothing of it. The show over, we went upstairs to the bar, which in the Gaiety Theatre is rather a big room. Cassie ordered our drinks, and we were talking about things that mattered to us, when in walked the English manager, a man about six feet high and weighing about thirteen stone. He was, to say the least of it, rude to Cassie. He said we had no right to go behind the scenes and all that sort of thing. Cassie never answered a word. The manager got angry, lost his head, and showered abuse on Cassie's big head. Cassie took not the slightest notice, but tried to keep up his conversation with me. Then the manager lost control of his arms as well as his head, and with one fist struck Cassie full in the face. We were all petrified except Cassie, who very slowly started to take off his great double-breasted coat of broadcloth, and quietly said to me, 'I am sorry, Orpen, this has happened. Would you be so good as to hold my coat for a moment?' I took it. Cassie turned round on the infuriated manager and said very quietly, 'I believe, sir, you struck me!' No sooner were the words out of his mouth than the manager rushed at him, his fists whirling about. And now a strange thing happened. In one second, without any blow being struck, Cassie had both the man's arms twisted behind his back; then he walked him doubled forward across the room, pushed his head with considerable force against the wall, then let him go, and he subsided quietly to the floor. Cassie walked slowly back and said to me, 'I am sorry. I think you would better finish your drink. They may get the police in, so we would better make a move. I don't think there will be any trouble, as I am nearly sure I have not killed him; but one never knows. After all, he hit me first, and I never returned the blow. Anyway, they know my address here if I am wanted.' Then, turning to a group of friends of the manager, he said, 'I am sorry your friend lost his temper. You would better go and see to him now. But if any of you wish to be put to sleep in the same way, it will give me pleasure to do the same to you before I leave. Nobody? No! Well, good-night, gentlemen.' And out we went quietly into the slush of a winter night in Dublin. Where is Cassie? Rumours came he was in the Russian army, that he had lost a leg, then an arm. Since then I have heard nothing; but I trust all is as well with him as his great heart deserves.

FRANK THORPE PORTER

Gleanings and Reminiscences

DUBLIN ❧ HODGES, FOSTER AND CO. ❧ 1865

CARRIAGE COURT CASES—DUBLIN CARMEN

When I assumed, by an arrangement with my colleagues, the regulation of the public vehicles, and the disposal of complaints in the Carriage Court at the Head Office, I announced my inflexible determination to cancel the licence of any driver who was proved to have been drunk whilst in charge of his vehicle on the public thoroughfare. I required the fullest proof of the offence, to which I awarded the highest punishment. I am happy to say that such cases were by no means frequent, but there were some, and they generally occurred at funerals. A Rathfarnham carman was summoned before me and was convicted, not only on the clearest evidence, but by his own admission. He was about my own age, and I remembered that when I was about eighteen years old, I was one day swimming in a quarry-hole at Kimmage, where the water was at least twenty feet deep, and was suddenly seized with very severe cramps in my left leg. I kept myself afloat and shouted for help, but I was unable to make for the bank, when a young fellow who had been swimming, and was dressing himself, hastily threw off his clothes, plunged into the water and pushed me before him to the side of the quarry. He saved my life, and I now beheld him in the person of the convicted carman. I related the circumstance from the magisterial bench, and then cancelled his licence, and remarked to those who were assembled, that when I treated the preserver of my life so strictly, others could not expect the slightest lenity at my hands if they transgressed in the same way. The poor fellow left the court in great dejection, and when my duties for the day were over, I dropped in to my friend Colonel Browne, the Commissioner of Police, and mentioned the circumstance to him. He said, 'You cancelled his licence, but I can give him a new one, and he shall get it tomorrow.' The licence was accordingly renewed without causing me the slightest dissatisfaction.

Most of my readers are aware that the Richmond Bridewell, which is now the common gaol of the City of Dublin, is situated near Harold's Cross; and that on its front is inscribed, 'Cease to do evil. Learn to do well.' A carman named Doyle, who lived at Blackrock, was summoned before me on charges of violent conduct, abusive language, and extortion. He was a man of very good character, and the complainant was a person of the worst reputation, who had been convicted of several misde-meanours of a very disgraceful nature. Frauds and falsehoods were attrib-uted to him as habitual and inveterate practices. He was sworn, and then he described Doyle as having been most abusive and insulting in his language, as having threatened to kick him unless he paid much more than the rightful fare, and as having extorted an extra shilling by such means. The defendant denied the charges totally, and declared that the accusation was false and malicious. He then asked me to have Inspector O'Connor and Sergeant Power called and examined as to the complainant's character, and whether he was deserving of being believed on his oath. From my own personal knowledge of the complainant's reputation, I willingly acceded to the demand, and desired that the required witnesses should be called from the upper court, where they were both attending. Whilst we were waiting their appearance, Doyle made a speech; it was very brief, and I took it down *verbatim*; he said:

'Your worship, if I get any punishment on this man's oath, it will be a wrong judgment. The Recorder knows him well, and he wouldn't sintence a flea to be kilt for back-biting upon his evidence. He has took out all his degrees in the Harold's Cross college; and if, instead of sending me to the Cease to do evil hotel, you had himself brought there, the door would open for him of its own accord, for there is not a gaol in Ireland that would refuse him. He swore hard against me, but thanks be to God, he did not swear that I was an honest man, for there is nobody whose character could stand *under the weight of his commendation*.

On the evidence of O'Connor and Power, I dismissed the charge, and subsequently spoke of the case, and repeated Doyle's speech, in festive society. When Boucicault produced his interesting Irish drama of Arra-na-pogue at the Theatre Royal, I was one of his gratified audience, and was greatly surprised at hearing the speech which had been originally delivered before me in the Carriage Court by the Blackrock carman, addressed to the court-martial by Shawn-na-poste, to induce a disbelief of the informer by whom he was accused. I subsequently ascertained that it had been given to Boucicault by one who could fully appreciate its originality and strength, my gifted friend, Dr Tisdall.

The Dublin carmen are far from being faultless, but, as a class, I found them generally very honest. Whilst I discharged the carriage business, I knew instances of considerable sums of money and articles of value, which had been left in their vehicles, being brought in and delivered up to the police. I do not know how such property, if unclaimed, is now disposed of; but in my time, I invariably, after the expiration of twelve months, had it delivered, subject to charges for advertising, &c. to the person who brought it. I may mention one very extraordinary incident. Before the opening of the Great Southern and Western Railway, the Grand Canal Company ran passenger boats to the towns of Athy and Ballinasloe. A boat for the latter place left Portobello each day at two o'clock. A Rathmines man, who was owner and driver of a covered car, was returning home one morning about 11 o'clock, when he was hailed, in Dame Street, by a respectably dressed man, who engaged him to drive about town, and to be paid by the hour. The hirer stopped at several establishments and bought parcels of woollen, linen, plaid and cotton goods, as also a hat and a pair of boots, for all of which he paid in cash. There was merely room for the hirer in the vehicle along with his ample purchases. Finally, he directed the driver to go to Portobello, adding that he intended to leave town by the passage-boat at two o'clock. When the car arrived at the end of Lennox Street, the driver was ordered to stop. The hirer alighted and told the driver to go round by the front of the hotel and wait for him at the boat. The order was obeyed, and the carman waited until the boat started, but the hirer did not appear. The driver apprised the police of the circumstance, and, at their suggestion, he attended the two boats which left on the following day, but no one came to claim the goods. They were brought to the police stores and advertised, the hirer was described and sought for in various hotels and lodging-houses, but without any result. It was ascertained at the establishments where the parcels were purchased that they cost twenty-seven pounds, and the carman ultimately got them on paying some small charges. He had not been paid his fare, nevertheless he was not dissatisfied. A rare case amongst his fraternity.

A.M.W. STIRLING

Victorian Sidelights

LONDON ❧ ERNEST BENN LTD ❧ 1954

THE O'GORMAN MAHON

C harles James Patrick O'Gorman Mahon was born on St Patrick's day, 1800, the son of a squire in County Clare. Claiming descent from the ancient Kings of Ireland, he styled himself 'The O'Gorman Mahon'; and into his subsequent ninety-one years of life he packed sufficient adventures to have filled the lives of several ordinary men.

Six-feet-three in stature, with a singularly handsome face and a rare charm of personality, he was possessed of a fascination which, to friends and foes alike, was all-compelling. Bold and reckless as he was impulsive and hot-blooded, he fought duels at the smallest provocation, and it is not known how often the result proved fatal to his antagonist. 'It is less trouble to fight a blackguard than to argue with one!' he maintained; yet, when unprovoked, he was the gentlest, as he was the kindest of human beings. Meanwhile what he willed, he achieved. Even the fashion in which he imposed upon the world the unwonted prefix to his name affords a minor instance of his ascendancy over his fellows: 'There are only three beings in existence entitled to *THE*,' he announced in the House of Commons. 'The Pope, the Devil and The O'Gorman Mahon!'

One of The O'Gorman Mahon's early exploits was long remembered in Dublin. He was sent to Trinity College with an allowance of £500 a year from his father, and soon became notorious for his dare-devil pluck, his truculent temper, and his wild Irish patriotism. No escapade was too dangerous for him to attempt, no prank beyond his ingenuity to devise; he was recognised as a firebrand by both dons and students alike, and beloved and feared by all.

At that date the students were wont to forgather at intervals for gay and rowdy supper-parties, strictly forbidden by the Provost. Such festivities were usually called oyster-suppers because the chief course consisted of oysters, which were washed down by copious draughts of wine and whisky-toddy brought in by the servants. Rumours of these revels, however, reached the ears of the Dons, and they observed that the servants of the young men were bringing in water from the College pump during the bitter winter evenings—a fact suspiciously suggestive of the consumption of whisky-toddy, for in those primitive days of the early nineteenth century there was no water laid on inside the buildings and all had to be fetched from outside.

By order of the Provost, therefore, the pump-handle in Botany Bay Square was removed in the evenings, thus preventing any water being fetched thence after dusk. A meeting of furious students was at once convened, and they determined that, if they could not have their beloved whiskey-toddy neither should the dons have any. There was only one efficient reprisal—to blow up the pump bodily; and only one person with grit and initiative capable of achieving this—the dare-devil young O'Gorman Mahon.

The latter was delighted at the mission, and, having by some ingenious fluke possessed himself of the twelve pounds of gunpowder necessary for his purpose, on a stormy winter's night, deemed suitable for his escapade, he fared forth into the bitter darkness of a raging blizzard. Despite the blinding sleet which was falling fast and the piled-up ridges of snow which barred his progress, and in some places reached as high as the first-floor windows of the College, The O'Gorman struggled valiantly to his destination; and so successfully did he achieve his object that he not only blew up the pump with a devastating explosion which shattered every window in the vicinity, but was himself flung, bleeding and stunned, into the furthest precincts of the Square.

After a time, picking himself up and ready to laugh at his mishap, he battled his way back through the continuous blizzard, often crawling like a mole though the barriers of snow, till at length, exhausted, he reached the College and was hauled up to safety through a window by his fellow-conspirators. But his appearance struck them with horror for he was barely recognisable, blackened from head to foot, his burnt clothes hanging about him in shreds, and every vestige of hair, even his eyebrows and eyelashes, scorched from his scarred face.

Meanwhile the pandemonium which had ensued throughout the city was indescribable. For long the inhabitants of Dublin had been in dread of an invasion from the Fingalleons, and now it was concluded this had come to pass. Rumour reported that the Bank had been attacked—even that a massacre was actually in progress, and while distracted crowds ran shrieking through the snowbound, dark streets, the soldiers were called out to protect them from the imaginary onslaught.

Large rewards were subsequently offered for the discovery of the perpetrator of the 'outrage'; but this was never divulged to the authorities though all the students were in the secret. Meanwhile, injuries and exhaustion, as well as disfigurement kept The O'Gorman confined to his bed, since the obvious oddness of his appearance made anything else impossible if he were to escape detection.

He had hidden thus for some days when the door-knocker of his room sounded, and he next recognised the voice of his tutor, the Rev. Dr Sands, afterwards Bishop of Killaloe, who proceeded to enquire after his pupil and was informed by Rush, the servant of the latter, that all communication with the sick man was impossible: 'And,' added Rush with a fine touch of realism, 'I myself am obliged to speak low to your Reverence for my master is in the last stage of typhus fever, and orders are that no human being be allowed to enter!'

'Well,' rejoined the reverend divine shrewdly, 'you mention to the doctors on their next visit that I have had some experience of fevers of this description, and I strongly recommend to my pupil *immediate change of air!*'

The O'Gorman, hearing this message, decided to act upon it, and accepted a standing invitation to some friends. That night, much muffled-up and disguised, he departed to County Kildare, where he remained shooting and fishing till near the end of the term and till his hair had grown sufficiently for him to risk inspection.

W.B. YEATS

'Dublin Scholasticism and Trinity College'

UNITED IRELAND ❧ 30 JULY 1892

I am writing in the National Library, and as I look around me I see a great number of young men reading medical, mathematical, and other text-books, many of them with their notebooks open before them. Opposite me is a student deep in medical diagrams, and on my right is another with an algebraical work on the bookrest in front of him. And as the readers are to-day, so were they yesterday, and the day before, and the day before that again, and back as far as the memory of any frequenter of the library can carry him. The glacial weight of scholasticism is over the room and over all the would-be intellectual life of Dublin. Nobody in this great library is doing any disinterested reading, nobody is poring over any book for the sake of the beauty of its words, for the glory of its thought, but all are reading that they may pass an examination; no one is trying to develop his personal taste, but all are endeavouring to force their minds into the mould made for them by professors and examiners. What wonder is it that publishers complain that no book is bought in Dublin unless it be the text-book for some examination, that alone among the great cities of the United Kingdom Dublin is deaf to the voice of genius—deafened by the roar of politics on the one hand and lulled into the deadly sleep of scholasticism upon the other.

Let it be admitted that we are a poor nation, and must seize upon every chance of making 'an honest penny' out of intermediate examinations and college scholarships, even at the expense of much travail of the soul, much blinding and deafening of the personal inspiration that is or should be in every one of us, and of most dire delution of the whole man. Let this be admitted, and yet the explanation does not lie here, for half the energy we have given to covering the roads with bicycles and to all manner of muscular occupations would have made us both a reading and reasonable people. I know poor clerks in London who read the best books with entire delight and devotion, while here in Dublin countless numbers of fairly-leisured and well-to-do men and women hardly know the very names of the great writers of the day. Nay, further, they do not know the commonest legends or the most famous poems of their own land. Here in this very library, called National, there are Greek grammars in profusion and an entire wilderness of text-books of every genera and species, and but the meagrest sprinkling of books of Irish poetry and Irish legends. The library authorities are little if at all to blame, for they would get them if they were asked for. The blame is upon the teaching institutions which have given us scholasticism for our god.

SIR JONAH BARRINGTON

Personal Sketches of His Own Time
Personal Recollections

2 VOLS. 1827 3RD VOL. 1832 ❧ REPRINT
DUBLIN, CORK, BELFAST ❧ THE PHOENIX PUBLISHING COMPANY LTD

N othing can better shew the high opinion entertained by the Irish of their own importance, and particularly by that celebrated body called the Corporation of Dublin, than the following incident. Mr Willis, a leather breeches maker in Dame Street and a famous orator at the Corporation meetings, holding forth one day about the parochial watch, a subject which he considered as of the utmost general importance, discoursed as follows:—'This, my friends, is a subject neither trifling nor obscure; the character of our Corporation is at stake on your decision!—recollect,' continued he, 'recollect, brother freemen, that the *eyes of all Europe are upon us!*'

One of the customs of Dublin which prevailed in my early days made such a strong impression upon my mind that it never could be obliterated. The most magnificent and showy procession, I really believe, except those of Rome, then took place in the Irish metropolis every third year, and attracted a number of English quite surprising, if we take into account the great difficulty existing at that time with regard to travelling from London to Dublin.

The Corporation of the latter city were by the terms of their charter bound once in three years to perambulate the limits of the Lord Mayor's jurisdiction, to make stands or stations at various points, and to skirt the Earl of Meath's liberties—a part of the city at that era in great prosperity, but forming a local jurisdiction of its own, in the nature of a manor, totally distinct from that of Dublin.

This procession being, in fact, partly intended to mark and to designate the extreme boundaries of his lordship's jurisdiction, at those points where they touch the Earl of Meath's liberty, the Lord Mayor thrust his sword through the wall of a certain house, and then concluded the ceremony by approaching the sea at low water, and hurling a javelin as far upon the sands as his strength admitted, which was understood to form the boundary between him and Neptune.

The trade of Dublin is comprised of twenty-five corporations, or guilds, each independent of the other, and represented as in London by a common council. Every one of these comprised its masters, journeymen, and apprentices; and each guild had a patron saint, or protector, whose image or emblem was on all great occasions dressed up in appropriate habiliments.

For this procession every member of the twenty-five corporations prepared as for a jubilee. Small funds only were collected, and each individual gladly bore his extra charges—the masters and journeymen being desirous of outvying one another, and conceiving that the gayer they appeared on that great day the more consideration would they be entitled to throughout the coming three years! Of course, therefore, such as could afford it spared no expense; they borrowed the finest horses and trappings which could be procured; the masters rode, the journeymen walked, and were succeeded by the apprentices.

Every corporation had an immense carriage with a great platform and high canopy, the whole radiant with gilding, ribbons and draperies, and drawn by six or eight horses, equally decked and caparisoned, their colours and flags flying in all directions. On these platforms, which were fitted up as workshops, were the implements of the respective trades, and expert hands were actually at work during the entire perambulation, which generally lasted eight or nine hours. The procession, indeed, took two hours to pass. The narrow-weavers wove ribbons which they threw to the spectators—the others tossed into the air small patterns of fabric they worked upon; the printers were employed in striking off innumerable hand-bills, with songs and odes to the Lord Mayor.

But the smiths' part of the spectacle was the most gaudy; they had their forge in full work, and were attended by a very high phaeton adorned in every way they could think of, the horses covered with flowers and coloured streamers. In this phaeton sat the most beautiful girl they could possibly procure, in the character of wife to their patron, Vulcan. It is unnecessary to describe her dress; suffice it to say, it approached that of a Venus as nearly as decency would permit—a blue scarf covered with silver doves was used at her discretion, and four or five little Cupids attired like pages, aiming with bows and arrows at the ladies in the windows, played at her feet. On one side rode, on the largest horse which could be provided, a huge fellow representing Vulcan, dressed *cap-a-pie* in coal black armour, and flourishing an immense smith's sledge-hammer! On the other side pranced his rival, Mars, on a tawdry-caparisoned charger, in shining armour, with an immensity of feathers and horse-hair, and brandishing a two-edged glittering sword six or eight feet long, Venus meantime seeming to pay much more attention to her gallant than to her husband. Behind the phaeton rode Argus with an immense peacock's tail; whilst numerous other gods and goddesses, saints, devils, satyrs, etc., were distributed in the procession.

The skinners and tanners seemed to undergo no slight penance—a considerable number of these artisans being dressed up close in sheep and goat skins of different colours. The representatives of the butchers were enveloped in hides, with long towering horns, and rode along brandishing knives and cleavers!—a most formidable looking corporation. The apothecaries made up and distributed pills and boluses on their platform, which was furnished with numerous pestles and mortars so contrived as to sound, in the grinding, like bells, and pounding out some popular air. Each corporation had its appropriate band and colours; perfect order was maintained, and so proud was the Dublin mob of what they called their *fringes*, that on these peculiar occasions they managed to behave with great decorum and propriety.

I never could guess the reason why, but the crowd seemed ever in the most anxious expectation to see *the tailors*, who were certainly the favourites. The master tailors usually borrowed the best horses from their customers; and as they were not accustomed to horseback, the scene was highly ludicrous. A tailor on a spirited horse has always been an esteemed curiosity, but a troop of a hundred and fifty tailors, all decked with ribbons and lace and every species of finery, on horses equally smart, presented a spectacle outvying description! The journeymen and apprentices walked, except that number of workmen on the platform. St Crispin with his last, St Andrew with his cross, and St Luke with his gridiron, were all included in the show, as were the city officers in their full robes and paraphernalia. The guild of merchants, being under the special patronage of the Holy Trinity, could not, with all their ingenuity, find out any unprofane emblem, except a shamrock of huge dimensions! the three distinct leaves whereof are on one stalk. This, by the way, offered St Patrick means of explaining the Trinity, and thereby of converting the Irish to Christianity, and hence the shamrock became the national emblem of Ireland. The merchants had also a large ship on wheels, drawn and manned by real sailors.

This singular procession I twice witnessed; it has since been abolished, after having worked well, and done no harm, from the days of the very first lord mayor of Dublin. The city authorities, however, began at length to think venison and claret would be better things for the same expense; and so it was decided that the money should remain in the purse of the corporation, and a wretched substitute for the old ceremony was arranged. The lord mayor and sheriffs, with some dozen of dirty constables, now perambulate these bounds in privacy and silence—thus defeating, in my mind, the very *intention* of their charter, and taking away a triennial prospective object of great attraction and pride to the inhabitants of the metropolis of Ireland, for the sole purpose of gratifying the sensual appetites of a city aristocracy, who court satiety and indigestion at the expense of their humbler brethren.

PROCEEDINGS OF THE ROYAL IRISH ACADEMY

VOLUME XVIII ❧ SECTION C. NO. 10 ❧ 16 JULY 1910

PROCEEDINGS IN THE MATTER OF THE CUSTOM CALLED TOLBOLL, 1308 AND 1385
ST THOMAS' ABBEY V. SOME EARLY DUBLIN BREWERS, &C.
BY HENRY F. BERRY, I.S.O., LITT.D.

Read 25 April. Ordered for Publication 27 April. Published 16 July 1910.

So little is known of the medieval religious foundations of this city, as far as their early history is concerned, and so few and scant are the notices regarding the buildings contained within their precincts, that any additional record which throws light on them is of interest. The great abbey of St Thomas the Martyr, which today is only recalled in Thomas Street and the adjoining Thomas Court, was founded in the western suburbs in 1177, under royal auspices, by William FitzAudeline, 'dapifer' of King Henry the Second. It was dedicated to Thomas à Becket, the murdered Archbishop of Canterbury, and was set apart for the use of Canons of the Congregation of St Victor, a Parisian institution, the members of which were canons regular of St Augustine. King Henry and his son King John specially favoured the abbey, and made it an object of their bounty.

Students of the civic history of Dublin are familiar with two awards relative to the custom known as tolboll, which was a certain proportion of the ale and mead manufactured and sold by brewers and taverners in Dublin, claimed under royal grants by this abbey. These awards dated respectively 1524 and 1527, are enrolled in the *Liber Albus* of the Corporation, and will be found in Sir John Gilbert's 'Calendar of Ancient Records of Dublin,' vol. i., pp.178–189. They are also printed in the 'Miscellany' of the Irish Archaeological Society, 1846, vol. i., page 33. They arranged differences between the Abbot and Convent on the one part, and the Mayor and Bailiffs of Dublin on the other. The former had filed a bill of complaint, claiming that King John had granted them, for their own use, such measure of ale and mead as he himself was wont to have of the taverns of Dublin i.e. the tolboll of a gallon and a half of the best, and as much of the second brew, which they duly received, until they were hindered in their right by the city authorities. The arbitrators awarded that none of the brewers in the city at the particular time brewed sufficient to justify the proportion claimed being exacted. Henceforward the abbey was to have the tolboll of every brew of not less than sixteen bushels (each bushel being sixteen gallons), and of none under twelve bushels.

King Henry the Second granted this custom to the abbey for a particular charitable purpose, which purpose is not disclosed in the proceedings already mentioned, and which had, most probably, passed completely out of memory. Certain documents in a register of St Thomas's Abbey, now in the Bodleian Library, Oxford (Rawlinson Mss., B.499), to which my attention was recently called, make the King's purpose clear, and afford such an interesting narrative of the circumstances (hitherto unknown) attending his grant of the tolboll, and of subsequent proceedings connected with very early brewers and taverners in Dublin, that, as original material, unnoticed by any of our civic historians, they seem worthy of being brought under the notice of the Academy. One of the extant ancient Registers of St Thomas's Abbey reposes among the Haliday collection of Mss. within our walls; two others are in the Bodleian, one of which was edited by Sir John Gilbert, the second being that in which the documents under consideration are to be found.

At fol. 22 of this Register is an *Inspeximus*, dated 24th September, 1388, of the record and process of a plea in Chancery, between the King and Brother Thomas, Abbot of the House of St Thomas the Martyr, Dublin, in the ninth year of King Richard the Second (1385), which supplies the following details:-

King Henry the Second granted to the abbey three gallons of ale from every brew for sale in Dublin, so that the institution might find and keep sixty poor people and scholars, in food, drink and clothing, in a house called the King's Alms House, for ever; but Brother Thomas had ceased to supply such alms. Very little is known of the original buildings of this great abbey, and it is important to find that such an alms-house stood within the earliest precincts. From the date of the grant the abbey was pleaded to have continuously found support for poor and scholars, until Easter, 39 Edward the Third (1365), when such was withdrawn. Abbot Thomas admitted that Henry fitzEmpress had founded the house, and that his son John was seized of a right to three gallons of ale, etc., which he granted to the abbey for the use of the canons. He brought into Court the King's Charter, and it may be noted that the copy of the Charter in St Thomas' Register contains the names of two more witnesses than the printed copies. They are Roger de Maudeville and Adam Herforde. *Gilbard* Pypard of the Register appears as William, and Roger de *Playes* as Ilanes, in the printed copies. The Charter was executed at Orbec, in Normandy.

The abbot, taking his stand on this grant, demurred to the plea that King John had made it for support of poor people and scholars in the King's Alms House, or that he and his predecessors had supplied such support. Thereupon, Richard Glynnan, the King's sergeant, averred that King Henry's grant had done this, and that the abbey had supplied support until Easter, 1365.

The following jury was then empanelled:-

John Passavaunt,
Peter Wodere,
Nicholas Serjeant,
Roger Bekeford,
} formerly mayors of Dublin.

Thomas Maureward,
Robert Sergeant,
William Herdman,
John Drake,
} lately bailiffs of Dublin.

Richard Crux,
Robert Fitzleones,
} of the 24 Jurats, Dublin.

Geoffrey Lexestre,
Richard Corr,
} of the Commons, Dublin.

They found that King John, son of King Henry, gave to St Thomas's Abbey (as before) in support of the canons, and not for maintenance of scholars or poor people in the King's Alms House, but that King Henry the Second had made a grant to the abbey, for the purpose of certain scholars and poor people being supplied with food, &c. in said House. The jury further found that the then King's Alms House was erected by the abbot, &c. forty years since, but they have no knowledge at what time same was first constructed, because this was done before their memory.

They also found that the abbot and convent, sixty years before, of their mere will, supplied in said House, of their own alms, forty, sixty, sometimes thirty scholars, &c., more or less; without this that they, by reason of any gift of lands, &c. made to them, found or ought to find such scholars and poor people in food, etc. Being asked for what time before the said sixty years the abbey first supplied scholars and poor people in the King's Alms House, they say they have no knowledge, in as much as the abbey, before their memory supplied such in the Alms House of their own will, without being compelled of anyone, 'as from relation of their parents and other old faithworthy persons of said city of Dublin they often heard.' For want of repair the Alms House fell down about twenty years before.

The jurors also found that King John, before his said gift, was seised to take of every brew of ale and mead for sale in Dublin, 3 gallons, and that the taking of same was that custom which he was wont to have in the taverns, etc. In addition, they found that the abbey took this continuously from the time of the gift; and they often heard old men say that the abbey had right and title to what they claimed, by pretext of said gift.

Another document, which appears at fol. 27 of the ancient Register, contains a record of legal proceedings brought by the abbey against certain brewers in Dublin, with the result in each case. These proceedings, as a matter of fact, are earlier in point of time than those already considered, but it seems more convenient to have had the origin of the tolboll first described. The various pleas recited at length in them are of interest as affording an insight into the nature of such as were used in courts of law in Ireland at this early period.

In the octaves and quinzaine of St Martin, 2 Edward the Second (1308), John le Hore, William de Vylers, John Hayward, John de Castleknock, Hugh de Castleknock, Hugh Silvestre, Richard Ethnarde, Mabila Arnalde, John de Silleby, Elena de Donne, Joan Tyrell, Thomas Corlice, John Coliz, Robert Milton, William Cornewalleis, Robert de Trapston, Blissina Lotrix, Walter de Nangle, Juliana Honicode, John Sampson, William Botiller, William Callane, Roger Barboure, Walter Shermane, and William de Topishane (brewers and taverners) were attached at suit of the King and of the Abbot of St Thomas's, to answer wherefore they hindered the said abbot from taking the custom of ale and mead (in this case a gallon and a half) granted by King John, which were made in certain taverns in Dublin, from Tuesday next before the feast of the Nativity of St John the Baptist, 30 Edward I, to 20 October, 2 Edward II, whereby the abbot avers that he has lost to the value of £100. The defendants declared that they were not bound to answer, as under royal charters citizens of Dublin were not to be impleaded outside the walls of the city, or any plea arising within it; and the mayor, John le Decer, sought that the plea should be brought within the walls. The abbot replied that as this matter concerned the alms of the King's progenitors, and his own, being drawn away, it might be brought anywhere, and that the citizens ought to answer in any place at the King's will for trespass committed against him. The brewers were ordered to answer; and on this they said that the tenements they now hold were waste and uninhabited places in King John's time, so that neither the King and his progenitors nor the abbot and his predecessors could have taken the custom where the present defendants' tenements are now constructed, and they sought judgment. Robert de Trapston and Blissina Lotrix answer that they hold their tenements of a church; Walter de Nangle and Juliana Honicode, of an inn, which are exempt from such custom. The court held that as their tenements did not join with the said church and inn, they were liable.

John Sampson, William Botiller, William Callane, and John de Castleknock answered that the abbot was in seisin of the custom of ale without hindrance on their part; but as they never made mead for sale, he could not have been in seisin of it. In this instance, the abbot was adjudged to have made a false claim, and so he took nothing by his writ. The defendant John Silleby had died.

Finally, the court ordered that the abbot should recover against John le Hore, William Donne (representing Elena de Donne), John Tyrell, Thomas Coliz (Corlice), Robert Milton, William Cornewalleis, Roger Barboure, Walter Shermane, William de Topishane, Robert de Trapston, Blissina Lotrix, Walter de Nangle, and Juliana Honicode, the said custom to be taken in their taverns, made after the making of the said charter, with damages against them.

Later on, the jurors came before the Justiciar, and assessed the abbot's damages against John le Hore at half a mark; William de Vylers, two marks; John Hayward, two marks and four pence; Hugh Silvestre, two marks and a half; Mabilla Arnalde, two marks; Elena de Donne, twelve pence; Joan Tyrell, twenty shillings; Thomas Coliz, half a mark; Robert Milton, half a mark; William Cornewalleis, half a mark; Roger Barboure, two marks and a half; Walter Shermane, half a mark; William de Topishane, a mark; and Richard Ethnarde, two marks and a half.

It will have been observed that several of the defendants were females; and in this connection it is remarkable that an enactment specially dealing with female brewers is found among the 'Laws and Usages of the City of Dublin,' enrolled in the *Chain Book* of the Corporation.

IRISH INDEPENDENT

VOL. 75. NO.57 ❧ TUESDAY 8 MARCH 1966.

Central Dublin Rocked by Explosion
NELSON PILLAR BLOWN UP
Gardai search rubble for possible victims

With a shattering explosion that rocked central Dublin, the controversial Nelson Pillar in O'Connell Street was blasted by explosives shortly before 2 a.m. today.

The explosion split the 121 ft high column half way up and toppled the 13 ft statue of Nelson which was blown off with the broken column.

Gardai and firemen searched furiously through the rubble which blocked O'Connell Street after the explosion, as it was feared that some people had been buried underneath.

Every available Garda and fireman in the city rushed to the scene, which resembled a battlefield.

Det. Chief Supt Bernard McShane was summoned from his home at Griffith Avenue to take charge of the investigations. Special Branch detectives were also called in.

WINDOWS SHATTERED

Shop windows were shattered in nearby Henry Street and North Earl Street. Pieces of masonry from the Pillar were showered into O'Connell Street and neighbouring streets.

The time of the explosion was pinpointed for Gardai by the CIE clock on the kiosk at the Pillar, which stopped at between 1.32 and 1.33 a.m.

The luckiest man alive in Dublin today is taximan *Stephen Maugham*, of 29 Shantalla Road, who was stopped at the traffic lights at the Pillar. The lights turned green and just as he was about to move off, he heard the blast and saw a cloud of rocks falling towards him.

'I was going to the Rotunda Hospital for a sample of blood for the Blood Bank,' he said. 'The lights were red when I got to the Pillar. I was waiting to move off. The lights turned green. I was moving off and I heard a terrific bang.

'LIKE THUNDER'

'There was an almighty flash and a sound like a clap of thunder. I had just time to get out. I accelerated into the street. The rocks were falling on my car and it was badly damaged.

'If the lights had not turned green at that precise moment I would have been killed. It was the luck of God.'

Shortly after 2 a.m. the Army Bomb Disposal Unit from Cathal Brugha Barracks was called out as Gardai feared another explosive might have been laid at the Pillar and had not gone off. A large crowd which had gathered by this time was kept a safe distance away by the police.

Mr Kevin Dunne, 10 Oakley Road, Blackrock, the manager of the Greenbeats Showband, which was playing in the Metropole Ballroom, had just left the dance. He was driving along O'Connell Street in a car with his girl friend.

COVERED IN DUST

'I was about 100 yards away going towards the Pillar. I heard a bang but I saw no flash. Then I realised I was covered in dust and I saw the roadway in front of me covered in rocks. I did not see anybody in the vicinity.'

Two girls, *Brenda Moore* and *Angela Martin*, both of Sheriff St were walking in Earl St, about 100 yards from the Pillar.

'We had just walked away from the Pillar a few minutes. We were about 100 yards down Earl Street when we heard a terrible explosion. It shook the footpath. We looked back and the Pillar was gone. The place was littered with rocks.'

Police were inclined to believe that the explosive was placed by experts. The explosion, it was stated 'went straight up,' causing the minimum of damage to surrounding property. If it had been inexpertly laid, a spokesman said: 'I dread to think of the havoc it would have caused within a mile radius.'

Eddie Gormley, of Coulson Avenue, Rathgar, was bringing a passenger home in his car. 'I was driving down O'Connell Street. I heard a deafening explosion and then I saw the rocks flying right, left and centre,' he said.

WILLIAM BOLGER
AND BERNARD SHARE

And Nelson On His Pillar

DUBLIN ❧ NONPAREIL, HERBERT PLACE ❧ 1968

A t 1.32 a.m. on the morning of Tuesday, 8 March 1966, the top of Nelson Pillar in O'Connell Street, Dublin was blown off by persons still officially unknown. The explosion ended a controversy that had waxed and waned ever since the proposal to honour the hero of Trafalgar was first mooted. 'The statue of Nelson records the glory of a mistress and the transformation of our Senate into a discount office', fulminated the *Irish Magazine* in September 1809. 'The life and work of the people who erected it are part of our tradition. I think we should accept the whole part of this nation and not pick and choose. However, it is not a beautiful object', said Senator W.B. Yeats a century and a bit later. 'Give him another arm and call him by another name—Robert Emmet perhaps,' suggested Padraig Colum. 'One of the finest Doric Columns in existence', claimed the Arts Council.

Francis Johnston, who built the GPO, was the consulting architect, though William Wilkins was usually given the credit, or otherwise, for the design. As the records show, the original concept was not carried out. The statue itself was the work of Thomas Kirk, a Scotsman who lived in Cork. The Pillar was of black limestone faced with Co. Wicklow granite. The statue was of Portland Stone, 13 feet high. The top of the statue was 134 feet 4 inches above street level.

For good or ill, Admiral Horatio Nelson dominated the principal thoroughfare of Ireland's capital city for 157 years. In his place there is now a *lieu vague* known to the man at the bus stop as An Lár. An Lár evokes few emotions, except perhaps that of bewilderment on the part of the unadvised visitor. Nelson, in his curious alien way, acted as a focus for the divergent views of Dubliners through a period of radical political and social change. To record those views in exhaustive detail is a labour we are happy to leave to an historian with a burning determination to remain unread. Nor do we attempt to provide answers to the enigmas which still surround both the rise and fall of the Doric abacus. What became of the coins which are alleged to have been buried under the foundation stone? Is it (or was it) Nelson Pillar or Nelson's Pillar? These and other problems we gladly consign to more curious readers

Nor does the following record make any claim to be impartial. The early sources are heavily Government-orientated. We have not recorded the resolutions tabled at Dublin Corporation meetings in August 1948, December 1953, November 1955, March 1956, and January 1960, nor the proposal of Mr Michael J. Quill, president of the Transport Workers' Union of America to replace Nelson by a statue of President J.F. Kennedy. The candidatures of the Virgin Mary, Saint Patrick and Mr De Valera have equally gone unrecorded. We have aimed, however, within a small and assimilable compass to pay a guarded tribute to a one-eyed adulterer who in a palpable if paradoxical manner made Dublin very much his own.

EVENING CORRESPONDENT
Dublin, Tuesday 16 February 1808
Yesterday, according to previous notice, his Grace the Lord Lieutenant proceeded to lay the first stone of a monument of Irish gratitude to the memory of the illustrious Nelson.

On this occasion the vast assemblage of persons of every description—the crowds which thronged the street—and the beauty, fashion and elegance, which filled the windows of every house from Cork Hill to the Rotunda bore sufficient testimony how sincerely the Irish heart beat in unison with those feelings of grateful admiration which the Monument about to be erected was intended to record. The different military corps, and other bodies, which formed the procession, kept assembling at the Royal Exchange from eleven until about one o'clock, at which hour, the departure of his Grace the Duke of Richmond from the Castle was announced by the discharge of a cannon.

MARY BYRNE

Dublin Speak

DUBLIN PUBLIC LIBRARIES ❧ 1989

The North Strand is a part of the inner city of Dublin. A gateway to Sutton, Howth, Baldoyle, Portmarnock and Malahide, covering a small area from the famous Five Lamps to Newcommon Bridge. No doubt its history goes back as far as Brian Boru, who probably trod this path on his way to battle. I was privileged to live here for a few years, not in Brian Boru's time—I may add! My story began in May 1941—It was a lovely summer—lazy, hazy days for children to indulge their dreams along the banks of the Royal Canal. No hint of the impending disaster soon to bring death and destruction. Our house, No.15 Charleville Mall, looked out on the canal, framed by several large old trees. You could idle the hours away watching the swans, ducks, and pinkeens enjoying the unpolluted waters of their habitat. Or the Lock Gates being opened and closed by Mr Lynch to allow the barges through. These were drawn by horses guided by the 'Bargie Man'. The only blight on this picturesque scene was an Air Raid shelter at the top of the Mall. As evening approached on that fateful night we sat on the steps of our house, some of us children playing skipping or hop scotch or just chasing a hoop with a stick. All were hoping the lamplighter wouldn't come too soon for he was our signal for bedtime. As soon as he appeared and climbed up his little ladder and lit the street gas lamp we were called in for supper and prayers. Tomorrow was Saturday—great—no school—a lie on in bed. Alas, that was not to be.

Sometime after 1.00 a.m, we were awakened by a heavy thud. The droning of an aeroplane hovering overhead caused panic among us. Then a deafening explosion followed and we felt the house shake. The windows were shattered and the broken glass flew all over the beds and the floor. Father jumped out of the bed first and cut his bare feet on the glass. His cries of pain terrified us. 'Don't move' he shouted, as he searched for his shoes in the darkness. We could hear the cries of women and children, the exploding sounds of burst gas mains, the footsteps running by our house and the aeroplane still hovering overhead. Oh God, will he drop more bombs? Eventually when mother and father and the four of us children were ready we made our way down the stairs in the dark. When the hall door was opened it threw some light into the hall and we could see the damage to the walls. The splits were so wide you could put your hand into them.

On reaching the street, there was smoke all around us and the dreadful smell of burning rubber, timber, etc.. was everywhere. Looking up we could see the night sky brightly illuminated from the flames that were leaping skywards and the beams of the search lights crisscrossing the sky. People were running to and fro, not knowing where to go and not knowing if more bombs were still to come. Someone shouted that the hall in the basement of the Library had been opened up and we would be safe there. 'But what about the Air Raid shelter?' father said. 'No one knows who has the key' was the reply. We thought this was very funny and in the following years whenever the topic of the Air Raid shelter came up, everyone would laugh.

The hall was packed and people tried to settle down. They were shivering from the cold and some of them were still in their night attire. Neither did they have time to bring the gas masks we had been instructed to use in the case of emergency. The women started the Rosary and that went on through the night. The men went off to see where their services could be of use. Word came back that the Nuns in the convent across the road were serving tea and cakes, so mother sent me, being the eldest of thirteen to get the tea. Meanwhile some of the men came back to tell of the widespread damage and the many casualties. More than twenty dead, several missing, and hundreds injured. Some people were still trapped under the rubble of the demolished houses. All the dead and injured were laid out on stretchers on the sidewalk, some moaning and crying. People were running around searching for relatives. The emergency services were trying heroically to extricate people buried in the debris. The injured were rushed to hospital in ambulances, taxicabs and cars.

Father returned and despite his badly cut feet he told us how he had been able to help Mrs Grenville from the debris of her one-storey little shop. The roof had fallen in and she was trapped, so he got her out through the chimney—I felt so proud of him.

Dawn was breaking around 4.30 a.m, and by this time we were bored with prayers and wanted to see what was happening outside, so a few of us slipped out and headed for the forbidden area. Running down

William Street I felt an air of excitement with the other kids—no fear, as such—maybe we were too young to realise the seriousness of the situation. The roads were covered with slates, broken glass, and other debris. The overhead tramway lines were all down. From where we stood we could see the massive crater the bomb had made in the road. Garda, L.D.F. and Red Cross were still searching through the rubble for missing people and firemen were trying to put out the burning shops and houses. All the items found in the rubble were laid out along the road and it wasn't long before looting started. We exchanged all the 'tit bits' of news we had gathered with each other. One said that a man had looked out of the window and his head was blown off. Another said the explosion had shaken the canal and hundreds of rats were seen running all over the place. Hearing that all the Brown family were killed was very upsetting, four of them were children and we knew the eldest girl. By now I was beginning to feel a bit scared, so that I just wanted to get back to my parents. Reaction was finally setting in.

At the end of the day there were twenty-seven dead, three hundred injured and five hundred homeless. The government declared a public funeral for the victims, many of them children. My parents tried to go back to our house, but were told it was condemned. We were among the five hundred homeless. I remember wondering 'what will happen to us?', Where will we go?, The most of the homeless were sent to Dingle Road, and Swilly Road, Cabra West—a new frontier, a new beginning.

MAJOR E.S.E. CHILDERS RE AND ROBERT STEWART

The Story of The Royal Hospital Kilmainham

LONDON ❧ HUTCHESON & CO. ❧ 1921

BULLY'S ACRE AND ST JOHN'S WELL

Within the boundaries of the Royal Hospital is one monument of antiquity whose memories are specially varied and interesting. It is said to mark the last resting place of distinguished Irish chieftains who were slain at the battle of Clontarf, and amongst these are included Murrough and Turlough, the son and grandson of Brian Boru, who, next to Brian himself, are the popular heroes of the great victory. According to the Munster book of battles by MacLaig, Prince Murrough was buried at the west end of St Maignend's Church, a long stone, on which his name was written, marking his tomb.

There now remains but the shaft (about 10 feet high) of what must have been a large cross, which may originally have been the 'termon' or boundary cross of St Maignend's monastery.

This shaft is of coarse granite, and upon the western side of it is graven a true lover's knot, said to be an ancient emblem of eternity—sculpture of the eleventh century, not later—which can be readily followed by the finger or observed with the eye when the sunlight falls at a proper angle. Some letters or symbols are also apparent on the opposite side, but they have not yet been deciphered or explained.

At one time 'the cross of Kilmaynan by the bounds of the lands of Kilmaynan' served to mark the extent of the liberties of Dublin in this direction, as appears from a charter granted by King Richard the Second to the city. From thence the Mayor and his officers, in their annual progress, 'rode downward to Bow Bridge, passing under an arch of the same through the water of Cammock'—though 'for their more ease they sometimes rode through the Prior of Christ Church his lands.' Several references are also made to the 'great cross of Kilmainham' in various other documents relating to the city. Its site is now included in the Hospital cemetery so well known in the popular traditions of Dublin as Bully's Acre.

By an inquisition taken of the Priory of Kilmainham in the thirty-second year of the reign of Henry VIII, it appears that the Kilmainham possessions consisted of a messuage, called the Castle-House, three parks and an acre adjacent called the Bayl-Yard: as an office existed among the ancient knights called bailiff, it is thought that he had charge of that part where Bully's Acre is situated, and so corrupted to Bully from Baily. The ordinary derivation of the name is from its having been a place where pugilists decided their quarrels, and called from thence the Bully's Acre. It contains three acres and a half (old Irish measure).

The burying-ground which has earned this remarkable appellation will naturally be presumed to be notable for something else besides the presence of one historic monument. And it is so in fact: Bully's Acre has a history peculiarly its own.

It would appear to have been used as a repository for the dead since the time of St Maignend. What an interesting register, were it in existence, of Irish monk, Irish prince, Knight Templar, and Knight Hospitaller, who have there been laid to rest!

In the neglect of the Kilmainham lands which ensued upon their possession by the Crown, the ancient cemetery came more and more into use amongst those who reverenced the memories of the Abbey of St John. And when the Royal Hospital was erected this privilege of sepulchre within its bounds does not appear to have been interfered with.

The most ancient monument which is still legible is a simple head-stone inscribed 'Here lieth the body of Hive Hacket and Elizabeth Hacket who died the year 1652.' Who these worthies were is not known, but the stone goes to prove the preceding assertion that Kilmainham was used by the populace as a burying-ground, between the time that the last Keeper left the ancient Priory to its ruin in 1617, and its re-birth in its present form in 1680.

Besides the interest which consequently centred in Bully's Acre as their chief burying-place, many of the people of Dublin, as well as multi-tudes from other quarters, found a greater attraction there in the presence of a holy well. Across the junction of St John's Road with the Circular

Road there still sometimes flows from Bully's Acre a tiny stream. It indicates the whereabouts of the springs which supplied the well of St John— 'the Siloam of Kilmainham once,' says Burton, 'now a neglected rill. Beside it in days of yore, the Asiatic templar spake of Jerusalem, and laved his hands.'

In the month of June, 1737, a complaint was made by the officers of the Hospital that their grazing fields were rendered almost useless owing to the traffic through them to 'a well near Kilmainham frequented by numbers of superstitious persons'.

The feast of St John the Baptist occurs on the 24th June, and upon that day the waters of the spring were supposed to possess special virtues for the purification of sin and disease. It is moreover at the middle of summer, and if the weather were propitious scant shelter might suffice for the day or night. With a people at once gay, careless, and devout, the natural consequences followed. A scene of piety mixed with revelry, debauchery, and dissipation came to be exhibited year after year. 'The fields,' says the contemporary record 'are generally by day and night full of idle and disorderly people; the grass is trod down; the cattle stray.' At an alehouse, too, the Black Lion, erected by a man named Flanagan on the brink of the well, a roaring trade was doubtless carried on.

A way leading from the city had been opened across the north side of the Hospital lands for the convenience of the Earl of Galway, a Lord Justice, when he dwelt at Island Bridge. This, it was stated, had been made into a common thoroughfare, and afforded access for the multitudes into the fields near the well. Repeated attempts to stop it up proved futile. Walls and gates erected in the daytime were levelled by the populace at night. The plan was therefore adopted of farming out Bully's Acre and the adjoining fields. They were obtained by a dairyman and publican named Cullen, of Gallow's Hill. He contrived to exercise some kind of control over the lands, and exacted a fee of from 3d to 1d for each burial, according to the size of the coffin and the circumstances of the parties concerned; but of course he in no way discountenanced the gay vigils which tended directly to his own profit as a publican.

Things went on in this fashion until General Dilkes became Master of the Hospital in 1755. 'He endevoured,' says Sir John Traill, 'to put a stop to the pernicious nocturnal revels. He applied to the magistrates, who frequently attended and dispersed them, and he completely enclosed the burying-ground by walls. He levelled the graves and removed the headstones. This had the desired effect. The frequent compliments to departed friends, by decorating their graves with garlands, and the worshipping of Brien's supposed monument ceased. These objects of respect and adoration being removed, St John's Well lost much of its wonted powerful attraction, and the burying-ground remained perfectly shut up for some years.'

After this success, General Dilkes wished further to recover for the Hospital the control of the road which led through the fields to Island Bridge, and erected gates across it. But it had long been enjoyed as an open thoroughfare by the public. Men of property took up the popular cause. Subscriptions were raised, and the opinion of eminent counsel obtained. Application was made to the Grand Jury of the county, who presented that the gates were a common obstruction and public nuisance. This presentment was traversed by the Governors of the Hospital, but it was sustained by the verdict of the King's Bench. An immense multitude had waited the result outside the courthouse. Immediately it was made known, they set off with pickaxe and crowbar to vindicate their rights. But General Dilkes had already removed the gates in anticipation of any such proceeding. Being thus deprived of a much expected pleasure, the mob raised a cry of 'Down with the wall of Bully's Acre!' This work of destruction, at once so congenial to their instincts, and so agreeable to their prejudices, was soon completed. And thus Bully's Acre again became a common land and was devoted to the same incongruous purposes as of yore.

The burial ground, thus exposed and neglected, was soon in a fearful condition. In 1769, upon remonstrance from the Grand Jury of the county, the Governors ordered the walls to be rebuilt. This, however, could not be accomplished, owing to the determined opposition of the populace. General Dilkes' life was threatened, if the work were not stopped, and application was formally made, by the Governors to the Lord Lieutenant, for protection.

One serious attack appears to have been made about this time upon the Hospital itself. It was headed by the 'Liberty Boys,' a band of roysterers hailing from the Coombe. They burst in the western gate, which the sentry, alarmed at the formidable gathering, had continued to close, but not without being himself seriously injured. He gave the alarm, and the more active of the pensioners were speedily gathered and armed. Headed by General Dilkes, these proceeded down the elm walk to oust the rioters. 'What a mob will do knows no man, least of all themselves,' says one who studied their qualities. On the present occasion, however, they were opposed to men who had seen service at Dettingen, Minden, and the Heights of Abraham. A critical moment soon came. Finding his men assailed with all the dangerous, if primitive, weapons of lawlessness and threatened by an occasional musket shot, the General ordered his front line to fire. The leader of the rioters fell dead, and a number of others were wounded. A hasty flight of 'Liberty Boys' ensued. This unfortunate occurrence doubtless deepened the current of popular feeling against the enclosing of Bully's Acre, and it was eventually deemed more prudent to abandon the design.

No further attention was paid to the graveyard until the year 1795, when its woeful condition was at length again taken notice of by the County Grand Jury. They presented a sum of money towards the expenses of a new wall. The legal title of the Governors to the control of the disputed ground was investigated and declared perfectly valid. A better spirit prevailed in all quarters. The privilege of free burial was continued, but interments were placed under proper supervision. The wall was erected; the so called monument of 'Brian Boru' set up again; and a stone fountain provided on the edge of the South Circular Road for the waters of St John.

A few years later the body of Robert Emmet was buried in Bully's Acre. No headstone, no tradition, points out the spot of interment. There is some dispute, however, as to whether the grave was not afterwards opened and the remains conveyed to St Michan's.

The grave of another popular hero, of much humbler claims, but at one time of equal celebrity, is well distinguished. Few Irishmen past the age of fifty but were familiar in their youth with stories and ballads respecting Dan Donnelly. No spot on the Curragh of Kildare is better known than Donnelly's Hollow. For there the representatives of Ireland and England, namely, Donnelly and Cooper met in a far-famed pugilistic encounter, and the Irishman was victorious. When he died some years after, it was thought fitting by the multitude that he should be honoured with that grave and monument commonly supposed to be Brian Boru's. 'The tomb of Murrough,' says the better informed *Dublin Penny Journal* (1832), 'received the mortal remains of Dan Donnelly; and the victor of Clontarf and the victor of Kildare sleep in the same grave. We remember well his triumphal entry into Dublin after his great battle on the Curragh. That indeed was an ovation. He was borne on the shoulders of his people, his mother, like a Roman matron, leading the van in the procession, and with all the pride of a second Agrippina, she frequently slapped her naked bosom, exposed for the occasion, and exultingly exclaimed—"There's the breast that suck'd him!"—"there's the breast that suck'd him"!!!'

Bully's Acre was finally closed as a public cemetery in 1832. Whoever curiously examines the tombstones will observe how many date from that year. For in the frightful pestilence of cholera which then raged, no less than five hundred interments took place here within ten days. The ground having 'been for some ages the last home of the poor inhabitants of Dublin,' was thus so dangerously overcrowded that nothing less than madness could permit the continuance of burials. A notice prohibiting such was accordingly issued by the Governors of the Hospital.

The observance of St John's day at the Sacred Spring had, too, by that time, fallen into popular disfavour, and about 1844 the stone fountain erected in 1795 had to give place to the Great Southern and Western Railway. On the west side of the South Circular Road an arched recess in the wall still affords a supply of the once venerated water. It was constructed in lieu of the stone fountain, and was practically the last compliment paid to the virtues of St John's Well.

Separated from Bully's Acre by the Western avenue is the 'officers' burying-ground,' appropriated in accordance with its title. It was once used for all inmates of the Hospital. Its most ancient tombstone, which bears a legible inscription, reads thus: 'Corporal William Proby, who died 28th July 1700.' Burton speaks of him as 'a hero, by tradition, of Ormond's wars; a musketeer at Baggotrath; and after (sic) crossed Boyne's flood; wounded at Schomberg's side.' He had been only admitted to the Hospital seven weeks before his death. Space forbids further details of the other interesting memorials in this quiet and secluded spot –

'Where, like an infant's smile, over the dead
A light of laughing flowers along the grass is spread,
And grey walls moulder round, on which dull Time
Feeds, like slow fire upon a hoary brand.'

Two small enclosures on the northern side of Bully's Acre are enclosed by walls and set apart for the old soldiers of the Hospital. Beneath the simple mounds formerly marked by iron numbered tablets of shamrock form, and now by simple white marble headstones, they are laid to rest with military honours, as to each in his turn from age, wounds, or infirmity, is brought a last release.

May there long be found shelter and comfort in this Institution for those who have served, as they have done, the greatest Empire of the age.

CHARLES DALTON

With the Dublin Brigade

LONDON ❧ PETER DAVIES LTD ❧ 1929

For us in Ireland '1916' is only another name for the Rising of Easter Week. I was thirteen years old in that year, having been born in January 1903.

I was playing around my home in North Dublin on that Easter Monday, when I heard that the Volunteers had seized the General Post Office and other buildings in O'Connell Street, and that they had erected barricades across the streets leading to the positions they occupied.

The news of the Rising came as a great surprise to me, and I was most anxious to go into town and find out what was happening. When we sat down to dinner, my father told us that a party of Lancers had ridden down O'Connell Street, and that they had been fired on by the Volunteers, a few of the soldiers and horses being killed.

He said there would be terrible work now, and, perhaps reading my thoughts, he told me that on no account was I to go into town. He advised my mother to lay in provisions, and to buy two hundred-weight of flour.

'God knows how long this trouble will last,' he said. 'It may be a case of every ha'penny being needed to buy food.'

I had a ha'penny in my pocket, and I put my hand in and gripped it tightly, as I was greatly affected by my father's words.

After dinner, I went out again and found my playfellows, and we decided that it would be dangerous to go into the city. We could hear the sound of the firing. So we began to play cards. The boys all condemned the Rising; they called the Volunteers 'hot heads' and other insulting names. This made me very angry. However, at the cards—in which I had been rather unwilling to join after my father's words, fearing to lose my ha'penny—I had the satisfaction of winning and increasing my capital to two pence. It gave me greater satisfaction that I who was for the 'Rebels' had beaten those who were against them. I felt almost as if I were helping my heroes who were making the real fight not far away.

As the days passed, the noise of the guns grew louder, and temptation got the better of me, so that I decided that I would venture to find out for myself what was happening.

I had not gone very far towards the city when I found my way barred by a cordon of military stretched across the North Circular Road. They would not allow anyone to pass except those who had entered the city to get bread at the bakery. There were no deliveries of bread made at all during that week.

I felt that I should love to join the 'Rebels,' but the sound of the firing frightened me. If only I had been older I would have helped in the fight, because maybe then, I thought, I would not have been afraid of the terrible noise made by the rifles and machine guns.

I rambled along close to the military line, not able to tear myself away. I was greatly disgusted to see women coming out of the houses to give jugs of tea to the British soldiers. That picture remained in my mind for a long time.

On the fourth or fifth morning I was talking to my mother in her bedroom. All the younger children were there too, for some reason. Suddenly the windows shook with the noise of a deafening explosion. I thought the city was being blown up, and I found myself trembling. Then I heard my mother laughing. 'Look, Charlie,' she said, 'your hair is standing on end.' I was far too frightened even to smile.

What had happened? Everyone in our road ran to their hall doors to ask each other the same question, which none of them could answer. But they all expressed some opinion. One said:

'It is the artillery. The Rebels will all be killed now, and the fighting will be over. That will be a good thing, anyhow.'

Another said:

'It is the Germans landing at Howth to help the Rebels.'

The next day we learned that the explosions were caused by the gunboat 'Helga,' which had been brought up the Liffey to shell the buildings occupied by the Volunteers.

That night, when we were all, as usual, gathered together upstairs to say the Rosary, and to pray for the Volunteers, we did not light any lamps, thinking it too dangerous to show a light. In the dark, with the unaccustomed feeling it gave me of something solemn and mysterious I prayed with great fervour, beseeching God to let my heroes win.

When we had finished praying I looked out of the window towards the city, where my thoughts always were, and I saw the sky all lit up with a red blaze. We thought the whole city must be on fire. This sight added to my feeling that everything was changed; that all that was safe, familiar, and commonplace had disappeared.

We had to wait until the next morning to find out the meaning of it. A man who passed by our house told us that the General Post Office was in flames, and that the Volunteers had surrendered. He had seen them lined up on the footpaths, he said, with a military guard around them.

I was terribly disappointed at this news. I had hoped with my whole heart that the Volunteers would win.

LORD ARDILAUN

Souvenir of the Opening of St Stephen's Green as a People's Park

The Echo and Evening Advertiser

DUBLIN ❧ 1880

St Stephen's Green—Past and Present

There is nothing in this world on which Time does not lay his heavy hand for good or ill—generally the latter, since his crumbling, crushing weight invariably involves effacement or decay. In regard to St Stephen's Green this rule is now singularly reversed, for the very spot of ground voted by Parliament in days remote, to be a 'public nuisance,' is now a delightful, inviting, health-giving oasis, in a 'desert' of pain, and disease, and death! Certainly it is a wondrous transformation, and the manner in which it has been effected will elicit the thanks and admiration of generation after generation, until Time has produced his 'last man,' and sped away with him to the 'new earth' of which no man knoweth. And through the flight of time, and long after 'Arthur Edward Guinness' has seen the 'new heavens,' his name will be gratefully 'spelled out' on the monument he now refuses, but raised to his undying honour by a coming generation, when no modest hand can restrain the expression of a people's gratitude.

The most notable references to the past and present of St Stephen's Green, on the occasion of its opening as a People's Park are as follows:-

On the morning of the Twenty-seventh July at about half past nine o'clock, the gates of St Stephen's Green were unlocked, and the Green was thus, without any ceremony, thrown open to the public. The event was one of the most interesting that has occurred in Dublin for many a long day, and naturally it formed the chief subject of conversation in the city. The work of transformation within the Green has been carried out with extraordinary completeness, and those who walked through it must have been hard, indeed, to please, if they were not delighted with the artistic skill displayed in the way the ground has been laid out. From whatever point of view one looks at the work, the scene presented is extremely picturesque. The pretty bridge, the little cascade, the brook, and lake, and island form a charming picture or rather a number of very charming pictures. A broad ride encircles the interior, and from it branch off bypaths leading to shady recesses, pleasant walks, and resting places. A more delightful recreation ground could not be imagined—to see the little children playing there, and enjoying themselves to their heart's content, is a scene that poor John Leetch would have loved to sketch.

Indeed the advantages which the Green presents as a healthy resort for the humble people of the city, and their little ones, cannot be exaggerated. The entire cost of the work was about £20,000, and the annual cost of maintenance will be about £1,200, to be found through the Board of Works by the Treasury. It is difficult to give anything like an adequate description of the alterations that have been carried out through the very great generosity of Lord Ardilaun. It is just four years since he made the munificent proposal to the Corporation to effect, at his own expense the project of making Stephen's Green a public park. The matter having received full consideration, the Municipal Council ultimately agreed to accept the offer. A bill to enable the works to be proceeded with was passed in 1877, so as to constitute the Green as a public park, and since then the design has steadily progressed towards completion. Many reasons tended to keep back the work—one of the chief causes being the unusually severe winters of 1878 and 1879, which destroyed many valuable and beautiful shrubs that had been collected and planted after much trouble and expense. All difficulties, however, were successfully and quickly overcome, and, indeed, it is not too much to say that anyone walking through the Green will be struck with some surprise that so much has been accomplished within so short a time. Whoever takes the trouble to read a description of the appearance of this part of the city when the site of this noble Green was a rough field called St Stephen's, on which the Lord Mayor had 'the privilege of grazing a cow,' and when two hundred years ago this same field was for the first time made level and laid out in walks, will be amazed at the changes time has wrought in the district.

In a little book entitled *Ireland before the Union*, by Mr M.J. Fitzpatrick, the following interesting incidents are mentioned:- 'In these days the appearance of the Sham Squire was a familiar object. He was daily to be seen with Buck Whalley on the Beaux' Walk, in Stephens'-green.... During periods of more repose snipe shooting is said to have been carried on in the swamp in the centre of the Green. On the site of this gaiety, scenes presenting a contrast of the most horrible character were enacted. Women were butchered, and in some instances burned alive on Stephens'-green.

'*Hayden's Dictionary of Dates*, Eighth Edition, p. 650, states that a Mrs Herring was burnt alive on St Stephen's Green, on October 24, 1773.

'The cook of a bishop, who poisoned a numbered of persons, was sentenced to be boiled alive—the only execution of the kind on record, but the incident was not contemporaneous with the above burnings.

'*The "Beaux Walk"* described by the octogenarian Sexton, and the permanent presence of the great Buck, helped to make its environs quite a Rotten Row. A scarce publication "An Heroic Epistle to Richard Twiss, Esq." makes some reference to it -

When city belles in Sunday pomp are seen,
And guilded chariots troll round Stephen's Green.'

At the end of the last or beginning of the present century the King's troops, and volunteers were exercised in the Green. The railings enclosing it were erected at a cost of £10,000, and in 1852 it was drained, and for the first time gave evidence of its being utilisable for the cultivation of trees. Since then it has been mainly used by the inhabitants of the Green, the desirability of opening it to the public being again and again discussed, and four years ago decided upon.

The plans for the transformation effected were prepared by Mr Thomas, C.E., and it is said that many of the most attractive details were suggested by Lord Adilaun himself. Perhaps the most charming feature in the design is the clear and beautiful stream which flows along nearly the whole length of the western and north-western sides, till it reaches the ornamental lake. This stream, varied in its course by a fall constructed most naturally, is supplied from the Grand Canal, by pipes from above Portobello Bridge, and empties itself into the Canal at Mount Street. The arrangement of the trees and shrubs has been remarkably well done, the rock-work is delightfully natural, and the grassy mounds have been placed in most effective and picturesque positions. Plots of grass-grown turf, cut in graceful forms, are intersected by pathways, sheltered by the cool shade of beautiful trees. The ride is about twenty-one feet wide, and there is scarcely a point in its circuit from which some new and beautiful aspect of the Green will not present itself. The island planted with elms, evergreens, and variegated shrubs and mosses of all kinds, and bordered by rockwork, admirably disposed, is a charming and refreshing feature in the landscape. Two gracefully designed fountains are placed in the midst of a lovely sward, in which are fashioned parterres, planted with choice flowers most tastefully arranged. To the east and west of the centre statue very pretty rustic pavilions, with sloping roofs, and provided with seats, afford charming resting places, and command capital views of some of the most attractive portions of the Green. At the south west angle stands the super-intendent's lodge, built of Farham bricks, and roofed with tiles in harmony with the picturesque character of the building. A few of the most interesting features of the new work have now been briefly indi-cated. It may be mentioned that the rockeries were made by Messrs Pulham and Sons, of the Artificial Stone Works company, London; the handsome lodge was erected by Messrs T. Millard and Son, Harcourt Street, from designs by J.F. Fuller, architect; the stone bridge across the lake was erected by Messrs Pulham & Sons, and the rustic pavilions, which are, indeed, a marvel of taste and skill, were also designed by Mr Fuller. The ironwork around the walks and drives is by Mr Martin, and it is satisfactory to know that nearly all the work has been executed by Dublin tradesmen.

EVENING MAIL

100 Years of Dublin

12 OCTOBER 1961 ❧ THE EUCHARISTIC CONGRESS

F ew occasions in the history of our city have been more memorable than the 31st Eucharistic Congress, held in Dublin in June 1932. Dublin was chosen for the venue of the Congress of that year because 1932 was then accepted, unquestionably, as the fifteen-hundredth anniversary of St Patrick's lighting of the Paschal Fire, at Slane.

The first Eucharistic Congress had been inspired by a desire among Catholics, in French speaking countries to propagate devotion to the Blessed Sacrament and the first Congress, held in 1881, had an attendance of 3,000 pilgrims.

The Congress hitherto largely confined to French and adjoining countries, apart from one Congress held in Jerusalem in 1893, was beginning to spread its wings, being held in London in 1908, in Malta in 1913 and in Montreal in 1910.

Prior organisation to the Congress in Dublin, of course, commenced well beforehand. The director of organisations was the first layman ever to occupy this position, Mr Frank O'Reilly.

HEAVY TRAFFIC

In the General Strike of 1913, Mr O'Reilly had organised stations where food was given to children of strikers. In 1922 he became secretary of the Catholic Trust Society, and had organised the Catholic Emancipation celebrations of 1928.

The control of traffic into, through and out of Dublin during the week, and in particular on the final Sunday, when Pontifical High Mass was to be celebrated by the Papal Legate, his Eminence, Cardinal Lauri, in the Phoenix Park, was under General Eoin O'Duffy, Commissioner of the Garda Siochana.

Rich and poor alike prepared for the Congress. Women's retreats culminating in a general Holy Communion were held in Dublin Churches and in Dun Laoghaire, between the afternoon of 5 June and the morning of 12 June.

They were followed on the afternoon of the 12th by retreats for men, also lasting a week, and ending in a general Holy Communion.

Public buildings were impressively illuminated, but even more impressive were the less expensive decorations, obtained by steady saving of sixpences and shillings in the poorer areas of the city.

The Evening Mail *of June 22 1932, observes: 'Richness and novelty have been added to the decorations in Ship street by the draping of many of the doorways. Here also the picking out in colours of the brickwork round the windows has added considerably to the variety and beauty of the scheme. Generous use of lime wash has had good results in Great Longford street.'*

PAPAL LEGATE

His Eminence, Cardinal Lauri, the Papal Legate, and his suite (including Monsignori—later Cardinals—Tardini and Spellman) arrived at Dun Laoghaire from Holyhead, in the Cambria on Monday, June 20.

Flags of all nations, Britain included were flying from the East Pier to greet them.

Cardinal Lauri was presented with an address of welcome by Alderman Devitt, the chairman of Dun Laoghaire Borough Council. At Merrion Gates. the train stopped, to permit His Eminence to receive an address of welcome in Irish, English and Latin, from the Lord Mayor, Alderman Alfred Byrne.

Visiting prelates to Dublin for the Congress, included Cardinal Bourne, Archbishop of Westminster; Cardinal Hayes, Archbishop of New York; Cardinal Van Roey, Archbishop of Malines; Cardinal Hlond, Archbishop of Orenen and Posen; Cardinal Dougherty, Archbishop of Philadelphia; Most Rev. Dr Forbes, Archbishop of Ottawa; Most Rev. Dr Jansen, Archibishop of Utrecht; Most Rev. Dr. Kelly, Archbishop of Sydney, to take a few names at random.

Midnight on June 22 found pilgrims attending midnight Mass with great devotion.

'At 4 a.m.' the Evening Mail *of June 23 reports 'rejoicing pilgrims were still singing their hymns in the streets though midnight Mass had been long over.*

'So intense was the demand for accommodation in the churches that thousands heard Mass kneeling on the pavements outside. A thousand bells rang out at the Elevation, and gigantic letters of silver grey flashed a message of faith in Latin across the sky.'

The morning of June 23 was notable by the fact that Solemn Pontifical Mass in the Slav rite, was celebrated for the first time in Dublin, in St Francis Xavier Church, Gardiner Street.

In accordance with the rite, the 'ikonostasis,' or screen, adorned with holy pictures and having three doors, was placed before the altars, so that the congregation could witness the Mass only through those doors.

The Slav rite differs from the Roman rite, in that the congregation stands, for the most part of the ceremony, and that a low bow is made in place of a genuflection.

MASS MEETINGS

A mass meeting of men was held in the Phoenix Park at 8 p.m. on the Thursday, and a mass meeting of women at 8 p.m. on the Friday, both being presided over by Cardinal Lauri.

Addresses on the Blessed Sacrament were given, in Irish and English, by prelates at both meetings.

The Bishop of Raphoe, Dr McNeely, addressed the men in Irish, while the Archbishop of St Louis, Most Rev. Dr Glennon (later to die in Arus an Uachtarain on his way from Rome) addressed them in English.

The women were addressed in Irish by the Bishop of Down and Connor, Most Rev. Dr. Mageean, and in English, by His Grace, the Archbishop of Manila, Most Rev. Dr. O'Doherty. The two Irish prelates are still alive.

FOR CHILDREN

The children's Pontifical High Mass was the highlight of Saturday's cere- monies. It was celebrated, in the Phoenix Park, by Most Rev. Dr. Kelly, Archbishop of Sydney, then aged 83, and was attended by Mr de Valera, Mr W.T. Cosgrave, Cardinals Bourne, Hayes, McRory, Verdier Van Roey, 30 Archbishops, an enormous congregation.

The Fifteen Acres was described by the Evening Mail of June 25 as having become 'a white and black carpet, white with the dresses and veils of the girls and the flannels of the boys, black where there were nuns and priests...'

A general choir sang at the children's Mass, made up of 2,000 boys and girls from 88 Dublin schools.

There was, of course, a tragic side to the Congress. Rev. Father Lindo de Touratio, a professor in a seminary at Viterlon, Italy was fatally injured outside St Andrew's Church, while accompanying a number of pilgrims.

He was knocked down by a motor car.

Another Italian priest, Father Francesco Alara, of Turin, took ill in Lower O'Connell Street on June 25. He was attended by a priest and was taken to Jervis Street Hospital, where he was found to be dead.

The priests were buried in Glasnevin cemetery on June 27.

The journey home from the final celebrations, too, was marked with tragedy for a party of pilgrims from Tullamore, when the lorry, which was carrying them back to Tullamore crashed into a bridge at Leixlip.

Two killed

Two pilgrims were killed, and more than twenty seriously injured.

The highlight of the Eucharistic Congress was afforded by the cere-monials of Sunday June 26, when Solemn Pontifical Mass was celebrated by Most Rev. Dr. Curley, Archbishop of Baltimore, in the Phoenix Park, and was followed by clergy and congregation moving in procession to the altar, specially erected on O'Connell Bridge.

Benediction of the Blessed Sacrament was imparted by the Cardinal Legate.

Pilgrims converged on the Phoenix Park from all parts of Ireland. Thirty-seven special trains arrived in Kingsbridge from the south, carrying about 40,000 pilgrims. More than 18,000 westerners arrived at Broadstone station, the terminus for trains from the west, by twenty-three special trains.

Special trains

Twelve special trains brought about 9,000 pilgrims from the south-east to Harcourt Street, while the largest contingent of all came from the North to Amiens Street. More than 56,000 people travelled, 14,000 of them from Belfast alone.

The Dun Laoghaire and Bray line had also increased and accelerated train services travelled into Westland Row.

It was announced at the ceremonies that the Holy Father, Pope Pius XI, would broadcast a message to the Congress, before the Pontifical High Mass, but the message did not come through immediately and the Mass was started.

Before the *Credo*, Cardinal Curley addressed the congregation in English, and his address was broadcast over 2 RN as the Irish broadcasting service was then known. The music for the Mass—the *Missa Brevis* by Palestrina—was rendered by a choir of some 2,000. The motet *Panis Angelicus* by Cesar Franck, was sung by John Count McCormack.

Towards the end of the Mass, the Papal message came through.

The congregation were overjoyed to hear the Holy Father's voice— and overawed in a manner inconceivable to our younger readers of the present day.

Indeed, the use of radio communications was a striking feature of the Eucharistic Congress. The ceremonies in the Pro-Cathedral were broadcast over the centre of the city.

All along the procession route, from the Phoenix Park to O'Connell Bridge, loudspeakers were connected at eighty-yard intervals—to enable the choir to control and lead the singing throughout the procession.

At the close of Mass, the procession left the Phoenix Park in four sections, one section converging on O'Connell Bridge, by the North Circular road, one by Thomas Street and Dame Street, a third by the North quays, and the fourth section, in which the Blessed Sacrament was carried, by the South quays.

Each section was headed by a cavalry officer and twenty men of the National Army in ceremonial uniform.

Contingents of foreign pilgrims, bearing their national flags, mingled with the pilgrims from Dublin, and from every Irish diocese.

The first section of the procession, headed by members of the Franciscan and the Dominican Third Orders, arrived at O'Connell Bridge from the head of O'Connell Street. They were joined by contingents, who converged on the Bridge from Burgh Quay, and from Westmoreland Street.

Between hymns, the Rosary was recited in the Phoenix Park, and relayed to the crowds thronging O'Connell Bridge.

The first of the procession had reached O'Connell Bridge by 4.30 p.m. And by 6 o'clock the prelates had reached the altar. But the first glimpse of the portion of the procession including the Blessed Sacrament, was not seen until 7 o'clock.

Shortly afterwards, the canopy, flanked by Army officers, with drawn swords, reached the Bridge. All around, people fell to their knees in adoration. Side by side, among the canopy bearers—the Civil War and its bitter consequences for a short while forgotten—walked the newly-elected President of the Executive Council, Mr Eamon de Valera, and Mr W.T. Cosgrave, whom Mr de Valera had lately replaced.

The Host was received into the Tabernacle. Soon the solemn ceremony of Benediction began.

Trumpets rang out in the Royal salute, as the Cardinal Legate raised the Monstrance, high over the heads of the kneeling multitude.

Then—for a few seconds—the city was still ... to burst into sound again as Cardinal Lauri led the congregation in the recitation of the Divine Praises.

A little later, bugles sounded the 'Disperse.'

The Eucharistic Congress had come to an end.

TIGHE HOPKINS

Kilmainham Memories

LONDON ❧ WARDLOCK AND BOWDEN LTD ❧ 1896

[On 13 October 1881 Charles Stewart Parnell (1846–1891) was arrested because of his involvement with the National Land League.]

The details of Mr Parnell's arrest have not, I believe, been published. He was staying at Morrison's Hotel in Dawson Street, and it was there that he was asked for, at seven on the morning named, by a trusted officer of the Dublin detective force. The waiter who was first interviewed declared that Mr Parnell had 'gone for a bath.' It seemed improbable, and the officer, disclosing his identity, gave the number of Mr Parnell's room (No. 20, for the next curious visitor at Morrison's) and requested to be shown up there. He was begged to wait 'just four or five minutes.' 'Not a minute, if you please,' was the officer's reply. It is very unlikely that Mr Parnell, had he been warned, would have taken advantage of the warning, but in 'four or five minutes' a sympathetic waiter might easily have drawn together a sympathetic crowd in the street, and the officer was single-handed.

However, he was shown up at once to No. 20. Mr Parnell, who was still between the sheets, presented himself at his door in a moment in nether garment and slippers. The situation being explained to him he inspected the warrant, and said he must have time to write two or three letters. For fifteen minutes the officer paced the corridor, and then, as the crowd which he had feared was beginning to gather in the street, he requested Mr Parnell to make a hurried toilet.

Hurried or not, when he came out of his room five minutes later he was as scrupulously dressed as always. The officer led him out boldly by the front door; there was no disturbance (to the chagrin, doubtless, of the sympathetic waiter), and they entered the cab which was in waiting. Mr Parnell behaved throughout with admirable dignity and composure, only for one moment showing signs of annoyance. He had written three letters, which he asked to be allowed to post with his own hand, a request

217

which was repeated several times. 'Presently, sir,' said the officer, biding his time. For the officer it was a journey of some nervousness. He was carrying to prison, under the fiat of a Government detested by the strongest party in Ireland, the most powerful and most popular man in Ireland, and he was unsupported by any kind of escort. The whole 'national' element in Dublin was vehemently against the law and its representatives, and as vehemently on the side of Mr Parnell and the Land League. A word from Parnell as he was being taken through the streets and it would have been a hard matter to arrive with him at Kilmainham. There were a number of persons gathered about the Kingsbridge station, and had he merely shown his face and said, 'I am under arrest,' the cab would have been wrecked. He said nothing, and sitting well back in the vehicle seemed anxious that no one should recognise him.

Just beyond this point a company of the Guards turned out of the Royal Hospital and marched behind the cab. It was here that the prisoner, for the first time, vented a word or two of temper. 'You said that I should post my letters,' he said to the officer beside him; 'you are deceiving me.' 'You shall post them in a moment, Mr Parnell,' was the answer. Kilmainham was reached almost immediately, and in the pillar-box against the prison, Mr Parnell dropped his letters.

Some dozen or twenty hawkers, labourers, and car drivers recognised him here, and seeing that he was under arrest pressed forward to touch and speak to him. He drew back, and would give his hand to no one as he passed into the courtyard of the prison. With no less hauteur he entered the prison itself, and standing erect in the outer hall scarcely condescended to recognise those of his acquaintances amongst the suspects who advanced respectfully to greet him.

Indeed, from the first day to the last the 'Chief' was as unapproachable in Kilmainham by the rank and file of his party imprisoned with him as he had always been in the lobby or dining room of the House of Commons. Within a few days of his arrival, in fact, there came to be an 'Upper' and a 'Lower House' in the prison. The Upper House was the portion in which Mr Parnell and his few associates met and took their exercise, and rarely indeed did one from the Lower House venture unbidden within this privileged confine.

Mr J.J. O'Kelly was the comrade whose society Mr Parnell most affected, but he spent a great part of his time in his own room, and wrote much. It is almost superfluous to say that no rule of the prison was ever infringed by him, and that his conduct was never less than exemplary.

The majority of the suspects were lodged in the central hall, but to Mr Parnell was allotted a good sized room in a quiet corridor of the prison, the two arched windows of which give on to one of the smaller exercise yards. Facing this room, by the way, is the cell in which the informer Carey was afterwards confined. The 'Parnell Room' which was never a cell, has been quite changed since that distinguished occupation, and is now used as an office of the prison and for consultations between prisoners and their legal advisers. Here it was that Mr Parnell wrote the letter to Captain O'Shea, which was to become famous under the name of the Kilmainham Treaty.

Parnell himself in Kilmainham loomed larger than ever in the popular imagination; his celebrity grew with the days of confinement; his name became trebly heroic. Gifts poured in upon him: flowers from London; fruits, game, and cases of champagne; books, bedding, slippers, dressing-gowns and coverlets of satin and eiderdown. His postbag was enormous: letters of condolence, sympathy, admiration, adulation, indignation, and vituperation. Some of his correspondents praised, exhorted or abused him in verse; and there was one tirade commencing -

O Mr Parnell, O Mr Parnell
Cease to do evil, and learn to do well!

A pseudonymous well-wisher, thinking perhaps that the seclusion of prison might conduce to a change of faith, sent him a very pretty little Roman Catholic manual of devotion, in ivory covers, with a copy of verses on the flyleaf signed 'Merva.' It was shown me by the gentleman, an ex-governor of Kilmainham, with whom Mr Parnell left it as a souvenir.

From first to last his behaviour in confinement was beyond reproach. He was patient of such restraints as his imprisonment involved, courteous and considerate to the least of the officials. To the majority of his companions in durance he was the sphinx that they had known before, unaltered and unmoved in that novel environment, and neither more nor less conciliatory than it was at all times and in all places his wont to be.

This singular chapter in the history of Kilmainham being closed, one may venture the remark that this particular phase of the policy of the Government towards the campaigners of the Land League was on the whole a mistake. It is easy talking fourteen years after the event, but one may look back upon it at this day and ask whether all those arrests in all parts of Ireland—many of them, no doubt, rather arbitrary and ill-considered—had any appreciable result in weakening the power of the League; whether, on the contrary, they had not a much more considerable result in strengthening it. The situation, however, will probably not repeat itself in our time.

DUBLIN THROUGH THE AGES

Municipal Politics and Popular Disturbances 1660–1800

ED. ART COSGROVE ❧ DUBLIN ❧ 1988
COLLEGE PRESS LTD ❧ SEAN MURPHY

H istorical writing on Dublin in the late seventeenth and eighteenth centuries has tended to concentrate on the city's architecture, its intellectual and cultural life, its place in national politics, or to be set in the context of the careers of outstanding figures such as Swift and Grattan. This chapter will deal with the municipal government and local politics of Dublin from the Restoration to the act of union, and with the popular disturbances endemic in the city during this period. It will be shown that conflict in the city council and violence in the streets were often related, and that in the latter part of the eighteenth century especially, there existed an alliance between city radicals and the mob.

The local government of the city and suburbs of Dublin was divided between several different jurisdictions or 'liberties' until the nineteenth century. The major part of the city, or the 'city liberty' was under the control of Dublin corporation. The other principal liberties were those of Thomas Court and Donore or the earl of Meath's, St Sepulchre's or the archbishop's and St Patrick's (the area still referred to colloquially as 'the Liberties'), and those of Grangegorman and Kilmainham. In addition, functions such as paving, fire prevention and collection of local taxes were the responsibility of the vestries or councils of the twenty or so parishes in the city.

The common council or governing body of Dublin corporation had evolved a uniquely bicameral or two-chamber structure. The lord mayor and twenty-four aldermen formed the upper house, while the lower house was composed of the sheriffs' peers, who could not number more than forty-eight, ninety-six representatives of the city guilds, and two sheriffs who presided jointly. The lower house was called 'the sheriffs and commons' or 'the commons' for short (which should not be confused with the parliamentary house of commons).

The majority of citizens had no say in municipal affairs, and catholics were effectively excluded from 1690 until 1840. The privileged protestant minority of freemen of the city were represented on the common council through the guilds, and they also possessed the right to vote in parliamentary elections. The number of freemen was probably about 3,000 in 1749 (as compared to a total city population of about 130,000), and though members of the established Church of Ireland predominated, presbyterians and other protestant dissenters may have accounted for nearly one-fifth of the freemen. The number of guilds was raised to its final total of twenty-five with the formation of the apothecaries' guild in 1747. The strongest and wealthiest of the guilds was the merchants' guild, which filled nearly one-third of the seats in the corporation's lower house. As the eighteenth century wore on, the guilds progressively developed the character of political clubs and their original primary function of regulating trade and crafts diminished accordingly.

The constitution of Dublin corporation was founded partly on the provisions of some of the royal charters granted to the city since 1172, partly on usage, ancient customs and bye-laws, and principally on the 'New Rules' of 1672. As Maurice Craig has shown, the Restoration in 1660 marked the beginning of a period of expansion for Dublin city. Due to the Stuart tendency to interfere directly in municipal corporations, it was also to be a period of dramatic change and upheaval in Dublin's local government. The New Rules were issued under a clause of the 1665 act of explanation which empowered the lord lieutenant to restrict the independence of Irish corporations. Riots in the late 1660s over the building of a new bridge were one of the main reasons for the issuing of New Rules for Dublin in 1672, and their principal tendency was to increase the oligarchic powers of the lord mayor and the aldermen. Under the rules, the corporation's upper house was granted a virtual monopoly of power in the election of principal corporate officers, and was enabled to vet carefully the guild representatives appointed to the common council every three years. Despite their unpopularity, the New Rules were resolutely implemented, and it was not until the 1740s that a systematic campaign for their abolition was to be mounted.

The common council held four quarterly assemblies at Christmas, Easter, Midsummer and Michaelmas, as well as meetings for additional or extraordinary business called 'post assemblies'. During each assembly, the lord mayor and aldermen and the sheriffs and commons met simultaneously but sat in separate rooms in the municipal headquarters, the Tholsel (a building which no longer survives but figures in Malton's prints). Business was submitted for consideration in the form of petitions, which if passed by both houses became 'acts of assembly' and were entered on parchment 'assembly rolls'. In addition to the powers conferred on them by the New Rules, the lord mayor and aldermen possessed by usage the right to fill vacancies in their own ranks. While both houses of the corporation could exercise an effective veto in the transaction of business in the assemblies, the lord mayor and aldermen possessed the more important power of deciding the agenda and frequently suppressed petitions not to their liking.

The corporation was also responsible for the administration of justice in the city, and the lord mayor and members of the board of aldermen were magistrates. In addition to their municipal functions, the sheriffs possessed important legal responsibilities, including the empanelling of juries. Newgate prison and the various marshalseas or debtors' prisons were administered by the corporation. Among the civil courts under corporation control were the court of quarter sessions, the lord mayor's court and the court of conscience.

The administration of justice in the liberties was the responsibility of the officers called 'seneschals' and the county magistrates. There was a rudimentary police system in operation throughout the city, composed of constables and frequently old and incompetent watchmen. The watch system was administered primarily by the vestries of the various parishes with the lord mayor exercising a loose supervisory control. Dublin was also a heavily garrisoned city, and calling out troops to restore order was the usual remedy when all else failed. However, the patchwork of often conflicting jurisdictions and the inadequacy of the watch system enabled lawlessness and violence to flourish in eighteenth-century Dublin.

The instability which beset Dublin corporation during the reigns of the later Stuarts came to a head during the mayoralty dispute of 1711–14. This municipal dispute was caused by divisions among the aldermen on the question of electing lord mayors and was also related to the struggles between whigs and tories which were a feature of the closing years of Queen Anne's reign. Aggrieved by the fact that though he was senior alderman he had been denied the opportunity of serving as lord mayor, Robert Constantine appealed to the government in April 1711. The tory government supported Constantine by using its powers under the New Rules to withhold approval from the lord mayors elected by the predominantly whig aldermen of Dublin corporation. The conflict led to a breakdown in the function of the corporation in 1713-14, and the 1713 general election in Dublin city was accompanied by whig-tory, protestant-catholic rioting of great bitterness. The mayoralty dispute was only effectively ended when the return to power of the whigs after the death of Queen Anne in 1714 restored control of the city to the aldermen.

BREANDÁN O RÍORDÁIN

Old Dublin Within the Walls

DUBLIN ❧ E & T O'BRIEN LTD ❧ 1973

The High Street diggings of the past few years within the walls of old medieval Dublin have shown us that in the earlier phases of our capital's history we had close ties with Scandinavia, Britain and France. Looking at the jewellery, tools and other objects found in the excavation sites we can also learn a lot about the trades and crafts of the tenth century and later. Breandán O Ríordáin of the National Museum of Ireland directed the diggings.

In early Christian times a number of churches were located near what is now the old centre of Dublin. The *Ecclesia S. Patricii de Insula*—which was known as the Church of St Patrick of the Island—lay beside the Poddle river close to the present site of St Patrick's Cathedral and nearby, on the western side of Ship Street stood the Church of Saint Mac Táil—better known by its Norman name of St Michel le Pole. St Columcille's Church in High Street was succeeded in the twelfth century by St Audoen's Church (named after a Norman saint who is also the patron saint of S. Ouen at Rouen).

In common with many other Irish churches and monasteries of this period it is very probable that settlements had grown up in their neighbourhood. But as far as has yet been established it was not until the invading Norsemen of the ninth century had set up a *longphort* on the Liffey in 840 A.D. that the long low hill (a boulder clay moraine of the glacial period) lying on the south side of the river became a place of continuing and increasing importance in Irish history.

As a result of the seafaring and trading activities of the Norsemen, Dublin became an international seaport, the international character of which is hinted at in Arabic, Norse, English and Irish sources. In common with the Norse foundations at Wexford, Waterford, Cork and Limerick it later became a focal point of the Norman invasion in the twelfth century.

Tangible evidence of the Norsemen came to light in the Kilmainham-Islandbridge district in the nineteenth century when a large Viking cemetery containing graves of both men and women was accidentally discovered in the course of construction of the Great Southern and Western railway in fields sloping down to the Liffey, southwest of Islandbridge village. The Islandbridge cemetery and graves found in the 1930s in the course of construction of the Longmeadows War Memorial Park contained typical Viking grave finds: iron swords, spearheads, axeheads, fragments of shields, weighing scales, lead and bronze weights, tortoise brooches, bronze pins, buckles and beads of glass and amber. Although these discoveries and others at Donnybrook and in Kildare Street had been made in the environs of the medieval city, little had come to light from the city area itself, with the exception of material of a miscellaneous nature recovered from street cuttings in the nineteenth and twentieth centuries.

Charles Haliday's comprehensive study of the early phases of Dublin's history, *The Scandinavian Kingdom of Dublin* (first published in 1881 and recently reprinted in 1969) includes an essay 'On The Ancient Name of Dublin'. In this essay Haliday refers to the nature of the soil in the older parts of the city—High Street, Castle Street and Fishamble Street. He mentions the discovery of squared oak timbers, shells, leaves and other materials which came to light in the course of laying underground sewers in the city streets in the nineteenth century.

More information on finding archaeological material is contained in a diary written by Thomas Matthew Ray in the years 1856–9. At that time workmen employed by the Corporation were laying sewers in Nicholas Street, Francis Street, Christ Church Place (formerly Skinner's Row) and neighbouring Streets. Thomas Ray not alone recorded the discovery of bone combs, bronze pins and other finds but also included sketches of the different strata revealed in the street cuttings.

Ray noted the depths at which various antiquities and other features occurred. His diary and a collection of finds which he had acquired were later presented to the Royal Irish Academy and are now preserved in the National Museum of Ireland. The Ray Collection and other groups of objects presented by Dublin Corporation and by various individuals during the nineteenth and early twentieth centuries are particularly significant because they demonstrate that finds of the Viking period occurred in almost all the areas within the bounds of the old town walls.

Many of these older parts of Dublin have not been redeveloped in modern times; consequently they retain, relatively undisturbed, much of the debris which has accumulated in the course of the past thousand years. For archaeologists and social historians a systematic investigation of deposits of this type adds information on what may be otherwise undocumented aspects of human activity.

Until 1962 no excavation of this kind had been undertaken in Dublin City except for a small area which had been investigated by the National Monuments branch of the Office of Public Works under the East Wing of Dublin Castle.

High Street, as the name implies, was the principal street in the medieval period. The proposed redevelopment afforded the National Museum of Ireland an opportunity of excavation in this area; with the cooperation of the Corporation of Dublin, who owned the properties, archaeological investigation was carried out for two six-month seasons in 1962 and 1963 on a plot of ground bordered by High Street, Nicholas Street and Back Lane.

The quantity and quality of archaeological objects and of structural features discovered at this stage were considered sufficient justification to excavate a larger site also bordering on High Street. This investigation— begun in 1967—was completed in 1972. Excavations were also conducted at Winetavern Street between 1969 and 1971 next to the site selected by the Corporation for its civic offices. Further work is currently in progress on this site and on another which lies south of the Cathedral between Ross Road and Christ Church Place.

The excavations reveal that the original ground surface lay in general some fourteen feet below the present street level. All the overlying deposit consisted of the debris and refuse which had accumulated in the course of hundreds of years. The upper part—deposits of recent centuries—had been in great part removed during the construction of eighteenth century house cellars but the lower part remained intact to an average depth of six feet over most of the areas investigated.

This compact dark-coloured layer had accumulated from the ninth to the thirteenth centuries and the samples of it which had come to light in the eighteenth and nineteenth centuries had been interpreted as evidence that Dublin had been founded on a peat bog. As a result of the recent museum excavations we now know this was mistaken; however the deposit fortunately resembles peat in its remarkable preservative qualities which have resulted in the almost-perfect preservation of articles made of highly perishable materials.

Results show that the earliest occupation on these particular sites occurred in Viking times and many of the discoveries of the lower levels are identical with objects and structures found in Norway, Denmark, Sweden and Northern Germany.

They include a gilt bronze disc-brooch decorated in a tenth century Norse style—known as the Borre-Jellinge style—of which about twenty examples are known in Scandinavia, and a small openwork quadrangular bronze brooch similar to some found in the Viking cemetery at Birka near Stockholm, in a ship burial near Bergen and in the Norse town of Hedeby near Schleswig in Northern Germany.

Other Viking-type finds include two decorated bronze needle cases (another example was found in the cemetery at Islandbridge), an ingot mould which has a matrix for casting Thor's hammer symbols, animal and bird-headed bone pins, single-sided combs and other miscellaneous items of amber, bone, bronze and iron for which many parallels exist in Scandinavia.

Apart from these there are some other finds, including small toy models of ships and boats and incised sketches of craft found on timber planks, all indicating contact with Scandinavia.

Connections with Anglo-Saxon England—York and London in particular—are indicated by the discovery of coins of Alfred and Aethelred and a number of decorated pewter brooches, close parallels of which occur in a hoard which was found at Cheapside in London.

Apart from the discovery of objects showing contact with Scandinavia and England the excavations also reveal evidence of many different trades and crafts practised by the townspeople. Metal-working was practised in Dublin from the ninth century onwards. This is shown by the discovery in the earliest layers of furnace slag and of baked clay crucibles in which the bronze was melted. Large numbers of bronze pins, some of which bear traces of gilding and tinning, have been found and they are probably the products of local workshops. That there was a school of artists is shown by the discovery of many carved bone 'trial pieces'—animal ribs and long bones bearing panels of animal interlacements and geometric motifs. The carvings range from preliminary sketches to designs executed in full relief. The finished designs are considered to have served as patterns for casting in metal the decorative panels used in metalwork of the period; many of these have survived in croziers and other reliquaries.

Two of the more interesting examples bear motifs in an Irish-Scandinavian style. On one example the main composition, that of two animals each forming a loop and semi-interlaced, in a close parallel to the design on a panel on the Shrine of the Cathach of Columcille, a shrine made between 1062 and 1098 and now preserved in the National Museum. On another example the carved panels of ribbon interlacements bear a close similarity to those on the shrine of St Senan's Bell or Clogán Oir, a reliquary associated with Scattery Island in County Clare.

One of the principal crafts practised in the Viking Period of Dublin must have been that of the combmaker. Large numbers of deer antler fragments, bone plaques (some blank and some with the teeth sawn) as well as many single-sided combs are evidence of the presence of comb-makers in the town in the tenth and later centuries. Most of the combs were made from the antlers of red deer.

But despite a large amount of worked and unworked antlers very few deer bones were found among the animal food bones. This and the fact that many of the antler burrs display natural ruptures indicate that shed antlers were the main source of supply. It is probable that people living in the neighbouring countryside collected the shed antlers in late spring and brought them to the town for sale to the combmakers.

The houses and workshops used and lived in by the combmakers, metalworkers, weavers and woodturners were mostly constructed in the post and wattle technique. The walls were formed of upright posts in the ground, which had horizontal layers of wattles or rods (generally of hazel, ash and elm) woven between them in basketry fashion. A number of doorways which survive show that on each side of the wooden threshold there was a stout jamb with grooves cut into its outer face into which the ends of the horizontal bands of wattlework which formed the side walls were slotted. Some of the smaller structures were probably workshops and the larger ones houses. The hearth was in the centre of the floor in a number of examples.

The number of bowls, trays and other utensils made of wood is noticeable during the earliest centuries of the life of the town. Apart from some French pottery in the eleventh century levels the use of pottery vessels appears to have been due to trading contacts between Dublin and ports in the West of England: notably Chester and Bristol as well as France in the twelfth and thirteenth centuries.

The existence of a wine trade with south-western France in the second half of the thirteenth century is confirmed by the discovery of numerous examples of imported wine jugs, of a type known to have been made at La Chapelle-des-Pots, Saintes, Cognac and other towns near Bordeaux in that period.

It is to the thirteenth century also that we may ascribe a large and extensive deposit of worked leather which was found on the High Street site. Much of it was shoe soles—worn, damaged or holed—which suggests that at this period it was not the practice to repair worn soles. It would appear that the uppers, cut away from the worn soles, were re-used to make new footwear: usually of a smaller size than the originals. The finding of such a large volume of leather in one sector—over one thousand soles, numbers of decorated leather knife-scabbards and large amounts of scrap leather—suggests that a community of cobblers worked in the same area of the town for at least a century.

An interesting sidelight on thirteenth century sanitation was the discovery of many timber-lined pits which had been used as cess-pits. These had later been used as convenient places for the disposal of refuse. Salvaged items included pieces of cloth, an iron gimlet with a lathe-turned wooden handle, fragments of glazed wine jugs including an almost complete example of an unusual and highly ornamented knight jug of Bristol ware and a hoard of over two thousand pewter discs which are considered to be tokens or tallies for use in inns and taverns where wine was sold.

The pits also contained plant remains and seeds; examination has shown that a large number of different kinds of fruit were eaten: strawberries, apples, cherries, plums, sloes, blackberries, rowan-berries, hazel-nuts and frochans.

Some objects recovered from the thirteenth century levels in High Street have associations with persons known from historical records. One example is a lead seal matrix bearing the name Adam Burestone and the figure of a centaur in bas-relief. Another example is the lead *bulla* which was originally attached to a Letter Apostolic issued by Pope Innocent III (A.D. 1198–1216). It was Pope Innocent III who, in 1199 gave the Canons of Saint Peter's in Rome the sole right of casting small pilgrim badges and an example of this kind has also been found in the course of the excavations.

The badge is made of pewter and it bears the figures of SS. Peter and Paul, the latter holding his emblem, a sword, and the former a large Key of Heaven with highly decorative wards. It is most probable that this badge was brought from Rome in the beginning of the thirteenth century by some Irish pilgrim who wore it as a souvenir and as proof of his pilgrimage.

As well as these a large body of artifacts of a miscellaneous nature has been recovered which illustrates many other aspects of the contemporary way of life. These include iron locks and keys for doors and chests, spindles and their whorls used in spinning thread, bone gaming pieces, iron knives, fish-hooks, and a considerable number of textile fragments including extraordinarily delicate pieces of netting which were probably used as hair-nets.

'F.E.R.'

Historical Reminiscences of Dublin Castle

DUBLIN ❧ SEALY, BRYERS AND WALKER ❧ 1900

The Lord Lieutenant has not a fixed tenure of office, but changes with the government. His Excellency and household generally go to reside at the Castle in early February, the season commencing the following Tuesday, when a Levée is held; on Wednesday evening at half past nine o'clock a Drawingroom. The following nights of that week banquets are given. The ensuing week a State Ball. The third week a second Levée and Drawingroom are held. Entertainments continue until 17 March (St Patrick's Day), when the season is finished with St Patrick's Ball. Any person who has attended either the Levées or Drawingrooms of the year can attend this Ball by merely sending their names to the Chamberlain's office.

All State ceremonies must take place at the Castle. When a new Viceroy is sworn in, part of the inauguration is in the Throne Room and part in the Council Chamber of the Chief Secretary's office. Upon a Lord Lieutenant leaving Ireland a farewell reception is held in the Throne Room. Those who have only contemplated the somewhat gloomy aspect of the Castle in the day time can hardly realise the change which the State Apartments present at night while the season festivities continue. The entertainments given are on a large scale, and numerously attended, as many as sixteen thousand, three hundred and ten people having been entertained in one season. But perhaps nowhere are the Viceregal hospitalities better described in few words than from the pen of one of the visitors, signed 'Madam,' taken from *Heart and Home* of 31 March 1892:

' "But how can it possibly be done?" was my ever recurring thought at sight of the supper room (*i.e.*, St Patrick's Hall), on the occasion of one of the delightful "Throne Room" dances which so often follow a big dinner at Dublin Castle. To account for my surprise I must give a brief sketch of that which gave rise to it. We had, in company with some one hundred and twenty-five others, dined with their Excellencies that night, and to a newcomer at the Viceregal Court the scene was full of interest. The large party of waiting guests, gaily-clad and be-diamoned women, many uniformed and be-medalled men, and here and there the well-known pale 'Viceregal' blue of the household facings, gave, beneath the yellow-shaded electric light of the drawing-room, more the effect of a large and brilliant "At Home" than that of guests waiting for their dinner. But the hum of conversation suddenly ceases, a lane is formed, and we bend low as their Excellencies, preceded by the State Steward, and followed by the Comptroller, pass through the rooms to St Patrick's Hall to the strains of the "Roast Beef of Old England." Each man, on arriving, having been given a card with his "partner's" name, and being introduced to her if necessary, it does not take long to marshall this long dinner party to the table, one glance at which causes my housewifely soul to imagine the time and pains which must have been spent in even setting forth so Brobdingnagian a feast. By a quaint conceit of the energetic Comptroller of the Household, the table takes the form of the centre of St Patrick's star—*i.e.*, a round table in the centre, and four long arms, like St Andrew's Cross, in fact, springing thence.

'The Viceregal party sit at each side of the centre, overshadowed by two huge spreading palms some sixteen feet high, placed in the inner hollows of the cross, while the centre of the table is filled by a tall group of arum, lilies, palms, ferns, and red tulips. The four 'arms' have islands of the same all down them, varied by full many a magnificent racing cup and centre-piece, trophies of Lord Zetland's success on the Turf; while between the countless dishes of dessert and bonbons was laid a beautifully-arranged scrolly pattern of flat sprays of arbor vitae, with, whenever it crossed or interlaced, a stalkless red tulip, the petals turned outwards to form a star. Fain would I dwell longer on this beautiful scene, with its background of grouped banners on the ivory walls, and tall, gold-crowned Corinthian pillars; would tell of soft music issuing from a 'leafy bower' in the gallery; of the radiance of the chain of electric lights, which, like a giantess's necklace, encircled the ceiling; but space is precious, and I have much yet to say, so pass on to the moment when we rise at the sound of the National Anthem. Our Most Gracious Majesty's health is proposed and honoured, one sees the svelte figure and blonde head of her Excellency "make the move," and with a bow to His Excellency's back as they near the door—a chance for the ungraceful of my sex, of which, I might say, they availed themselves to the uttermost!—we women file back to the drawingroom, where the other guests invited for the dance are beginning to arrive. But on this my rule, never to write of the society in which I happen to be moving, forbids me to dwell so I will return to St Patrick's Hall soon after midnight, and repeat my surprise to find the beautiful, elaborate table which we left at 9.30 (and the gentlemen, of course, even later) gone, "like last year's snow," and in its place a large round centre table for their Excellencies, etc., and several smaller ones, all beautifully arranged with flowers and an elaborate supper, while the tall palms—no joke to move—form groups, with others of their kind, at the end of the room.

'"But how can it be done?" I say feebly, little thinking that my breath will be further taken away by hearing that during the five weeks' season last year, over 15,000 guests were entertained at the Castle; and judging from what I have seen on many occasions there, well entertained too. Nevertheless, and in spite of the lavish hospitality of recent and present Viceroys, we can all recall timeworn sneers and jokes about "the Castle entertainments."

"What amount of truth such held in days of yore, I know not; but in the present 'reign' they can but engender surprise between romance and reality, and for once on the side of the latter.

'Little, however, did I think, as I sat there lost in admiration of the arrangements, the absence of confusion at the tables, the excellent waiting, and liberal supply of everything, that a fortunate chance would soon afterwards give me a glimpse of "the way the wheels go round" which so smoothly work this machine of gigantic entertainment in the shape of a visit to the Viceregal kitchens. I was not surprised to hear that the giant fire consumed some two tons of coal a day during the high pressure of entertaining, and gladly we fled from the scorching monster into the cool seclusion of the "chambre de composition," where were marble slabs spread with regiments of daintily decorated timboles and other entrees, and on the centre table were large groups of tiny white statuettes moulded *in suet* (of all unlikely materials), each of which formed the centre of a "compotier" for the ball supper. The courteous French chef seemed not the least flurried by the fact this was required for some 800 persons, indeed, cheerfully observed that, "it is only a little dinner of sixty-five persons to-night," while I looked respectfully (for the first and probably the last time in my life) at 800 cutlets, egged and breadcrumbed, ready for frying, and some 150 cold fowls. We pass into the "vegetable and fish kitchen," admire a splendid 39-lb. salmon *en passant*, peep into what appears to be a good sized butcher's shop, but which turns out to be "one of the larders," then into a sanctum sanctorum, where are the "telling effects" for the supper table at "St Patrick's Ball." The Saint himself, under a barley sugar dome, ships manned with little blue sailors, windmills, and full many a "quainte conceite" flow from the ceaseless hospitalities of Dublin Castle during the winter season.'—Madam.

How different the strange social gatherings of the past. Let me, in conclusion, place a reminiscence of Viceregal hospitality before you of the early Georges—it is taken from the records preserved in the Record Tower. The document states that the Lord Lieutenant generally invites the city to dine with him soon after Twelfth Day. The Gentleman Usher sends the Lord Lieutenant's footmen with cards of invitation. The Lord Mayor and Corporation meet at the Tholsel at half-past three o'clock, and come to the Castle. The mace and sword are carried before them as far as the

Presence Chamber, where they are received by the Gentleman Usher, who conducts them into the Privy Chamber. Then the Gentleman Usher acquaints the Lord Lieutenant that the Lord Mayor and Corporation are come, and his Excellency goes from his chamber attended by the Aide-de-Camp and Gentleman Usher, into the Privy Chamber to them. The Steward, Comptroller, Gentlemen of the Bedchamber, Gentlemen at Large, and Pages, attend in the Presence Chamber, to be ready to go before the Lord Lieutenant to dinner. When dinner is on the table, the Steward and Comptroller with their wine staves, acquaint the Lord Lieutenant of it, who proceeds to dinner with the Aide-de-Camp, Steward and Comptroller, Gentleman Usher, Gentleman of the Bedchamber, all Gentlemen at Large and the Pages. A band of music plays in an ante-room during dinner. At dinner the Lord Lieutenant drinks the company's health. When the two courses are removed and the dessert is set on the table, the Lord Lieutenant calls for servers of wine; he being first served by one of the Pages, and all the company having their glasses filled, the Lord Lieutenant rises, and the company also, and drinks 'The King,' followed by the 'Prince of Wales,' the 'Duke and all the Royal Family.' Then follow 'The Glorious Memory of King William,' and afterwards 'The First of July, 1690,' at which toast the band plays 'Lillibullero.' Water is called for. Then the Lord Lieutenant drinks the following bumper toasts:- 'Prosperity to the City of Dublin,' 'Prosperity to the Linen Manufactory of Ireland', 'Prosperity to Ireland and the Trade thereof.' The Lord Lieutenant then rises, grace is said, and he takes his leave of the Lord Mayor, etc. recommending them to the care of the Steward, Comptroller, and Gentleman Usher. As soon as the Lord Lieutenant is gone, the Lord Mayor or the Recorder, etc., are conducted from the dining parlour by the Steward, Comptroller, and Gentleman Usher into the cellar, where a table is laid with glasses. The butler fills a large glass with wine, which he gives to the Lord Mayor, who puts a piece of gold into it and drinks the Lord Lieutenant's health, and passes it to the Recorder, and so it goes round all the company, each putting a piece of gold into it. When this is over, they return to the dining-room and take their seats, the Lord Mayor at the head of the table, the Comptroller and Gentleman Usher at the foot. The Steward gives the first toast by calling to the Comptroller or Gentleman Usher, so the Steward calls for everyone's toast, and the company pass the evening.

The Steward, Comptroller, Gentleman Usher, and such gentlemen of the Lord Lieutenant's family as are to stay to entertain the Lord Mayor, are to be provided with dinner in the Steward's apartments at two o'clock. All other gentlemen attending go to the green cloth. When dinner is over at the Lord Lieutenant's table, 'if the Lord Mayor, Recorder, Aldermen, and Sheriffs are not sufficient to fill the table, the Lord Lieutenant invites as many gentlemen as will fill it, who are best acquainted with the citizens.'

It appears that the system of the Lord Lieutenant entertaining his guests in the cellar was an old English and Irish sort of hospitality. Each man going to the cellar with a glass in his hand could drink from whatever hogshead he pleased. It is recorded that some gentlemen who were imbibing longer than usual, sent a request to the Duke of Ormonde to provide them with chairs. 'The Duke, however, sent as an answer that he could not encourage any gentleman drinking longer than he could stand.' The custom was given up in the Viceroyalty of the Earl of Halifax, the Lord Mayor, Sir Timothy Allen, begging his Excellency to excuse them from going to the wine cellars.

Some two hundred years ago the Viceregal Levée was held on Sunday, and the other entertainments were characteristic of the times. On a Drawingroom night, as recorded in the note of ceremonies, some few candles were to be lighted in the Presence Chamber, Privy Chamber, and Drawingroom at half-past six, and only when the ladies are coming were the rooms fully lighted. An officer, since discarded, was the Lady Lieutenant's Usher, who was to be in waiting at seven o'clock, and whose duty it was to take a list of the ladies to be presented and submit their names to the Lord and Lady Lieutenant. The Lady Lieutenant entered the Drawingroom at eight o'clock, and after the ladies to be presented were first received by her, the Lord Lieutenant was informed when this was over, and then entered the Drawingroom, the ladies being again presented.

The Lady Lieutenant played at cards on Drawingroom nights, while her pages attended behind her chair. It is also recorded that on ball nights the ladies scrambled for sweetmeats on the dancing floor.

When we read this I fear we must confess that the Castle doings of the present time compare favourably with the past, and tarnish the halo, which in imagination we so frequently paint, around that familiar phrase, 'The good old times.'

M. SARRAT

History of Ancient and Modern Dublin Or a
Visitor's Guide to the Metropolis of Ireland

DUBLIN ❧ J. CHARLES, 57 MARY STREET ❧ 1831

A nother custom which prevailed among the citizens, was that of electing annually an officer who was denominated, the mayor of the bull ring. He was appointed guardian of the bachelors of the city and during the year of his office had authority to punish such as frequented brothel-houses, and such infamous places. He took his name from an iron ring in Cornmarket, formerly Newgate Street, to which the butchers fastened their bulls for baiting; and when any bachelor citizen happened to marry, the mayor of the bull ring and his attendants conducted the bridegroom, upon his return from church, to the ring, and there, with a solemn kiss, received his homage and last farewell; from whence the new-married man took the mayor and sheriffs of the bull ring home to dinner with him, unless he was poor; in which case a collection was made, and given to him at the ring, on receiving his homage. But this office seems to have been ludicrous, and established merely by custom, without any foundation of authority.

The dress formerly worn was in accordance with the times. The men wore the *truis*, a sort of trowsers made of weft with various colours running in stripes. It extended from the loins to the ancles, fitting close to the limbs. They wore a kind of shirt, called *cota*, made of thin woollen stuff plaided, or linen died yellow, which was open in front, and fell so far below the waist as to admit of being occasionally folded about the body, and fastened by a girdle about the loins. The *cochal* was their upper garment, which reached to the middle of the thigh and had a large hanging hood of different colours; it was fringed with a border like shagged hair, and being brought over the shoulders, was made fast on the breast by a clasp or buckle. The *fillead* was a kind of mantle, which being thrown on the shoulders, spread over the whole body. The mantles of the higher classes were made of the finest scarlet cloth, bordered with a silken or woollen fringe; but those of the inferior orders were of frieze of a dark colour, with a fringed or shagged border sewn down the edges. The head-dress was a conical cap called the *barrad*, nearly resembling that of our present grenadiers. The feet were covered by the *brogue*, made of half-tanned leather, and consisted of a single sole, level from toe to heel, which they bound to the foot by a latchet or thong. They paid great attention to their beards and the hair of their heads; the latter they threw back from their foreheads, and permitted it to flow about the neck in what they called *glibbs*.

The female dress differed little from the male, except that the mantles of the former were longer and worn over a long gown. The unmarried women went bareheaded, with their hair either hanging down their back, or filleted up and fastened with a bodkin. The married wore a veil or kerchief on their head, made of fine or coarse linen, according to their circumstances.

The mantles and glibbs were such peculiar objects of abhorrence to the English, that Henry VIII in 1539, issued a proclamation prohibiting, under certain penalties, the wearing of *glibbs*, or hair upon the upper lip, called *crommeal*; also the wearing of mantles, or any garment dyed with saffron, in order that the Irish might be induced to a conformity 'with them that be civil people.' Hats were not introduced into Ireland until the beginning of the seventeenth century, and the first Irishman who wore a wig, was a Mr O'Dwyer, who lost his estate by opposing Cromwell, from which circumstance he got the appellation of 'Edmund of the Wig'.

At the time of the English invasion, the Irish soldiers were armed with short lances, darts, and broad axes, exceedingly well steeled; the latter they are said to have used with such dexterity, that the whole thigh of a soldier, though cased in complete armour, has been frequently lopped off by a single blow. In the reign of Edward III the Irish infantry consisted of gallowglasses and kerns; the former wore an iron head-piece, and a coat of mail, and were armed with a long sword and a pole-axe; the latter were a kind of light infantry, who fought with darts and javelins, and sometimes with swords, and a species of knife called skeyns. Another military weapon is mentioned which they called *krann tabhal*, a wooden sling with which they cast stones to a great distance, with great dexterity and preci-sion. Fire arms were not known in Ireland until the year 1489, when six muskets were brought from Germany to Dublin, and presented to the Earl of Kildare, then lord deputy, who put them into the hands of his guards, as they stood sentinel before his house in Thomas Street.

The Irish placed their chief confidence in that impetuous fury with which they attacked the enemy; they generally advanced to the sound of military music, and the martial cry of *Farah, Farah* which is conjectured to mean *fall on*, the word in the Irish language signifying force or violence. Afterwards, when factions universally prevailed, every chief of a sept had his peculiar war cry, which generally terminated with the word *aboe*, which is supposed to have meant the cause of the chieftain; thus the cry of the O'Neils was, *Lamh-derg-aboe*, that is, huzza for red hand:—the O'Briens, *Lamh-laider-aboe*; huzza for strong hand—the Bourkes, *Galriagh-aboe*; huzza for the red Englishman:—the Hiffernans, *Ceart-na-suas-aboe*; huzza for the right from above:—the Knight of Kerry, *Farri-buidhe-aboe*; huzza for the yellow troop:—and the Fitz-Geralds, *Crom-aboe*; huzza for Crom, supposed to be the castle of Crom, in the County of Limerick. The war cries of particular families were productive of such evils, that an Act of Parliament was passed in the year 1491, for their abolition.

The qualifications necessary to gain admittance into the Irish army, in the third century, were quite in conformity with the marvellous exploits which have been attributed to the soldiers under the command of Finn MacComhall. Every candidate was required to possess a poetical genius, to defend himself unhurt against the javelins of nine soldiers, to run through a wood pursued by a company of militia without being overtaken, to leap over a tree as high as his forehead, and to stoop easily under another as low as his knees. He was also obliged, after taking the oath of allegiance, to promise that he would never marry a woman for the sake of her portion, never offer violence to a female, never turn his back upon nine men of any other nation, and that he would be charitable to the poor.

GEORGE
BERNARD SHAW

John Bull's Other Island

LONDON ❧ CONSTABLE AND COMPANY LTD ❧ 1907

PREFACE FOR POLITICIANS NOVEMBER 1929

At Easter 1916 a handful of Irishmen seized the Dublin Post Office and proclaimed an Irish Republic, with one of their number, a schoolmaster named Pearse, as President. If all Ireland had risen at this gesture it would have been a serious matter for England, then up to her neck in the war against the Central Empires. But there was no response: the gesture was a complete failure. All that was necessary was to blockade the Post Office until its microcosmic republic was starved out and made ridiculous. What actually happened would be incredible if there were not so many living witnesses of it. From a battery planted at Trinity College (the Irish equivalent of Oxford University), and from a warship in the river Liffey, a bombardment was poured on the centre of the city which reduced more than a square mile of it to such a condition that when, in the following year, I was taken through Arras and Ypres to shew me what the German artillery had done to these cities in two and a half years, I laughed and said, 'You should see what the British did to my native city in a week.' It would not be true to say that not one stone was left upon another; for the marksmanship was so bad that the Post Office itself was left standing amid a waste of rubbish heaps and enough scraps of wall were left for the British Army, which needed recruits, to cover with appeals to the Irish to remember Belgium lest the fate of Louvain should befall their own hearths and homes.

Having thus worked up a harebrained romantic adventure into a heroic episode in the struggle for Irish freedom, the victorious artillerists proceeded to kill their prisoners of war in a drawn out string of executions. Those who were executed accordingly became not only national heroes, but the martyrs whose blood was the seed of the present Irish Free State. Among those who escaped was its first President. Nothing more blindly savage, stupid, and terror-mad could have been devised by England's worst enemies. It was a very characteristic example of the mentality produced by the conventional gentleman-militarist education at Marlborough and Sandhurst and the conventional gentleman-diplomatist education at Eton and Oxford, Harrow and Cambridge. Is it surprising that the Russian Soviet Government, though fanatically credulous as to the need for popular education, absolutely refused to employ as teachers anyone who had been touched by the equivalent public school and university routine in Russia, and stuck to its resolution even at the cost of carrying on for some years with teachers who were hardly a day ahead of their pupils?

But the Post Office episode was eclipsed by an event which was much more than an episode, as it shattered the whole case for parliamentary government throughout the world. The Irish Nationalists, after thirty years of constitutional procedure in the British Parliament, had carried an Act to establish Irish Home Rule, as it was then called, which duly received royal assent and became a statute of the realm. Immediately the British officers on service in Ireland mutinied, refusing to enforce the Act or operate against the northern Orangemen who were openly arming themselves to resist it. They were assured of support by their fellow-officers at home. The Act was suspended after prominent English statesmen had taken part in the military manoeuvres of the Orangemen. The Prime Minister publicly pledged himself that Belfast, the Orange capital, would not in any case be coerced. In short, the Act was shelved under a threat of civil war; and the Clan na Gael, which in America had steadfastly maintained that the constitutional movement was useless, as England would in the last resort repudiate the constitution and hold Ireland against the Irish by physical force, and had been rebuked, lectured, and repudiated by the parliamentary Home Rulers for a whole generation for saying so, was justified. The Catholic Irish accordingly armed themselves and drilled as Volunteers in spite of the hostility of the government, which meanwhile gave every possible assistance to the parallel preparations of the Orangemen. An Irish parliament (or Dáil) sat in Dublin and claimed to be the national government. Irish courts were set up for the administration of Irish justice; Irish order was kept by Irish police; Irish taxes were collected by Irish officials; and British courts were boycotted. Upon this interesting but hopeless attempt to ignore British rule the government let loose a specially recruited force (known to history as the Black and Tans) with *carte blanche* to kill, burn, and destroy, save only that they must stop short of rapine. They wrecked the Irish courts and produced a state of anarchy. They struck at the Irish through the popular co-operative stores and creameries, which they burnt. The people found a civil leader in Arthur Griffiths and a military one in Michael Collins. The Black and Tans had the British government at their back: Collins had the people at his back. He threatened that for every creamery or co-operative store or cabin or cottage burnt by the Black and Tans he would burn two country houses of the Protestant gentry. The country houses that were not burnt were raided at night and laid under contribution for needed supplies. If the occupants reported the raid, the house was burnt. The Black and Tans and the ordinary constabulary were treated as enemies in uniform: that is, they were shot at sight and their stations burnt; or they were ambushed and killed in petty battles. Those who gave warnings or information of any helpful kind to them were mercilessly executed without privilege of sex or benefit of clergy. Collins, with allies in every street and hamlet, proved able to carry out his threat. He won the crown of the Reign of Terror; and the position of the Protestant gentry became unbearable.

Thus by fire and bullet, murder and torture and devastation, a situation was produced in which the British government had either to capitulate at the cost of a far more complete concession of self-government to Ireland than that decreed by the repudiated Home Rule Act, or to let loose the military strength of England in a Cromwellian reconquest, massacre, and replantation which it knew that public opinion in England and America would not tolerate; for some of the most conspicuous English champions of Ulster warned the government that they could stand no more of the Black and Tan terrorism. And so we settled the Irish Question, not as civilized and reasonable men should have settled it, but as dogs settle a dispute over a bone.

Future historians will probably see in these catastrophes a ritual of human sacrifice without which the savages of the twentieth century could not effect any redistribution of political power or wealth. Nothing was learnt from Denshawai or the Black and Tan terror. In India, which is still struggling for self-government, and obviously must finally have it, a military panic led to the cannonading of a forbidden public meeting at Amritsar, the crowd being dealt with precisely as if it were a body of German shocktroops rushing the British trenches in Flanders. In London the police would have broken a score or two of heads and dragged a handful of ringleaders to the police courts. And there was the usual combination of mean spite with hyperbolical violence. Indians were forced to crawl past official buildings on their hands and knees. The effect was to make British imperial rule ridiculous in Europe, and implacably resented in India.

In Egypt the British domination died of Denshawai; but at its deathbed the British Sirdar was assassinated, whereupon the British government, just then rather drunk after a sweeping election victory secured by an anti-Russian scare, announced to an amazed world that it was going to cut off the Nile at its source and destroy Egypt by stopping its water supply. Of course nothing happened but an ignominious climb down; but the incident illustrates my contention that our authority, when it is too far flung (as our patriotic rhapsodists put it), goes stark mad at the periphery if a pin drops. As to what further panics and atrocities will ensue before India is left to govern itself as much as Ireland and Egypt now are, I am in the dark until the event enlightens me. But on the folly of allowing military counsels to prevail in political settlements I may point to the frontiers established by the victors after the war of 1914–18. Almost every one of these frontiers has a new war implicit in it, because the soldier recognises no ethnographical, linguistic, or moral boundaries: he demands a line that he can defend, or rather that Napoleon or Wellington could have defended; for he has not yet learnt to think of offence and defence in terms of airplanes which ignore his Waterloo ridges. And the inevitable nationalist rebellions against these military frontiers, and the atrocities by which they are countered, are in full swing as I write.

Meanwhile, John Bull's Other Island, though its freedom has destroyed all the romantic interest that used to attach to it, has become at last highly interesting to the student of political science as an experiment

in political structure. Protestant Ulster, which armed against the rest of
Ireland and defied the British Parliament to the cry of 'We wont have it,'
meaning that they would die in the last ditch singing 'O God, our help in
ages past' rather than suffer or tolerate Home Rule, is now suffering and
indeed hugging Home Rule on a much more homely scale than the
Home Rulers ever demanded or dreamt of; for it has a Belfast Home
Rule Parliament instead of an Irish one. And it has allowed Catholic
Ireland to secure the Irish parliament. Thus, of the two regional parliaments which have been established on a sectarian basis, Protestant Ulster
has been left with the smaller. Now it happens that Protestant Ulster is
industrial Ireland and Catholic Ireland agricultural Ireland. And
throughout the world for a century past the farmer, the peasant, and the
Catholic have been the bulwark of the industrial capitalists against the
growing political power of the industrial proletariat organised in trade
unions, labour parties, and the ubiquitous sodalities of that new ultra-
Catholic Church called Socialism.

From this defensive alliance the Ulster employers, blinded by an
obsolete bigotry and snobbery, have deliberately cut themselves off. In my
preface of 1906, and again in my 1912 preface to a sixpenny edition of
this play called the Home Rule edition, I exhorted the Protestants to take
their chance, trust their grit, and play their part in a single parliament
ruling an undivided Ireland. They did not take my advice. Probably they
did not even read it, being too deeply absorbed in the History of Maria
Monk, or the latest demonstration that all the evil in the world is the
work of an underground conspiracy entitled by them 'the Jesuits'. It is a
pity they did not begin their political education, as I began mine, by
reading Karl Marx. It is true that I had occasion to point out that Marx
was not infallible, but he left me with a very strong disposition to back the
economic situation to control all the other situations, religious, nationalist,
or romantic, in the long run. And so I do not despair of seeing Protestant
Ulster seeking the alliance it repudiated. The Northern Parliament will
not merge into the Oireachtas; for until both of them are superseded by a
completely modernised central government, made for action and not for
obstruction, they will remain more effective as regional parliaments than
they would be as national ones; but they will soon have to take counsel
together through conferences which will recur until they become a

permanent institution and finally develop into what the Americans call Congress, or Federal government of the whole island. No doubt this will be received in Belfast (if noticed at all) with shouts of 'We wont have it.' But I have heard that cry before, and regard it as a very hopeful sign that they will have it gladly enough when they have the luck to get it.

REV. G.N. WRIGHT

A Historical Guide to Ancient and Modern Dublin

LONDON ❧ BALDWIN, CRADOCK AND JOY ❧ 1821

The city of Dublin is encompassed by two canals, communicating with the Liffey, near its mouth, on the north and south sides, where extensive docks are attached to them. Upon passing the canal bridge, on the north side of the city, a flat but highly improved country is expanded to the view. On the road leading to Howth harbour, not far from Clontarf, is Marino, the seat of the Earl of Charlemont, consisting of about 100 acres richly wooded; in the centre of which stands the Casino, a beautiful structure, designed by Sir W. Chambers, and a rich specimen of Italian architecture. In this demesne there are several objects worth the attention of the visitor, viz the hermitage, and Rosamond's bower.

In the neighbourhood is Killester, the seat of Lord Newcomen, a beautiful demesne of about 50 acres, with an excellent house. In the garden are graperies and pineries of great extent. Near the village of Clontarf, about one mile from Killester, stands Clontarf Castle, the seat of George Vernon, Esq., a stately edifice, possessing noble apartments, excellent gardens, and surrounded by a highly improved demesne. A few miles farther to the north is Malahide Castle, the seat of Colonel Talbot, Member for the County of Dublin. This ancient building, and the grounds attached to it, were given to the Talbots by Henry II; much care and pains are used to preserve that air of antiquity which every object about this interesting spot possesses. The oak parlour is not only a great curiosity, but a strong testimony of the skill and address of artists in the days of other times.

Turvey House and Park, formerly the seat of Lord Kingsland, but now belonging to the Trimleston family, is an extensive demesne, and thickly wooded, but no farther interesting. There is another magnificent residence at the north side of the city, three miles from Dublin, Santry, the seat of Sir Compton Domville, Bart., remarkable principally for its great extent.

Near Malahide, is the Church of St Dolough, an object of great interest to the antiquarian; this ancient building, which is roofed with stone, and in excellent preservation, is of such a style of architecture as to render it a matter of considerable difficulty to reconcile the date of its erection with any exact period; there are many holy wells of various forms and properties around.

On the hill of Howth, which is such a prominent feature in the scenery at the north side of the city, is Howth Castle, the seat of the Earl of Howth: the house is an ancient castle modernised, and is much disfigured by being so constantly and accurately white-washed. In the residence of this ancient and noble family, some relics of the greatness and heroism of their ancestors are still preserved: here may be seen the double-handled sword, with which Sir Tristram committed such havoc amongst the Danes.

The Abbey of Howth is a beautiful and interesting ruin, and contains some curious tombs; and on the island of Ireland's Eye, about three quarters of a mile from the pier head, are the ruins of the Monastery of Holm Patrick; upon this little detached piece of land, there is a castellated rock, which, seen from the shore, never fails to deceive the stranger; and on the shore along which the Dublin road winds, are the ruins of Kilbarrick Abbey.

To the south of Dublin lies a country not exceeded by any outlet in the empire, a spacious inclined plane reaching from the foot of the mountains to the seaside, thickly studded with villages, lodges, castles, demesnes, villas, etc. from Dublin to the base of Sugar-loaf Hill, a distance of twelve Irish miles.

The villages of Black Rock and Dunleary have long and deservedly been celebrated as bathing places, and the retreat of all the citizens on

Sundays. Near Black Rock are innumerable seats, commanding delightful sea and mountain views, the most splendid of which is Mount Merrion, the seat of—Verschoyle, Esq.; the demesne, which is enclosed by a high wall, contains 100 acres beautifully wooded, and commands a view of the whole County of Dublin, part of the County Wicklow, with the scalp in the foreground and in cloudless weather, the mountains of the County Down may be distinctly seen from these grounds. Sans Souci, the seat of Mr La Touche; Leopard's Town, the residence of Lord Castle-Coote; Stillargan, and many other equally magnificent demesnes, adorn this neighbourhood.

More to the west are Rathfarnham Castle, formerly occupied by the Marquis of Ely, whose property it is; Bushy Park, the seat of Robert Shaw, Esq. MP for the city of Dublin; Marley, the seat of the Right Honourable David La Touche; and Holly Park, the property of Jeffrey Foote, Esq.

Along the banks of the Liffey, west of the city, is a beautiful view of a country in which are some very elegant demesnes and splendid mansions. Leixlip Castle and the Salmon Leap are romantic and beautiful objects, and the aqueduct thrown across the Rye, by the Royal Canal Company, is a great artificial curiosity, being 100 feet high. Near to Dublin, along the banks of the river, are several very beautiful plantations and residences. Hermitage, formerly the seat of Colonel Hanfield, is particularly picturesque and romantic. Palmerstown, one of the seats of the Right Honourable Lord Donoughmore, is a princely dwelling.

Lutterils Town, the seat of Luke White, Esq. MP, formerly the property of Lord Carhampton, is one of the most extensive demesnes in the county of Dublin.

JAMES COLLINS

Life in Old Dublin

CORK ❧ TOWER BOOKS ❧ 1978 FACSIMILE EDITION
FIRST PUBLISHED 1913

A s we leave the quay side on our way to Arbour Hill, we pass over the 'Croppies' Acre.' Thousands of Dublin citizens, year in and year out, on their way to the Phoenix Park, gaze on the Esplanade in front of the Royal Barracks, not knowing the fact that this was in '98 known as the 'Croppy Hole'. The late Dr Thomas Willis, father-in-law of our respected City Coroner (Dr Louis Byrne), after great research, located beyond doubt its exact site, and published privately the following 'Memorial of the Croppies' Acre':

'In the year 1798 the Irish Government had information that an attack would be made on the city of Dublin by a large body of United Irishmen, then collecting on the north side about Swords and Santry, and on the south about Rathfarnham and neighbourhood. Although ignorant of the exact point to be assailed, the Executive (greatly alarmed) took speedy measures to defeat the project. The men assembled at Rathfarnham were dispersed by Lord Ely's Dragoons, strengthened by a large detachment of Yeomen. Those on the north side were routed by Lord Roden's Fox Hunters (so designated from the splendid horses), supported by some Light Infantry. These bodies were dispersed after feeble resistance. Some of the insurgents were sabred, and some prisoners were made. Nevertheless, the insurgents did make several simultaneous attacks upon various forts and garrisons with surprising pertinacity. However, the metropolis had little reason to be alarmed at such fitful and desultory attempts. The Yeomen, Infantry, and Cavalry, being placed on permanent duty, scoured the surrounding districts, and had frequent encounters with small bodies of insurgents. Rathfarnham, Crumlin, Saggard, Tallaght, Clondalkin, Rathcoole, Kilcock, Maynooth, etc., were the scenes of the petty warfare. The prowess of the Yeomen was estimated according to the number of prisoners and mutilated bodies which they brought into the city, and it is worth mentioning that we have no record of a single man of the various corps having been killed or wounded in any of these inglorious raids. Lord Cornwallis, writing to the Duke of Portland, states "that any man in a brown coat who was found within several miles of the field of action was butchered without discrimination".—(Cornwallis Correspondence, vol. ii, page 357) Every day beheld prisoners brought into the city; nor was it unusual to see a procession of carts, in which were piled the mutilated corpses of peasantry. The prisoners were hanged from lamp-posts, and the dead were, in some instances, stretched out in the Castle Yard, where the Viceroy then resided, and in full view of the Secretary's windows. "They lay on the pavement as trophies, cut and gashed in every part, covered with clotted blood and dirt."—(Barrington, vol. ii, page 260) "And at other times the sabred dead were suspended in Barrack Street."—(Musgrave, page 224).

'To avoid expensive interment, the authorities selected a piece of waste ground on the south side of Barrack Street, within about fifty paces of the Infantry Barracks, as a convenient repository for the corpses of the Irish rebels. This unhallowed spot was thenceforward known as "Croppies' Acre", or "Croppies' Hole". It now forms part of the Esplanade. It extended in the year 1798 from the rere of the houses down to the river, and was then waste, and covered with filth. The diminishing breadth of the river by walling in, the making its course more direct between the bridges, and the formation of the Esplanade, have very considerably altered the appearance of the ground, and have obliterated every vestige of "Croppies' Hole". However, the site and exact dimensions can be very accurately ascertained from maps of the period, also from very many persons still living who have a perfect recollection of the ground, and who remember reading the names of the deceased rudely carved on the surface of the stones which formed the boundary wall on the west side of that unconsecrated cemetery.

'Those strangled at the Provost Prison, and on the different bridges, together with the sabred bodies of the peasantry brought into the city almost daily, were all flung into the trenches formed in that filthy dung heap.

'"The day will come (says Dr Madden) when this desecrated spot will be hallowed ground, consecrated by religion; trod lightly by pensive patriots, and decorated by funeral trophies in honour of the dead whose bones lie there in graves that are now neglected and unhonoured."

'Names of some of those whose remains moulder in "Croppies' Hole":

'Ledwich, brother of the PP of Rathfarnham; hanged on Queen's Bridge, 26 May 1798.

'Wade, from Rathfarnham, hanged on Queen's Bridge, 26 May, 1798.

Carroll, cotton manufacturer, hanged on Church Street Bridge, 26 May, 1798.

'Adams and Fox, hanged at Provost prison. (Musgrave, Appendice XV)

'Fennell and Raymond, hanged on Church Street Bridge.

'Esmonde, Doctor, brother of Sir Thomas Esmonde, hanged on the scaffold north side of Carlisle Bridge, then in process of erection. His corpse was carried back in a cart and flung (O'Kelly, page 63) into a heap of offal in "Croppies' Hole", 14 June 1798.

'Byrne and Kelly, killed at Rathfarnham. Their lifeless bodies and three others were hung the morning after their death from lamp irons in Barrack Street, and afterwards consigned to "Croppies' Hole". (Musgrave, page 224)

'Teeling and Matthew Tone, hanged at Provost Prison. (Teeling, 2nd Narrative, page 245.—Speeches from the Dock, page 71)

'Bacon, hanged on Carlisle Bridge.

'Several poor men, employed as lamplighters, were hanged on the bridges for neglect of duty, and blood began to flow without any mercy.

Barrington, vol. 2, page 261.'

In addition to the foregoing in the printed matter, the following notes are in the copy I possess, written by the late Edward Evans:

'Note.—"Croppies' Acre" was situated 147 feet from the boundary wall of the Esplanade, on the west side of Liffey Street (west), and 155 feet from the boundary wall of the Infantry Barracks. The area from east to west was 312 feet, and from north to south 170 feet. (This minute description of "Croppies Acre" is in the handwriting of the late Dr Thomas Willis, and now in my possession.—E.E.)

'Michael Rafter, Esq., CE, City Hall, has kindly supplied me with the following particulars of the site of "Croppies' Hole":

'1 May 1884—The position of the "Croppies' Acre" can be found as follows:—Exactly midway between Albert Quay and Barrack Street, in the Esplanade, and opposite the centre of the Royal or Central Square, in the northern corner, from whence keeping in the centre of the Esplanade for 104 yards due east, runs the northern boundary, between which and the river lay the field in question. This field is shown on Roques' Map of Dublin, published about 1760, as being at the end of Flood Street, and its measurements on that map correspond with those given above.—(Michael Rafter, Surveyor and Civil Engineer)'

P.J. DILLON

The Fingal Road and Some Who Travelled It

DUBLIN ❧ M.H. GILL AND SON LTD ❧ 1930

BRIAN BORU

A day of glory and of sorrow for Ireland is the day that follows on Clontarf. From the Liffey to Binn Eadair—the Hill of Howth—the Danes lie thick in death, and the tide that breaks on the shore still casts up the corpses that have been tossing the waters of Dublin Bay. The Viking demon that has tormented the body of Ireland for centuries has been exorcised, but, alas! the voice that, under God, cast that Demon out, is silent. The hand that wielded the sceptre is still; Brian Boru, the High King of Erin, is gone to Heaven; and it is his obsequies that we take part in, on the road that leads through Fingal.

Brian fell by the hand of Bruadar, in his tent overlooking Clontarf, Good Friday, 1014. And the men of Erin raise him on the bier, and they set out on that mournful pilgrimage to distant Armagh, where he is to lie till the Judgment. And as the cortege proceeds the memories of the deeds that the dead King had accomplished crowd thick and fast, and the might of mind and the greatness of the man stand out. As the thunder-cloud emits out of its own blackness the livid shaft of lightning that illumines the earth, so Death, out of *its* darkness, throws a search-light on the earthly career of its victim. And so, too, as they go *forward* on his last journey, they go *backwards* over the journey of his life. *Forward* by Drumcondra and Santry, solemnly and slowly and reverently they bear him. *Backwards* go their thoughts to his youthful exploits against the Danes, when, with a chosen band of Dalcassians, he fought a lone hand against the enemy. They dwell on the vengeance he wreaked on the murderers of his beloved brother Mahon, on Danes and on traitorous Irish alike, on the lustre he brought to the Kingship of Munster, which came to him as successor to Mahon. And the *caoine* rises. Brian the Valorous! Brian the merciless avenger of treachery! Brian the champion of Christianity against the Pagan! Brian the exemplary High-King who died penniless, and desired with his last breath to be buried in Ireland's primatial Church at Armagh. May his name be honoured for ever in Erin.

Onward his cortege moves on the Fingal Road. The news of its coming has spread far afield, and groups gather here and there to see it pass. From Raheny, and Baldoyle, and Cloghran and Kinsealy, they make their way to swell the throng that accompanies the monarch's remains to Swords—Sord Coluimcille. There in the monastery they rest, under the care of the monks, that first night—for the remains of his valiant son and his gallant grandson are with his own—while unceasing prayers ascend to Heaven for the souls of the dead King, his natural heir and the heir to his heir. And the people outside in the ancient town of Swords tell and retell the stories of his prowess: how he released his own kingdom of Munster from the thraldom of the foreigners; how he drove them out of Limerick and out of Connacht; how he gave them a blow from which they reeled for long on the bloody field of Glenmama. They recall the tales told them by their fathers of the grinding tyranny that the Irish had groaned under, when the barbarous invaders plundered and spoiled and ravaged and burned; how the people were harried by ruthless tax-gatherers, who wreaked their will on man, on woman, and on beast, so that it was not, as their chroniclers put it, 'in the power of one of the men of Erin to give the milk of his own cow, or the equivalent of one hen's laying of eggs, in succour or in sincere kindness to his elders, but to preserve them carefully for some foreign steward, or bailiff, or soldier'.

While it is still early in the April morn, the funeral train resumes its progress along the Fingal Road. Before long, they are abreast of another way that leads to Lusk, by which, on another Easter week, nine centuries later, another Munsterman, Thomas Ashe, is to march along to try conclusions with the foreigner. Think of it: two Easter weeks, nine hundred years apart and two, but linked together, through undying loyalty to Roisin Dubh, by Brian Boru and Thomas Ashe, and Kilmainham, and Ashbourne and the Fingal Road.

Now the mourners' train has reached Balrothery—Baile an Ridire. The 'hungry Hamiltons' are not yet to descend on that district for some centuries yet to come, and Balbriggan is not in being. So we proceed by the old highway of the North, and cross the Delvin into Meath. Those who, for sufficient reason, are obliged to drop out of the cortege, are replaced by others, as contingents from Naul, and Garristown, and Stamullen, and Ardcath and Cnoc na gCeann, join it at various points along the way.

And now a temporary deflection is made from the main thoroughfare, so as to reach the monastery at Duleek, where the second night's halt is made. Again the bier is placed before the High Altar, and throughout the watches of the night the monks chant the prayers for the dead. When, with the light of another day, the funeral train sets out again from Duleek, we accompany it but a little way. We detach ourselves from it at Drogheda, watching it withdraw itself from us across the Boyne. As it recedes further from us and still further, the cadences of the mourners, rising and falling on the quiet morning air, grow faint and fainter. And so, we watch the spirit cortege out of sight, moving onwards to Dún Dealgan, 'the Gap of the North', to halt at last with its gift of kingly dust to the consecrated bed that has been hollowed for it at Armagh.

There is one other moral. Somewhere, across that road from Dublin to Belfast, along which Brian's coffin was borne on men's shoulders, subtle brains have constructed what they call a boundary. Brian ruled at Kincora; Brian triumphed at Clontarf; Brian lies buried in Armagh. In a notable panegyric at the graveside of O'Donovan Rossa, Padraig Pearse, apostrophising the English Government in Ireland, said: 'Fools! fools! fools! to think that you can destroy the Irish instinct for Freedom, while you leave us our Fenian graves.' And Brian Boru, glorious victor of Clontarf, and High-King of all Ireland, lies buried at Armagh, separated from us of Leinster and Munster and Connacht, even part of Ulster—separated from us by what? Fools! Fools! Fools!

G.F. CUMING

Some Old Dublin Conveyances

PERIODICAL NOT KNOWN

We find it difficult to picture Dublin without its splendid tramway services, linking up, as it does, every part of the city and suburbs and facilitating our many little expeditions on business or pleasure. We prefer not to picture Dublin without its trams. Nor can we imagine it without motor, taxi or private motor-bicycle, or 'push-bike'—not to mention the ubiquitous 'per-am!' Yet there was a time when none of these things were, and life went on—without them.

Let us glance backwards for a moment and see how the citizens of Old Dublin got about town. The mere man, for the most part, trusted to 'shank's mare', in other words, his own two feet. The well-to-do and their families patronised the sedan chair and at one time every family had its own chair; while sedans were for hire on the streets. In 1771 there were about four hundred of them for hire in Dublin and, as it was at that time 'deemed a reproach for a gentlewoman to be seen walking in the streets' they were naturally much in demand by the ladies. Sedans were introduced into England by Charles I, who, when prince, brought them from Spain.

The sedan-bearers were familiarly known as 'Christian Ponies', and there is a well-known story of a Connnaught man who, having hired a couple of these 'ponies' to bear him to his destination, stepped into the chair, only to find that the bottom had fallen out of it: but far from demurring, cheerfully walked all the way, and on getting out, remarked to the bearers: 'Only for the honour of the thing I might as well have walked!'

Hackney coaches were regulated and controlled in 1703 and the number limited to one hundred and fifty. They were copied from the English, but one-horse vehicles had been in use in Dublin long before there was anything similar in England. Cross-Channel passengers in the old days landed at Ringsend and the 'Ringsend cars' did good business between it and Dublin, and also by conveying parties to Irishtown, then a fashionable resort for sea-bathing and cockle parties. The Ringsend car consisted of a seat suspended in a strap of leather between shafts and without springs. It was distinguished by the noise made by the creaking of the strap, which supported the whole company.

Next comes the 'noddy', so-called because it had an oscillating movement backwards and forwards. It was a low vehicle, capable of holding two, and covered with a salash. The 'noddy boy', who was usually a full-sized man, occupied a seat that protruded back so that he sat, as it were, in the lap of his company. The saying: 'Elegance and ease like a shoeblack in a noddy,' was probably levelled at Higgins, the Sham Squire, who had been a shoeblack in his early days. It will be remembered that he took his prospective father-in-law and his fiancée for a drive in a noddy on one occasion.

The jingle was a four-wheeled vehicle which rattled like the bells of a waggon team. The 'jaunting car', modified and improved, is still a popular mode of conveyance in Dublin and throughout the country. It is, I fancy, exclusively an Irish means of transport. It is said that the witty Duchess of Gordon remarked after the passing of the Union, and the consequent exodus of the aristocracy, that there were but two titled men now who attended her soirées—Sir John Jingle and Sir John Jaunting-Car, alluding to Sir John Stevenson, the great musician, and Sir John Carr of pocket-book celebrity.

OLIVER ST JOHN GOGARTY

As I Was Going Down Sackville Street

LONDON ❧ RICH AND COWAN LTD ❧ 1937

DUBLIN HAS ONE ADVANTAGE: IT IS EASY TO GET OUT OF IT. Unlike London, which is bottled on three sides and uninteresting on the fourth, Dublin has the country and the streamy hills very near, and nearer still the sea. It is but three minutes' drive to Ballsbridge, which was widened recently by 'Contractors', which is about as much of a 'Bull' as the statement that the Sussex heights are downs. And Ballsbridge is by Serpentine Avenue, in which you can get a horse for an hour's canter on the wide sands of Merrion. One must choose the time when the tide is out, or at least not fully in. And as the tides—uncharacteristically—of Dublin are predictable and punctual, there is rarely an hour of a morning when the sands are covered. The morning sky is a sight worth more than a morning's sleep. Before the reek ascends from the old houses in which now nearly every room holds a fire—so different from the days when one family held a whole house—there is always a glint of sunlight to be found at the edge of the distant tide. The little waves that cannot rise to any height on the level sands may be the better part of a mile away, but you can canter for five minutes before you meet them and watch them bearing rainbows and spreading on the tawny sands their exquisite treasures brought, as it were, overseas from the inexhaustible and sunny East.

On the right is the smooth outline of the Dublin mountains, rising like cones and rippling into nipples like the paps of Jura, where Wicklow shows Bray Head. The Golden Spears are softened and magnified in the golden morning haze and the greater nearer mass of the Two and Three Rock mountains is half translucent and unreal. Far away, twin steeples catch the light at Kingstown; and the great house at Monkstown, built where the Dún or stronghold of Leary stood, begins to blink its windows at the sun. The outline of the little granite town between the hills and the sea is the colour of the sand, and recalls some such sight as must have gladdened pilgrims' eyes when dawn showed them Florence or Fiesole. But the irregular formation of the Wickow Hills preserves the mind from forming a pattern or formula for their formation. They are subject to no one design as the herring-bone ridges of the Apennines; and they will never by repetition offend or limit imagination. And yet in the morning light they rival the hills of Italy in the beauty of their form; at other times their beauty must depend, like all Irish mountain scenes, on the play of shade and light. The uncontaminated breezes flow in with the gentle tide. Howth is amethystine yet, and the long, high horizon is unbroken by a sail. I can see the parallel valleys shared out from a central ridge running along half Italy, steeped in monotonous and assured sun. Here, before I turn, all may be changed. The luminous mass may be angry brown and fuming at its edges with luminous vapour. The whole canvas may be erased.

The morning sky along the coast may be seen as late as 9 a.m. on a morning of February or March. Dublin is, during the months from October to March, a winter resort. The summer gives us delights in their proper season. It is only the winter months that would lie heavy were it not for the advantages the town has of egress to the wilds. We inhale the Atlantic vapours and they turn us into mystics, poets, politicians and unemployables with school-girl complexions; thus these vapours have lost their enervating and transforming powers before they reach England. And yet her only thanks is to send us for April her eastern winds, whose influence is influenza. No one makes allowance enough for us who live in this vat of fumes from the lost Atlantis.

You must not think that Merrion is like this every morning at the beginning of the year; certainly not, but I have seen it thus on occasions when beauty reigned in the air and made it receptive. All we have to do is to dwell on such moments of beauty. The other moments matter little, and should be dismissed as interlopers and of evil origin. It is the same with life: few moments are allotted to us free from concerns or boredom. These can be counted on the fingers, but as they shall have to stand for us for whatever is desirable and tolerable in life, engrave them in golden letters on the marble of memory and let the rest be forgotten, or remembered, by the happy moments' foil.

It costs one hour's sleep and half-a-crown to ride out to meet the winnowing tide at Merrion. You could not do it for that in Rotten Row, nor there, for all the money in the Treasury, could you make sure of being alone. There may be a corpulent and cheery bookmaker striding the foundation of his profession along by the sea wall, but he will not come near you. He will think that you are melancholy mad or that your horse is restive: that you are better left alone. One thing is sure: you will not waken Dublin, which insists on nursing its misery while shutting its eyes to its delights. Your horse will be hard to hold once he is turned. He sees the squat tower of Irishtown Church. He knows the slip that leads to the roadway. He wants to get back to his stables. No matter how far you may take him beyond them, he will gallop back.

It will not take me long to get through my hospital work this morning, I thought, as I was breakfasting. I shall have time to read the morning papers, particularly the *Daily Express*, for things have come to such a pass now that we have to look into an English paper for uncoloured news and for news suppressed at home. Either through pity for the Government, or an endeavour to leave it unembarrassed, the two untied papers 'go easy with the news'. A leader or two criticising finance, or such impersonal theme, is the furthest the criticism goes. The Government here has freedom from the Press. This is compensated for by the fact that it owns a press, which has no freedom from the Government, and so the whole round earth is every way ...

If I am late I shall have to talk to Sir Chalmers, the historical surgeon at the hospital. He is an asset to us, for without him the tradition of surgery which comes down from Nelson's hard-battling fleets would be broken. He is a type of the old and lost school of the days when a doctor had first of all to be a gentleman. After that he could be qualified. How few could be qualified were such a condition to be made primary! A genial man, a great host. 'That's sloke and piping hot ... with the mutton ... with the mutton .... What was this I was about to say? Oh, yes! I believe in top-dressing women, and in helping them, if occasion arises afterwards. And why not, poor creatures? The under sex.'

Sir Frederick will be there, he whose memory goes back so far that he has forgotten his survival in the present. And the 'workers' of the Staff will, mercifully, be engaged. Thank goodness, my line of work seldom involves calamities. In the scramble for beds no one has as yet suggested 'slabs' for me. I will be discreet and ask no questions about the winner of the over-night's Sweep. Well, I know, but unofficially—which covers a multitude of inquiries—that there is a Sweep nightly in most of the wards, and he who draws the 'stiff'—the first to die in the morning—wins. Thus it is differen-tiated from horse-racing, which is gambling; but Death is certain! 'When we beat the Incurables, I was in the Hospice for the Dying. We beat them by nearly ten degrees.' The degrees were degrees of temperature. Rival nurses took the temperatures of a selected team from the ward in each hos-pital, added them up and reported. 'We beat them by ten degrees, and if Mr Purvis Puris is operating to-day, we'll knock hell out of the Fever Hospital next week.' Such are the advantages of surgery over Medicine!

There are nineteen hospitals in Dublin, and all of them unmergeable into one. That is due to the fact that many grants and endowments were denominational. There is a greater vested interest in disease than in Guinness's Brewery. This explains why it would give rise to far more trouble than it is worth to run the nineteen into one. Besides the unem-ployment it would create and the disease it would end! Disease is not always a heartbreaking and melancholy affair, as might be supposed. Where there are so many hospitals for so small a city the diseases thin out, as it were, in proportion to their deadliness; they tend to become chronic and tolerable. The cheeriest of people I have come across are cripples or invalids of some sort. A robust or 'hearty' person is looked on somewhat as askancely as he would be in Magdalen or 'The House'. The same applies to an independent spirit... I sometimes feel that even I am wanting in popularity.

'So St Vincent's beat us. I am sorry to hear that, Sister. Who had we running against them?'

'The Grattan Ward.'

'And they?'

'Their Gynaecological.'

'They must have had a few puerperals, for they won by 6.80° over our side: we were playing eleven. I hope none of them rubbed their ther-mometers on their sleeves or put them on the hot-water bottles..... I have known that kind of thing to happen, and it's not fair. When patients take such an interest in these inter-hospital sports competitions, which help them to bear their trouble and add interest to the weary hours, they should at least play the game.'

'There was no cheating. I took the temperatures with my own thermometer.'

'Sister, this is an excellent report.'

'But, sir, I am afraid there is to be a Board inquiry.'

I was puzzled. I felt that I had been putting my foot into it if the inquiry involved the sister.

'A Board inquiry? What about?'

'About these inter-hospital matches. Matron says they are disgraceful, undignified and full of unbecoming levity.'

'I will make a point to attend that meeting.'

'We'll all be grateful if you will, sir. I need not say how grateful I will be, for it was I who took the temperatures.'

But I had no time to compose a defence because one of the physicians came in, with 'Look here, I'd be glad of a word with you.'

'Yes. Out with it.'

'The hospitals are going to blazes. It seems that for some months most unseemly competitions in temperatures have been going on: whole wards vying with each other, not only in their own hospitals, but against wards in other hospitals. It will bring us into disrepute and lead to a collision with the other Staffs. We are holding a meeting in the Board Room this afternoon at four o'clock...' (Just as I might have guessed, when I cannot be there, I said to myself.) 'A Board meeting to find out what is to be done.'

'It's quite clear: reduce your temperatures on the medical side, and we will look after our surgical side, so that our hospital will be scouted out of the Senior League or whatever it is; and let the others set their own houses in order.'

'That's all very well; but Matron says we must show our authority and maintain discipline by administering a stern rebuke.'

'I'm perfectly sick of authorities and administrations of stern rebukes. If I go to that meeting, I warn you I will blow it sky high. What sort of Sadists are you, that you must stuff your authority into patients, when probably all they want is a clyster? Anyway, this department, which was built for me by the Irish Hospitals' Sweep, is hardly the place to deprecate sweeps in hospitals. If it ever occurred to you to ask yourself whence comes the amazing courage of the half-fed sick poor that makes ailing and terrorised patients face operations—all the more appalling because of ignorance exaggerating terror—and makes them 'frivolous', as you call it, in the face of Death, you will find it is due to this camaraderie and good-human-natured joking among the patients themselves. The alternative is disciplined efficiency run to such lengths as would turn the establishments for the relief of pain and the cure of disease into vivisection societies. Let them have all the fun they can, and good luck to them. They are better men than I would be if faced with half of their disabilities—of which not the least is the arbitrary discipline planned to exalt "Authority". Every little pettifogging (no, no, that is not the word, for they don't leap as to the tabor's sound and they have no joy in the jumping), every trumpery little commissar is trying to bolster up his lack of personality and character by becoming a disciplinarian and an authority. And now they want to put a stop to the only game in which it may be truly said that the side which is beaten is not disgraced. Some women have no gumption; they would offer to nurse St Anthony through his struggles with the flesh.'

'Well, you are busy now, but we can go into the matter thoroughly at four o'clock.'

My own character must be weak somewhere, I thought, after Crowningshield had taken himself off. The moment I gain a point I feel like a bully and I want to apologise. Now, Crowningshield is a nice fellow if not driven by 'Authority'. I do not want to hurt his feelings. The more I dwelt on that the more I saw he was right in a way: most of us are—because there is something to be said for discipline in hospitals, something to be said for measures against frivolity in the ante-room of Death.

I remembered what happened to a beautiful young woman whose father took up Spiritism, or whatever they call it, late in life. The growing girl was taught that Death is not, and that the supersession of breath was no more than 'passing over'. After two attempts to poison herself, she jumped from a high bridge into a shallow stream and drove her splintered thigh-bones into her beautiful body. Once we relax the fear of death something happens to Life. It would appear, then, that Death is an astringent to Life. It is verily. This is borne out by the fact that those who are near Death fear it not so much as those who are in the fullness of health and the enjoyment of life. These are conscious of what they have to lose, and so the contemplation of the opposite condition becomes frightful. Death holds life together. We are borne onwards by the black and white horses.

Long ago I was greatly shocked when I saw patients for operations being trundled on a tumbril of sorts into the anaesthetic room *en route* to the theatre, where they would be operated on by a man whose job it was, and who neither knew their names nor circumstances. But the reverse of the picture converted me. Were the surgeon to know that perhaps he had under his knife the breadwinner of a family of eight would it help or hinder him? It would be in degree like operating on a relative. And where was the sympathy to end? Surely you could not permit dirty friends to accompany the sick man up to the moment he was put to sleep. There is plenty of discipline where it is wanted. Try to relax it where it is not. The whole problem of the treatment of the sick appeared at one time to me to be full of wastes, overlappings and abuses. Suppose, for example, forty little hunchbacks are gathered together under the new disease description of 'Surgical tuberculosis' in a mansion sold for the sake of the rates. Any syndicate who owned the premises could call it the only hospital for the exclusive treatment of bone tuberculosis, a staff of sixty could congregate—proprietors, doctors, nurses, laundry-maids, porters, wardmaids, etc. That is one and a half supers carried on each little hump! Why is this not scandalous? Because the expense falls on no one in particular, and one and a half persons to serve each hump is not as good as two, or even three would be. The more, the sooner the hump may disappear.... No one in particular is paying for the upkeep of this imaginary example of a hospital. But many get their living out of it, and each child gets an extra chance of life. So long as we consider life precious, this must continue. Humaneness is our claim to existence in a civilised mode. The higher the type the more humane. Humanity is all that matters to human beings. There is so much of it among the British people that it overflows into the animal world, as is witnessed by the Societies for the Prevention of Cruelty to Animals and the pampering of dogs. The corollary: disregard of animal suffering is a disregard for human life; as soon as animals are maltreated it will not be far until children, women and men will suffer. It is a good thing to have an overplus of humane feelings. The multiplication of small hospitals might be objected to if they were a drain on the community. The Empire of Austria had but one for the whole of its wide and mixed territory. The conditions there were the next thing to inhuman. There were no nurses, as we know them, for there were no middle-classes whose daughters would enlist. Old street-walkers took their places, and, what is worse, took the places and performed the duties of qualified men. And if a student wished to get into personal relationship with a teacher, without which it is hard to learn, he had to go round the corner to a little half-private hospital run by the nuns of some Order. Any personal sympathy with the patients was out of the question because of the system and because of the multiplicity of languages. The different departments were marked by coloured stakes: red for surgery, blue for midwifery, yellow for eyes, etc. And the flag that announced no deaths was never flown.... We have discovered a way to deal with diseases and to subordinate them to man. We keep disease in its proper place. If Death walks the world, why not make it walk the streets and suffer us to be its souteneurs like George Moore's *Alfred aux belles dents*? Yes! We must meet it with a serious aspect. Let us make disease 'keep' us all.

Thus we make disease pay for its own upkeep, but keep those concerned with its cure or treatment. Those who fell victims to suffering—the dead—have endowed most of our hospitals. The rest of the upkeep of hospitals falls now on sportsmen, no longer on the Banks. The Banks have thus lost the last link that bound them to humanity, and sportsmen gained the first links which give them possibly something in common with religion—Hope and Charity. The Archbishop of Canterbury points to an eternal reward after death, and bids his followers live in Hope. The Hospitals' Sweep sells us Hope of an earthly reward three times a year. Thus the Archbishop and the Bookmakers have a common interest: both hawk Hope; but the hoping sportsmen, seeing that they are not required to die tri-annually before chancing into their reward, endow the dying so that they may take their eternal chance. The Archbishop requires that men should spend their lives righteously and in corporal works of mercy. The horsey people propose that you should live your own life and spend ten shillings, and the Sweep will look after the mercy by endowing charities. It is Cantuar *v.* Centaur.

Three great inventions came from Ireland—the invention of soda water whereby whiskey outdoes champagne, the invention of the pneumatic tyre whereby was made possible the evolution of an engine to scale the blue, and the invention of the system whereby disease is made to support patient, nurse and doctor, and horses to carry hospitals!

There are proportionally to population not half so many hospitals in London, and this in spite of the many vocations which lead to disease. This is only apparent. The truth is that every Englishman's house is his hospital, particularly the bathroom. Patent medicine is the English patent. Liverpool to London, judging by advertisements for food, sauces, soups, purgatives and hygienic porcelain, is an intestinal tract. Millions have been made out of patents for purgatives, not to include the patent medicines which are intended to deal with the various results of eating too much. And most of these patent medicines, very nearly all of them, are taken in the bathroom. The most amazing results are advertised. You can lose pounds of flesh by taking a patent form of Glauber's Salts, or put on pounds (only if you are a lady) by the same taking. Agonising aches in people unseen and unheard of by the patentees disappear, regardless of idiosyncrasy, or a positive Wassermann. And the Englishman believes all this. He believes that a purgative can fatten or make him thin; he believes that either there is only one kind of ache or that one medicine can cure various kinds. His empty churches would be filled twice over by the faith he wastes on the permutations and importance of his lower bowel. And yet, in spite of his faith in one medicine for many unseen and unknown diseases, he cannot accept miracles; he burks at the infallibility of the Pope, but unquestioningly accepts the infallibility of the pill. 'Just as much as will fit on a threepenny-piece' instead of as many angels as will stand on the point of a needle. So Faith has fallen in England to the level of the lavatory. And yet it cannot be said that it gives rise to less appreciation of love of righteousness, for it makes *Mens conscia recti*. But it saddens me to think of the pent-up faith misdirected that liberated could rise to Heaven in ministers with flying buttress, curious pinnacle and soaring belfry. Perhaps, fearing lest he be made to hop on the Day of Judgment, the Englishman is keeping something in reserve.

DOUGLAS GOLDRING

Dublin Explorations and Reflections
By an Englishman

DUBLIN AND LONDON ❧ MAUNSEL ❧ 1917
(PUBLISHED ANONYMOUSLY)

One of the most delightful aspects of Dublin life is its frugality and lack of ostentation. There is no 'money standard' in Dublin, for no one, luckily, appears to have any money. An income of £600 or £700 a year, on which in London a single man with a moderate liking for the play, for dancing, and for entertaining his friends at restaurants would before the war have found it difficult to manage, in Dublin would be considered affluence. For one thing, the play, such as it is, is accessible for a few shillings; and the restaurant habit does not appear to have been developed at all. Dubliners are thrown entirely on their own wits to make their social life diverting, but it is safe to assert that Dublin hospitality (which is traditional) loses nothing from the fact that it lacks the oppressive opulence of London entertainment. Speaking from my own limited experience, I must say that I have never passed more amusing or delightful evenings than in the houses of friends in Dublin.

One of the reasons for the moderate standard of living in Dublin may be found in the fact that—except for the brewing of porter and the manufacture of whiskey and of biscuits—the city appears to have no industries. So far as I have been able to observe, the population of Dublin (not counting the brewers, &c.) is made up chiefly of doctors and priests, with a sprinkling of *rentiers*, a great horde of officials, and, finally, perhaps the largest proportion of abjectly poor people which is to be found in any city in Europe of the same size. The principal source of livelihood, alike for rich and poor, is undoubtedly that fine old crusted institution, the 'Money Office'. The particular form of 'Money Office' which supplies the necessities of the very poor has three golden balls hanging decoratively on its façade. Inside the establishment there is a long counter marked off by little partitions. Behind the counter wait the assistants who receive the quaint bundles presented to them—a patched woollen shawl, perhaps, enveloping a man's shirt, boots and Sunday trousers—and deliver in exchange to their owners the few shillings or pence necessary to support life or to procure forgetfulness. Among the very poor it is always the women who visit the pawnbroker, and every 'Money Office' has its long list of regular clients.

The 'Money Offices' for the intellectual and upper classes are naturally of far superior design, and no tell-tale golden balls detract from the dignity of their exteriors. They are maintained by the Government. They are housed in magnificent quarters. Merrion Street, Ely Place, Stephen's Green all contain these admirable institutions in which, for a certain number of hours each day, the intellectuals deposit their bodies, receiving for this act, from a grateful State, incomes ranging from about £200 to £4,000 per annum. Could one possibly conceive a more excellent, a more sensible, arrangement? I wish we had something of the kind in England, some such happy combination of ease with dignity for the deserving. In Dublin the road, for the educated young man, winds up hill all the way; and there are jobs for all who come. What in Heaven's name the Irish cultured classes would do if it were not for the lavish inefficiency of English administration I cannot imagine. Perhaps they would be forced to live by threatening to expose each other's washing!

The nervous strain occasioned by depositing oneself in these more elegant and Governmental 'Money Offices' does not seem so excessive as to preclude the diversions of scholarship. In no other town have I encountered so many learned persons as I have in Dublin, or perhaps I should say, so many people able and willing to give 'mixed company' the benefit of their erudition. The literary people, in particular, are sometimes tremendously impressive and awe-inspiring; so much so that it is occasionally rather a shock to trace them back not to a shelf of profound and epoch-making treatises but only to a few newspaper paragraphs or a single slender sheaf of verses. I cannot imagine a don at an English University, however distinguished he might be, inflicting his particular subject upon a collection of people composed largely of women and of obvious ignoramuses like myself. But in Dublin I have heard a 'nut of knowledge' keep an entire room in silence while he spouted ancient and modern Greek, and discussed the origins of Sanskrit, disgruntling a rival 'nut' who knew something of these subjects, but couldn't get a word in edgeways, while the rest of us displayed on our faces that expression of 'rapt attention' which we hope the other person will mistake for intelligent interest. Dropping Sanskrit for the moment, the Philologist went on to the derivation of names, relentlessly 'deriving' all our names for us. One man had a name which was 'patently Norse'; the name of a second was derived from the 'low German'; and that of a third was a 'French corruption'.

'Now I have a nephew with rather a curious name,' said a quiet woman with white hair, who had not previously spoken. 'He was christened Judmar ...'

'Judmar!' screamed the Philologist, 'Judmar! Why that's obviously from the Kalmuck Jud*marah*, meaning 'shining warrior'. It occurs also in Tchali. I remember coming across the name of Jud*maroosh* when I was living in Kajmackalan, among the Tchalis. Clearly the same name; but you note the subtle difference?'

We all sat around noting, as intelligently as we knew how, the 'subtle difference'.

When silence returned, the elderly lady continued in the same tones: 'He was called Judmar because his mother had two favourite aunts, Judy and Mary....' I was unable to hear how the Philologist extricated himself, but I feel sure that he did so with the greatest *aplomb*.

The collection of 'knowledge,' or intellectual *bricabracologie*, is no doubt as valuable a hobby as any other, but to make a custom of displaying the treasures of the collection at all times and in all seasons seems to me to have about it a certain flavour of provincialism. Another indication of provincial pedantry is to be found in the pronunciation of that, alas, household word, 'margarine'. In Dublin, even the people who sell it to you by the half-pound, pronounce the g hard, with one eye firmly fixed on the word's Greek derivation. It is almost as if they were speaking English like a dead language which they had acquired at Extension Lectures. In England, however, English is still far too much alive to permit such a barbarity as pronouncing 'margarine' with a hard g (thus turning it into an ugly word) when by pronouncing it with a soft g it makes quite a tolerable addition to the language. All the professors of all the universities may denounce this practice till they are blue in the face, but it will not make a penn'orth of difference; the community as a whole will continue to trust its ear, and to disregard everything else. If the word is to be assimilated into the English language it will be pronounced in the way which to the majority of English-speaking people seems most agreeable, and that sooner or later, inevitably becomes the *right* way.

D.L. KELLEHER

The Glamour of Dublin

DUBLIN AND CORK ❧ THE TALBOT PRESS LTD ❧ 1929

George's Court is deep in a swamp of slums. Hope ends at the confines of such a place and hell is near. In the one-room flats around children learn by observation such mysteries of existence as pass comfortable folk by till manhood or sudden disaster is at hand. Birth and death are too hackneyed even for a joke, since you sleep so often in the odour of them here. So this little girl of ten is as cute in the year of grace 1728 as half the psychologists in the colleges elsewhere. For she has happened into a world egregiously full of misery and hunger. That bricklayer father of hers, an honest dullard fellow, is dead already these five years, and this elder girl must set out and be day-labourer herself, dragging water from the Liffey to the houses of wealthy folk, a darling little face and flowing hair, for ever smiling under her pitcher of red-brown ware, until the Court knows her as the 'brave little woman', and rich customers of hers, seeing the cherub-cheeks at their kitchen window, silently lament the saving ugliness of their own well-groomed girls. So the Greuze picture shines to and fro, until one day, in Fownes Street, a certain tight-rope dancer catches sight of the seraph, and, scenting profit in the face, hires her for the troop of small children out of whom a new vogue of drama is about to spread in Dublin. And behind Lord Justice Whiteside's house in a booth in Fownes Street here is the ex-water carrier, aged ten only, Polly Peachem in 'Beggar's Opera,' one of the sensations of the theatrical hour. A rare little diva she is, joining her mother, the orange-seller, after the 'show', at the corner of Fownes Court, counting and packing the unsold oranges and helping home with the burthen then. Gallant, lofty little soul, those dancing curls supple and sweet about thy head, no serpents coiling in them yet, nor meshes spread for men's eyes. Though later *via* Smock Alley, and Drury Lane, and the salons of London, fame will track thee down, and infamy wait like a jackal for the dead. Poor Peg Woffington, indeed, Dublin builder's daughter, who soon shall need the builder's skill again. For down there at Teddington-on-Thames, nor yet forty years old, at the end of all thy exotic nights the carved tomb claims thee:

Oh, shining hair, and mouth of all delight,
Not love nor glory shorten now the night!

W.J. LAWRENCE

The Gael Magazine

DUBLIN ✺ 12 DECEMBER 1921

MORRISON'S HOTEL

It may safely be said that no Dublin hotel ever had a longer existence or a more picturesque record than Morrison's. For eighty years on end it stood at the eastern junction of Dawson and Nassau street, yielding to the sojourner within its gates an old-world comfort not to be paralleled in any of our more modern caravanserais. Built in 1819, by Arthur Morrison, who had previously presided over the fortunes of a smaller hotel in Frederick Street, it passed in its day through many hands, but was affectionately known as Morrison's to the end. Truly the man who could thus impress his name on cold stone, making it (as Wren made St Paul's) his memorial, must have been a genius in his way.

Although Dublin boasted some thirty-seven hotels at the time of its erection, Morrison's soon acquired the premier position and held it, despite occasional challenges for over half a century. Numberless were the celebrities who had been sheltered by its hospitable roof. In the autumn of 1824, that marvellous little man, Edmund Kean, greatest tragedian of his century, made Morrison's his resting place, while fulfilling a long and prosperous engagement at the vast new Theatre Royal in Hawkin's Street. More interesting still, perhaps, is it to find that it was there, on St Stephen's Day, 1838, a public dinner was given to Michael Balfe, composer, who had then just crossed the threshold of his distinguished career. The tickets were a guinea each, and about a hundred gentlemen assembled to do honour to their compatriot. On the following day a delegation waited upon the brilliant melodist at the same place, and on behalf of a numerous body of admirers, presented him with a gold snuff-box of Irish manufacture.

Nor were these the only happy experiences Balfe was fated to have at Morrison's. In October, 1848, when Jenny Lind came to town to delight cultured music-lovers by her singing in Italian opera, both she and Lumley, her impresario, honoured the historic old Dawson Street hotel with their patronage. With them came the amiable composer of 'The Bohemian Girl', as conductor of the operas. The details of the frolics indulged in by the triad at Morrison's during their stay are best given in the words of an eye-witness, no less a person than old R.M. Levy, the well-beloved orchestra leader of the old Theatre Royal:-

> 'Two off-nights occurred during the engagement, and on each of those vacant evenings the great stars had a reunion amongst themselves, the writer receiving a special invitation as 'one of the family'. It would be difficult, indeed, to imagine any unstudied or unrehearsed entertainments more delightful and unconventional than those two, of which music formed but a limited portion, dancing, forfeits, and cards (for very limited stakes) filling nearly all the time. Jenny Lind could dance nearly as well as she could sing. Balfe inherited the art, and was capital on the "light fantastic". A mock ballet was organised, the great soprano filling the role of the maiden, and the composer and conductor that of the lover. The corps de ballet

consisted of the company, Mick, the waiter, being once pressed into service, when he entered in his professional capacity. Mr Lumley, a model manager in appearance, was placed on a throne to decide on the merits of the aspirants, and was supposed to offer an engagement to the most accomplished. The ballet proceeded most seriously, Monsieur Naudaud and the writer contributing the music alternately, each as he passed the fiddle to the other, joining the dancing troop. At the end a discussion occurred, carried on most gravely, as to the respective merits of the two principal characters. The great manager was undecided. His means would only allow of the engagement of one. The question was put to the vote—a plebiscite. The votes were equal. What was to be done? The manager decided that one great test of skill should take place, each to perform an elaborate solo. Balfe led off and danced "like an angel". Then "enter Jenny Lind" with all the air and grace of a Taglioni. She proceeds. An adagio and fascinating allegro, tripping "solo" to follow, astonished all the lookers-on. Rounds of applause, bouquets, etc., etc., and, to conclude, great Jenny wins the day. The evening concluded with a set of quadrilles, Mlle. Lind singing the quadrilles, seated in a corner on the music stool.'

Of Arthur Morrison himself little has come down to us: we do not know when he was gathered to his fathers. But a story told of him in Colonel Maurice Moore's biography of his father, 'An Irish Gentleman: George Henry Moore', redounds to his credit. Once upon a time there was an old country priest whose motto was 'The best is always the cheapest'. Circumstances occasioned a visit to Dublin, where, strangely enough, he had never been. Before setting out he made careful inquiries as to the best hotel in the city, 'the best being always the cheapest'. He was told Morrison's, and to Morrison's he accordingly repaired, so far living up to his maxim as to ask for the best room. In those days the famous hotel was mostly patronised by well-to-do country gentlemen who paid their fat bills complacently without any scrutiny of the items. That sort of habit does not tend to make a hotel enter into a competition with its rivals, and Morrison's was expensive. Moreover, it was essentially the rendezvous of the ascendancy, and as no Catholic priest had ever honoured it with a visit before, the poor old gentleman was an object of some curiosity. But, happily ignorant of all this, his reverence ordered the best dinner, and asked which was the best wine, smiling as he brought out his little homely maxim. He enjoyed himself thoroughly for a week and then packed his bag to return home by mail-coach. He had a last glass of port while he was waiting for his bill, remarking as he eyed the purple fluid, 'the best is always the cheapest.' Possibly that he might have an opportunity to say goodbye to his customer, Mr Morrison always brought the bill himself, and he made no change on this occasion. When the poor old priest saw what he had to pay he dropped into a seat with a sinking heart. He had not the quarter of the money required with him. To his surprise, however, Morrison said, 'Sir, you are the first Catholic priest who has ever entered this house, and you will do me an honour if you will consider yourself my guest.' To which the good priest's reply was, 'Mr Morrison, I thank you. I came to this house because I thought the best was the cheapest, and I was right.'

Even in the days when sheer old age compelled it to yield pride of place to its bustling young rivals, the Shelbourne and the Gresham, Morrison's still continued to add to its picturesque history. One recalls that Parnell was stopping there when he was arrested by Mallon, the detective, on the morning of 13 October 1881, while dressing before breakfast, and carried off to Kilmainham for complicity with the Land League. But leases have an ugly trick of falling in, and in 1899, full of honours and years, Morrison's disappeared to make room for an up-to-date commercial building.

MICHAEL O'LOUGHLIN

Invisible Cities: The New Dubliners

DUBLIN ❧ RAVEN ARTS PRESS ❧ 1988

I began commuting from Finglas into the city when I was four years old. There were no schools available in Finglas at that time, so my mother used to bring me to the bus stop and deliver me to the care of a friendly bus conductor. He kept an eye on me, and made sure that I got off at the right stop for Strand Street School. I saw nothing strange in this arrangement; I didn't regard the bus conductor as a stranger. One aspect of growing up in a working-class suburb is that you assume every man is like your father, every woman your mother. It is more than a question of neighbourliness or community, you see the world as your family. Then you grow older and discover that in the more advanced societies this is not the case. This is a heart-breaking discovery from which you will probably never recover.

Travelling from Finglas into the city, the bus has to travel along the high stone walls enclosing Glasnevin cemetery. This was where the dead lived, a quiet suburb straggling down the hill to the Tolka river. It was a suburb of the dead among the suburbs of the living, characterised by its trees and grass, its rustic vistas, in the midst of the grey concrete streets. Over the years, I became familiar with the cemetery. My grandfather died and was buried there, and distant relatives of whom I have no living image. We visited their graves on quiet Sunday afternoons. One of our neighbours on the street was a grave-digger, who worked there. Every day he would come home, wearing a clay-coloured suit, and boots caked with grave-earth, and a broad-rimmed brown felt hat. With his squat round form and smiling red face between his hat and jacket, he reminded me of a healthy earthworm.

I came into closer proximity with the cemetery when I was twelve years old, and started attending a school in Glasnevin. For the next five years, I traced its edge four times a day. From the upstairs window of the bus you could look down into the cemetery, at the rows of headstones stretching into the distance. A friend once told me that, as the bus sped from Finglas into town, he looked down and glimpsed his own name, which was a very uncommon one, written on a stone. Perhaps unwisely, he returned to look for it one day, unsuccessfully. For me, going to school in Glasnevin was not just a literal displacement, but one in time and culture. It was an exile, a five year sentence to a gulag archipelago of the spirit. In one sense, Finglas could be defined in terms of absences, but it was also full of life and possibilities, the thousands of children on its streets were emblems and bearers of a kind of hope. The schools were crowded and noisy, but they were guided by a talented generation of progressive-minded teachers. I left this raw, invigorating air to be delivered into the hands of a nineteenth-century establishment, a slaughterhouse of the sensibilities, a wilderness of discipline and religion. Its aims were clear: to produce a class of Catholic civil servants, teachers, doctors. It was about power. It was also a linguistic displacement. Although they had all been born in the surrounding suburbs, they sometimes spoke with country accents, and sometimes in Irish, a badge of caste, a denial of the city I came from. Architecture, wrote Nietzsche, is the rhetoric of power, and I could hear what Glasnevin was saying to me, with its solid red-brick houses tightly grouped around defiantly ugly churches. These were the people who had triumphed, who had added the halfpence to the pence and prayer to shivering prayer till they had built a country in their own image. I never entered their houses without sensing something rotting and damp, every house seemed to contain something which had died a long time ago, and never been taken out. Years later, I came to live in one of these houses. One night we found a strange parcel hidden behind one of the shutters, probably left there by the Catholic spinster who had died shortly before we came to occupy the house. It was wrapped in a pair of old nylons, stained with something which could have been blood. When we opened it, gingerly, we found a few hundred old and disintegrating pound notes, mixed with holy pictures and relics. It was almost too apt, a metaphor made flesh.

Just across from the school was the main entrance to the cemetery, and a large grey wall equipped with watchtowers to guard against the body snatchers who once haunted it. Every day, I saw the hearses drive through the gates. The big clock above the gates ticked out the minutes of my life as I came and went from Finglas. Someone, perhaps in 1966, had painted in big white letters on the wall: *EIREÓIMÍD ARIS*. It became something of a catchphrase in the school, but the joke was not immediately obvious to us. We sat in class and analysed 'The Windhover', but no one saw fit to tell us that its author lay in the earth a few hundred yards away, an outlandish stress in the long lines of the dead.

I left school and left Finglas, and my early commutings became a rehearsal for future displacements. But I was surprised to find that Glasnevin cemetery which had always been such an oblique, if huge, presence in my mind, had somehow become central to my thoughts. I had become a haunter of cemeteries, scrutiniser of stones, a connoisseur of their poetry. I went back to look at Glasnevin Cemetery, but it was as if I had never seen it before. It lay spread out before me like a printed text, which I had learned to read, all my life I had been carrying this book, whose contents I somehow knew. Now my eyes could pick out the pathetic pomp of the bishops' tombs, my ears were attuned to the ironies of the Republican Plot. Here was the official story of Ireland, laid out in sentences and paragraphs of stone, from the phallic pun of O'Connell's monument and the surrounding crypts, each figure carefully selected and placed in his niche, the mot juste, to celtic crosses commemorating some obscure writer of patriotic ballads.

But beyond this, around this, another story begins. This one is silent. Tens of thousands of graves, some almost vanished without trace, some whose names you can just decipher, with their dates. Here and there you can find a simple cross of wood without a name, or a wordless stone, with perhaps in front of it, a dusty plastic flower in an old milk bottle. There are patches of bare earth covered with fine, hair-like grass, where graves used to be, now vanished, silent forever. Here are buried the people who built the city, who worked in it and died, and were wiped out of history, leaving nothing behind but their children, perhaps, or an intonation, a verse in an anonymous song. I thought of how they must have laboured and suffered, and what the hopes were which kept them alive, and if they had been justified. I compared their silence to the rhetorical stones I had just seen. I stood there, my thoughts mired in bitterness and frustration, when an image came into my mind, one I recognised but had almost forgotten.

Somebody had once shown me a book he was translating from the Serbo-Croat, about a group of people called the Bogomils. Originally, the Bogomils were a sect which was widespread throughout the Balkans from the tenth century onward. It was a neo-Manichean heresy which spread like wildfire among the peasants and ruling class alike. Eventually, it was stamped out, as an international movement, but survived among the peasants in the backwaters of what is now Yugoslavia, until at the end of the fourteenth century, when it was absorbed into Islam. What is known about this obscure sect is that it mingled Manichean ideas with a radical social approach. They avoided all outward show, had no priests, no churches, no books, no painters. They would have vanished from history if it weren't for one thing. Scattered across the plains of Bosnia and Herzegovina, they left enormous, mysterious necropoli, suburbs of the dead. The significance of these is not clear to commentators. They consist mainly of simple blocks of stone, arranged randomly on the earth, some of which carry unsophisticated but enigmatic carvings. They often show groups of people doing ordinary things, such as dancing, or hunting. Looking at photographs of these stones, I felt a strong sense that they were telling me something about myself which I couldn't quite grasp. But the images became embedded in my memory, waiting for the right moment to reveal their significance. Standing in Glasnevin Cemetery, an image came back to me from the Bogomil tombs. It was a crude carving of a man facing the viewer, with an enormously enlarged hand raised up, palm outward. Some commentators have traced this gesture back to ancient

Persian religions. But now it seemed to me to be exactly what it seemed: a hand raised in greeting and benediction, hail and farewell, a message of peace from the dead to the living. I realised that you can deprive people of everything, their rights, their hopes, their selves, but you cannot deprive them of their death, which is theirs inalienably. Standing among the Bogomil graves of Glasnevin, I felt that their silence was a message more benevolent, more hopeful, than any rhetoric.

For me, Glasnevin Cemetery will always be the green, secret heart of Dublin.

PEREGRINE PALAVER

Dublin Penny Journal

DUBLIN ❧ 4 AUGUST 1832

TERENURE

To the Editor of the Dublin Penny Journal

Sir—The citizens of Dublin of the middle and poorer classes are rather unkindly treated by some of the noble and affluent among their countrymen, who with a spirit of exclusiveness unknown in many other countries, debar them from a sight of those parks, palaces, and pleasure grounds within which they repose. Often have I, when coasting along a park wall, whose jealous coping towered far above my head, wished that the niggard possessor had half a day's residence at the bottom of a dry well, just to teach him, in rather a different style than Parnell's angel taught the miser, not to begrudge the king's lieges a sight of his improvements. Not a few act as if they thought another man's enjoyment would lessen their own, and as if another's breathing the common air of heaven in the neighbourhood of their demesne, would taint the atmosphere within their own enclosures. In this way, not long ago, a heavy-pursed man, who had purchased a fine property in the county of Wicklow, did not feel himself quite snug in the midst of lawns, glens, waterfalls, and rocks, until he had excluded vulgar eyesight by a twelve-feet wall. Surely his lordship was mistaken in supposing that thereby he kept Satan from leaping into his paradise! Alas, the foul fiend had already taken possession of a narrower and nearer enclosure—his head-quarters were beneath his lordship's ribs, and his name was selfishness.

Now Ireland is, of many countries under the face of the smiling sun, most remarkable for this exhibition of the effectual working of *appropriation*. In England a *silver key* will open many a proud man's gate; and even if you have not money to bribe gate-keepers, and housekeepers, you may get a glimpse of the demesne either over or through the park paling. But here stones and lime are so plenty, that the great man can *wall* away at a cheap rate; and Mr and Mrs Grundy of Grafton-street, who, after being pent up for weeks at measuring tape and posting ledgers, have ventured to take a day's pleasure in the country, are compelled to travel on a fine day in July, amid clouds of almost animated dust, arising from an equally almost suffocating road, their horse kicking under the bites of horse-flies, and themselves sweltering under a blistering burning sun—in vain do they stretch their curious necks to come at the rural scenery on either side— high walls—(oh, I hate high walls) and beltings of lofty trees almost shut out the very mountains from the view, and they go on, coasting demesne after demesne, that they cannot see and dare no more enter, than a cruiser may venture on the cliff-bound and battery protected shores of a hostile kingdom.

Now, there *are* exceptions to these remarks, even in Ireland, and Saxon and stranger though I be, I have met instances of it which have pleased me exceedingly. Walking in the neighbourhood of Terenure, situated in one of the numerous pretty outlets of Dublin, I was struck with the number of carriages, jaunting cars, and pedestrians, either standing at the gate, or issuing in and out of the demesne. 'Why,' says I to myself, 'is there an auction going on here? Perhaps some of our great merchants— some eminent distiller, brewer, or notary public, has, after enclosing this park for himself, figured in the Gazette—his bubble has burst, and here are his creditors now gathering in their 2s 6d in the pound, and bringing to the hammer all that his soul rejoiced in!' But it turns out quite the reverse. TERENURE is the demesne of FREDERICK BOURNE, Esq., a gentleman who, having acquired his property by the public, is desirous that the public should see how he disposes of a portion of it, and therefore his gates are open to all who may choose to walk in, and his capital and his taste, and his science are laid down here that the meanest and the humblest citizen, may see, enjoy, and admire.

On entering Terenure, you perceive that it has no natural beauties. The grounds are flat and fat, producing a rich abundance of lofty elms— the house is not remarkable—but the large gardens, fraught with all the glories of Pomona and Flora, form the grand attraction. No expense has been spared—all that care, labour, science and taste, can do, has been done; the well-constructed conservatories supply the natural defects of our climate by means of the newest mechanical inventions—hot water circulating through all parts, and communicating a genial warmth, such as neither steam nor hot air burnt in the old way, by passing over heated iron, can impart; and then the beautiful flower plots—such beds of roses—such amaranthine odours, as neither Damascus itself, nor those Sabean vales that gave the Arabian prophet an idea of his sensual paradise—can surpass!

The pleasure I enjoyed in walking through these gardens was greatly enhanced by the idea of the perfect disinterestedness of their owner. If you walk through a highly-cultivated farm—and a well-cultivated farm is a beautiful sight—though you may be struck with the well-contrived arrangements—with the teeming luxuriance of the crops—with the simple yet perfect adjustment of the machinery, yet you say to yourself, the proprietor will have his *profit* in all this—it will amply *repay* him. But not so the florist. His beds of hyacinths—his stages of auriculas—his Dutch tulips and Turkish anemonies—all that the Cape, Australia, or China, can supply—instead of yielding something to boil in the pot, very seriously extract from the pocket, as I daresay the proprietor of Terenure can well tell. But who would begrudge him riding so innocent, so beautiful, and so accommodating a hobby? He is spending the money acquired by speculations which have been beneficial to Ireland, *in* Ireland, and giving employment to many not merely in the way of his business, but in the bent of his pleasure. His demesne is open to all—no greedy gardener is allowed to traffic his civilities for shillings—all is as open and as free as at the *Jardin des Plantes* at Paris.

Now, if any of your readers have been in the habit of reading the valuable Penny Magazine published by the Society for diffusing Useful Knowledge, they may remember seeing an extract from the Quarterly Review, in which it is said that though on the continent the people are freely admitted into museums, parks, galleries, &c., yet, owing to the propensity of the English to mischief, they must be excluded as much as possible from these places of public entertainment. Without discussing this point, I would only say, that the owner of Terenure has to guard against a circumstance which is unknown in the French gardens, already alluded to; but grieved am I to say, that Irish florists have a propensity of appropriating what is rich and rare—even at the risk of a breach of the eighth commandment. But mind, I do not say this of the middle classes—no! the simple citizen, who knows not the difference between a rose unique and a blush rose, or a tag from a jonquil, or an anemone from a ranunculus, walks, admires and touches not: but it is your tasty LADY or GENTLE-MAN against whom the accusation comes, those who *know* the value of a rare flower or plant, who have their own floral snuggery, their own well-guarded paradise, who cannot see a black or a white moss rose, or any other splendid expensive monster of the kingdom of flora, without feeling a longing desire, and casting a lingering look. Oh, ye gardeners and collectors, beware of such—war-hawk—watch well the one we *hint* at; Barrington himself was not so light-fingered. Such greediness will grasp at one of the most prized and gorgeous of your garden beauties—let gardeners in such a demesne as Terenure beware of a lady coming in a carriage, with her fair hands enveloped in a muff; oh the supple nimbleness of those fair fingers; oh, the convenient concealments of that capacious muff—Mercury himself invented muffs—so admirably adapted to cover a billet-doux or a bulbous root—a piece of lace or a fat fowl—a round of ribbon or a pound of sausages! Suppose by way of illustration, one fine day in spring, just before the show of flowers at the Rotundo, a well-appointed yellow chariot drives up in rapid style to Terenure, and the footman alights, and a *lady* walks in to see the grounds. Furthermore, suppose that Mr B. on liberal thought intent, himself comes out, and volunteers to show this fair fashionable all the blooming exuberance of his gardens—for mind you, reader, it is delightful, really delightful, to exhibit rarities belonging to oneself, and to descant with science, taste, and ardour, on the distinctive qualities of each fine thing, under the chuckling feeling that all this is MINE—exclusively MINE! But when this is done in the presence of a pretty woman, whose sparkling eye flashes with a perfect understanding and tasteful community of sentiment—when the rich red lip, rivalling the very rose that is the subject of discourse, expresses its admiration and pleasure in honied words—who could stand this? Why, Argus himself would not know whether he was standing on his head or his heels—and his eyes, had he a thousand instead of a hundred, would be glewed up with the gum of pleasurable confidence! Just further suppose the pair to walk from bed to parterre, and from parterre to conservatory, and from conservatory to hot-house—when lo, the serene repose of confidential communication is set ajar by a whisper from one of the numerous gardeners—a man from the 'north countrie', who with provincial shrewdness, says, *en passant*, 'Master, your best auricula has left its ain place—maybe yon unco *lady*, could tell you something about it, for if I'm no mista'en, she has it, pot and all, in her *muff*!' What was Mr B. to do?

Was he so gruff to seize the *lady's muff*, and drag the auricula into day light? No; feigning an excuse that it was necessary to shut the garden in order that the workmen might go to dinner, he, with continued affability, led the lovely lady plunderer towards her equipage, and handing her in, said with great suavity, 'Madam, you have done me the honour to admire the auricula I intended for the show of flowers—I am highly gratified— you are taking it home to show to your friends—I am better pleased—but as the confinement of your muff may injure the delicate mealy efflores- cence for which the plant is celebrated, pray allow me to disengage it from its *happy* prison; here, Tom Turfington', calling to the watchful guardian, 'you can, if the lady chooses, attend her home, and as soon as she has admired this auricula, and displayed it to her friends, bring it back—I must always prize it the more on account of the discriminating partiality with which it has been honoured.' The worthy gentleman made his bow, and retired—the detected and doubtless abashed lady resigned the auricula into the hands of Tom Turfington, and drove off; and Tom and his fellow gardeners have ever since evinced a watchful jealousy of lovely ladies who come provided with muffs, especially on a warm Spring day, and who talk knowingly—look around surreptitiously—and with pretty paws play pickingly among the flower beds.

Now, this little story is *perhaps* a pure invention of my own; and I tell it just to show that the owners of improved grounds and fine gardens are not *entirely* to blame when they exclude the public from their properties. If *all* visitors would, like the French, learn that delicate abstemiousness of using the sense of seeing, without putting forward the pawing propensi- ty—if they would neither pluck, derange, carve names on trees or scratch bad verses on glass, there might be many other estates thrown open to their inspection, and kept, like Terenure, for them to walk and wander in. As it is, Mr B. deserves no small credit for keeping open his demesne for the pleasure of the citizens of Dublin, affording, as it does, so delightful a rendezvous for parties of pleasure, who every day may be seen ranging through the grounds, and enjoying, with a relish which none but a citizen can so peculiarly feel, that exquisite delight which flows from an after- noon spent not in the bustle of business, but amid the delights of TERENURE.

I am, Sir, yours truly,
PEREGRINE PALAVAR.

ERIC WHELPTON

Book of Dublin

LONDON ❧ ROCKCLIFF SALISBURY SQUARE ❧ 1948

I n the eighteenth century Dublin was, I believe, the third or fourth biggest capital in Europe, and certainly the second city in Great Britain both in size and in the splendour of its public buildings. That, at least, was the considered opinion of many travellers who had done the Grand Tour and were still contemptuous of Gothic and Mediaeval architecture. To-day, Dublin, with its 500,000 inhabitants, has the great advantage of not being swamped by mile after mile of suburbs on all sides. A few minutes' drive by car or bus and you can find yourself more or less in open country. Some streets, even in the centre of the city, have a horizon of sky, others seem to lead up directly to the Wicklow Mountains. From the last bridge on the Liffey and even from the O'Connell Bridge, if you look straight downstream, there is a glimpse, though a narrow one, of the sea.

From Collinstown, the airport, the approach is perhaps not too impressive, but after a few minutes of driving through more or less rustic roads, one finds oneself in Georgian streets, rather dilapidated it is true, but full of well proportioned brick houses with graceful fanlights. Clearly this northern quarter has seen more prosperous days, but it has, in a sense, a touch of Hogarth's London, for there were few new buildings and I noticed a slender eighteenth-century type of spire and some classical façades to complete the setting.

As our car speeded on rather swiftly I noticed the surging crowds, rather dingy, even compared with the London crowds, but obviously cheerful and full of animation. The men especially were talking and gesticulating in interested conversation. The women seemed more silent and far more sedate. Immediately I was reminded of an Irish friend who had said to me: 'You cannot spend ten minutes in Dublin without being struck with the unforgettable beauty of the women. You won't find their like anywhere else in the world.'

He was right. The Dublin women have perfect skins, good features and eyes of inexplicable brilliance, but they scarcely seem conscious of their good looks, and they appear to be devoid of personal vanity. It is perhaps because of their beauty that they do not seem greatly interested in clothes, or it may be that they are really and sincerely modest. Even after a few hours in Dublin I have been impressed by the absence of sex con-sciousness among the Irish. Most of the bars are for men only, there seem to be few lovers in the streets or elsewhere, and the gawky lads at street corners do not whistle at passing girls. Yet there are women everywhere, and I am told that there are twice as many spinsters under the age of thirty as in England where the number is already unduly high. In a sense the moment one is in Dublin one seems to have returned to the nineteenth century both in environment and in ways of life. Possibly this old–fash-ioned atmosphere can be explained more simply by the fact that if the Irish are more or less untouched by the modern spirit, it is because, like many ancient races, they are untouched by the changes of time, and they are of course fairly isolated from the rest of the world. I am told that until quite recently there were old people who could remember seeing sedan chairs in the streets of Dublin. A trifle, perhaps, but fairly symbolic of the whole place.

After threading its way through some fairly shabby streets our car came out into O'Connell Street, impressive in its broadness and monu-ments which are not, however, particularly good in themselves.

It was six o'clock in the evening when we crossed the O'Connell Bridge. To the east, the dome of the Customs House was outlined sharply against indefinite pinkish-grey clouds. The lower part of the building was less discernible since it is screened by an iron railway bridge, embellished by giant letters advertising a product whose name I have fortunately for-gotten. The streets were full of people hurrying home, and there were more bicycles than I have ever seen before. In these surging crowds it was difficult to discern individuals, and yet here and there a face or a figure would stamp itself on my mind: A tall, dark man with fine, clear-cut fea-tures, wearing the most tattered and torn coat in the world with regal dig-nity—not a beggar, I should say, but just an onlooker with a slight con-tempt for his fellow men. A young woman on a bicycle, crossing herself devoutly as she passed a church. She was indescribably beautiful, and yet she seemed completely abstracted from her surroundings. Then, walking slowly on the pavement, an oldish woman in nondescript garments, who epitomised for me the suffering mothers and wives of Dublin that have been immortalised for us in Sean O'Casey's plays. It is probably unnecessary to describe her face, lined and worn, with marks of sorrow and patient endurance, eyes still bright, and well modelled nose and mouth.

Our car stopped. Since Dublin was crowded we had booked at hazard rooms in an hotel which could scarcely be described as luxurious or cosmopolitan. It was frankly shabby and not up-to-date, but we were glad in a sense to stay somewhere where we should see something of the Irish people unadorned and unaffected.

My first impression was that the clock had been set back sixty years and that we were in the London of the 'eighties, staying at an inn that had been modernised with the railways. To complete the illusion there seemed to be swarms of porters, waitresses and chambermaids eager to make themselves useful. The decorations were certainly Victorian, especially of the sitting-rooms, which were, thank Heaven, completely devoid of chromium plating. Our bedroom was, to put it mildly, frankly inconvenient. No bedside lights, switches by the door, and insufficient hanging cupboards. A succession of trains rumbled nearby and drowned all conversation. The dining-room downstairs was also nineteenth-century provincial in appearance, and we both of us blenched when we were offered high tea...

Irish high tea, we soon discovered, is not a meal to be despised or treated lightly. If the atmosphere of the lesser Dublin hotels is Dickensian, so is the fare. We had the choice of every kind of grill or egg dish imaginable, each of them the equivalent of two or three courses elsewhere and excellent of their kind. If there is no regional cooking in this country, you can at any rate rely on the Irish to treat eggs, bacon or ham in the best possible manner, and their omelettes are superb. Tea, a drink which I detest to take with meat, has in Dublin a peculiar quality which makes it acceptable at any time. I can only suppose that the local water makes it infinitely more palatable than elsewhere.

Within a few hours we ceased to worry over the lack of modern conveniences which were more apparent than real. In this hotel as everywhere else in Ireland the service was excellent and everyone was kindly, friendly and courteous. Irish servants are anxious to please, interested in your well-being, and genuinely glad to see you happy, and these characteristics appear to be shared by all their compatriots.

After consuming an enormous high tea, we went for a short stroll round the town. We passed through street after street of Georgian houses, with rarely a modern building to break up their alignment and perfect composition. There were fine large squares, beautifully kept up, with painted porches and graceful fanlights, and then, quite nearby, equally noble houses in almost derelict condition. Through the open doors we could see moulded plaster ceilings crumbling away above wrought-iron banisters, unpainted and chipped panelling and a general air of decay. And yet somehow or another the impoverished tenants of these houses seemed to belong to this setting. In many cases they looked shabby and ill-clad, but rarely sad or despairing, for they were always talking cheerfully.

CHIANG YEE

The Silent Traveller in Dublin

LONDON ❧ METHUEN & CO. ❧ 1953

'An old lady,' wrote a correspondent of the *Dublin Evening Mail*, 'who lives alone on a very minute income, lost a goldfinch some months ago. She was very fond of it, and still misses its company. I wonder if anyone would be kind enough to give her one to replace it? She has a cage...' Someone, I recalled, had told me that there is a bird market in Dublin, open only at week-ends, situated somewhere in the old part of the city. Immediately I decided to visit it. But I had better confess that my motive was not to buy a goldfinch for the old lady, or even for myself; her wish would doubtless be fulfilled by one of her compatriots: I am but a silent traveller.

In China the love of birds is innate, and there is a bird market in almost every city or large town. The Chinese love birds as the British love horses and dogs. Not that the British do not love birds, but it is a different kind of affection, one which seldom lends them to buy birds to keep as pets; and on the overcast Saturday morning my chief difficulty, I perceived, was going to be to find the Dublin bird market at all. Neither my host nor my hostess knew where it was. The maid suggested that it *must* be near Bride Street, but as she had never been there she could not be certain. I decided to follow this clue, and set off.

As I approached St Stephen's Green I noticed that the morning mist had fused the leaves and twigs of the trees which line the boundaries of the Green in a mysterious pale green mass. Between the trunks and railings, red and yellow dots of flowers appeared, but the much-too-grey sky did not allow the sun to touch them to gaiety. They wore a wan rather than a brilliant smile. Dublin is no great distance from London, and its climate, and therefore its light, cannot be very different. Yet Dublin buildings look cleaner and brighter than London's, even on a dull morning, chiefly perhaps because they are not shadowed with soot.

Presently I came into York Street, where my feet, as on former occasions when I had walked there, refused to carry me quickly. The elegant if not always well-preserved doorways of the houses on one side of the street made me dawdle. There are many attractions in Dublin, but I found the variety of doorways all over the city appealed to me more than anything. It is said that Dublin has more Georgian houses than any other city in the British Isles. A friend of mine who lives in Bath disputes this, and I know no way of resolving the point; I am no student of architecture and can discuss neither the number of Georgian buildings nor the merits of their style. I will only make the comment that to me it seems that the Georgian architects were the pioneers of town-planning. Before the eighteenth century no one planned *streets*. Houses, mansions, churches, yes: but not streets. There is a lot to be said for the neatness and order of some parts of Dublin. The doorways along York Street, however, varied though they are, have not been uniformly kept in condition. How so many of them came to lose their distinction I do not know. Many doors stood wide open and I wanted to look inside, but when, having selected one house, I set foot on the step, I was driven away again by the formidable chatter and laughter of some women leaning on the railing. One of them was holding a baby, whose crying did not interrupt her gossip, and I could not bring myself to interrupt it either.

I moved on into Aungier Street, where I enquired for Bride Street. An elderly gentleman whose red face and white hair suggested liveliness and good humour answered me jovially: 'Oi doan't know what y're going to Bride Street for—there is no bride for ye, young man. But just look at that house! It's the house where the Irish poet and song-writer Thomas Moore was born in 1779. He wrote and published his first sonnet in his fourteenth year, addressed to his schoolmaster, Mr Samuel White. His book *Irish Melodies* is very well known. Ave coorse, ye may know it already. Oi thought I'd tell ye. Bride Street? Ah, ha. Ye just walk along this street towards the east and then turn to the right, pass through to the end and there ye will find Bride Street. Oho, "Bless the Bride". Goodbye. Good marnin'....' Many people have helped me to find my way during my silent travels, but none have been so humorously amiable as this one.

Following his directions, I presently found myself in Bride Street. It appeared to be a purely residential quarter. Not a single shop could I see. Wherever could the bird market lie? Hardly anyone was about—just one elderly woman trying to carry a big dustbin into a house. There were no elegant Georgian doorways, but the street was clean and quiet. I trotted on, looking vaguely from side to side. At the corner of Upper Kevin Street a man lurched out of a building which the strong scent from his nostrils identified as a public-house. Another man, with a pipe, stood idly by the kerb. He knew what I was after and directed me to one of a row of small houses on the other side of Bride Street. I crossed and entered the wrong house. It was rather dark and there was a spiral staircase against the wall not unlike an Edinburgh close. While I paused, baffled, my informant reappeared and conducted me to the right place.

I found myself outside a house very similar to the one I had entered by mistake. But there was no staircase inside, only a narrow corridor blocked with people. A boy shook a box at me and said: 'Penny for admission.' I dropped a coin in the box and was allowed to pass through the corridor into a small courtyard. It was oblong in shape and big enough for more than twenty of us to stand in it though at pretty close quarters. There was only one woman in the little crowd, but many boys and girls. My flat face caused a stir and I felt that all eyes were turned on me. One elderly fellow with a shock of white hair and a massive moustache remained unmoved; he was too interested in a healthy-looking male chaffinch in one of the seven cages hanging along the high wall on one side of the courtyard. He smiled, laughed and even made a faint noise as if joyously whispering some words to the bird. Presently the interest in my face waned and attention was once more turned upon the activities of the birds in the cages. The old folk were the most excited. The birds consisted of three chaffinches, two goldfinches, five canaries and two blackbirds. Of the crowd, I could not distinguish which were buyers and which sellers. It seemed to me to be a cage-bird *show* rather than a market. Then I over-heard two men discussing the price of a chaffinch and a goldfinch. I had not known that chaffinches and goldfinches were ever kept as cage-birds. Doubtless their beautiful plumage is the reason. The attention of a few of the younger spectators was not fixed continuously on the birds: first furtively, then openly, they were staring at me, as if I were a bird. The thought of being a bird appealed to me and I giggled. The youngsters responded with broad laughter, in which the elder folk joined. It was a delightful moment.

There was not much talking among the crowd. Everyone seemed quite content to look at the birds. I took out my sketchbook and began to draw a pictorial note. Two or three of the boys jostled me slightly and one elderly man told them not to be a nuisance. This touched me; I felt it was I who was causing the disturbance in their otherwise peaceable occupation of cage-bird watching. I thanked them, and when my sketch was finished I left.

As I walked home I reflected upon the differences between the Irish and Chinese in their ways of enjoying the company of cage-birds. Here in Dublin the cages hung along a wall and the company looked at them. In my childhood in China, as I have described in my book, *A Chinese Childhood*, my grandfather used to take his cage-birds for a walk every morning. His destination was a wood about a mile from our house, and he often took me with him. Arrived at the wood, we would find scores of cages hanging from trees, the birds singing joyously, for in China only song-birds were ever kept in cages; and we would hang up our birds too. Conversation would largely concern the birds. Nobody could have resisted the charm of the scene.

In the West, I believe, song competitions are held annually for cage-birds, but I have never heard them. They cannot, I fear, be very popular, for if they were one would hear the birds being rehearsed. And what a charming setting Kensington Gardens in London or Dublin's St Stephen's Green would provide for that!

My love of birds has often induced envy in me for the matchless freedom which their wings give them. Their struggle for life and avoidance of accidental death is as great as ours, but when they fly to warmer climates for the winter they are not troubled with passports, visas and Customs examinations. They carry no baggage, and even their homes they use only while rearing their young. It is true they are sometimes caged for the amusement of human beings, but do not men cage themselves—in homes and offices and labour camps? No bird has ever caged itself.

It is sad but inevitable that it is just those creatures—birds or human beings—which possess the most striking qualities or powers that are caged and confined. Some pertinent words on this theme were written by the Irish natural philosopher, the Hon. Robert Boyle (1626–91) in an essay on a glow-worm in a Phial:

If this unhappy worm had been as despicable as the other reptiles that crept up and down the hedge when I took him, he might as well as have been left there still, and his own obscurity as well as that of the night, had preserved him from the confinement he now suffers. And if, as he sometimes for a pretty while withdrew that luminous liquor, that is as were the candle to this dark lanthorn, he had continued to forbear the disclosing of it, he might have deluded my search and escaped his present confinement.

Rare qualities may sometimes be prerogatives without being advantageous. And though a needless ostentation of one's excellencies may be more glorious, yet a modest concealment of them is usually more safe, and an unseasonable disclosure of flashes of wit may sometimes do a man no other service than to direct his adversaries how they may do him a mischief.

Boyle's philosophy can be summed up in a Chinese proverb:
Showiness invites trouble; modesty has advantages.

Boyle concludes:

And as though this luminous creature be himself imprisoned in so close a body as glass, yet the light that ennobles him is not restrained from diffusing itself, so there are certain truths that have in them so much of native light or evidence, that by the personal distress of the proposer it cannot be hidden or restrained, but in spite of prisons it shines freely, and procures the teachers of its admiration even when it cannot procure them liberty.

I cannot imitate Boyle's rotund sentences, but the idea he expresses is familiar to me and it is a great truth. Did not Confucius's most famous disciple Mencius say: 'It is possible to subdue others by force, but not their minds'? And is not this something to be remembered to-day by those who exercise great power?

INDEX